PENGUIN

The Brave and

Dilan Dyer is the internationally bestselling author of the Princess Crossover series. Constantly on the move, she has lived in countless cities across five countries and dreams of a camper van to take her life on the road. She just needs to find one big enough for her pets, her vintage teacup collection and her staggering TBR.

The Brave and the Reckless

DILAN DYER

PENGUIN BOOKS

PENGUIN BOOKS

UK | USA | Canada | Ireland | Australia
India | New Zealand | South Africa

Penguin Books is part of the Penguin Random House group of companies
whose addresses can be found at global.penguinrandomhouse.com

Penguin Random House UK,
One Embassy Gardens, 8 Viaduct Gardens, London SW11 7BW

penguin.co.uk

Penguin
Random House
UK

First published 2025
001

Set in 12.5/14.75pt Garamond MT
Typeset by Falcon Oast Graphic Art Ltd
Printed in Great Britain by Clays Ltd, Elcograf S.p.A.

The authorized representative in the EEA is Penguin Random House Ireland,
Morrison Chambers, 32 Nassau Street, Dublin D02 YH68

A CIP catalogue record for this book is available from the British Library

ISBN: 978–1–405–97851–4

For every gifted girl grown into a woman struggling to find her path. It's okay to fuck around and find out. (Maybe even fuck a cowboy in a mask and find out.)

Content warnings

While this is a fun romance, some of the following themes may be triggering to some readers:

Alcoholism (side character); chronic illness, financial struggles; hospitalization due to chronic illness; parental control; parental death (in the past); parental neglect.

If you would like more information about the sexually explicit content in *The Brave and the Reckless*, you can turn to the end of the book.

Please read at your own comfort level.

The Brave and the Reckless

Chapter One

BRAVETOWN

History meets imagination when you take the railroad roller coaster into unknown territories, swing through the saloon doors to dine with the cowboys of the Old West, and join the sheriff in his fight against a notorious bandit.

Are you brave enough for the biggest adventure of your life?

ESRA

I must have hit my head when I face-planted in the parking lot, because when I sat up, the sun was covered by a cowboy. Hat, horse and all.

"Are you all right there, ma'am?" he asked with a perfect twang to his words.

I felt around my head for a bump but couldn't find anything. I blinked and blinked but the cowboy and his horse remained. Not a hallucination triggered by too much sugar and country radio. Very much a guy in white boots atop a white steed.

I probably would have been less shocked to see a "cowboy" in pink crotchless chaps on an inflatable horse riding the F train through Manhattan. I knew how to

I

handle *city*-weird. This guy . . . he was weird because he was too picture-perfect. He was country. He was ready to be photographed and slapped on a *Greetings from Tennessee* postcard.

"Ma'am?" he asked again after I'd been staring much longer than appropriate.

"Yeah, no, all good. Carry on. Or *ride* on? Yee haw?" I wasn't making sense. We both knew that, but judging by his tight-lipped polite smile, he thought I was drunk. I was actually just grappling with the reality of this place and a serious case of road-trip legs. In my defense, when he'd seen me stumbling out of my car and kissing the dirt, that was mostly thanks to those damn bumpy roads jostling me around until my joints were simultaneously numb and jittery. Sea legs, country version. We were in the middle of fucking nowhere, halfway between Nashville and Memphis, and I'd stopped feeling my toes an hour ago.

"Can I help you find your way?" With his white hat, sleek dark hair and round nose, he kind of looked like that old cartoon my brother had been obsessed with as a kid. Lucky Luke. He just needed a piece of straw hanging from the corner of his mouth.

"I'm good, Lucky. I'm going in there." I pointed at the old farmhouse at the end of the parking lot and pushed to my feet. Once I'd dusted off my knees, I grabbed my fluffy candy-heart backpack that read "bite me", and the enormous red slushy I'd picked up at a rest stop.

"It's Lucas, actually."

I snorted and quickly hid my laugh behind the plastic cup. Lucky *Luke*, indeed. "Do you work here?"

"Yes, ma'am."

"Amazing. Me too. Well, not yet, but in a few minutes. Still gotta sign some papers. That *is* the main office, right?"

"Yes, ma'am," he said again, but this time his polite smile wavered, and his eyes narrowed on my crop top. I glanced down to double-check. Big sparkling letters across my chest read "Retired Porn Star". That's what I got for dressing in a dark rest-stop bathroom.

"You think I should change, Lucky?"

"Yes, ma'am." Instead of taking the cue to stop staring at me, his gaze dropped to my bare legs. Lucas was so far from my type. For one, he was too young, probably my age – around twenty-three. Young guys always wanted to talk about dreams and ambitions. Ugh. On top of that, his initial concern had seemed genuine. And I didn't do genuine. "Take a picture, it'll last longer, Lucky."

"I'm so sorry, you have something on your, uh . . ."

I looked down to find a Dorito stuck to the inside of my thigh. It left a perfect triangular indent when I picked it off, laughing. "Thanks. Here, don't eat it all at once." I held the chip out to him, and he actually bent down and took it from me. Such a nice boy.

I also didn't do nice.

"See you around, Lucky."

"Uh, yes, I've got to get going now, but you have yourself a nice day." He clicked his tongue and that mountain of a horse trotted away.

"Fingers crossed," I mumbled before climbing back into my car and rummaging through the explosion of clothes on my backseat. The clean-smelling choice came down to a blue shirt with white rhinestones spelling out the word "feral" or a pink one that read "u can't pick

3

ur father but u can pick ur daddy". I chose the blue one and hoped that the HR department here wouldn't take things literally.

After turning the legroom between the driver's seat and the backseat into my personal changing room, I typed out a quick message.

Esra: I'm here

Sinan didn't reply. Hell, he didn't even read the message. It stayed stuck on "delivered" the whole way from my car to the farmhouse. Of course he didn't reply within seconds. He wasn't Mom, ready to swoop in and handle every situation for me – even something as minor as introducing myself to my new employer. Nope. My brother had told me when to be here, where to go, who to talk to . . . I'd wanted my independence, and I was getting it. I just low-key wished he would drag me through the door. Instead, I had to will my own two feet into action.

I grimaced at the rough wooden stairs and tested one with the tip of my sneakers. It groaned, but despite its weathered state, it seemed to hold.

It's all for show. I had to remind myself of that. The farmhouse seemed to have been here for centuries and looked ready to crumble, but that was the point. Bravetown was meant to look like it belonged in an old Western movie. Apparently, the theme reached past the amusement park's entrance and included the adjoining admin buildings.

The inside only looked marginally more modern thanks to phones and computers. The decor was still very *Little House on the Prairie*. A receptionist closed her fist over her headset's mic just long enough to throw me a visitor's badge and send me to an office upstairs to find Renee Barlow. I tiptoed past closed doors with little name plaques beside them, inscribed with important-sounding job titles, and my eyes roamed over the wood-paneled walls and all the framed articles on them: Bravetown's grand opening twenty-four years ago, expansions and changes to the park as its popularity grew, and apparently a TV show based on the park that came out in the early 2000s. I'd have to look that up.

"You must be Esra!" A chipper blue-haired Bravetownee pulled me from my exploration back to the real world – or as real as it seemed to get in this place.

"Yep," I replied and blinked past her to the office door beyond her desk. Renee Barlow. Perfect. "I'm here to see Renee. It's my first day."

"You're a little early, but that's okay. I have some papers for you to sign right here." She beamed at me as she handed me a clipboard. "Can I get you anything while you wait?"

"I'm good. Thank you." I scanned the papers, expecting an NDA or something, but finding a work contract instead. Huh. I knew scooping ice cream wasn't exactly rocket science, and Sinan had probably vouched for me, but I'd expected a bit more formality. The contract said something about visible tattoos, face piercings and unnatural hair colors being forbidden for employees in the park, and I dragged my eyes back up to the young woman in front of me. She was dressed in a white blouse and a plain blue maxi skirt with buttons down the front, looking ready to be whisked away by an Old West cowboy, but the hair was definitely *unnatural*. It brought out her piercing, icicle-blue eyes though. "I love the hair, by the way."

"Oh, thank you. I won't lie, I was aiming for a light gray, but it'll wash out." She shrugged.

"If you have a pool at home, that'll do the trick. I had a pink clip-in streak as a kid, and the chlorine turned it salmon beige real quick." I wasn't sure how much of a luxury pools were around here, but my parents had always insisted on getting the best money could buy. That included a *nice* condo in a *nice* apartment building, with a pool, in a *nice* part of the city.

"Thank you! I'm Vivi, by the way. It's really good to meet you. Sinan has told us so much about you."

"He has?"

"Well, more about you coming to Bravetown than about you, really. He's so excited for you to start here." Vivi dove behind the counter and produced a huge canvas tote with the theme park's logo embroidered on it in pink and purple. "Your official welcome pack. If you wear your staff shirt or jacket around town, you'll usually get a discount when you grab coffee or something, but you're not allowed to wear it around the park. There's a strict dress code, but Renee will—"

The door to the office swung open, cutting Vivi off mid-sentence.

". . . really. I swear, any of them would be great as Annie. I'm so sorry. Genuinely. So sorry." A blonde girl backed out of the office, then dashed past us without a second glance.

"Sure you are, and I'm Britney Spears," someone, presumably Renee Barlow, replied, barely loud enough for me to hear, let alone the girl already jogging down the stairs at the end of the hallway.

6

Vivi tucked a stray blue lock behind her ear with one hand and shooed me toward the door with the other. I left my signed contract with her alongside the tote bag. I'd pick that up later.

Inside the office, a middle-aged woman with a ginger bun and a freckled, tanned complexion sat behind a simple wooden desk, pursing her lips at the papers in front of her.

"Hi," I said and closed the door behind me. Hopefully that blonde girl hadn't soured her mood to the point of making this harder for me than it had to be. "I'm Esra Taner. I'll be working in the ice cream parlor this summer. I was told to come see you first."

"Who told you to come see me first?" She raised her brows without looking up. As I stepped closer to the chairs by her desk, I could see that the papers weren't just papers at all; they were full-page photographs of women's faces, their pearly-white smiles beaming off each one.

"My brother, Sinan, and the guy at the entrance to the staff parking lot. Peter. His name was Peter. I think."

"Right. You're Sinan's little sister." She pinched the bridge of her nose and inhaled deeply before finally blinking up at me. Her eyes roamed up and down, and I regretted not bringing a more suitable shirt. "Green."

"What?"

"You're getting a green costume. Come with me." She breezed past me, and I had to jog to keep up with her long strides. We went up to the next floor, where half the hallway was taken up by overflowing clothing rails, some labeled with names, others with sizes. She pushed through a door into what looked like an actual costume warehouse. The walls were lined with clothing up to the ceilings.

"You can either be in the park in regular clothes and act like any other visitor, or you're in costume and stay in character. That means you pretend it's the Old West. You don't know what phones are, or words like 'yeet' or 'rizz' or whatever else is trending online at the moment."

"Sure, okay," I muttered and let my eyes travel over a row of corsets. I *so* didn't want to spend my summer stuck in one of those.

"Stand there."

I climbed on to a little round pedestal. Renee walked over a second later with a tape measure and started circling me to get my sizes.

"So I put on a costume, pretend it's *ye olden days* and I scoop ice cream all day. That's it?"

"You'll get three costumes," Renee explained while scribbling my measurements on to a tiny notepad one after another. "You get at least one full day off every week, so that's when your costumes get taken care of. That means if your day off is on Wednesday, you bring your clothes to the costume department on Tuesday after your shift, make sure to tell Gina if there's anything that needs mending, and you'll get them back fixed and washed Thursday morning."

"I gather that you're not the costume department."

"No, I'm the park director, have been for ten years. So all of this is my vision. I know who wears what, goes where, plays which role, and it's all cohesive." She narrowed her eyes at the notepad in her hands. "How tall are you?"

"Five-six."

"Wait here."

Not that I had much of a choice . . . Renee dashed out the door, and I was left alone on the pedestal, staring at my reflection, surrounded by historical garments. Not exactly how I'd pictured my summer playing out. I'd envisioned more beaches and cocktails while I figured out my crap. Alas, my parents had decided to freeze my credit cards, and hanging out at a theme park still beat my father's idea of a summer well-spent interning at his office. I didn't even know exactly what his firm did. Numbers on computers. I'd take breeches and cowboys over that any day.

"Try this." Renee came back with a heap of fabrics on her shoulder and held out a harness for me, black straps and sturdy buckles.

"I need a few more drinks before I get that freaky."

Her lips twitched up, but she schooled her features quickly to reply in a neutral tone: "It goes under the costume."

Well, I preferred a harness to a corset, so I stepped into the leg loops and secured the clips around my waist. "What kind of ice cream parlor are we talking? Will I be dangling from the ceiling?" If so, that would be a problem. I wasn't dangling material.

Renee opened a blue dress for me. Hadn't she just said I was going to wear green? "Would you consider yourself pretty?"

"If we're being technical, I think I'm more hot than pretty," I said while lacing up the dress. The top half was thickly lined with some sort of sturdy padding. "You know, more trophy wife than girl next door. It's the big eyes and big . . . other things that are probably not appropriate to mention in front of my new employer. But pretty works if you just think not-ugly."

"You talk," Renee fumbled around my waist and pulled

the metal harness links through two little gaps on either side of the dress, "a lot."

"Funnily enough, you're not the first person to tell me that, but hey, that just means I'll make great small talk with all the customers."

"Change of plans. You're not selling ice cream. You're my new Annie."

"Hard-knock life?"

"The Pretty Annie Lou. She's the mayor's daughter, gets kidnapped by Ace Ryder, the lawless cowboy, during the big showdown, before she gets rescued by Kit Holliday, the sheriff."

Those sure were a lot of words that had just left her lips. They just didn't make sense to me. Renee must have tracked my blank stare, because she heaved a big sigh.

"We have a bunch of well-known characters that inhabit Bravetown. They have lives and stories. We sell a ton of kids' books about them, but you can get the gist from the website. Bravetown only works because it feels real. It's not just the movie set of a Western. It's an actual Old West town with backstory and townspeople who are beloved by our regular visitors. During our summer season, these characters put on a show every day. Twice on weekends. No show on Wednesdays."

"Like, you want me to be in a play?" Maybe I should have paid a little more attention to Sinan's stories about the park. He worked as a Deaf Interpreter on the accessibility team here, but he usually just gushed about how adorable the kids were that he got to work with. I was pretty sure his fiancée was the only reason I wasn't an aunt to at least three babies yet.

"Trust me, you don't need any acting chops. Annie Lou has all of two lines. I just need you to fit in the costume, because finding someone else and having a reinforced costume sewn for them takes time that I frankly don't have." Her words got choppier and choppier until she pressed the last ones through gritted teeth.

I *was* getting the blowback from the blonde girl that had fled Renee's office earlier. She'd said something about Annie. And Renee had been looking through headshots when I'd walked in.

Talk about being in the wrong place at the wrong time. Starring in some Western live action show did not sound like the relaxed summer I had planned.

"I don't mind switching things up, but . . ."

"Stand up straight."

Her tone left little room for protest, so I did as I was told.

"The hem is two inches too long, but that's a quick fix," she muttered and scribbled on to her notepad. "Shoe size?"

"Eight?" I wasn't sure why it came out as a question.

"Easy enough." She beelined for a shelf in the corner and came back with three shoe boxes. "Try these ones first."

It was a pair of plain brown boots. Not the kind of cowboy boots you'd wear at a Taylor Swift concert, but definitely fit for the gravelly roads outside. I slipped my feet in, and they welcomed my ankles home like a comforting leather hug. Snug enough to offer some stability, loose enough not to leave any blisters or bruises.

"These are great. But I don't think I'm real damsel-in-distress material."

"You run away from the bad guy, and he whisks you on

to his horse. Which is where the harness comes in. It's not that hard."

"Oh, yeah, I don't do horses." I definitely shouldn't do horses. I'd been excused from PE my whole life. I didn't have a gym membership; I had a physical therapist. Heck, my parents hadn't even let me ride a bike. "Bad idea."

"Frankly, Esra, I need a Pretty Annie Lou. I don't even need a new ice cream girl. Sinan asked me to give you a job. This is a job. Take it or leave it."

"Oh." A smart person would have said something like *"With all due respect, I'm physically incapable of performing a stunt like that, even if it seems easy to you"*, or *"Thank you but I'll have to decline"*, or even *"Bestie, putting me on a horse is an insurance liability you don't wanna deal with."* But despite spending the last four years acing my way through college, I wasn't smart. I didn't want to keep driving on these painfully bumpy roads to maybe, possibly, find someplace else to spend the summer. And I didn't want to intern at my father's firm. So I only said, "I'll take it."

Chapter Two

CAREERS – STAFF HOUSING

The shortest commute possible: Bravetown is excited to offer its staff members modern housing on-premises. Employees can benefit from low rent prices on private studio apartments.

Just joining the workforce? Young people and junior employees may even qualify for a room in our free house-share program.

Rules and regulations apply.

NOAH

The rules were right there. Black on white. Laminated. Taped to both the backsplash of the shared kitchen and the refrigerator. You'd think that would be impossible to ignore, but you'd be wrong. Clearly, labeling my bread and peanut butter and putting them on the cupboard shelf with my name on it wasn't enough. And while I didn't mind sharing, the peanut butter sandwich thief had the nerve to leave the counter covered in crumbs and abandon their plate with the bread crust still on it.

What self-respecting adult cut the crust off their bread?

Lucas sauntered into the kitchen in one of his sheriff costumes, white hat still on. He got a kick out of riding through town like that. Any tourists that made their way out here had come for the theme park. Even if they stayed at the one motel we had or Berta's B&B, they'd flock to Bravetown eventually. Which made Lucas, also known as Sheriff Kit Holliday, a local celebrity. Technically, we weren't supposed to be in costume outside the park, but Lucas put on the white knight act to get girls, and Renee turned a blind eye because it helped draw undecided people into the park and steer excited fans there earlier.

I didn't care so much about the costume as I did about the crumbs on his vest.

Were those peanut butter sandwich crumbs?

"Don't glare at me like that. I stocked up this morning." Lucas lifted his hands in mock surrender before he pulled a bag of Doritos from his designated shelf.

Fair enough. Lucas had been working here almost as long as I had. He wasn't exactly a stickler for rules, but anyone who'd spent more than one summer at the park understood the bare minimum of keeping the peace in the staff housing complex.

"Fucking seasonals," I muttered and screwed the lid back on to my peanut butter jar.

"Absolutely planning on it," Lucas replied with a grin. "I mean, did you see that redhead waitress she hired for the saloon?" When I rolled my eyes at him, the idiot winked at me. "Don't get your panties in a twist over some bread, Noah." He chuckled and strolled out the door.

"It's not about the bread. It's about the principle." And now I was talking to myself while wiping off counters. Great.

I was getting too old for this place. Most people who worked here all year came from town, had their own homes and families to get back to at the end of the day. I hadn't meant to make this my permanent residence, but I'd moved in at twenty-four, and five years later, I was still here.

Two more years. I'd done the math. Two more years and I could move back home.

I slammed the cupboard shut harder than needed, earning myself a puzzled look from Austin, who sat at the huge dinner table with his chunky headphones on and his phone propped up in front of him.

I booked it upstairs before I'd start ranting about shared living etiquette to him. Even considering how to word it made me feel too petty for a Tuesday night. I was going to hit the shower and just eat at the staff gathering later.

We were two weeks away from summer season officially starting. Which equaled opening earlier and closing later, live shows, busloads of tourists rolling in daily, and right now a shit-ton of work to get the park prepped. I'd spent the entire day in the stables, and if I showed up to the saloon like this, the whole place would smell like horse shit by the time Renee had finished her big welcome speech – which was the same each year, but the new seasonals didn't know that.

Staff House B was three floors, the upper two allocated to bedrooms and bathrooms. Each floor held six bedrooms, two bathrooms. Sharing the bathroom with two other people usually wasn't a big deal. I twisted the handle, found it locked, and would have just come back in five.

This time, however, an unfamiliar chipper voice inside yelled, "One second!"

"It's fine," I replied. My mood had soured, but I wasn't so much of a dick that I'd rush some new employee off the toilet.

"Don't worry," the door swung open and a cloud of steam evaporated into the hallway – *someone* had probably used up all the hot water – "the bathroom's all yours."

I glanced down at the short woman in front of me. Soft. Everything about her seemed soft, and it wasn't just the fluffy towel wrapped around her chest, or the billows of steam behind her. Her big brown eyes took up so much of her heart-shaped face, she almost looked like a doll. Dark waves grazed at her delicately sloped shoulders, and her damp skin glistened like copper. Even her brows were smoothly curved black arches. Not a jagged line on her.

And despite all of that, my eyes latched on to the fluffy fabric that covered her from chest to knee. "That's not your towel."

"Huh?" She glanced down, water dripping from her wet hair, then grinned back up at me, a deep dimple in her right cheek. She tapped her finger against my embroidered initials on her midriff. "Yes, it is. Look: N.Y. New York. That's where I'm from."

"That might be, but it's still not your towel."

"Who are you? The towel police?"

"No, I'm N.Y. Noah Young."

"Oh, you're *Noah*." She said it as if the name meant something to her.

"Yes," I huffed, not giving a fuck if it did, because I was already so over people taking my shit.

She slapped a hand against her gleaming collar bone. "Esra."

Right. I'd forgotten she was meant to come today. Sanny hadn't shut up about it for two weeks straight. Once you got over the fact that this girl was wet and almost naked and in the middle of stealing my towel, she actually looked a little like her brother. Beyond the dark hair and light brown skin, they shared the same downward slant to their eyes. "Okay."

"Sinan's sister," she clarified.

"Yes, I understand. That's still my towel."

"I'll bring it back later."

Somehow, I doubted that. "Did *you* take my peanut butter?"

"Towel *and* toast police?"

"Is that a confession?"

"You're not much fun, huh?"

"Not when I'm being stolen from."

"Well, I can't give back the sandwich, but *god*. Here." She untucked the top of the towel. I realized what was happening just in time to drag my gaze to the ceiling before the fabric rustled distinctively. "Take it."

"What on earth are you doing?" I gritted the words out through clenched teeth. This was beyond ridiculous. Knowing who she was, I could have excused her taking my food. She'd come in from out of town and she'd been hungry, and Sinan had clearly talked about me enough for her to recognize my name in the kitchen. She'd felt safe enough to take that food. That made sense. This towel bit was beyond irrational.

"What do you think I'm doing? Giving your towel back. Take it already."

"Jesus. Put it back on before someone sees you. This isn't *that* kind of community housing."

"Take your damn towel, N.Y., Noah Young." When I didn't reach out to take it from her, she groaned. "Fine. Be difficult."

The towel rustled again but this time it dropped to the floor, the edge of it hitting my boots.

"I'll tell Sanny that you got me naked on my first day here," she chirped from a few steps away.

"I did no such—" Her words caught me off-guard enough for my gaze to swing down, just to find her disappearing into one of the bedrooms, catching the last perfect curve of her ass before the door slammed shut.

My first thought was that her brother might just kill me for even a split second of staring at her ass. He had never talked much about Esra beyond childhood stories, but I'd always gotten the sense that the silence was more protective than secretive. She had her own life, and it wasn't his to broadcast to strangers.

My second thought was that this girl radiated trouble. And she'd just moved into the room next to mine.

Chapter Three

THE RATTLESNAKE SALOON

Saddle up and ride on over to the Rattlesnake Saloon, where a finger-licking menu of quick bites awaits you by day, and we kick up our boots with barroom dancing by night!

No park admission required.

Esra

Esra: What am I walking into?
Sinan: A saloon.
Esra: Very funny.
Sinan: Free food.

He knew me too well. He also hadn't talked to the sandwich police yet apparently. I wasn't as hungry as I could have been, but I'd still spent the last ten days on the road on a tight budget for gas and snacks, so *any* food was a good idea. While I had no intention of copying our parents, either sticking to the trendiest dietician's advice on bland, fat-free foods or serving classic four-course dinners, the novelty of jerky and ice cream for every meal had worn off a little.

Walking into Bravetown was surreal. Sure, I was holding

my tiny supercomputer of a phone, and wearing a pair of denim shorts that would have gotten me jailed for impropriety way back when, but those things faded to insignificance when I stepped through under the wooden arch with the town's name on it. The entry to the park was a dusty circular plaza. In its center, a statue of a cowboy on a rearing horse greeted visitors, while the sides were lined with old wooden buildings, their slabbed facades faded shades of brown and red and the porch roofs wonky enough to seem at risk of crumbling. Not old. Old-looking. None of this was older than twenty-five years.

The large buildings to my left were marked as ticket offices and visitors' information. I would have loved to linger on the way the light flickered in perfect rhythm in the upstairs windows of the former, or on the silhouette of a woman walking back and forth in mechanically paced steps behind the curtains of the latter, but I was part of a crowd heading the opposite way. I didn't want to get trampled while gawking.

The people around me were chattering and huddling together, and they looked like they all belonged there in their faded Wranglers and their scuffed boots, half of them even wearing freaking cowboy hats. And not the pink-tassel, bachelorette-party kind. My chunky platform loafers alone branded me as the new girl when I'd figured they'd look at least somewhat professional for a staff meeting.

My footwear musings were cut short by the Rattlesnake Saloon. Maybe I'd get used to Bravetown one day soon, but I stumbled in my steps and almost face-planted for the second time today. The Rattlesnake was in all actuality a saloon. Music and voices spilled through the swinging half-doors, barrels outside served as standing tables on the porch, and three real-life horses were tied to a rail-and-trough fixture on the side.

My mind did the same backflip it had when I'd seen Cowboy Lucky this morning. People had come here on their horses, because of course they had freaking horses as an actual means of transport.

I wasn't given much chance to check out where the path led past the saloon. I just got a glance at the closed ticket gates before I was shuffled forward by an old lady who told me to "stop dilly-dallying" as she shooed me inside.

The inside of the Rattlesnake was still Old West, but a bar was always going to be a bar. There was a stage at the far end, draped in heavy red and blue curtains, a large round space right in front of it, covered in chairs and tables that could probably be removed to create a dance floor, and all of it was ringed by booths and upper-level balconies with more private seating. Behind the booths, a long bar ran along the wall, a woman with honey-blonde curls juggling bottles like it was a sport.

"Ez! Esra!"

My head swiveled in the direction of my brother's voice. Sinan was standing in one of the booths, waving both arms over his unruly head of dark hair, grinning from ear to ear. His fiancée sat behind him, smiling and just waving with her hand raised to shoulder-level.

The second I made my way over, his arms wrapped around my shoulders and he pulled me against his chest. It started as a hug but then his embrace tightened bit by bit until my face was smushed against his chest, and I flailed my arms and grunted.

"You've gotten so tall," he fake-wept against the top of my head.

"You stink," I grunted even though I could only smell his laundry detergent.

He released me with a huff.

"Hi, how are you?" Zuri slipped around Sinan and wrapped me into a much gentler hug. Zuri gave the best hugs. She'd come to New York with Sanny a few times, so I'd had my fair share of Zuri Hugs, and I'd have made Sanny marry her for those alone. She was a bit taller than me and while I didn't lack assets, Zuri was all lush curves that made every hug extra-cozy. Most of her black curls were wrapped into a high bun, drawing all the attention to her soft face, shimmery gold highlighter making her dark skin glow. "How was the drive?"

"It was good. I saw the world's largest chicken."

"What?" She laughed and pulled me next to her on to the bench.

With Sinan sitting across from us and the saloon filling with people and noise, I automatically started signing alongside my words. Sanny's hearing aids had a setting for crowded spaces like this, but it wasn't always the most reliable. "The world's largest chicken. Okay. Technically, it's the world's largest chicken *sculpture*. But it's huge."

"That's why you took almost two weeks to get here?" Sanny asked.

"I also saw the world's largest chest of drawers. And a big chair. It's not the world's largest anymore, but it was at one point."

"That sounds like fun," Zuri said, signing the words as she spoke them. Her hand movements were still a little slow, but she was learning. She actually meant what she was saying, too, while Sinan was chuckling and shaking his head.

"How do you like your room?" he asked.

"It's tiny." It took everything in me not to grimace. "My closet at home is bigger than that room."

"Don't worry," Zuri laughed, and the tight coils that had escaped her bun bounced around her face. "You'll spend hardly any time in your room anyway."

"I don't plan on working that much." Now I did grimace.

"There's always something going on either here or in town. Once you get to know everyone, you'll always be busy. The saloon is open to the public like a regular bar most of the time, so people from town don't need to buy a park ticket to just come here and hang out."

"That's good to know." I grinned and wiggled my brows.

"Esra, no." Sanny glowered at me across the table.

Zuri signed "sorry" with her right hand, while grinning into her drink and taking a swig.

"Don't start telling me *no*. I could have stayed home for that."

"I care about this place," he replied. "Don't make me regret getting you this job."

"You can still care about it when summer is over, I leave, and everyone just accepts that your sister is a slut who parties too much."

Sanny's mouth fell open and Zuri snorted a laugh. She held a hand up to her face as some of her drink blubbered back up. "Oh god," she coughed, still laughing, "you're really going through with this whole *wild summer* plan, huh?"

"I don't know what you mean." Fluttering my lashes, I gave her an innocent smile.

Before either of them could come up with a retort, our attention was drawn to the stage, where Renee Barlow tapped a finger against the mic until everyone fell silent. She started a welcome speech, but I barely paid attention. Zuri's words echoed through my mind. *Wild summer.* It was so much more than that and it irked me that apparently my entire family had boiled it down to this. "Out of control" were the words my father had used after I dropped out of med school and went on a two-week bender in Malibu. That I had "lost my way" had been my mother's diagnosis when I'd started staying out overnight without telling them where I'd been. (Usually, the bed of some guy from some crappy rock band I'd seen playing at some shitty bar. Usually a drummer. The calloused hands just worked for me.)

But I wasn't *wild* or *out of control* or *losing my way*.

It was the complete opposite. I was in full control. For the first time in a long time, I was doing what I wanted. I was finding my way. I'd spent the last decade of my life sticking to a predetermined script to get into a *great* college and a *great* med school and a *great* medical residency program. None of that was on the cards for me anymore, and in a weird way, it was freeing to see your future go up in flames.

Sue a girl for having fun and getting laid when she finally has the chance to make her own decisions.

"That's you." Zuri pushed her elbow into my ribs.

"Hm?" I blinked and focused back on the room just in time to hear my name being called out again. Renee was on the stage with a couple of other people, pained expressions plastered across their faces.

"Go. She's introducing the new hires."

"Oh, got it." I shuffled out of the booth, took a quick swig from Sinan's beer, and beelined for the stage. "Hi, hello, oh thank you," I laughed when Renee offered me her hand to help me up. I was not going to look like a deer caught in the headlights, even if the stage lights were blinding. This was going to be my summer of fun, no matter where I was spending it. I plastered on my biggest smile and waved into the silhouetted crowd like I was winning a beauty pageant.

Judging by the snickers and mumbles in the front row, people were picking up on my shirt. After my shower earlier, I'd had exactly one left that didn't reek of sweat and car. The pink one. The one that said "u can't pick ur father but u can pick ur daddy".

Renee introduced a few other people, and by the end there were around twenty of us up on stage. Most of us were just here for the summer; two were new permanent hires. Those two were the only ones that got lengthy introductions that included their job titles – the blonde barkeeper called Adriana, and an older accountant named Donna. Apparently corporate emails weren't a thing at Bravetown. I was just grateful that she hadn't introduced me as her new Annie Lou.

I still had to mentally prepare for the lecture Sanny would give me for accepting a job that involved climbing on to a horse.

Once we were dismissed, I followed Adriana to the bar.

"You're Sanny's sister, right?" she asked and slapped a napkin down in front of me.

"How do you already know that?"

"Wild Fields is small," she said, shrugging, "and you two look alike."

"Not much," I mumbled, because I almost looked like a carbon copy of our mom, while Sanny was all our dad's straight lines and height. Contextually though, there probably weren't many Turkish people in this town. Safe to assume we were related. "So you're from here?"

"Kinda, yeah." Adriana shrugged and didn't elaborate. She just set my drink down in front of me. I hadn't ordered anything specific, just as fruity and girly as possible. She'd delivered. The drink in front of me was pink and garnished with pineapple and orange slices, and glitter dust swirled around in the cup.

"What do I owe you?"

"Tap your staff pass here." She held up a little white scanner. "First alcoholic drink is free tonight. Soft drinks are always free for staff members."

Good to know. That would save me some money. I laid my card against the scanner, but Adriana didn't give me any sign of it working even after the machine beeped. She just blinked.

"Did it work?"

"It says cast member," she replied.

"Huh?"

"The display says cast member, not staff member." She narrowed her gray eyes at me, her freckled nose scrunching up. "Did you steal someone's pass? Is this your second drink?"

"No," I said but before I had a chance to explain, she swiped my card from my hand, turning it to read it in the dim light.

"Esra Taner, that's you all right." Adriana returned my pass with pursed lips. "You should get that looked into. Different passes open different doors, so you might need it reprogrammed or something."

"I thought you were new here too."

"Kinda. Yeah." This time, she grinned. "Long story that involves a lot of tequila and poor life choices."

"Sounds like my type of story. Tell me some other time?" I glanced over at our booth, because I still had so much to catch up on with Sinan. Including my new job. My brother and his fiancée were no longer alone though. Noah Young, peanut butter and towel officer extraordinaire, had sat down next to Sanny.

Not going to lie, I was a little disappointed that he had so valiantly avoided looking at my body earlier. Whenever Sanny had mentioned his friend Noah who worked with him at Bravetown, he'd forgotten to mention that Noah was tall, like easily 6'3", had strapping muscles, a sharp jawline and ink-black hair. Right above his left brow, that hair had one perfect white streak in it. Not the turned-gray kind, and not the peroxide kind, but a white patch caused by lack of melanin.

I turned back to Adriana. "Actually, do you have peanuts back there?"

"Sure."

She poured me a small bowl of nuts. It wasn't exactly a whole sandwich, but hey, it would have to be enough to make amends.

With the official part of the evening over, people were crowding between tables, chatting and laughing, swinging with the music pouring from the speakers. They almost

27

made me spill my drink and my nuts twice by the time I was close to our booth.

". . . back to your parents. It's not your job to keep her out of trouble." Noah's voice cut through the noise, halting me dead in my tracks.

"She's my baby sister. Of course it is," Sanny replied, and my stomach dropped a little. I was grateful for his help getting a job, but I didn't need to be kept out of any trouble. I wasn't looking for trouble. I was looking for some fun. And I was done letting the people around me keep me from it.

"She's a grown woman," Noah said, "and she's obviously careless and irresponsible."

"Noah," Zuri pleaded, but didn't interject beyond that.

"I'm just saying, don't let her blow through your life like a tornado. You're trying to build something here."

Fuck Noah Young and his stupid haughty opinion. Over what? Some bread and a towel? I'd even given the damn towel back. Asshole.

And fuck Sinan for not defending me.

Wild.

Out of control.

Losing my way.

Tornado.

I turned on my heels and headed back to the bar, clanking the peanut bowl back on to the counter. Adriana turned to me with raised brows after serving someone their beer. "What's wrong?"

"My brother's best friend is being a total dick," I grumbled and climbed on to one of the barstools. I shoved a whole handful of peanuts into my mouth. Ha. He wouldn't get any of them.

Adriana bent over the bar to glance toward where Sanny was sitting. "Noah?"

"Yeah," I grunted through the nuts.

"Don't worry. Noah doesn't really like anyone. He's more of a mutual-tolerance kinda guy. I'm pretty sure your brother is the only exception because he's real damn hard *not* to like."

I currently despised him, but I could admit that she was right. Sinan was a goddamn ray of sunshine, always had been. He made friends easily, helped anyone who needed him, and never said "I told you so" even if he had given you sound advice before you made your own stupid mistakes.

"What about you?"

"Me? Oh, nobody except Renee likes me," she laughed, but there was a sad undercurrent of truth to her words. "These people wouldn't come near me if I wasn't handing them their drinks."

"I think we should be friends," I said, because I was feeling a kinship with my fellow disliked person.

"Sure," Adriana grinned, "but only if you can hold your liquor."

I pointed one finger-gun at her and used the other hand to tip my drink back. I gulped down the sugary concoction like it was air and I'd been suffocating. When I set the glass back down, only ice cubes clinked against its sides. "You just found yourself a new friend."

Chapter Four

WILD FIELDS

If you're ready to take your adventure past Bravetown's borders, why not visit our charming neighbors in Wild Fields? Take a walk around the lush town square with its historic gazebo, and dip into the surrounding cafés and restaurants for a refreshing taste of modern American small-town living.

Esra

"Bart's Mart doesn't take cards?"

"By George, she's got it." Adriana grinned and pushed her sunglasses up to her head. They did little to keep her wild blonde mane at bay. "There's an ATM around the corner. Casey's Supermarket does take cards, but for some reason there's never any bathroom stuff. There are shelves for toothpaste and shampoo and all that, all right, it's just never in stock."

She had parked the car on a corner of Wild Fields' town square, from where we had a perfect view of both supermarkets. They each occupied a corner of the square, and I couldn't help but imagine a diagonally opposed turf war that cost them their credit card readers and toothpaste stock.

"ATM and Bart's it is," I said. "I do need toothpaste."

Adriana led the way. Her long skirt flowed in the breeze, creating a perfect carefree image paired with her cream crochet top and dozens of necklaces and rings. She pointed out the side of the square where three restaurants and two cafés lined up, and called it the food mile, even though it was definitely not a mile.

Everything in Wild Fields looked shrunk. All the buildings were close to the ground. The tallest ones we walked past were three stories high. And with everything built so low, there was just So. Much. Sky. Everywhere. No matter where I turned, I could see the horizon and, above it, miles and miles of emptiness. I kept staring at all that blue and the streaks of cloud. Driving across country and having all that sky above the road and the rolling hills in the distance was one thing, but this whole town was topped by azure.

Adriana had to grab my elbow and pull me in the right direction, or I would have walked right past Bart's Mart.

I'd only taken fifty bucks out of my account, because there wasn't much more in there in the first place, but walking the aisles with Adriana soured my stomach. Those fifty would be a tight stretch across two weeks. Who knew that cereal was this expensive? God, I'd have to use the rest of my Moroccanoil shampoo in droplets for the rest of the summer if I considered *that* cost.

"You look a little pale," Adriana mumbled through a mouthful of M&Ms while we were checking out and the number on the cash register kept climbing and climbing.

"I'm going to sound dumb, but I've never bought my own groceries," I replied, and tried to smile at the lady behind the register who silently raised her brows at me.

She'd started scowling the second Adriana had stepped up to pay and hadn't stopped since.

"Awww, I popped your cherry," Adriana laughed and made the cashier's frown deepen.

"You could have bought me dinner first, you know?"

"Gosh, you're high-maintenance." She playfully rolled her eyes at me. "Back in my day, it was a beer on the front porch and then you hopped in the car together."

The cashier cleared her throat.

"To go grocery shopping together for the first time," Adriana clarified with a grin that betrayed her blatant lie.

I bit my lip to stop myself from laughing. At least having her here made it easier to stomach the $43.68 I had to put down for a bagful of bare necessities. And that was with the 5 per cent staff discount I got for wearing my Bravetown employee polo shirt.

"You weren't kidding about nobody liking you, huh?" I asked as I buckled my precious groceries into her backseat.

"Yeah," she shrugged. "But it's fine. I still like Wild Fields and everyone who lives here. They'll fall back in love with me sooner or later. I just have to get them all drunk first."

She'd told me that she'd left when she was nineteen and only returned a few months ago, but I hadn't gotten the story last night, and it didn't look like I was getting it now. "Where did you learn how to bartend?"

"Nashville."

"You don't like talking about yourself, do you?"

"Nope."

We fell back into her car, and Adriana drove down a few streets branching off the town square, where she pointed out City Hall, the local dive bar, a books-and-plants-and-gifts shop, and a hair salon to avoid at all costs unless I wanted to walk out bleach-blonde.

"Okay, tell me about Bravetown," I said when we were done with the Wild Fields tour after all of ten minutes. "I haven't really paid a lot of attention to Sinan's stories over the last four years."

"We can talk about *you* if you want."

"Nope." I chuckled as I threw her response back at her. I didn't think she'd be the kind of person to throw shade at me, but I'd gotten plenty last night and didn't care to repeat that. I was just going to ignore Noah Young's presence. He no longer existed in my world. I was manifesting a blissfully dreamy summer where opinionated, controlling, gossiping assholes had no air to breathe.

"Fine," she smirked. "The most important thing for you to remember about Bravetown is that it belongs to Wild Fields. There's no big corporation or random gazillionaire behind it. If you don't work in the park yourself, you have a relative who does. Farming isn't as lucrative as it once was, and the alternative would be commuting into the city every day. But the tourism around Bravetown brings in enough money to keep the whole town afloat. It's beloved because it kinda belongs to everyone a little bit."

"I'm sorry, who went 'we hate commuting, so let's build a theme park'?"

"It's a whole thing. I'll send you a video."

I'd treated myself to exactly one thing at Bart's Mart – my favorite Reese's (the mini cups) – and crawled into bed

33

with my strictly rationed portion of three of them at the end of the day. This wasn't half bad. I had the best chocolate and a nice, firm mattress. Sure, my room was nothing but a shoe box with a twin bed, a sturdy chest of drawers that creaked every time you opened it, and a tiny desk that currently functioned as my laundry hamper, but I'd spent quite a few nights sleeping in my car on the way here. This was already an upgrade.

After Adriana took me back to the staff housing complex, my last day off had passed in a blur, sorting away my groceries and unloading everything that I had stuffed into my car.

I wasn't on full duty yet. I had two weeks to learn the ropes before the big summer-season opening weekend. Not ropes. Reins. They'd put me on a horse. I really should look up this whole Annie Lou showdown thing.

Opening the link Adriana had sent, I propped the phone up against my pillow and let the video play. It was an old news report on Bravetown's first anniversary. The colors were too bright and too dull all at once in that 2002 way reserved for old sitcoms.

The video showed a reporter in a crisp white shirt paired with a bolo tie standing beneath Bravetown's wooden arch, the cowboy statue right behind him.

"I'm standing at the entrance to what may look like a Clint Eastwood movie but is actually the gate to the thrilling adventure that's Bravetown, an Old West theme park, just an hour and a half outside Nashville. The history of this park is quite unique," the reporter said, big microphone up to his nose, "because it starts with a last wish. With us here, to share this inspiring story, is Bravetown's park director, George Barlow."

The camera zoomed out to show the man standing next to the reporter. George Barlow was an old white man in a suit. He wasn't distinctive beyond the bright-red cowboy hat on his head and the tiny round glasses on his nose, the lenses the size of a dollar. Doing some mental math, I figured he had to be Renee's father or uncle, or something along those lines.

"Thank you," he said, holding his own microphone low enough for his voice to crackle. "We are so proud to celebrate one year of brave guests at the park, and it's all thanks to a man called Bob Horton. There are some people who leave a lasting impression in your life, and Bob was one of those. He had a big heart. He was like Wild Fields' honorary uncle. He was at all the birthdays, all the graduations, all the weddings. He had no family of his own, but everyone knew him. Everyone loved him. You saw his bright-red hat from a mile away." George tapped the brim of his own hat. "His passing left a hole in all of our lives. Little did we know that he had big plans for our small town. You see, he had all this farmland that he left to the city, along with more money than any one person could spend. None of us knew that he'd won the lottery in the eighties. Bob was the type of man who wore the same shoes until they came apart at the seams."

The video showed some grainy pictures of a brightly smiling man in a red cowboy hat and a variety of denim shirts.

"And he left his estate to the town of Wild Fields with a stipulation, didn't he?" the reporter asked, clearly guiding the park director to his point.

"He did, indeed. Bob's will stated that we had to use his

money and his land to create a place where people would gather and have fun. He wanted to bring people together. When we cleared out his house, we found hundreds upon hundreds of these old pulp Western novels, and that's how the idea for Bravetown was born. A place that honors Bob and his last wish."

"Let's take a look at what the brave people of Wild Fields have created in his honor," the reporter said, and the camera swiveled over to the Rattlesnake Saloon.

Now Adriana's words made sense. Bravetown belonged to Wild Fields. It had started with one person who loved the town and its people enough for them to build a whole theme park in his honor.

I was going to skim the comments for some gossip on that backstory but one of the suggested videos caught my eye. *Ace Ryder vs. Kit Holliday – The Showdown*. Dated one year ago. I clicked on it and threw another peanut butter cup in my mouth.

The video started with a shot of the Bravetown entry sign, then cut to two men in some sort of duel. One of them was the guy I'd met on my first day in the parking lot. Same exact costume. White hat to white shoes. The other appeared to be the bad guy, dressed in a black hat, black leather coat and a dark bandana drawn over his nose. The clips were edited to a fast-paced country-rock song, cutting back and forth between the two.

It was over in less than a minute before the next video started on auto-play. That one was all about Ace Ryder, the lawless cowboy. The guy dressed in black. It showed clips of him in the park from all sorts of angles, all grainy, clearly filmed with phone cameras that weren't meant to be zoomed in that much. It also showed him riding after a girl in a familiar blue dress and whisking her on to the horse mid-gallop.

I was so not up for that. No matter how hot a villain was doing the whisking.

Chapter Five

ACE RYDER
THE LAWLESS COWBOY

Ace Ryder is an infamous bandit known for his silver tongue and his quick draw. With a heart as cold as the night, he robs banks with his gang of outlaws and vanishes into the shadows on his black steed before the sheriff can catch him.

Will you be brave enough to face him?

NOAH

"I call dibs," Lucas announced from the tack room, where he'd just disappeared with Canyon's saddle.

"You call dibs without knowing who it is?"

"Eh, better safe than sorry." You could practically hear him shrug through the wall. "If I've already hooked up with her, the dibs lapses. If she's from around here and I haven't hooked up with her yet, she's probably a drag anyway, but I got dibs just in case she isn't. And if she's new, she has to be hot to play Annie, so I got dibs."

"That's messed up." I rolled my eyes and turned to Tornado, who huffed and shook his head. Clearly the horse agreed with me. "He's messed up," I repeated, voice lowered as I led him out of the stables.

"What's messed up is that I gave you four years to pull Lindsey," he called out. "I never invoked dibs. And now she's off to sing on a cruise ship and neither of us got in her pants."

"Lucas, Lindsey shot you down on your first day here." I wasn't going to point out that Lindsey was also on a cruise ship with her girlfriend who she'd been with since sophomore year in high school. He'd never had a chance.

"Send me a picture."

"Not happening."

Once outside, I mounted Tornado and directed him toward Bravetown's Main Street. It had been a while since I'd taken him out this early in the day. He was the calmest horse I'd ever encountered but his ears still twitched with the break in routine.

Between all the useless yapping, Lucas had indirectly said something true though. I'd known Lindsey for years even before doing the show, this town was small, and there weren't that many candidates to replace her. Certainly not with the short notice Lindsey had gotten to make her way down to Florida for her onboarding. Maybe Tornado had every right to be twitchy.

We turned the corner to the large town square at the end of Main Street, where the artificial mesa formation jutted high into the sky behind the bank and the town hall – and I felt *it*. The same way you feel a horse about to buck in the way its shoulders shift and its muscles tense. The way the birds go into a frenzy before a thunderstorm. The split second of thick air and anticipation before a catastrophe.

". . . your picture on the website," Renee was saying, fixing her red hair into her signature messy bun atop her head.

"Full costume, I'm assuming," Esra replied. I'd half-expected her to have run off already. I hadn't seen her at all since her on-stage introduction on Tuesday in a very inappropriate and very see-through shirt, and Sanny had texted me last night to ask if I'd heard from her. All I could tell him was that there was a carton of almond milk with her name on it in the fridge.

"Yep. Full makeup, costume, everything. We'll take a few group shots too."

"Like a whole photoshoot? That sounds so cool. You know, I've seen those over-the-top shoots on *Top Model* with the sets and the costumes, but I never really thought I'd be in one." Esra grinned and clapped her hands together.

The staff pictures were *not Top Model*. Probably no point in explaining that to a girl in skin-tight daisy-print leggings and a T-shirt that said "If you're rich, I'm single". The harness clipped around her thighs and waist didn't make that outfit any less ridiculous. It just drove home the point that she had taken over from Lindsey.

"Shit," I muttered. We were still two buildings away, but Tornado neighed his agreement loud enough to draw attention.

"Ah, here we go," Renee said, turning to fully face me.

Esra's gaze roamed over the horse, the corners of her mouth straightening out, posture clenching. Double shit. That wasn't the look of the kind of rich girl who had gotten private horseback riding lessons all her life.

I dismounted a couple feet away from the two women. "Good morning, Renee. Esra."

Esra's chin jerked in my direction, eyes reluctantly

tearing off Tornado and narrowing on me. "What are *you* doing here?"

"Oh good, you two already know each other." Renee smiled. "Noah plays Ace Ryder. The bandit that kidnaps Annie. Noah, Esra will be our Annie this year."

"So I have to share a horse with *him*?"

"Yep."

The chain of expletives running through my mind only remained unspoken because Renee started walking up the steps to the bank building. Meanwhile Esra was back to staring at Tornado like he might eat her. I wouldn't even blame him.

Leaving Tornado tied to the hitching post by the building, I followed Renee to the bank.

"Noah, I've already talked Esra through the opening of the show on the way over. Ace and the bandits causing chaos on Main Street, some of the stunts, all the townspeople fleeing into the buildings. How Annie and her father run into the bank before you and the boys follow. Then you all run out with the money and Annie as a hostage. We'll do some full runs with everyone next week. For now, I just need the two of you to get the kidnapping right. Esra is two inches shorter than Lindsey, so you'll have to adjust, too."

I nodded but turned to Esra. "Do you know how to ride a horse?"

"Nope."

"Seriously, Renee?"

"Oh, don't worry," Renee waved me off as if this wasn't begging for catastrophe. "You just have to get her on the horse and buckle her in."

41

"Why am I buckled in exactly?" Esra asked.

"So you don't fall off when the horse rears," Renee replied.

"That horse? Rearing? Like . . . ?" She pointed down the street, and it took me a second to realize she meant to point toward the park entrance and the statue of Old Bob on a rearing horse. The color was draining from her face.

There probably wasn't a person more ill-fitted for this job than this girl. She wasn't the first out-of-towner working here, not the first one from a big city either. Heck, she wasn't even the first person in her family to be employed here. But you needed a certain rationality to make it work, and I could come up with a lot of words to describe Esra Taner, but rational wasn't one of them. She'd get herself thrown off the horse before even getting in the saddle.

"Just rewrite the show," I said. "We'll do it without Annie Lou. She's clearly out of her depth."

"Hey, you don't get to decide my depth." Esra glared at me. "I'll get on the damn horse."

"She'll be fine," Renee insisted with a nonchalant wave of her hand, like I had no reason to be concerned here, "let's just give it a shot. In the version we've done the last few years, Ace uses Annie as his human shield when he leaves the bank." Renee stepped from the bank doors down the stairs, holding her arms as if she was holding an invisible hostage at gunpoint. She then jogged down the stairs, her voice growing louder as she went through the scene. "When he fixes the bags of money to his horse, Annie runs off. Ace races after her and hauls her on to the horse as she's running."

Esra opened her mouth, but Renee silenced her with a raised hand.

"I don't think that's realistic." She jogged back over to us. "Not only because you don't have the experience but because you are shorter, and those two inches Noah would have to bend down further could very well be the two inches that pull him off the horse."

This time, I was about to speak because I wasn't falling off any horse anytime soon, but Renee cut me off. "What we're going to do instead is Annie running off – not as far as we have done up until now – and you, Noah, will lift her on to the horse and then mount behind her. The sheriff and his men follow, gunfire, explosions, and you ride off to the hideout."

"You want *him* to grab *me* and lift me on to the horse?"

"Yep. Let me go get Tornado in position." Renee beamed.

"And here I thought I was in for a touch-starved summer," Esra muttered under her breath.

She was a lawsuit waiting to happen.

"Don't worry," I said. "Nothing about the way I'll touch you is going to fix that. It's rough stunts. Hard work."

"Maybe I like it hard and rough."

I rubbed the bridge of my nose, willing myself not to dwell on that response in detail. "This job isn't a joke."

"Don't worry. With that face, nobody will ever think you're joking."

"Excuse me?"

"No, not yet." She twirled around, her glittering hair clips winking in the sun as she beelined toward the bank's doors. "It's empty!"

"Yeah, it's just a set for the show."

"All right, all right." Renee popped up next to us, and grabbed both of us by the elbow. "Ace brings Annie out, bandits run off. He's holding a gun to her head to get her to the horse."

"Gun?" Esra asked.

"Prop," I replied.

"Down the stairs." Renee kept directing us and I knew better than to be anything but a puppet in her hands. "Ace turns, Annie runs." Renee left me by Tornado's side and pulled Esra further. Squinting at the distance between us, she dug her heel into the ground and marked a deep groove. "Run from Noah to this spot for me and pretend you're in a long skirt, so no big leaps."

Esra had to run back and forth around two dozen times before Renee was happy with the distance. At least Esra didn't question her. She just followed each command to run, faster, slower, glance back, faster again.

Renee's mind for the park was unparalleled. She knew each button on each costume, knew where every character was at any given time of day, and had the show choreographed down to the second. Once Esra managed to run the distance to the count of eight, I jumped in to run the same distance in half the time.

"Okay, great. And then Noah is responsible for the horse part. He'll hoist you up there," Renee called from where she was watching on the front steps of the town hall. "Give it a go."

I stepped up next to Tornado, rubbing his neck, and waited for Esra to follow. She kept two extra feet of distance between her and the horse. Any mild praise I'd afford her for running back and forth on command evaporated at the sight of her pinched lips and crossed arms.

The park offered horseback riding to its guests, so I'd put many bloody beginners on horses.

Esra was worse.

Esra was like the prim nanny or the third wife who got dragged along with the overeager kids and hated even the idea of sitting on a horse. I'd seen plenty of her type, too.

"This is Tornado," I said in my calmest visitor-friendly voice.

"He's big," she grumbled. "His head is like . . . half of me."

"Not quite, but yes, he's big. Come here. Say hi." I waved her forward and showed her how to pet his neck.

Esra stretched her hand out and Tornado immediately swung his head around to meet her halfway, more than happy to make a new friend. Esra jumped back, clamping her hands against her chest. This was going to take a lot of work. The horse sniffed at her, and each huff from his nostrils tightened the set of her shoulders.

"I'm not sitting on that."

"Fine by me," I said with a shrug.

"In the saddle, Esra," Renee yelled over.

"Can we rehearse the other part first?" Esra called back. "Where he drags me from the bank. I feel like I can really channel my kicking and screaming resistance right now."

"Get on the horse, kid."

Esra huffed, shot a sideway glance at me, then propped her hands on her hips, rolled her shoulders back and jutted her chin into the air. She looked like she was posing for some superhero comic cover.

"What are you doing?" I asked.

"Nothing." She shook her head, then her limbs, and plastered on a stupid big smile that was all teeth and crinkles around her eyes. "It's fine. Lift me up, cowboy."

"It's probably easier if I'm behind you. Lindsey always made a show of kicking her legs, because you need to swing your leg high to get the skirt over the saddle." I stepped around behind her and pretended not to notice the ruffles along the seam of her leggings that ran right down her ass. "Ready?"

"For a little roughing-around? Always."

"Oh, for god's sake." My hands dropped from where I'd been about to grip her waist. "Try to be serious for a few minutes, so you don't get anyone hurt."

"Up," she commanded, arms stretched away from her sides like a damn cheerleader. At least she wasn't running away from the horse.

"Yes, ma'am." I grabbed her waist right over the thickly cushioned harness straps and lifted her up. I immediately tracked my mistake. Lindsey had been slightly heavier, and I'd given Esra the same momentum up the horse. She swung higher than I'd meant her to and landed harder in the saddle. Eyes screwed shut, she let out a squeaky huff. "Shit. Sorry."

"Are you?" she gasped and pried one eye open to look at me. "You won't get rid of me that easily, you know?"

"That's not . . ."

"Oh god." She blinked and turned her head, tracking her new position in the saddle. Her hands flailed out by her sides.

"Hold on to the horn," I said, and tapped the front

46

of the saddle to point out the vaguely mushroom-shaped handle for her.

"Not the reins?"

"I'll be taking the reins."

"Right."

I pulled on the straps with thick carabiners on each side of the saddle. "These are your buckles. They connect to your harness to keep you on the horse. I'll buckle you in when I'm sitting behind you. You just hold on to the saddle and try not to fall until then, okay?"

Esra shook her head. "I want to get down."

"Foot in the stirrup, here."

"No, I don't think that's . . . This is too high." Her voice jumped higher. "Can you get me down? I want to come down."

"I'm trying to show you how to get down. Your foot goes here." I pointed at the stirrup again.

Instead of listening to me, she started twisting in the saddle as if she was trying to dismount by sliding off her stomach. This girl was trying to break her neck. I curled my fingers into the harness, trusting that she had it fixed and fitted to her measurements, and hauled her off the horse. Even knowing what a lightweight she was, the way I could maneuver her body with a few straps was way too fucking effortless. Definitely not a realization I should dwell on.

At least Esra's scowl made *that* easy. As if I'd been the one doing something wrong.

"When I tell you to put your foot in the stirrup, you put your foot in the stirrup," I grunted.

"Let go of me." She pushed against my arms, and I released the harness I hadn't realized I was still holding.

"You can't fuck around like that. A horse isn't some jungle gym."

"Noah," Renee intervened, placing a hand on my shoulder, "language."

I hadn't noticed her coming over.

"He should lift me off the horse," Esra said to her without missing a beat, "when we get to the hideout. Ace should pull Annie off the horse instead of making her dismount. Makes more sense. Otherwise what's stopping her from kicking him in the face when he's standing next to the horse, and just riding off on her own with all the money he stole?"

"His gun should be intimidating enough, no?" Renee asked, clicking into the show as if Esra hadn't just risked her neck because she couldn't even stay in the saddle for two minutes.

"Not with everyone choosing bear over man," Esra said.

"What?"

"Most women would choose being trapped with a bear over being trapped with a man," I supplied, not sure how to feel about the fact that I was actually tracking Esra's train of thought.

"I'd rather take my chance kicking my kidnapper in the head and maybe getting shot," Esra explained. "It's better than a guaranteed kidnapping."

I had to unclench my jaw, because her words mirrored a couple of comments we got online. "If Ace pulls Annie off the horse and into the hideout, she can still try to fight back physically instead of going just because he points a gun at her head," I conceded.

"Fine. Fine." Renee waved her hands around, clearly

48

not quite following the bear argument, but not invested enough to start a discussion. She must have seen the same comments about Annie being too passive though. She had a better handle on our reputation on social media than me. "Ace pulls Annie off the horse when he dismounts. We'll save that for another day. Let's wrap it up for today. I expect both of you to be here at the same time tomorrow."

"Okey-dokey."

"Sure," I said.

"Here, take this." Renee pulled a park pass from her pocket and handed it to Esra, who had somehow inched further and further away from Tornado. "It'll allow you to skip the queues and there's a bunch of meal vouchers on it. Your job this week is to get familiar with the park. Ride the rides, try the snacks, meet the characters. Guests will ask you a whole lot of questions when they meet Annie, so you better know this place like the back of your hand."

"You mean I get paid to ride roller coasters?" She perked up. "I can totally do that."

"All right, head back the way we came in, so you're out of sight before the park opens. You," Renee pointed her finger at me, "walk with me."

Esra turned the pass over in her fingers, whipping her phone out and taking a selfie with it. She'd fare much better as a visitor than as a character actress.

Falling into step beside me, Renee headed along toward the stables. She tapped away at her phone screen until we were about halfway, then her head whipped back up. With one glance back over her shoulder, she made sure we were out of earshot before hitting me with a tight-lipped frown.

"We both know that your stables aren't ready for your

horses yet, so they need my roof over their heads. And we both know that it would take me a whole lot of time that I don't have if I had to replace you. So level with me. Can you lift her on and off the horse?"

"Yes, but—"

"Do you think you'll be able to keep her in the saddle for five minutes?"

"Yes."

"Without the characters, Bravetown is just a bunch of old buildings. Without Annie, Ace is just a thief. If I thought there was any chance we could survive without having Annie in our show, do you think I would have hired the first girl who fit the costumes? Annie has been a Bravetown staple since day one. I don't need the two of you to get along. I need a thirty-minute show, six days a week."

"Seriously? Nobody else fits the costume?"

"Not unless you want us to get sued by concerned parents who didn't sign up for nip slips with every bounce on that horse."

"Jesus, Renee." I rolled my eyes at her. She wasn't quite old enough to be my mother, but there was still something off about hearing her talk about *nips*. "What are you saying?"

"Suck it up."

"Your pep talks are incredibly inspiring."

"Noah, you don't need inspiration. You need to be slapped across the back of the head with a reminder that this is the job you signed up for to pay for the job you actually want. You have a whole lot of people rooting for you, so *suck it up* and focus on the end goal."

Two more years. I had to cling to that. Two years wouldn't get me quite to the finish line, but I'd have my family's old ranch fixed up enough for me and the horses to move in.

"Fine," I muttered, "but next summer, at least find an Annie Lou who isn't afraid of horses."

"She'll be great. I have a feeling about this one." Renee grinned and winked at me before breaking off and returning to the emails on her phone.

Yeah, I had a feeling, too. The foreboding kind.

Chapter Six

MOUNTAIN PASS RAILROAD

The road to Bravetown has never been easy. Many adventurers have tried and failed to cross the dangerous mountain pass. Nowadays a railroad leads straight into town, but don't be fooled. Passage won't be smooth. The mountain terrain is steep, and dangers still lurk around every sharp turn. Be prepared to encounter wild animals, sudden rockslides and menacing bandits.

Esra

My right hip shot a sharp dagger up my side with every step from the park to the staff housing grounds. I'd made sure to wait until Renee and Mr. Grumpy Cowboy had rounded a corner before I'd hobbled back.

Okay, so maybe I had underestimated just how badly this could go for me.

As it turned out, falling off the horse wasn't the only thing to be concerned about. Being thrown on to it? Also not something my joints enjoyed.

Where other people had naturally resistant tissue around their joints to secure them and keep them in their sockets at safe angles, my tissues were weak, and my body just stretched every which way. Joints weren't meant for that lack of support. Back home, I had a whole variety of braces for my wrists, ankles and knees, which were always the first to cause issues, but how the hell was I supposed to stabilize my hips?

Even though everything desperately needed a wash, I squeezed myself into my tightest yoga shorts, followed by a pair of leggings and my snuggest pair of jeans. I'd survive walking around with a coffee stain on my right thigh.

The compression actually helped the pain, and a glance in the mirror confirmed that the layering did wonders for my ass. Win-win. I'd just sweat like a pig.

Definitely not a problem big enough to derail my perfect summer of freedom. If I'd even mentioned so much as a new, unfamiliar twinge in my hips to my parents, they would have already booked me in with my doctor and found a way for me to never go near a horse again. As if I wasn't able to deal with a little bit of pain after all these years.

Plus, even with the jeans plastered on like a second skin, I still managed to slide my priority park pass in one of the heart-shaped back pockets. That was basically fate, right?

Wrapped up tight, I waddled my way back to the park. My first stop was a popcorn cart disguised as a Conestoga wagon, where white cloth covered modern machinery. The delicious smell of sugar and butter had beckoned me closer even from outside the turnstiles. The man inside the wagon greeted me by name. He'd probably been at the saloon for the big on-stage welcome. I only smiled and nodded, and thanked him when he handed me a sparkling pink plastic bucket shaped like a cowboy hat, with a matching pink lanyard to carry it around my neck. It was the most perfect popcorn bucket ever. The other option, besides paper boxes, would have been a boot-shaped-bucket. *This* was much better.

Smiling to myself, I wandered along Main Street, shoveling down handfuls of the best popcorn I'd ever tasted. Possibly made better because it was (a) free, (b) from a glittering hat and (c) the first thing I'd eaten all day.

Despite the summer-season opening still being two weeks away, crowds began filling the shops and the attractions. Kids ran around in Western costumes, horse balloons tied to their wrists, swinging horseshoe-shaped pretzels through the air. I'd need one of those later. Meanwhile their parents snapped pictures and pointed between buildings and the park map in their hands.

I had a map saved on my phone, alongside a PDF with information on every attraction and character in the park, thanks to Vivi from the main office.

Between the slow crowds and my own standing-and-reading outside buildings, my hips got a fair amount of rest. By the time I made it to the far end of the park, where the deep ochre mesa formation jutted into the sky behind the railroad station, I even felt good enough to be thrown around on a tiny high-speed train.

The staff members here were dressed like old-timey train conductors, in dark blue uniforms with gold buttons. After checking my pass, they waved me past the main line and into the train station through a separate line. Just like the inside of the saloon, everything in here was perfectly on-theme. Old suitcases were piled into a corner, train schedules hung on the wall and a *Wanted* poster at the end of the queue warned people of Ace Ryder and his gang of bandits.

I was almost at the roller coaster when annoyed exclamations behind me made me turn.

"I'm so sorry. I'm just here to make sure my little sister doesn't have to ride alone." Sanny apologized to the family behind me as he climbed over the banister. His arm curved around my shoulders to prove to a red-faced mother that we really did belong together. Still smiling, he turned to me, brows raised. "Something you want to tell me?"

Wow. Word spread fast. Hadn't expected Noah to be that much of a gossip. Instead of confessing to my new job, I blinked up at Sinan, all innocence and fluttering lashes. "Did you know that the mountain pass is completely artificial? The park was built on flat land. They just built a mountain for the roller coaster."

"I got the same info folder you did, Ez." Sinan rolled his eyes at me. "I'm talking about Annie Lou."

"Oh, yeah." I shrugged as if I hadn't even considered that answer – let him feel ridiculous for the lecture he'd undoubtedly prepared. "Renee decided I'd be a great fit for the role. I'm surprised this place doesn't do understudies."

"I love you, but you can't even ride. How do you expect to pull off the stunt? You'll end up getting hurt."

"I'll learn."

"Esra— thanks, Paul." Sanny maneuvered us past a conductor, through the turnstile and into one of the carriages. "Here, sit on this side. You'll get the better view."

I took my seat and stowed my empty popcorn bucket away between my feet. "Look, I'm grateful you got me a job here, but you have to actually let me do the rest from here on out. I can look after myself."

"Can you?"

"Yes." I rolled my eyes at him. Sanny was five years older than me, which meant Mom and Dad had always roped him into their overbearing ideas of keeping me safe. He'd eased up a lot when he'd gone off to college here in Tennessee, but a certain protectiveness had been ingrained in him so young, I wasn't sure he'd ever let it go. Still, I'd try to get him there. I wasn't going to spend my whole summer appeasing his worries. "I'll come to you if I need help. Promise. Just let me do the thing."

"Mom and Dad are going to kill me." He took his hearing aids off and pocketed them deep in his jeans before folding the safety bar down across our laps.

A whistle blared through the air, Paul waved a paddle above his head, steam blew from the front of the train, and then we tore off. The roller coaster seized around the corner and rattled up the mountain. I got a panorama of Bravetown and blue skies for all of two seconds before we plunged into the belly of the mesa formation. An explosion sent a ravine of rocks our way and the train zipped around another turn right before they hit us. We went back up, past bears and coyotes, and tore down at breakneck speed.

The wind whipped tears from my eyes as I screamed and laughed at the same time.

My brain rattled around my skull, my lungs pumping hard to make up for the screaming.

The train eventually slowed down, and the station came back in sight. Right before we rolled in, the barrels next to the tracks sprang open. A group of life-sized dolls, dressed like outlaws, jumped forward, screaming – and I screamed back. Somewhere a flash went off.

It took me a moment to compute that I'd just been photographed during a jump scare. The same moment it took for the train to stop in the station and the bars to spring open.

"That. Was. Brilliant," I gasped as we exited the building.

"I love the mountain pass," Sanny laughed as he repositioned his hearing aids. "Definitely in my top three rides here."

"Can we ride again? Wait, no, what are the other two?"

"Journey Downstream and Bootlegger's Barrels."

I waved my priority pass through the air. "How much time do you have?"

He checked his watch. "I have like an hour before I have to get in costume."

"Good thing we can skip the queues."

"Good thing, huh?"

I nodded. "And then I need to get one of those horseshoe pretzels."

Sinan jogged up to the photo kiosk and got our picture, complete with a little paper frame with cacti and tumbleweeds on it. While I was screaming my ass off, hair all windswept, he was cheesing directly into the camera. He also brought back a plastic yellow star pin, which read *BRAVE* where it usually would have said *SHERIFF*. I fixed that to the lanyard of my popcorn bucket.

Journey Downstream turned out to be a little boat ride. For a few minutes we disappeared from the park and drifted through nature's wilderness. Much to the delight of the three kids on the boat behind us, Sanny knew all the animal animatronics by heart and rattled off wildlife facts like their personal tour guide. If the giddy little giggles hadn't been infectious already, Sanny's terrible bear puns would have done me in. I bear-ly made it off the boat dry because I laughed so hard I almost slipped off the dock.

Bootlegger's Barrels was a spinning-teacup kind of carousel – which always turned competitive between us. Losers got dizzy. We turned the center console as fast as we could, knuckles turning white. Maybe, just maybe, I should have had a more substantial breakfast than sugary popcorn. Before I even got dizzy, my stomach twisted. I let go of the wheel and grabbed the seat instead, squeezing my eyes shut.

Sinan laughed and bellowed out a lyrically incorrect version of "We Are the Champions" until the carousel stopped.

With my tummy still spinning, I was suddenly also very aware of the dull throbbing in my right hip that I'd managed to ignore through sugar and adrenaline.

Linking his arm through mine to keep me upright, Sanny sighed. "You know, you don't have to wait until you need help before you come talk to me, right?"

"Huh?" I doubted he meant my hip. He was only supporting my weight because he thought I was dizzy.

"If you ever need to talk about . . . stuff."

"Oh, I'm all right." I patted his shoulder. "Just figuring things out. You did all the figuring-out in high school. I never got to. Did you know that I'd never even been to a party with alcohol before this year?"

"Really? Never?" He raised his brows. "Fine. Just don't

make a mess. Please. This is more than a theme park. It's my actual life and my actual friends. And don't get thrown off the horse."

"Don't worry. I'll be buckled in."

"I feel like you'd somehow find a way around that."

I rolled my eyes at him. "Don't you have to go slip into a tasseled vest or something?"

He shot a look at his watch. "Dammit. Come watch the show later?"

"Sure."

He gave my arm one more squeeze before tearing off through the crowd.

I had to eat something before the show. And I had to sit down. Preferably in that order.

The show was a children's play on a small stage between the coffee cart and the candy store. It was a watered-down version of the bank robbery and the showdown between the outlaws and the sheriff.

Sanny stood in one of the front corners of the stage and interpreted everything. He'd introduced himself as Carl, explained his role and a few words in sign language, like sheriff and bandit, before the actors had come onstage. He translated the whole show with more energy than a single person should have, with big movements and dramatic facial expressions. The kids were eating him up.

Out of all the other people on stage, I only recognized Kit Holliday, the sheriff, aka the guy who had selflessly accepted my thigh-Dorito when I first arrived.

At least I was spared another encounter with Noah. I had yet to see him in his costume, and I wasn't sure my brain would survive the clash of Ace Ryder swaggering across my screen and winking into the camera, and Noah goddamn Young with the broomstick up his ass.

"What are you doing?" My concentration was shattered by a voice that sounded an awful lot like its owner had a broomstick up his ass.

I set my jaw and refused to look up from where I was bent over the washing machine, trying to decipher the faded instructions above the detergent drawer. "Reading."

"Scoot over," he grunted and set down his laundry basket.

"I can do my own laundry." I scowled. "I watched a tutorial. I separated by colors, and I checked all the labels to get the temperature right."

The tutorial had been for a washing machine with a little glass door in the front though, and this one opened on top, and had a completely different detergent compartment. I didn't even want to admit how long it had taken me to figure out which one of these contraptions were washers and which ones dryers.

"Give me a break," he muttered, earning himself a withering look. "Move before you end up flooding the entire house."

"I'm pretty sure that only happens in the movies." Although, to be fair, I'd only seen gunslinging cowboys in movies up until a few days ago. "Right?"

Noah raised his dark brows in response, that one streak of white hair falling across his forehead. Ugh. Fine. The alternative was another tutorial, but my phone was in my room, charging. And my hips would prefer to avoid another upstairs trip from this tiny laundry room in the basement and back.

Grimacing, I stepped aside and gave Noah control over my washing machine.

"Pre-wash detergent for heavily stained clothes, regular detergent, fabric softener," Noah explained while pointing out the different boxes in the drawer. He plucked the bottle from my hands and pulled a different one from the floating shelf above the row of machines. "You're washing colors, so you use this detergent. One cap of it in the middle slot." He poured the soupy blue slime into the detergent compartment, then grabbed yet another bottle from the shelf. I tried to mentally catalog all of that. "A splash of fabric softener is enough."

"Not that one." My hand jutted out to cover the detergent drawer as soon as I recognized the dumb purple flowers on the bottle. Lavender threw me back to the hospital, to being poked and prodded and scanned. They may have intended the scented pillowcases to be calming, but there were only so many nights you could spend alone in the children's ward before the smell started to elicit Pavlovian nightmares. "I don't like the smell of lavender."

"All right," he sighed and switched to a different fabric softener with pictures of honeycombs and milk on its label. Better. "Is this one to your liking, princess?"

"Yes, peasant boy, that's agreeable," I bit back. I hadn't even asked him for help. He had absolutely no right to give me attitude.

"Shut the drawer, hit start, set a timer on your phone." He rattled the instructions off as he started the machine for me. "Come back on time and put your stuff in the dryer, or someone will throw your wet clothes out to use the washer themselves."

"Stop talking to me like I'm stupid. I'm doing this for your benefit. You have to get up close and personal with me tomorrow morning. I'm just making sure I don't reek of sweat."

"You're a grown woman. You should have enough self-respect to *want* to wear clean clothes."

"I have enough self-respect not to let you talk down to me like that." I turned on my heels, and wished my hair was long enough to whip it in his face as I pushed past him, out of the narrow room.

Fucking unbelievable. Excuse a girl for trying to learn a new household skill in her twenties.

Huffing and grumbling, I marched into the shared kitchen and yanked the cabinet doors open. My dinner plans consisted of pesto pasta and my nightly ration of Reese's Minis – until my eyes zeroed in on Noah's name on his shelf. And how it was freshly Sharpied on to every single one of the items on his shelf.

Sandwich, towel and laundry police.

Ugh.

I grabbed bread and jelly from my own shelf, but he had this huge jar of peanut butter from some obscure brand I'd never heard of. I narrowed my eyes at the label. Organic and zero sugar? And he was calling *me* a princess. Bet he ordered that online or something.

I lathered a thick layer of his fancy-schmancy peanut butter on to my bread, then heaped an extra spoonful of jelly on to the sandwich to make up for his lack of taste.

I screwed the lid back on and eyed his neatly organized shelf. With this big a jar, I wasn't sure he'd even notice a portion missing. And I wanted him to notice. Maybe it was childish, but I considered it payback for being a dick to me all day. And what was the point if he didn't know revenge had been taken?

I put the jar on my sparsely stocked shelf instead. Right next to my cheap off-brand sugary peanut butter. Perfect.

"Dorito girl."

I bit my lip to suppress the gleeful grin as I turned and closed the cupboard.

The parking-lot cowboy, aka Lucky Luke, aka Sheriff Kit Holliday, leaned in the doorway, clad in plain jeans and a Marvel T-shirt. "Fancy seeing you here, Lucky."

"I live here. Top floor. Last door."

"Don't recall asking for directions, but thanks."

"You might feel like you need them at some point in the future." He grinned and pushed himself off the door in a strangely rehearsed fluent move that involved entirely too much hair flipping.

It reminded me why I preferred drummers over frontmen.

"Sure, let me know when you're throwing a party and I'll stop by."

"Will do." He winked at me, but it lacked that confidence I'd seen from Noah in the Kit vs. Ace videos – and I immediately hated myself for taking note of that. Noah had the confidence, but more than that, he had the *nerve*.

"When you do, make it worth my while, okay? No half-assed parties on my watch." I grabbed my plate and beelined for the door. I didn't even hear Lucky's response to that.

The first couple of stairs toward my room were fine. But my hip buckled by the halfway point. By the time I made it all the way up the stairs, I was leaning against the wall, needles piercing through my right side. The rest of my night had just become a strictly horizontal endeavor.

I dumped the plate on my nightstand and crawled into bed, jeans still on. The coffee stain on my right thigh mocked me like a schoolyard bully, pointing right at me and laughing.

If Noah made even one dumb comment tomorrow about my laundry staying in the washer overnight, I'd hide his stupid fancy peanut butter somewhere he wouldn't find it.

Chapter Seven

THE PRETTY ANNIE LOU
THE MAYOR'S DAUGHTER

Annie Lou is a gentle beauty beloved for her kindness. With a warm smile and a heart for helping, her caring nature has made her a true town treasure. Annie brings a touch of sweetness to the Old West.

Always remember: In the face of adversity, kindness can be the bravest act of all.

NOAH

There was a chance Esra was conducting a social experiment to see how many inconveniences it would take to make me snap. Hadn't she been in med school? Maybe she hadn't dropped out. Maybe she was part of some sort of psychological-torture study. I was merely a guinea pig trapped in her maze.

At least that would explain why I'd found my peanut butter among her things, right next to her own, when I'd gone to make dinner – and her laundry in a wet heap on top of the dryer when I'd gone to pick up my own dried clothes. I'd told her to be back in time or someone would unload the washer for her.

I should have let her deal with the mess the next morning. The water dripping from her leggings on to the floor had started to pool though, and I actually cared about keeping the living conditions here a few levels above a camping ground's shared amenities.

When we met up again in the park for our next practice session, she didn't so much as acknowledge the fact that she'd woken up to a basket of dry and folded clothes (including her current T-shirt, with weird naked baby angels all over it). Instead of showing gratitude, she pulled a face every single time my hands wrapped around her waist to lift her on to the horse.

Renee watched the first few lifts from various vantage points before making us change our moves and the way we were angled to the horse. She then went back to watch the new lift from her chosen locations. We repeated that process until she clapped her hands from the steps of Miss Clementine's Café and jogged across the square. "What if we tie her hands?"

"No," I replied without missing a beat. "She can barely keep herself upright as is, and Tornado isn't even moving yet."

Esra jutted her chin out from where she was leaning sideways in the saddle. "How on earth did someone like you end up working here?"

"Someone like me?"

"This place is fun. You're . . . you."

"The *fun* is for visitors," I pointed out. "Those of us who work here actually treat it as a workplace."

"Sanny still has fun in the park." She raised her brows at me as if I should take that as a challenge. "I just think you should enjoy the job you choose."

"Makes sense coming from you. Is that why you dropped out of school? Wasn't fun enough?"

"Yeah, I thought it would be so much more fun to spend my days around you and your smelly cow." She crinkled her nose down at Tornado, who huffed and shook his head as if he understood the sentiment.

"Wow, we've stooped to insulting my horse? Very mature."

"I think we're done for today," Renee interrupted us, levelling her gaze on me. "Save your breath for tomorrow. We'll hook you both up to microphones, so we can practice the full scene."

I was close to defending myself by saying that Esra had started it, and I was actually okay to keep going, but considering I'd criticized Esra's maturity, *"she started it"* didn't seem like the way to go.

I forgot my maturity later that night though, when I opened the kitchen cabinet. I'd only meant to cook myself dinner, but Esra's shelf taunted me. She had a couple necessities, but everything else was quick snacks and pure sugar. Eyeing her jar of peanut butter, I ran my hand over my chin.

This was stupid. What was that saying about an eye for an eye leaving everyone blind?

I turned to shoot a look at the empty kitchen doorway. I listened for any footsteps. Nothing. Nobody.

Setting my jaw, I grabbed the bag of Reese's from her shelf, only to hide it behind my own jar of peanut butter. That was for calling Tornado a cow. Besides, that stuff was unhealthy anyway.

BRAVE

67

My immaturity earned me intense eye contact the next morning. I could have chalked up the death glares she greeted me with outside the bank building to her superb Annie Lou acting skills, but I had a feeling they were chocolate-related.

"Good morning." I plastered on a smile for Renee's benefit. "How were the rests of your days yesterday?"

"Fine, fine, thank you." Renee waved me off, twirling her pen through the air while she hunched over a stack of paper.

"Loved my afternoon in the park, loved the Haunted Mines ride," Esra replied, squinting at me, "but my dinner was lacking a little something."

Yeah, fuck, maybe it was immature, but vindication tasted better than any peanut butter chocolate confection could. It took every drop of restraint in my veins to keep my lips tight as I nodded and hummed an understanding note.

"Okay, here we go." Renee shoved a sheet of paper at each of us. "Commit to memory, please."

We each had four whole lines of dialogue in the revised scene before Esra's escape on foot. Short enough to memorize in the twenty minutes it took Renee to fix a mic pack to Esra's obstructively tight daisy-print leggings, snake the small beige headset under her hair and around her ears, and explain the control switch on the pack. I hadn't touched that switch once. Our microphones were controlled remotely during the show. That switch was just for emergencies, and allowed us to switch between normal mode, intercom or turning the mics off altogether.

"Say something for me, Esra," Renee said, clipping on her own headset.

"I swear by Apollo the physician, and Asclepius the surgeon, likewise Hygeia and Panacea, and call all the gods and goddesses to witness, that I will—"

"Got it," Austin's voice cracked through our earpieces. "Thank you, Homer."

"Hippocrates, not Homer," Esra replied as she turned in a circle. Instead of finding the source of Austin's voice, her eyes landed on me. Her head dropped sideways, waves of chocolate hair spilling over her shoulder as her forehead wrinkled in confusion and her big doe eyes rounded out.

It wasn't even the full costume. Merely the part that would influence the microphone. There was no need to look at me like I'd grown a second head just because I'd pulled a black bandana over the bottom half of my face.

"Noah," Austin prompted.

"I'm saying words. Test, one, two, three. Testing, testing."

Esra's head snapped back upright, and she silently mouthed: "Boring."

"Thanks, good to go," Austin said.

"Okay, while exiting the bank, there's still a lot of shooting noise from the other bandits who run out before you two," Renee explained as she walked us over to Tornado's side, her voice carrying through the intercom of the headsets, "but when Annie Lou runs away from Ace, your microphone is turned on, so feel free to huff and puff a little."

"Huffing and puffing, got it."

"And when you scream for help, use an *indoor* scream. Or it will crackle on the speakers."

"Indoor screaming." She nodded. "Okay."

"Noah?"

"Villain voice, I know." I tipped my hat at her before I turned toward the saddle, so I could act distracted enough to give Annie Lou her chance for an escape.

Renee backed away and counted us in. In my peripheral, Esra took two tentative steps backward, then booked it. Fast, raspy breaths filled my headphones. Her voice carried on them like a wordless whisper, every exhale uniquely hers. The sound raised the hairs on my arms. Before I could seriously contemplate that phenomenon, Renee cued me in, and I did my best exaggerated double take before chasing after Esra.

I was ready to grab her, but my muscles locked up. In that instant, her body's shape etched itself into my memory. The slope of her neck and shoulders, her waist accentuated by that thick leather harness, those curved hips covered in purple flowery spandex, down to her slender calves. Fuck, I probably would have memorized her ankles if they hadn't been covered by her costume boots.

It was one second of realizing I was about to handle her body like a prop.

That one second was enough for me to miss my cue and for her to overstep her mark.

Fuck.

I wrapped my arm around her middle and hauled her to me. Esra's back collided with my chest, air whooshing from her lungs. Her ribcage deflated beneath my fingertips, and her deep rasp filled my ears louder than it should have.

"You'll have to run faster than that, gorgeous," I growled. The words and Ace Ryder's low, scratching voice came automatically.

Esra stilled against me. My headphones fell quiet. She didn't move a muscle, not even her lungs.

Maybe I'd grabbed her too hard. Shit. I'd been off-beat, distracted, when I should have been more careful.

"Fight him, Annie Lou," Renee called through the headsets.

"Oh, right," Esra muttered. Her body rippled against me with a new surge of energy. Then the screaming and kicking started. "Let me go! Help! No, stop! Help!"

I carried most of her weight as I hauled her back, only to whirl her around and cage her against the horse. I shaped my fingers to a gun in the absence of props, tilting Esra's chin up. Her slender throat was completely exposed as she swallowed.

"Get on the damn horse, Annie Lou."

"I'm not going anywhere with you, *criminal*," she spat the word, her amber eyes like flames in the sunlight.

"Have it your way." I lifted her on to the horse like we'd practiced, her feet kicking through the air, and mounted behind her in one swift move. I leaned in close as I buckled her in. "Hold on tight. Don't want anything to happen to a pretty little thing like you."

"You should worry about yourself," her voice hitched with the perfect amount of panic, "because Sheriff Kit Holliday is going to come for me."

"Let him come."

I tapped my heels against Tornado's sides and he tore off. In the show, there'd be more gunfire behind us. We raced to the other end of the town square, before a sharp 90-degree turn. Esra squeaked into her mic. She got a few moments to collect herself, during which I pretended to fire at a group of barrels marked "gunpowder" in the town square.

Instead of a fake explosion of said barrels, we only got Austin's voice on the headphones: "Boom."

I dug my heels in and Tornado got up on his hind legs. His muscles rippled under us, all calm and precision. I just flexed my thighs to stay in my seat. The whole thing looked more impressive from the stands thanks to the fireworks and Tornado's height.

"Fuck, fuck, fuck, fuck, fuck," Esra muttered. Maybe the trick wasn't as unremarkable to someone who had never sat on a horse. She clenched up to the point of shrinking in front of me. Using my hold on her waist and my weight against her back, I pushed her forward, leveling our center of gravity.

We were back on the ground in an instant, but her breathy chant of *fuck*s didn't stop until Tornado halted in front of the gray building that was Ace Ryder's designated hideout.

"Great. Esra, exactly like that," Renee's voice crackled through the headphones, "Noah, you came in two seconds too late. Come back here and let's go again. Austin, let's make sure Esra's microphone is set to intercom as soon as the horse begins to move."

"What about the dismount?" I asked.

"Let me see you get the chase right first," Renee replied.

We trotted back to the bank building, where we dismounted. Well, I dismounted, and then I had to lift Esra off the horse. I bit back any comment on how she should at least learn that much about horseback riding because her face had taken on the same shade of gray as the dust under my boots.

"You don't have to hold on that tightly," I said when she

flexed her fingers, marked with deep red grooves. "You're buckled in, remember?"

"Leave me alone, Young." She glared at me. "Let's just go again."

I wasn't entirely sure if that was still about her chocolate, or if I'd offended her some other way. But less talking, more working sounded great to me.

On the second go around, I grabbed her right on cue.

"You'll have to run faster than that, gorgeous."

"Let me go!" Esra started wriggling and kicking without hesitation this time, probably giving me a bruise or two on our way back to Tornado's side. "Help!"

"Get on the damn horse, Annie Lou."

"I'm not going anywhere with you, *thief*." The way she spat that word was *definitely* about her chocolate. At least she didn't see me smirk behind the bandana. This woman was turning me into a sadist.

"Have it your way, ma'am." I set my jaw and hoisted her on to the horse. When I slotted in behind her, she whipped her head around, hair flicking me in the face, and glared over her shoulder. "Hold on tight. Don't want anything to happen to a pretty little thing like you."

"Pause and freeze," Renee interrupted. "Amazing. I love the hostility. Esra, good improvising. I think *thief* works better than *criminal*. Noah, can you wrap your arm tighter around her waist, so we don't see the left buckle?"

I shifted closer, my thighs framing Esra's and my chest snug against her shoulder blades, just to brace my arm around the entirety of her waist.

"Stay like that." Renee jogged backward while we stayed frozen in spot. At least, I stayed frozen because I had a modicum of patience. Esra huffed and whipped her hair around again. This time, I managed to duck.

Fine. She wanted to sulk over some chocolate? Two could play that game.

"At least you don't reek of sweat," I muttered into the narrow space between us.

"What's that supposed to mean?" She shifted back, her elbow jabbing me in the arm, as if she hadn't been the one to bring up the smell of her sweat a few days ago. "For your information, I shower every day."

"Yeah, don't worry, I noticed you hogging the bathroom for hours on end. I meant because of your dirty clothes . . ."

"That works." Renee clapped her hands, clearly interrupting us on purpose. "Again! From the top. We're not stopping until you're ready to do all this in costume next week. You'll get there quicker if you stop bickering like little schoolgirls."

Austin cackled on the intercom, but both Esra and I remained quiet. We both obviously wanted to get this over with sooner rather than later.

"Have you actually tried talking to her?" Sanny laughed and dragged the paint roller up the wall. Light blue that had faded to gray over the decades disappeared under a slick coat of white. We'd only done one wall so far, but it already brightened up the entire hallway. "Did you actually have a conversation about what you expect from a roommate?"

"She should know that it's a shared living space, so there's—"

"Why *should* she know?" he cut me off.

"It's common sense," I replied as I traced around the door to my childhood bedroom with a paint brush.

"Sure. Common for you. I'd like to see you navigate a Friday-night dinner with my parents compared to her, and then see what Esra says about *your* common sense."

"I think I'd manage. I have manners."

"Oh, really?" He laughed and leaned on the paint roller, raising his brows at me. "Are you able to tell apart a salad knife from a butter knife?"

"That's not common sense, that's just rich-people nonsense."

He hummed a non-committal note. Sinan had gone to college in Nashville and had started working in the park shortly after graduating. Sure, when I'd met him, he'd been a bit clueless about living in a small town, but he'd already lived in a dorm for a few years then. I didn't actually know what he'd been like straight out of high school, silver spoon still in his mouth.

"If my mother invited you for dinner at seven, would you know to arrive half an hour earlier because it's *common* in their circles to have an aperitif before dinner?" he asked.

"Are you just making shit up to make me feel like a small-town hick?"

"I wish I was." I was saved from more quizzing on etiquette by the buzzing of his phone. Sanny wiped his hands off on his overalls before pulling his phone from his pocket. He flashed me the caller ID, the photo of a middle-aged version of his sister. "Speak of the devil."

Sinan clicked a button on his hearing aids and disappeared down the narrow stairs at the backend of the hallway. His voice carried up from the kitchen, but with the call being in Turkish, I couldn't make sense of anything but his tone. He sounded like I did when approaching an agitated horse, both hands raised, every step toward it calculated. I chuckled. His mother probably wouldn't appreciate the comparison . . .

By the time he reappeared, his dark hair stood up high and had a couple of paint flecks in it.

"You good?" I asked.

"Yeah . . ." He plastered on a smile and shrugged, but just when he grabbed the paint roller to keep working, he turned on his heels. "You know my parents have called me more often in the few months since Esra dropped out of med school than they did in the four years I've worked here. I actually counted in my phone log."

"Shit. That sucks."

"Yeah." He pursed his lips, eyes narrowing on the paint bucket. There was something else he wasn't saying, but I realized that I didn't actually know enough about his family to figure that part out — and he clearly wasn't ready to spill.

Sighing, I grabbed the beer bottles from the top of the folding ladder and held one out to him. "If it makes you feel any better, my parents haven't called in years."

Sinan blinked at the bottle in my hand, then up at me, and it took a moment, but he barked a chest-deep laugh. "Are you kidding? That's dark."

"Does it make you feel better though?"

"Yeah," he chuckled, and took the beer. "Dark, man."

I shrugged and dipped my brush back into the paint

to cover up the pencil marks by my door that marked my height growing up. My father had left me this place and not a cent to maintain it when I'd been way too young to take on the responsibility. Almost a decade later, we were finally on track to get it back up and running. Sanny had even offered to invest his trust fund, but friends and loans usually didn't mix well. Instead, we painted, and we refinished the floors, and we fixed the fences on the paddock.

By the time we opened for business, this place was going to look nothing like the miserable house I'd left.

Chapter Eight

Esra

"What do you think?" Vivi leaned back, blush brush in hand, to let me admire her work.

My reflection somehow looked like I belonged on a pop music stage in a sparkling leotard, while simultaneously oddly like I just sprang fresh-faced from the last season of *Bridgerton*. "I'll never be able to replicate this on my own."

I wasn't bad at makeup, but this kind of full beat was levels beyond my winged liner, shimmery highlighter and contouring stick essentials. Even the guys masked in bandanas had sat down at the brightly lit vanity tables to do their foundations and brows in layers. They'd been so much quicker than me, who had to be tutored step-by-step. They were all off to get their staff photos taken within minutes. Picture day saved me from the humiliation and *pain* of horseback riding, but this was yet another part of the job that I was not equipped for.

"I filmed a tutorial, don't worry," Vivi said.

"You filmed a makeup tutorial just for me?"

"Yes, well, partially." She tilted her head from side to side, blue tresses swinging over her shoulders. "I thought it would be good for you to have, but I also just posted it online in case anyone wants to do their own Annie Lou makeup. Obviously, the pink lipstick I use in the video won't look the same on you, because you're a deep winter and I'm a light spring, but just stick to this shade and you're good." She waved the little tube of Russian Red in my face until I plucked it from her hands.

"I have no idea what you just said but will not stray from this lipstick," I promised.

"Perfect, just give me a shout when you run low." She swiveled around to grab her makeup bag. The momentum in her turn knocked against the table and my thermos cup wobbled off the edge. Both of us dove forward to catch it, fingertips knocking together and completely missing the cup. "Oh shit. Sorry. Darn it."

The cup clattered to the floor, last remains of iced coffee splashing from the lid on to my skirt.

"It's okay. I've got it," I said as I dipped down to pick it up, saving us from knocking our heads together too.

"I'm so sorry," Vivi squeaked, hands still flailing through the air. "Oh god, your costume."

"It's fine," I assured her. "You can barely see it. I'll pose strategically."

"I'm so, so sorry. I can run and get you one of your other costumes."

"It's a teeny-tiny speck, don't worry. Really."

Vivi was still biting her lip and staring at the stain, so I pulled out my phone to get her mind off the little faux-pas and told her to cue up the tutorial.

I gasped at the video on my screen. "Vivi, this has like thirty thousand views."

"Hmm? Oh, yeah." She shrugged and filled a Ziploc bag with Annie Lou makeup items.

"Are you internet-famous or something?"

"No," she laughed, "I'm probably one of the few people here who isn't."

Before she could elaborate, the door to the fitting room flew open. It smashed into the wall, startling the guy strapping on the undertaker costume.

"Coffee delivery," Adriana trilled in a perfect high note.

She spotted us at the vanity table and beelined over, handing out cups from paper trays as she went. She had braided little golden beads into her blonde curls that clicked against each other and against her dozen necklaces as she went. "Don't you look pretty, Annie Lou?"

"Thanks," I laughed but shut up when I caught Vivi's pursed lips. She muttered something about not liking coffee and scurried off. Adriana shrugged off the cold shoulder and placed the trays on my vanity table. I raised my brows at the various cups. "What's all this?"

"Told you I'm buying everyone's affection back with drinks. Figured they didn't have to contain alcohol for it to work." She grinned and handed me an iced coffee. "And you get one as a reward because you already like me."

I narrowed my eyes at the milky concoction, because my coffee order nowadays usually contained a lot more whipped cream and razzle-dazzle. "Thanks, but I . . ."

"There's like twenty pumps of caramel syrup in that." She rolled her eyes at my stunned expression. "Please, you shop for groceries like a teenager who's home alone for the weekend."

"Thank you." I took a sip and glanced down at the phone in my lap, Vivi's video playing in silent mode. "Okay, before I embarrass myself in front of everyone. Vivi just said something."

"What did she say? Do you need me to fight her? She's Renee's daughter, you know, so fighting her could lose me the only other friend I have."

"No," I laughed, "appreciate it though."

I told her about the tutorial and Vivi's insinuation afterwards.

"I sent you the video, didn't I?"

"You sent me some old news report," I said, recalling the video about the theme park's history.

"And the algorithm didn't send you down a whole spiral of fan videos?"

"I watched a few, but . . ."

"Oh, sweet summer child." She checked over both her shoulders, narrowed her eyes at the other three people in the room, then grabbed my hand. "Come with me. Let Aunty Adriana tell you about the birds and the bees."

We settled on a bench outside. This small corner of the park had been closed off for the day, and a photographer had set himself up a short way down the street.

"Richard, daddy mayor, started the whole thing by posting actually educational content. You wanna be on his team on trivia night," Adriana explained, and opened Richard's profile on her phone. I'd met him earlier because he plays Annie Lou's father. Online, however, he seemed to explain the Old West in full costume. "Heather kind of blew up, well . . . because she's hot and can do stunts in a leather corset." I'd not met Heather yet. She played the female bandit in Ace Ryder's gang. But her profile was one thirst trap after another. "Vivi does a lot of behind-the-scenes things, but she only posts once in a blue moon. But still, so many park fans just want to know how the machine runs." The most recent video on Vivi's account was the makeup tutorial. Even the other few had a decent number of views. "Lucas's account is the biggest, and it's where things get interesting for you. How do I say this without you losing faith in mankind?" Adriana grimaced as she brought up Lucky Luke's profile – which boasted hundreds of thousands of subscribers. "People wanna bone Annie. People wanna get boned by Kit, as well as Ace. And more than anything, they want Kit, Ace and Annie to bone. In any constellation, really. Kit and Ace is probably the most popular ship. There's fanfiction. Don't read the fanfiction. Lindsey – she was Annie before you – said it really fucked with her head."

"Don't sugarcoat it or anything," I muttered as I reached over and scrolled down dozens upon dozens of videos. He had to be posting multiple times a day.

"Sorry, but I figured you'd discovered the Bravetown fandom by now. That Bravetown show from like fifteen years ago only had three seasons, but it's turned the whole park into a cult classic." She brought up her browser and had a fanfiction window open with a single bookmark click. It brought up hundreds of results. "Noah also has socials, but it's just him in costume reacting to fan videos. Lindsey had an account, too. Mostly singing musical numbers in Annie Lou costume though. You could totally start one. As far as I know, there's a couple of rules Renee makes people follow, but it's a good side hustle. Do you have any special talent?"

"I can recite the Hippocratic oath in three la—" I cut myself off when her words finally registered. "I'm sorry. Hold on. Noah has an account where he actually posts videos and engages with his fans?"

"Yeah, people get a kick out of being roasted by Ace Ryder. Here."

Adriana switched apps again and handed over the phone, opened to Noah's profile. A familiar dark-hat-and-bandana combination greeted me. All the videos were split-screen, one half Noah-as-Ace and the other half a different video. Some of those showed random women's faces as they yelled at their phone cameras, others were videos of Noah filmed in the park. It was like a Brad Mondo cowboy special. Ace Ryder barely reacted. He raised his brows, crossed his arms, shook his head in disapproval and tsk-ed at the videos. At the very most, he pulled the bandana off his face and smirked in a way that made even my stomach clench – so his fans were probably fainting.

"Wow. Thank you. Oh, this is brilliant. Do you think he'd hate being called an influencer? A thirst trapper?"

"You know, your job would probably be easier if you tried to get along with him," Adriana giggled. We'd texted extensively the last couple of days, so she was all up to speed.

"Where's the fun in that?"

"That's the spirit. That's why we're best friends already."

"Oh, okay." My chest seized at those two silly little words. I blinked. I'd never really had a best friend. Fuck, I'd barely had friends. First I'd been in and out of hospitals, and then I'd been too focused on school. Since dropping out, I hadn't really stayed in one place long enough to even make friends. "Am I getting a friendship bracelet with that title?"

"Sure." She grinned. "I'll get you one."

"Ez, you're up!" Sanny waved his cowboy hat at me as he walked over from the photo set. "Hey Adriana!"

"Hey Helper Carl!" she called back, offering him a big smile. "Did you serve face?"

"Oh, I served," he laughed and did a strange vogue-esque hand move around his face. Goofball.

"Sanny, we're friends with Adriana now. Get on board," I said.

"Okay, cool. Pals. Amigos. Besties." He gave us both a thumbs up and slipped back inside.

"Thank you," Adriana mumbled, a rare heavy note in her voice. "You didn't have to."

"I know a thing or two about needing a fresh start," I said. "I got you."

"Shoo! Go, before I lose all my hard-earned goodwill by keeping you."

I handed her phone back and headed over to where the real Ace Ryder and Kit Holliday were already posing. A couple of lights and reflectors had been set up to create a brightly lit area outside a nondescript building. A gray horse stood tied to one of the posts. Barrels and crates were arranged for sitting, leaning, posing . . .

One of the photographer's assistants guided me by the elbow to stand between Luke and Noah, and plucked the plastic coffee cup from my hands. Noah's eyes narrowed at the stain on my skirt, and he scoffed. I stuck my tongue out at him in response.

"Very mature," he uttered behind his bandana.

"Better immature than a jerk," I replied.

"Okay, quiet, please," the photographer yelled over while she fumbled with her camera. A minute later, she was all over us. My bubble of glamorous photo shoots in costume burst instantly. She moved us around like dolls, fixing my arm, nudging my shoulder and tilting my chin, even positioning Luke's hand around my waist inch-perfectly. The guys had to glare at each other. All I had to do was smile into the camera. Easy enough.

At least for a few minutes.

Then my cheeks started to twitch painfully from smiling. And with the way my weight was all on one leg, the dull throbbing in my hips reminded me of too many hours in the saddle this week. I hated this kind of pain. It lurked on your mind just enough for the discomfort to nag at your every thought. Especially when you had nothing to do but stand still and look pretty.

"Okay, thank you!" the photographer called out, waving her hand at us. All three of us let out a sigh, muscles relaxing, shoulders sloping. Now *that* would have been a funny video to post.

Alas, my relief was short-lived. One of the assistants

pulled Luke from the set and turned me by the shoulder to face Noah.

"Okay, okay, we're trying to show that Annie is more than just a damsel in distress, okay?" The photographer gesticulated wildly. "Like he's your kidnapper, but you're not just all scared and helpless, okay?"

"What are we doing?" I asked. Judging by Noah's raised brows, he was as clueless as me.

"Promotional pics, okay? New Pretty Annie Lou. New spunk. New spirit. Okay, so try crossing your arms, lifting your chin. Noah, you stay tall and menacing, okay? Just stare at each other."

Could someone take the word *okay* away from this woman?

She got back in position, camera in front of her face, and I turned back to face Noah. Nope. Ace Ryder.

Something had shifted in him. It was more than just the black leather duster that accentuated his broad shoulders, or even the dark waistcoat and holster that lay tight over his chest. The costume was pure movie-villain magic, but something in his stance was different. He was different. Just like the shift in his voice. He wasn't just dressing up. Somehow, he was less *Noah*.

My stomach tightened. I suddenly understood the fanfiction.

Before I could even muster up the will to cross my arms and glare at him, I snorted a giggle. Fuck.

The photographer cleared her throat.

"I'm sorry," I gasped. Avoiding the visual confusion of Noah-as-Ace, I focused on my feet while I knotted my arms and squared my shoulders. The second I glanced up again, Ace's cold eyes stared back, burrowing through me. I giggled. Shit. "I'm sorry. I'm not a good enough actress for this."

"Get your shit together, princess," Noah said, the words low and rumbling, caught halfway between his own voice and his character voice. It sent an unwelcome shiver down my spine. He leaned down, far enough for the corner of the bandana to feather over my neck. Voice even lower, so only I could hear him, he said, "Touch my stuff in the kitchen again, and I'll tell Renee the show would be better if Annie fled on horseback and Ace stole the sheriff's horse to chase her."

He was threatening me. In the middle of this damn photo shoot, when I was trying to concentrate, he had to bring up his stupid peanut butter. He knew the one thing I would *not* be able to do was keep myself on that damn horse. And fuck. That chase would actually make for a more interesting scene than me running off for ten seconds with my skirts in my hands. Had to give him credit for creativity, even if it was working against me.

"I never wanted to touch your *stuff* in the first place," I hissed. "Besides, you're the one who got his hands all over my underwear when you folded it."

"Don't flatter yourself," he chuckled and leaned back. "Others needed the laundry room. I told you to get your clothes out on time. And it was one ratty pair of men's boxers."

"You even memorized my underwear? That's sick."

He rolled his eyes at me. "Bite me."

"I neither want to *touch*, nor *bite* your *stuff*, Young."

"Okay, that's great. Awesome. Got it," the photographer

called out before Noah could retort. "Can I get Annie Lou alone, please? Okay, Noah, you're done for today."

I blinked at the woman with the camera, and when I turned back, Noah had pulled down the mask and held his hat in his hands. He was back to being all Noah.

"You played me," I gasped as the realization hit me. "You made me angry at you."

"I'm getting the job done," he replied and turned without another glance in my direction.

Once again, I wasn't even given the chance to do something myself. Nope, Noah just had to swoop in – in the name of efficiency – and do things the rudest way possible.

Un-fucking-believable.

It took me twenty minutes to put on a smile the photographer deemed sweet enough for Annie's portrait. Noah Young was making me scowl so hard, I'd end up calling my mom's Botox guy before even turning twenty-four. Ugh. Stupid, annoying, grumpy cowboy.

Chapter Nine

THE STALLIONS – LIVE SHOW

Meet the rowdiest cowboys in town! Join the Stallions for a wild ride at the Rattlesnake Saloon. This 90-minute live show promises an unforgettable blend of comedy, music and dancing.

First Wednesday each month, 9:30 p.m.

18+ only.

No park admission required.

Esra

By our third day practicing in costume, I was no longer as easily flustered by Ace Ryder. I had too many other things to focus on. Mostly my feet. The first day, Noah had been faster at wrangling me down the bank building's steps than I'd anticipated, and I'd twisted my ankle. The second day, I'd stepped on my dress when coming off the horse and my knee had clicked sideways. At least the layers of skirts had hidden that from all the others that had joined our rehearsals.

The last money in my bank account had paid for a couple of cheap bandages at the Wild Fields pharmacy.

Beneath the dress and the underlayer of leggings, I looked a little like a mummy now. I'd have to get my hands on proper braces soon.

At least it kept me focused. I didn't want to end up at the hospital. Sanny would drive me back home himself if it got that bad. And home was the last place I wanted to go. Bravetown, and playing Annie Lou, may have come with its own rules and expectations, but I was reveling in the small things. Last night, I sat on the kitchen floor at 1 a.m., eating cereal straight from the box, watching Netflix on my phone – and nobody had questioned it or admonished me for my unhealthy life choices.

"I've got it." I swatted Noah's hand away as he reached for my waist to pull me off the horse at the end of costume practice, day three. I lodged my foot into the stirrup and swung my other leg back over the saddle to get off.

"Been secretly practicing?" he asked.

"You just underestimate me." *That*, plus fifty instructional videos on YouTube and three episodes of *Free Rein*. The latter being surprisingly entertaining for a children's show, but not as educational as I would have hoped.

I still floundered for a hold when I lowered myself from the stirrup to the ground and dropped the last ten inches, my ankles shooting flames up my legs in protest. I grimaced and took a wobbly step back from Tornado.

"You good?" he asked.

"Just a very tall horse with a very high saddle."

"How are your abs?"

"Never had any complaints. I'd show you, but I'm a little tied up." I drummed my hands against the lacing down the front of my dress.

He rolled his eyes. "I can lower the stirrups if that makes it easier for you to get in and out of the saddle, but you'll be less snug up there. You'll need more core strength to stay balanced when we're riding."

"My abs might not be *that* good."

"Look, when dismounting, try not to drop your weight all at once. Lower yourself until you've got ground under your tiptoes, only then take the weight off the foot in the stirrup." He stepped around behind me and I strangely knew exactly what was about to happen. I read it in the shift of his shoulders and the flex of his hands. A moment later, I was hoisted back in the air. I automatically kicked my feet out, sending my skirt flying high, allowing me to slot into the saddle. "Try it. Slowly."

"Are you giving me free lessons, Young?"

"Just making sure we don't lose another Annie before summer season starts," he huffed.

"Lovely." I sighed and assessed the position of the stirrups. "How do I go from swinging my leg through the air to crouching in the stirrup?"

"Imagine you have one foot on a ladder, and you don't know where the next step is. You'll keep your weight on the foot that has a hold."

"I don't remember the last time I was on a ladder," I muttered, but tried anyway, visualizing some sort of step ladder beside the horse.

"Steady," Noah whispered, only for his hands to snap around my waist when I lost my balance a few inches off the ground. His arms absorbed my drop, saving my ankles from another hit. Before I even had my full balance back, his hands were off me. "That's it. There you go. Good effort."

"You had to catch me," I protested. Nothing about this dismount deserved the word *good*.

"Still. You made an effort."

I worked my jaw and rolled my ankles. Effort was all fine and dandy, but it didn't help the fact that I'd be limping up the stairs to my room just to get to my Advil. *Good effort* still meant I'd failed. "I think I'll let you do the heavy lifting for now."

"As you wish, princess," he said, but for once, there was a chuckle to his words. The *princess* wasn't as deprecative as usual.

I still rolled my eyes at him before turning on my heels.

For my last day off before becoming the official face of the Pretty Annie Lou, Zuri insisted on taking me shopping. She'd offered to let me raid her closet, but we both quickly realized that her clothes were too big to fit me and not big enough for a cute, oversized look.

Between the two boutiques in town, I only ended up with a Wild Fields baseball cap and a blue flannel. I wasn't a flannel kind of girl, but Noah wore either his Ace Ryder costume or a flannel pearl snap. Next time he complained about my clothes, I'd find a way to use my new flannel to get him back.

I let Zuri pay for my shopping. Only because she wasn't even hiding her attempts to ask about my plans for returning to school (not happening) or moving back home (*so* not happening) or at least calling my parents (big nope). If Sanny could send his fiancée to pry, I could let her buy me clothes.

She also paid for my cocktail when we ended the day at the Rattlesnake Saloon.

The place was packed. Queue-out-the-door kinda packed.

We had to push past a few people and flash our staff badges just to get upstairs to a designated premier-access balcony, and the staff section behind it. The chatter and music mounted at peak volume under the vaulted ceiling, people shouting louder and louder just to hear themselves over the other groups shouting at each other.

Even the staff section was tight by the time we plopped down at a table with our drinks. Vivi and another girl, who I didn't recognize, were already seated.

I shot a quick look around, but I didn't recognize anyone else besides Adriana behind the bar. Considering how busy it was, there should have been a few more familiar faces.

"Where is everyone?" I asked, joining the communal shouting match.

"What do you mean?" Zuri asked.

"Sanny, Lucas, Austin or . . ." I squinted. My eyes skipped from our table to the next. A group of middle-aged women. The next table was surrounded by more women, all styled to the nines, one of whom I recognized as Heather, the leather-corset thirst-trap queen. One demographic was noticeably in the minority though. I leaned over the balcony to check the crowd in front of the stage, too. "Men. I mean men."

Zuri giggled. "Not here tonight. Or on any first Wednesday of the month."

"There'll be men, don't worry," Vivi said, and leaned over to pat my hand. "They'll just be on stage."

93

Ah.

Okay.

I was halfway through my cocktail when the lights dimmed. All that chatter had nothing on the screams that suddenly tore through the saloon. My options were to cover my ears or roll with it – and the second seemed like more fun, so I whooped and hollered alongside everyone else when the Stallions took the stage.

In all his stories about Bravetown, my brother had forgotten to mention that the entertainment included a Magic Mike cowboy show. Okay, it wasn't quite Magic Mike, but it was a dozen shirtless men in cowboy hats and boots, dancing and doing strangely wholesome comedy bits.

Vivi explained that the show was officially classed as burlesque.

It still involved just as much body glitter as a strip show.

"Hold my seat," I yelled over the squeals of hundreds of women. On stage, two guys dance-battled to a Kacey Musgraves song around a girl with a bachelorette sash and crown. I needed a refill for the second-hand embarrassment of audience participation.

Zuri was already slightly wobbly on her feet when she followed me to the bar. That girl could not hold her liquor. Adriana took our orders, as well as Zuri's car keys for safekeeping.

I didn't notice the man approaching until a tall glass was plonked down right in front of me. Condensation pearled down the sides, but the drink was clear. "Here," Noah barked.

"Noah!" Zuri squeaked and threw her arms around him in a happy hug. I almost got jealous. Zuri Hugs were the best and Noah barely returned it, patting her shoulders. So undeserving. "Whatcha doin'ere?"

"Just checking up on you all," he replied.

"Sanny?" Zuri asked, eyes going big. She leaned around him to check for my brother's presence.

"Nope, just me."

"Aw man." She deflated. God, that was cute. Watching cowboy strippers with eight-packs do body rolls, and still missing her fiancé. "I'm 'onna call him," she announced before she grabbed her freshly made drink and sulked back to the table, phone in hand.

"And what's this exactly?" I picked up the glass he'd served me and sniffed. Nothing. He was either serving me water or pure vodka. Most likely water.

"Final costume rehearsal tomorrow. You shouldn't be hungover for that." Rationally, I knew he was shouting because of the volume of the crowd, but his stupid authoritarian demeanor needled me even more this way.

"I figured it out," I replied and grabbed my caipirinha instead of the water.

"What?"

"Your zodiac sign. It explains so much."

Noah heaved a deep sigh, leaning on the counter and tilting his head. "Astrology is a scam. You know that, right?"

"You're a buzzkill sun, party-pooper ascending and killjoy moon. Deadly combination." I grinned. "My condolences."

"Do you always become more annoying when you drink?"

"I don't know. Let's find out." I lifted my glass but before it could touch my lips, his hand folded over mine. Warm fingers plucked the drink from my hands. Before

I knew what was happening, he downed it himself. His Adam's apple bobbed in his throat, and in four gulps my drink was gone.

"Hey," I yelled, "I had to flash the bartender to get that for free."

"Best tits I've seen in a while," Adriana piped up from behind the bar and winked at me. "Didn't expect the piercings."

We all knew it was a blatant lie, but Noah's eyes still dropped to my chest. My white shirt fittingly spelled out the words "No Bra Club" across my boobs. Cheeks tinge-ing red and lips pulling into a straight line, Noah forced his eyes to the stage. As fate would have it, there were some actual pierced nipples there. They just belonged to a guy.

Noah pinched the bridge of his nose.

"Can you please make me another one?" I batted my lashes at Adriana.

"Noah, do you want to pay by card or do you want to flash me your nips?" she cackled.

Noah set his jaw and slapped his cast member ID on the counter. "At least drink the water, too," he growled and slid the full glass closer to me.

He hadn't come to check up on us. He'd come to the show to check up on *me*. He thought I'd fuck up tomorrow by getting blackout drunk tonight. "Do you always come to these? Do you have a favorite down there?" I asked. "Let me guess, the guy with the slutty little glasses. Gives the illusion of being a goody-two-shoes, right?"

Noah ignored me and turned to Adriana, leaning both elbows on the counter. I blamed the alcohol for noticing the flex in his biceps. "How long's the show?"

"Another hour or so," Adriana replied as she served me my replacement drink.

Noah checked the clock on his phone and ran a hand over his eyes and down his face.

"Go home, Young. I don't need a babysitter."

"Fine."

I shook my head at this ridiculous man. I did take both my cocktail and the water back to the table though.

"I've got her," Adriana huffed as we slotted Zuri into her passenger seat. Three drinks over three hours and she was going to have the worst hangover tomorrow. Lightweight.

"I love you," Zuri mumbled, patting Adriana's arm, eyes already falling shut.

"I love you too. Now buckle up." Adriana chuckled and winked at me over the top of her car door. "Told you. They're all falling back in love with me one drink at a time."

"You're a genius." I grinned and shook my head. I wasn't drunk but that little shaking still made my world spin, and I had to close my eyes for a second to stay upright.

"Are you sure that you're okay to get home?"

"I'm fine," I said, "it's like five minutes."

The walk over to staff housing would actually be good to burn off a bit more of that alcohol.

"Okay, text me when you get home."

"I'll text Sanny that you're on your way," I said and waved them off. Once Adriana's car was off the lot and on the street, I sighed and turned to the shadows. "Stop creeping. Let's go home."

"I'm not creeping," Noah said.

"You could have gone home already. Instead, you followed us out the bar and you're waiting for me in a dark parking lot. That's creeping," I said and started toward our housing complex.

His feet pounded into the pavement as he jogged to catch up with me. Hand on the small of my back, he directed me to the inside of the sidewalk, so he could walk by the curb.

"What are you doing?" I asked.

"Sidewalk rule," he said.

I just blinked at him with raised brows. That had to be the most outdated crap I'd heard in a long time. As if he could somehow protect me if a car came barreling toward us, just because he was a big muscly manly man walking thirty inches closer to the street.

He sighed at my expression. "It's just good manners. Like holding open a door or pulling out a chair."

"Good manners, huh? And you keep calling me a princess." I shook my head and narrowed my eyes at the dimly lit street before us. It was awfully quiet. My ears were still ringing from the saloon. My pulse still racing. "We should go skinny-dipping."

"Esra," he moaned, more exasperation in those four letters than I ever thought possible.

"Climb up on a hay bale," I said, desperate for anything more fun than crawling into bed and scrolling on my phone. "Teach me how to ride a tractor. Uhm . . . line dance."

"You want to learn how to line dance?" he asked.

"Well, what is it that you country boys do for fun, huh? Tip cows?"

He smirked. "Sure, let's go tip some cows."

"Really?" I turned on the sidewalk. Too fast. My ankle didn't stop the spin, twisting too far. My vision was too blurry. I felt my leg give before I could stop it.

"No, not really," Noah grunted as his hands wrapped around my waist, in the exact same spot they always did. He kept me upright. Except this time, his fingers dug into the naked skin between my jeans and my crop top. While any other man might have lingered, well-mannered Noah Young dropped his touch the second I was steady again.

Ugh. Boring.

"Shoot at cans?" I suggested. "Blow up heads of lettuce with fireworks?"

"Jesus," he sighed and started walking again. "What kind of hillbilly redneck shit do you think we get up to here?"

"Well? What do you do for fun?" I asked.

He opened and closed his mouth. He furrowed his brow. For a minute or so, we walked in complete silence while his face scrunched up more and more with each step.

"Noah, do you have *fun*? Not just a little amusement. Actual fun?" I asked as we crossed on to the staff housing lot.

"Sure," he replied stiffly and opened the door for me. "Time for bed, princess. Big day tomorrow."

Ugh. Bed. I crinkled my nose at him. "Party pooper."

"Buzzkill sun, killjoy moon, I know."

Chapter Ten

NOAH

I'd told her.

This was beyond any common sense Sinan may have prescribed her.

I'd fucking told her.

My knuckles turned white around the handle of the kitchen cabinet as I stared at her latest bullshit. Instead of groceries, glasses of water lined my shelf, all of them filled to the brim. She hadn't even put my stuff on her shelf. It was just gone. Replaced by water.

"Do I want to know?" Austin asked as he reached past me to grab a box of cereal from his own, perfectly intact supply.

"Esra," I grunted.

"You two realize I can still hear you fighting when I switch your mics from speakers to intercom, right?"

"So?" I glared at him, and he just raised his free hand and backed away.

He wasn't even supposed to be at the receiving end of this glare. He hadn't caused a stupidly restless night by asking too many questions. He wasn't keeping me from my tea.

I huffed and tracked back upstairs. I rapped my knuckles against her door hard enough to hurt.

"Who is it?" Esra sing-sang from inside.

"The prime suspect if you were to go missing today."

Her laugh carried through the door before she opened it. "Did you just make a joke, Young?" She blinked at me with those big brown eyes, not a fucking care in the world that she was standing in front of me in her underwear. Pink and white, mismatched.

"Jesus, Esra." I tipped my head back, blinking at the ceiling. Even so, the sight of her chest, lined by pearly silk, was burned into my corneas. It was all over the ceiling. Fuck her "no bra club" T-shirt. This bra was made to spotlight her smooth bronze skin and rounded— *Hell, no.* "Put on some clothes."

"For the record, you came to my bedroom. You act like you've never seen me naked before," she laughed.

"I haven't . . . That's not . . . You should . . ."

"Cat got your tongue?"

Judging by the rustle of fabric, she was getting dressed. I still didn't dare to look. Not that it helped. I still saw the smattering of freckles on her stomach behind closed lids every single time I blinked.

"Food," I huffed, not trusting my brain to produce a single worthwhile thing.

Maybe I was having a stroke.

"Food. Four-letter word. Nutritious substances that are eaten and digested in order to survive and grow," she replied, voice dripping with false sweetness. "You can look."

I lowered my chin and found her wrapped in a fluffy bathrobe, standing by her desk – which had disappeared under a heap of clothes. If I'd trusted my brain more, I'd have told her that there was, indeed, a chest of drawers for her to use. And a laundry room for the towels that littered her floor. "Where. Is. My. Food."

"Hmm." She smirked. "In the kitchen, I'd assume."

Her words flipped the switch, and all images of bras disappeared from my mind. "For the love of god, I'm about to throw you through the air. You don't want me to do that on an empty stomach."

"If you're out of food, I can share. PB and J? Cereal?" She blinked innocently.

Suppressing every urge to yell at her, I gritted my teeth, spun back around and left. She wanted to play her stupid pranks? Fine. Nothing good would come out of me staying in her mess of a room.

"It's rude to leave without saying goodbye," she called out after me. "Oh, hey Lucky."

"Hey . . . Oh come on, Noah," Lucas piped up. "Not cool. I had dibs."

"What?" I whirred back around. Esra leaned in her doorway. Lucas must have just come downstairs and now stood next to her, looking like a wet puppy. "I didn't sleep with her."

"Don't worry," Esra cackled, "he starts panicking every time he sees me naked."

"Every time? As in multiple times? Still not cool. *Bro code*, man." He stormed past me, sulking like a petulant toddler.

"I can't believe you didn't respect his dibs, Young," Esra said, loud enough for Lucas to still hear.

"No dibs disrespected!" I yelled and followed Lucas back downstairs to the kitchen. "I didn't sleep with her. I have no intention of sleeping with her. You know what, Lucas? You have my blessing. You two are perfect for each other." I tore open the cabinet again, hinges creaking, and started dumping glass after glass of water in the sink. Half of it spilled over, soaking my sleeves and the counters. But who the fuck cared in this house anyway? "Just keep in mind that you did hook up with Zuri before she and Sanny got together, and now you intend to stick it to his little sister. If he wanted to kick your ass for that, the real sheriff would probably side with him. But who cares? Fuck consequences, right? Fuck consideration for other people and the fact that they're just trying to live their lives."

Lucas sank into a chair and rubbed a hand over his chest. "Jeez, you're worse than usual."

"Worse than usual? Meaning what exactly? That I, for one, actually don't treat this place like a fucking high school field trip?" I emptied the last cup and stared at the mess on the counter. Someone else could deal with that. "I'm out of here."

A few minutes later, I stomped through the hallways in the main office building. I thought that maybe, possibly, the fresh air would calm me down. Instead, each step had just hiked my pulse up more. The actual fucking audacity. Didn't this count as bullying? Sexual harassment? Something?

Renee's office door was closed, but Vivi glanced up from her desk when I stormed in, and that was good enough for me. "I can't work with that woman," I grunted.

"Who?"

"Esra."

"Why?" She tilted her head like a fucking bird. Like she hadn't been there last night when Esra had ordered a third drink even though she'd already been wobbly on her feet.

"She's immature and irresponsible." And half-naked in her room, etched into my memory.

Vivi laughed, then clapped her hand over her mouth. "Sorry. Why do you think my mother will care?"

"She should. I mean, if the show goes wrong because Esra can't treat it like a serious job, people could get hurt. Between the horses and the explosions . . ."

"From what Mom's told me, she's doing all right during the shows."

"She's spoiled."

"Have you gotten into method acting?" Vivi sighed and propped her hands on her hips, leveling me with a completely neutral stare that she had from her mother. It had the unique ability to make you feel like a little kid being questioned about the cookie jar, even if you never touched the cookie jar. "Hating the mayor's daughter and the cushy life she stands for while becoming more and more of a hermit who doesn't see himself as part of society? Is that what you're doing?"

"What the fuck? Where did that come from?" I wasn't a social fucking butterfly, but I wasn't a hermit either. "That's not what's happening here."

"If you say so . . ." Vivi pursed her lips. "My mom's already in the park to set up for the final rehearsal. So if you want to complain about Esra being too immature to work with, you'll have to head over there."

"Great," I huffed. Despite having a new destination, I couldn't move. I could only stare at Vivi's desk and the little digital picture frame that played a slideshow of party pictures. Just because I wasn't out line dancing or blowing up lettuces or skinny dipping on a Wednesday night, that didn't mean I was a hermit. "I know how to have fun."

"Oh-kay?"

"I know how to have fun," I repeated with a grunt and stormed out.

Esra had laughed. I'd confronted her about my missing food, and she had laughed. Was I supposed to find that funny? I'd stolen her drink last night, so she stole my food this morning, and now we were all in on the joke and having a jolly time laughing about it?

I paused in my tracks outside. Behind the main office building, some of the park's attractions poked out above the trees and roofs. The Ferris wheel, disguised as a wooden mill, and the Mountain Pass Railroad were the tallest. I hadn't been on either in fifteen years. Hell, I hadn't been on any of the rides since then. That still didn't make me a hermit who didn't know how to have fun or take a joke, right?

Chapter Eleven

HAPPY HARRY'S HORSE RANCH

Visit happy rancher Harry to get a tour of the stables, where you might just catch a glimpse of Kit and Ace's iconic horses. Ready to saddle up yourself or want to take a leisurely ride down Bravetown's Main Street? Harry's Ranch offers pony, trail, wagon and carriage rides for Bravetownees of all ages.

Trail rides require pre-booking. Inquire here.

ESRA

I wasn't ready for tomorrow. Or Saturday. Or Sunday. The whole weekend would be a disaster. I had to do two shows a day on weekends. That equaled double the disappointment.

Rehearsals hadn't gone horribly, but with the rest of the show's cast surrounding us, I'd spotted enough costumed cowboys grimacing to get the message. My Annie Lou sucked. Running a few feet sucked. Of course it did. They were used to a tall blonde Annie twirling through the fucking air as she was hauled on to a running horse – and they got me instead.

I stomped across the dark park, using my phone's

flashlight to guide me past closed shops and restaurants.

I hadn't signed up for this. I was meant to be scooping ice cream in exchange for a room. No more than that.

The stench gave away the stables before I could double-check the park map on my phone. Then came the lights. I stopped dead in my tracks and narrowed my eyes at the building, and the porch lights glowing warm orange beside the doors. Slipping my earbuds into my pockets, I listened for any signs of life. Only horses huffing and puffing. Neighing? Nickering? I should brush up on my vocabulary.

I opened an app I hadn't used in months. So long, in fact, that it was still opened to the to-do list for my M1 biochemistry course. My stomach cramped in a familiar way and I quickly archived the whole M1 folder. I'd never complete the first year in med school, so no point in keeping it around. In its place, I created a folder called *Summer*, and a list titled *Bravetown*.

Summer > Bravetown

To Do
- Research horse noises

Appointments

Notes

I added a little horse emoji, just to make it more fun. When I closed the app again, some of the anxious flutter in my chest had subsided. Give a girl a good task-management app and her mood would improve tenfold.

Phone back in my pocket, I continued toward the stables.

The inside smelled even worse than the outside. One might think New York sewers in summer would have prepared me for the stench of horses – one might be wrong. At least the inside was partially lit by dimmed lamps above the doors. Horsey night-lights. Cute.

With the collar of my shirt pulled up over my nose, I passed the stable boxes until I found a plaque with a familiar name. He was barely visible in the shadows of his little wooden cubicle, but Tornado's ears twitched when I stopped in front of his gate.

"Hi," I whispered. I pulled the shirt off my face. Sure, this was a horse, but it still felt impolite to let him know that his home smelled like ass. "Sorry for dropping in unannounced."

Tornado made a huffy noise and turned, walking over. He tilted his head, dark eyes staring right at me. I shifted my weight. I'd had a bunny as a kid, but when Flopsy had looked at me, he only saw a treat dispenser. Tornado saw me, my treat-less hands braced on top of his gate, and he waited and watched and breathed.

"You're really scary, you know?"

Tornado let out a chuckling sound and shook his head. Apparently I was having a two-sided conversation with this horse. He disagreed.

"Yes, you are," I muttered and lowered my chin to my hands, looking into the stable. "You're tall. You're the kind of horse people fall off and get hurt real bad. And I'm an expert in the getting-hurt department. I mean, even just sitting on you hurts."

Tornado took another step toward me, and I forced myself to stay still. I'd come here to make peace with him before our first show, so I couldn't run off just because he got too close. Maybe it was silly, but if I got hurt, I didn't want it up for debate whether it was the horse's fault. And that started with me making sure Tornado didn't hate me.

"Anyways, I just wanted to tell you that whatever happens tomorrow, it's not you, it's me, okay? I'm the one who sucks."

The horse tilted his head at me, nostrils flaring only inches from my face. Hot breath fluffed through my bangs. I squeezed my eyes shut and tried to breathe through my mouth.

"Sorry for robbing you of a really cool stunt."

Tornado huffed and nudged his nose against my elbow. Hard. My arm slid off the gate. I managed to catch my balance just in time for him to nuzzle his forehead into the hand that had dropped into his stable.

"Oh, you're not subtle at all, are you?" I chuckled and ran my fingertips up and down the smooth hair on his forehead.

"He's a shameless flirt."

I screamed and jumped at the voice. Loud enough for Tornado and some of the other horses to join in, neighing and squeaking. Heart beating in my throat, hand clutched to my chest, I turned to see Noah standing a few feet away. That white streak in his jet-black hair had dropped down on to his forehead. His pearl snap had been untucked, and his sleeves were rolled down but still creased from being pushed up all day. He was *still* out here, while I was already in my fluffy PJ pants and a heart-print tank top.

"Are you stalking me?"

"I was here first, just about to close up," he said, brows raised.

"So just eavesdropping?"

Noah sighed and reached past me, broad chest a few inches from my face, highlighting just how much height and muscle he had on me. A light inside the box flickered to life and Tornado's door clicked open. "I just *overheard* you."

"How much?"

"Apologizing for robbing him of a stunt. Why? Was there more? There's a church in town if you need to confess in a more private setting, you know?" He had one hand on Tornado's cheek, rubbing it while he held the gate open for me. "Come on."

I glanced down at my sneakers. Formerly cute and white, they'd gotten layered in dust from the days spent in the park. Might as well get stable dirt on them.

Noah closed the gate behind me, then guided me with a hand between my shoulder blades to Tornado's side. "Do you know how to braid?"

"Yeah."

"Here." He pulled a long string of wooden beads from his pocket and dropped them into my hand. Some of them had a vague blue or green sheen to them, but it looked like time and sunlight had gotten to them. They were fixed with a thick knot to a metal hair clip at one end. "It's a good luck charm. Tradition before the first show of the summer. You can braid it into his mane."

"I see." This was more touchy-feely than I'd meant to get with Tornado, but braiding hair and beaded charms would definitely make us BFFs.

I ran my hair through Tornado's silky black tresses until I found a strip that looked right. Noah didn't say anything about my choice, but I felt the weight of his attention on me. I focused solely on my fingers, weaving the most precise braid of my life, just so he had no reason to complain about it.

"You're not getting cold feet on us, are you?" he asked when I was halfway down the braid.

"No," I scoffed. Despite my nerves, I wasn't going to run off. I'd never thrown in the towel just because things got a little uncomfortable.

"Good." He ran a hand up and down Tornado's neck. "A lot of people love and need Bravetown, and the shows are a big part of that."

"No pressure."

"It's a lot of pressure, Esra. We're constantly aware of how much the entire town depends on the survival of the park and the tourism it brings."

"Will you lay off?" I finished the braid off with the little rubber tie at the end of the string of beads and turned to face Noah.

"No, not until you realize how big of a role you play here." His mouth was set in that stern line that sharpened the shadows across his face.

"You're going to die of a heart attack real soon if you don't lighten up a little." I rolled my eyes at him, but after all the concerned looks I'd earned today, his words still nagged at my gut. *I was supposed to be scooping ice cream.* If I had wanted to constantly be reminded of what a letdown I was, I would have stayed with my parents. Instead I was stranded in the middle of nowhere, where I only knew my brother, having to scrape the last cereal from the box until my first paycheck came through. And I wasn't even getting any free ice cream out of it.

My thought spiral was interrupted by Tornado twisting his neck and pushing his big soft face against my chest. I froze with my hands in the air. "What's happening?"

Noah furrowed his brow. "He's calming you down."

"What? I am totally calm." My voice hitched an octave, betraying my blatant lie. "At least I was before your horse started motorboating me."

"I'm training him to be a therapy horse. Here. Feel this." Hands raised slowly as if he was approaching a wild animal – me, not the horse – he inched closer and folded his fingers around mine. He guided my hands around Tornado's head to the underside of his jaw. His touch was too slow and too gentle and too warm. My spine straightened. I knew this kind of touch, and I didn't want a pity party.

"I don't want to be calmed down," I hissed and shook his hands off. "I am perfectly calm and happy and content. I had an offer to spend the summer on a yacht in the south of France, you know? I mean, the dude was like sixty and I wasn't crazy about that, but I chose this damn cowboy park over sunshine and champagne."

"Just. Feel."

I rolled my head and groaned. As annoyed as I was with Noah, I'd come here on a mission to make friends with Tornado, so I stroked the silky hair under his jaw. It took a second for the slow thrumming to register against my fingertips. "You want me to feel his pulse?"

"Yes."

My fingers stilled over the steady beating. I instinctively started counting. "It's so slow. Is he okay?"

"He's fine. Just feel it."

Tornado huffed and nudged his forehead deeper into me, forcing me to hold on tighter to him to stop from tumbling backward. His head was the size of my entire torso. Which meant feeling his pulse turned into a full horse hug. I sighed and slid my second hand closer to the first, tracing the slow beat beneath his hair. Even a clock ticked faster.

I counted again, but by the time I got to twenty-three, my mind wandered to Tornado's warmth seeping into me. I started again and made it to seventeen before I got distracted by the way his coat was all silk in one direction and a little stubby the other way. By the third time I counted, I barely made it past ten before my eyes fell shut and my breathing started matching Tornado's slow in- and exhales.

I wasn't sure how long I stood there, but when I blinked, my skin was warm, my muscles soft, and the light seemed too bright.

"Go home. Get some sleep," Noah said, voice low.

Right. I'd forgotten he was here. My arms fell off Tornado and the horse shook his head, taking a step back. I raised my brows but couldn't even look at Noah. Something had passed between me and his horse, and it was strange and vulnerable, and I didn't want his judgy glare to ruin it. "So I'm well rested and don't fuck up the show tomorrow?"

"I didn't say that."

"Sure," I muttered and slipped out the box's gate, still not meeting his gaze. "I'll see you tomorrow, Young."

I had not gotten any sleep.

Actually, I'd gotten like two hours of sleep. Non-consecutively.

I wasn't ready to disappoint a whole town and the whole damn Bravetown fandom.

I shouldn't have scrolled last night. I had ended up spending most of my waking minutes on the videos Noah was reposting, and then the various hashtags, and then everything that had been posted about the previous Annie Lou. They loved her. There were very few people who criticized the character for being outdated or too much of a damsel in distress. Especially since more and more female characters had been added over the years. The Pretty Annie Lou was the OG. She was Snow White. You didn't criticize Snow White for being saved by a prince.

And people wondered about me. At least the concept of me. The new Annie Lou. Lindsey was posting content from working as a performer on a cruise ship. People had figured out that there was no way for her to be on the open ocean and in Bravetown simultaneously. To the fans, Lindsey's replacement was one big mystery.

On any other day, I would have been expected to make my rounds in the park for an hour before the show. I'd gotten scripts to memorize and very clear instructions on how to interact with the little kids. It was supposed to make it that much more of an emotional journey when Annie got abducted.

For my big debut, however, Renee wanted me to come on to the scene without a soft launch beforehand.

There were closed-off walkways for staff, so I stayed behind the scenes as I made my way over to the changing rooms. I peeked from the first-floor windows at the massive crowd that was gathering in the park. The last two weeks had seemed busy, but it was nothing to the mass of visitors now gathering under the bright sun.

You could tell exactly where some of the cast members were out to take pictures with and chat to the visitors, because people crammed around in circles, phones raised above their heads. Every one of them was accompanied by at least one or two other staff members in bright-red cowboy hats, keeping the crowd under control.

My stomach tightened. I'd have to do that tomorrow. And if I fucked up, someone would post it on their socials.

I closed my eyes, balled my hands into fists, and reminded myself of the feel of Tornado's soft coat and his slow heartbeat.

"Did someone here order some liquid courage?" Adriana popped her head into the dressing room with a big toothy grin. She poked one arm through the door, a bottle of Jack in hand.

"I think I'll throw up if you make me drink that right now."

"Sugary courage?" She slipped in fully and held her second hand up, holding a huge bag of Reese's Pieces.

"I love you."

She dropped the candy on the vanity in front of me before scanning the name plaques and leaving the whiskey at Lucas's assigned space. She grabbed one of the tissues and pressed a lipstick kiss on to it, draping it artfully around the bottle.

I raised my brows at her.

"If he asks, tell him it's from a secret admirer but you didn't recognize her. It's going to drive him mad all summer." She laughed and plopped into the seat next to me. "Ready for your close-up?"

"Nope."

"Want a pep talk?"

"Sure."

"You're in. You're part of Bravetown. No matter what happens out there, for better or worse, this town sticks together. We got you. It takes a lot to make them hate you. I know that first-hand, okay? You can fuck up your stunt. You can forget your lines. You can probably make a child cry by saying the wrong thing and you'll get a slap on the wrist at most. Nobody's going to kick you out if you're not perfect on your first day."

"Okay, come on, what did you do?"

Adriana sighed. "I'll tell you if you don't fall off the horse today."

"Deal."

I finished my makeup while Adriana chattered about the summer cocktail menu they were doing at the saloon. She helped me fit my microphone around my ear and under my hair to make it as invisible as possible. My apron had a hidden pocket on the inside, where I dropped my phone and the mic pack after switching it on.

"Hello?" I tentatively pressed the earpiece.

"Hey Esra," Austin's familiar voice replied, "are you on your way?"

"Leaving the dressing room now."

Adriana walked with me to the point where I could slip into the back of the town hall building and use it as my entry point into the park. She drew me into a tight hug. "You've got this."

"Thank you." My voice came out shaky and I had to force myself to leave her hug and push through the staff door. "I'm in the town hall," I whispered into my mic, not entirely sure how soundproof the building was.

"Ez?" Sinan's voice crackled through my earpiece.

"Yeah?"

"Break a leg."

Before I could reply, a whole chorus of voices chimed in, wishing me luck and offering words of encouragement. Maybe Adriana was right. They'd all seen me suck yesterday and they were still cheering me on.

"Thank you, guys," I muttered.

Alongside Adriana's words, Noah's voice suddenly echoed through my head. The whole town needed this park, the show, the characters . . . This support was a two-way street, and I wasn't sure I could hold up my end.

"Everyone's in position," Renee said, "whenever you're ready, Esra."

I wasn't ready. This was too much. I never wanted this amount of responsibility.

"Have fun out there."

I blinked at the four words – and the familiar voice they'd come from. Noah Young telling me to have fun? Had I already fallen off the horse and hit my head?

I shook my head, trying to lose the echo of people from my mind.

I was going to go out there in my silly costume and run around and scream and ride a horse. I got to play cowgirl dress-up. That *was* fun. The rest didn't matter.

"Here we go," I sighed and pushed through the doors.

For a moment, I was fine. The bright sunlight drowned out everything else as I stepped outside and skipped down the stairs on to the dusty road like I'd done count-less times over the last week. Then the cheering filtered in. People had been waiting for the Pretty Annie Lou, and they greeted her with applause and whistles. And I wasn't allowed to look. They were all watching from the sidelines of the town square. The weight of their eyes pressed down on my shoulders and lashed around my lungs like a corset. Fighting every instinct to stare back, I focused squarely on Richard, who played Annie's father, as he called me over and delivered some lines about Bravetown.

The first part of the show ran smoothly. I didn't have any lines. While the storyline of Ace and the sheriff was set up, I was passing out plastic flowers from my apron to some of the other cast members in the town square.

But then the robbery started. I shrieked at the first explosion because it was twice as loud as the rehearsal.

I wasn't supposed to shriek. Shit.

I twisted around, trying to find Richard, finding my way back into the story where he hauled us into the bank — instead, I found the audience. Hundreds of people. Watching. Waiting. Staring at us. At me.

I wasn't supposed to look at them. Fuck.

"Run! We'll be safe in there!" Richard's lines and his hand around my elbow snapped me back into the moment. We hauled up the stairs of the bank and through the doors. As soon as we were out of sight, he dropped my arm and gave me a curt smile and nod. A few more people filtered in behind us. Then the doors fell shut and a small orange light above it flickered on. Our signal to wait.

Right now, the bandits were causing mayhem outside. They had stunts that involved knives and fire, and some serious horseback acrobatics, getting the audience riled up.

I closed my eyes and mentally replayed my fuck-ups from outside. At least the horror on my face must have looked hyper-realistic.

Before I had the chance to chicken out and look for the nearest escape route, the door flew open again, and a group of masked bank robbers swarmed inside. They all gunned for the cart of canvas bags with big dollar signs printed on them. Except Ace Ryder, who stepped in last, who stood tallest, and whose icy blue eyes found me across the room instantly.

My insides twisted thanks to the strange mixture of dread and being on the receiving end of such intense focus.

I had to remind myself to breathe when he stepped up right in front of me, those cool eyes the only visible feature of his face.

"All set?" he asked, his voice dropping low between a whisper and a growl that was nothing like Noah. But his hands were all Noah's when they slid around my waist, the same path they'd taken every day, and he tugged on the metal loops to double-check my harness.

"Sure," I mumbled.

The rest of the bandits stormed outside again, whooping and hollering. One of them tossed Noah one of the money bags on his way out. My gaze flicked to the orange light glowing above the door. As soon as the bandits and some of the sheriff's men had raced off in one direction, I'd get my big moment in the spotlight.

"Ace and Annie in position, please," Renee's voice announced on the headset.

"Don't fuck this up, princess," Noah rasped.

And just like that, my nerves turned from trembling taut strings to blazing fuses. "Screw you," I hissed.

The orange light above the door died. Noah pulled his prop gun from his holster. And we were off.

I blinked and it was over.

Every step landed perfectly timed. Every word dropped from my tongue as rehearsed. Before I even had the chance to worry, we were boxed into the hideout, door shut, another orange lamp telling us to stay put.

I did it.

A wide grin split my lips and I pressed a hand against my racing heart. Relief and pride surged through my veins like pure adrenaline. So much energy. I wanted to scream and jump and run around the room. Alas, this place was maybe eight by eight feet and an old table from the saloon was crammed against the back wall, eliminating any chance of sprinting in circles.

I whirled around, at least wanting to yell at someone that *I HAD DONE THE THING,* but all I got was the starkly contrasted silhouette of Ace Ryder, leaning by the frosted window with his arms crossed and the black bandana drawn over his face. The rush dropped from my head, plummeting to my abdomen, where the ecstatic surge kept tingling. I locked my jaw and turned away. Stupid goddamn shadows shouldn't be allowed to slant this sharply over a man's body. Not a man. Not even Ace. Noah. Ugh.

Crossing my arms as well, I sat on the tabletop and waited.

If everything went according to schedule outside – the sheriff fighting the bandits to get to the hideout – we were stuck in here for seven minutes.

I considered pulling my phone out, but the windows were only covered in a cloudy sepia film, so the bright light from a phone screen might still shine through. Points for Esra Taner for mindfulness, thank you very much.

I swung my feet, and I blew a loose strip of hair from my forehead, and I inspected each of my nails, and I traced the knots in the wooden tabletop.

"So . . . do you come here often?" I asked when I was close to fainting from boredom.

Noah's head tipped, barely an inch, just enough to look at me between the brim of his hat and the bandana. His pale eyes speared through all the darkness shrouding him, and that tingling adrenaline somersaulted in my stomach. I pressed my hand flat against my belly, trying to calm it down.

It was a completely normal physiological response. Adrenaline was just another hormone, and it easily tricked the body into states of attraction. It was so common, they had a name for it. The misattribution of arousal.

Remembering the textbook definition, however, didn't stop my body from putting me through it. Couldn't it at least misattribute on to someone else?

"Hungry?"

"Huh?"

Noah's eyes dropped to where my hand pressed into the folds of my costume.

"Sure," I muttered and shook my hand out, fixing my

eyes back on the orange light. To be fair, my eating habits weren't exactly the best these days, with my stocks running low, but earlier on my phone had happily pinged with a bank notification. It wasn't much, but it was a bit more money than I'd been promised for selling ice cream. As soon as I was out of costume, I'd be ordering the biggest and cheesiest pizza Wild Fields had to offer.

My stomach did actually rumble at the thought.

Good job. I patted my belly, thankful for its noisiness. At least that saved me from having to explain getting the adrenaline hots for Ace Ryder.

"You should really prioritize a healthy breakfast when you know how physically demanding the show gets."

I rolled my eyes at him. "Says the man with the gargantuan peanut butter jar."

"It's organic peanut butter without any artificial additives. It's a good source of protein, unsaturated fats and fiber," he said without moving an inch, but his voice was taking on that grating arrogance.

"Wow, Young," I huffed, "you even suck the joy out of a PB and J."

"Ace and Annie, about thirty seconds. Stop bickering and get in position." Renee's voice sounded through the headset. Damn. I'd forgotten that we were on intercom. Had Sanny heard all that? I hadn't been pretending to be Noah's biggest fan or anything, but I didn't want my brother to think I was going to mess up his life and his friendships here. I wasn't exactly sure how it worked, but hopefully he was connected to the actual show's dialogue and busy interpreting that in sign language, not creeping on the intercom.

Noah mumbled a *sorry* that clearly wasn't for my benefit and pushed himself off the wall.

I hopped off the table and straightened out my skirts.

Ace and Kit were about to duel it out. Once Ace was in chains and off to the jail, I'd fling myself into the sheriff's arms and be reunited with daddy mayor. And we'd live happily ever after. Or at least until tomorrow at 4 p.m.

"Let's go," I huffed.

Chapter Twelve

CHARACTER MEET & GREET

From outlaws to sheriffs, meet the walking legends of Bravetown. Snap an unforgettable photo, listen to tales of their Wild West adventures and let them inspire your bravery.

Click here for Meet & Greet schedules and locations.

NOAH

Summer being in full swing meant more time at the park, less time for the ranch. Usually, I managed to get a few hours out there in the early morning or late afternoon, away from the noise and the people. My family's ranch was just a few minutes' drive away, but between the wide green pastures, the tree-lined perimeter and the rolling hills behind it, it was perfectly secluded. Perfectly peaceful. Just me and a few tools. Sometimes Sanny came out to work alongside me. Time moved differently there. Life moved differently. I didn't _hate_ life at the park, but I _loved_ living on the ranch.

Besides taking up more of my time in general, summer season at Bravetown also meant being roped in at the park with few breaks during normal business hours.

"Please don't put me on hold again, Sally. I only have about five minutes left," I pleaded with the woman on the other end of the phone call. Instead of an answer, I got elevator jazz.

I hung up and shoved the phone into the hidden pocket on my holster. Tornado nudged me in the shoulder as I closed the gate to his box. He must have sensed my seething annoyance.

Sally was supposed to tell me which form I had to fill out, so we could accept monetary donations for the ranch. Apparently, I'd filled out the one meant for charities. How hard could it be to get the correct PDF sent to me? I couldn't afford a lawyer to file all this crap for me yet, but god forbid any government website contain clear instructions. Tomorrow, I'd end up wasting my day off on phone calls and buffering websites instead of mounting new light fixtures in the bedrooms on the ranch like I'd planned.

I rolled my shoulders back and left Tornado with an extra apple before heading off to the side entrance of the park. I'd pick him up in an hour for the show. Anna and CJ were already waiting for me at the gate to accompany me into the crowd. It had seemed ridiculous to me, at first, to have two people shadow my every move. But they were worth their weight in gold as soon as a kid started barfing up their sugar overdose or some fan took their parasocial attachment to Ace Ryder a little too far.

"Can you tie a good solid knot? You know we have to tie people up when we rob banks," I told the little guy who had proclaimed he wanted to join the outlaws. He was in a gray cowboy costume, save for the eye patch and the three-pointed pirate hat.

"I tie my own shoes," he huffed with his hands on his hips.

"Hmm, all right." I lowered myself to one knee. "Can you make a really scary face? A bandit has to be scary."

He responded with a teeth-baring grimace and clawed-up hands that seemed more appropriate for a Halloween monster costume contest. He even added an angry growl.

"That is mighty scary," I said. "I have to try that."

I mirrored him, only for him to lift his claws higher and growl even louder.

There. Photo moment for the parents. I kept my own growl going for a moment or two, then outstretched my hand into the space between us. "All right, Harry, you're hired. Your bandit name will be Harry the Horrible. Me and the other outlaws are robbing the bank later and I need you to watch very closely, so you know what to do next time, got it?"

"Awesome." He beamed and slapped his sticky, sugary hand into my palm.

The kids' enthusiasm never ceased to be infectious. It was so simple. Tiny pirate bandit growling at his enemies to scare them.

"Come here, Horrible Harry," his mother cooed from the sideline of the photo space.

"It's Harry the Horrible," he corrected her, hands propped back on his hips.

"Okay, Harry the Horrible," she laughed. "Come on, Gracie, your turn."

"I don't want to," a young teen girl with blonde ringlets groaned. "I'm way too old for this."

Harry cackled and turned back around to me. "She lo-o-oves cowboys."

"Ohmygod, can we go?" She hid her face in her hands while her mother shoved her closer to me by the shoulders.

"I did not buy you that costume for you not to get a picture, honey."

I hated these moments. Pushy parents of teenagers who were old enough to make up their own minds. It was a fine balance between coaxing a shy kid into a fun picture and knowing when to stop making it an even more embarrassing moment for them.

This one, however, was in costume indeed. She was dressed like Annie Lou, blue dress and white apron. Ah. The big blonde ringlets made sense. That was how Lindsey used to wear her hair as Annie.

"You look strikingly familiar," I said and snapped my fingers against my hat to tilt it back. "Have I held you for ransom recently?"

"Ohmygod," she hissed, face tinting bright red, but she stepped forward, shooting her mother a scathing look over her shoulder. "Fine."

"And you? Are you ready to join your brother and me on our next raid?"

"No." She stood next to me, arms crossed, and turned toward her mother's phone camera. "You should take me for ransom next time though."

"A volunteer hostage? That's a first."

"Only because it's way more believable. That new Annie Lou is so boring and ugly. Like, why would Kit even want to rescue someone like her? Ugh. He deserves so much better."

Thank god the girl stomped off and past her mother before I had to come up with an in-character response to that. Even so, CJ held the line back, giving me a moment before the next kid could come through, and caught my eye with a little double tap to his name plaque. Asking if I needed a break.

This was only the third time someone had mentioned the recast to my face over the last week. The first one with this kind of vitriol. Nothing compared to the number of videos and comments I'd been bombarded with. Part of it seemed somewhat legit, people not liking how Annie got handled like a ragdoll. The other part of it was completely baseless, because they claimed Esra was unfit to play the *Pretty* Annie Lou – and it always boiled down to Lindsey having been pale, blonde and blue-eyed, all of which didn't actually account for her prettiness.

Fuck. If you asked me – and a couple of people had, I'd just not answered – Esra was more than pretty.

Regardless of all her infuriating tics, she had those big brown eyes ringed by thick lashes, those pouty cushioned lips, that bunny crinkle on her nose when she made a face . . . Anyone calling her ugly was either blind or stupid. Esra was a pain in the ass, but she was beautiful.

I waved CJ's concern off with a flick of the wrist, and the next kid in a bandit costume came jumping toward me. He hollered and threw his hand up in the air for an enthusiastic high five. I couldn't help smiling as I slapped my hand against his. This was more like it.

Esra

My legs caved before my butt even touched the chair. I dropped on to it like a sack of flour. My skirts fluffed out around me.

Done. Six days. Eight shows.

And the reflection in my vanity mirror showed as much. My eyes were a little down-slanted, but those bedroom eyes just looked ready for bed now, with heavy lids and thin creases underneath them. It wasn't even pure physical exhaustion. It was the mental exhaustion of constantly having to be aware of my movements. My focus slipped today, just for a second, and my right knee folded sideways when I'd run into the bank. Because of the stabbing pain, I'd barely been able to kick my leg up high enough to make it on to Tornado.

While everyone around me started taking off their costumes and makeup, I went online and ordered myself some knee and ankle braces. Just cheap generic ones. Still better than having to call my mother and ask her to send me my perfectly fitted expensive ones. She probably wouldn't send them anyway. Not without demanding something in return. It was my own stupid oversight, not packing them when I rarely went a month without spraining something. I'd just never been away from home long enough for it to even cross my mind.

I confirmed the order just as Lucas sank into the chair next to mine.

"Hey Lucky," I said and exchanged my phone for a makeup wipe.

"Hey, gorgeous." He grinned widely, and I had a feeling those pearly whites worked on a lot of women. "We're celebrating the start of the summer season tonight."

"Yeah? Who's we?" I asked as I scrubbed my face. I usually didn't care much about guest lists, but the last week had been a crash course in parasocial relationships, and I'd banned myself from checking the online chatter within two days. *Ignorance is bliss* and all that. So I wasn't crazy about celebrating anything if it involved Lucas bringing a bunch of Kit Holliday groupies to the staff house. Especially if I was limping around on a bad knee.

"Just the cast members. Almost everyone else has to work tomorrow. Over at House C, where Heather, Charlotte, Griggs and all live."

"Okay, sure." I beamed up at him. "House party?"

"House part-ay!" He hollered and pumped his fist in the air. The display of a cowboy sheriff acting like a frat boy was comical enough to make me laugh and distract me from my twisted knee for a moment.

Exactly what I needed. Mindless nonsense.

"Perfect. Count me in."

People cleared out of the room within minutes. Even the ones who usually hung back to chat were out of their costumes, or at least out of their makeup, in a flash. Apparently I wasn't the only one eager for a break. I hung back, waiting for the Advil to kick in, because I wasn't sure how much weight my knee would support right now.

"Esra?"

I glanced back over my shoulder, catching Noah's gaze. He stood in the door, hand on the light switch. He'd changed into one of those plaid pearl snaps and some jeans, and raised his brows as if I'd personally offended him by dilly-dallying.

"I still need a minute. I'll switch the lights off on my way out."

"Something wrong?"

"No," I said, because I definitely wasn't gonna give him more reasons to treat me like a blister on his heel.

He glanced back and forth between me and the door. "Do you need me to get Sinan?"

"Oh, for crying out loud," I snapped, "I just need a minute to myself. Can you give me a minute?"

His hand dropped from the light switch. Instead of leaving, however, he sighed and took a seat at the vanity next to mine, usually occupied by Heather. The chair settings didn't fit him, but he didn't mess with them, just awkwardly folded his long legs under the table as he pulled his phone out.

"What are you doing?" I asked, wondering if he'd come up with some insane reason why I wasn't to be trusted alone in the dressing room.

"Checking my messages." Noah shrugged.

Fine. I'd be game for any kind of distraction, and I didn't want to check my own socials, so I swiveled my chair around to face him. "How many fan videos did you get tagged in today?"

He cocked his chin and narrowed his eyes at me. "I thought you needed a minute to yourself."

"Humor me."

"Only one today."

"I expected more from the Ace Ryder fans," I mused.

"They're more active in the evening."

"Can I see?"

Noah opened his profile to the posts he was tagged in and handed the phone over. The video was a fun little outfit transition from a girl wearing athleisure in her modern bedroom to wearing a full Wild West outlaw costume on Bravetown's Main Street. I scrolled to the next one, which was a video of a young woman going to the character meet and greet and pretending to interview the infamous Ace Ryder for a newspaper. I had to give Noah credit for staying in character through some of her ridiculous questions.

I kept scrolling, finding fan edits, park trip vlogs, clips of the stunt show, merch hauls. All from the last few days. Who knew theme parks were such a hot topic online?

"Okay, we need to talk about the changes they made in Bravetown this summer, because this – is – not – *it*," a young woman yelled at the phone camera on the next video I opened, clapping between the last few words to emphasize them. When she said "this", a grainy picture of Noah lifting me on to the horse popped up.

"Sorry, I didn't realize . . ." Noah grabbed the phone and locked the screen before the video could go on.

"It's fine. I don't care." So much for *ignorance is bliss*. I'd have to down a couple of tequila shots later to get back to bliss.

"Let's go. It's been more than a minute." Noah unfolded himself from the chair with surprising grace.

"I'm going to make some ungodly ambiguous sounds when I get up, and it's just because every single one of my muscles is sore from sitting on that horse. So don't get turned on. That's not happening." I grinned and wiggled my brows. The painkillers had kicked in, but I wasn't taking any chances.

"Do you talk to everyone like this?" He pinched the bridge of his nose.

"No," I laughed. He was so easy. "But I think if I try hard enough, I might make that vein on your forehead pop someday."

Noah sighed and turned away.

My muscles had stiffened with that deep-rooted ache that even Advil couldn't touch, and while my joints were pain-free, they resisted enough to make me groan as I rose to my feet. "Ugh." I bent and patted my knees through my skirts just to make sure they were stable enough to carry me.

"You sound like an eighty-year-old."

I glanced up to find Noah raising his brows at me.

"Oh, you're one of *those* guys." I scrunched up my nose. "Grandma porn? Whatever floats your boat, I guess."

"Jesus, that's not what I—"

He shut up when I started laughing. So. Easy.

"Are you coming to the party tonight? We can get you drunk. Maybe that'll help you loosen up a little."

Chapter Thirteen

THE HATTERY

Add the finishing touch to any outfit with a hat from Bravetown's Hattery. Ride off into the sunset with one of our ready-to-wear models or experience true tradition with a bespoke hat made just for you while you watch the masters at work.

Noah

While the cast parties tended to unravel into a drunken stupor, they usually started out fun enough. People crowded into the living room and kitchen. Zuri, who wasn't part of the cast but had come with Sinan, brought home-made pizza rolls, while Lucas showed up with three dozen bags of chips that were just beyond their expiry date, warning people not to ask questions. Austin sat in the corner with his headphones on and his laptop open, supplying the room with a mix of background music and sing-along hits.

And Richard, who had shown up in a sequined blazer and his white hair styled in a high quiff, brought out some trivia cards. He turned the sofa into his personal game show, where both winners and losers got drunk.

Most of us circled the sofa, waiting for the show to start.

"No, I'm on her team, I'll just sit over here," Sanny shouted over the chatter, pointing at his sister.

Esra perched on the sofa, rubbing her hands together, completely focused on Richard and his quizmaster cards. Her tank top proclaimed "born yesterday" in big pink letters.

"All teams must sit together for group rounds," Richard said and waved Sanny to the other side of the L-shaped sofa. Five people would already be a tight squeeze on there, but seven made it look like a tin of sardines. "We need one more person." Richard pointed at Sanny, Zuri and Esra's corner of the sofa. No wonder people didn't want to be on a trivia team with someone who was *born yesterday* . . .

"Noah!" Sinan waved me over before I could pretend to be too busy sipping my beer.

"No, thanks," I replied and turned to find someone or something to turn my attention to instead. Vivi, who'd been watching next to me, just pointedly held up a hand as a sign not to talk to her.

"Noah, I love you. I respect you. But you get your butt over here so we can start," Zuri yelled, already hyped up on the sugary concoction in her cup.

Sanny laughed and planted a kiss on his fiancée's cheek, while she aggressively patted the three inches of sofa beside her.

"Fine. One sec." I grabbed a bottle of water from the fridge to switch to once I'd finished my beer, before I resigned myself to my fate.

It took some shuffling. Zuri ended up snuggling into Sanny's lap, and I was wedged between him and Esra. Her knee bounced against mine, her whole body vibrating. She didn't even spare me a glance or make a snarky comment about my water. Instead, her knuckles were turning white from gripping the red claxon squeaker for our team.

"Is she okay?"

"No, she's insane," Sanny snorted, earning himself a slap on the chest from Zuri, "but yes, she's fine."

"First round," Richard announced. "Each correct answer earns you a round of shots for the team. The shots will remain on the table in front of you. First team to collect four rounds wins. If a team gets an answer wrong, the opposing team has the chance to answer and steal a round of shots from the first team. Any questions?" People stayed silent or shook their heads, so Richard continued: "The category for this round: History."

"Shit," Esra muttered under her breath. Her knee bounced faster.

The first question was something about the Civil War and Esra honked her signal before Richard had fully ended the sentence. She bounced up and down on the sofa when the first round of shots appeared in front of us. She was just as fast with the second question, about something called the Silk Road.

The third question was about the California Gold Rush, and Lucas hit the green squeaker at the other end of the sofa – maybe half a second before Esra squeezed the red one. The other team got that question.

Esra glared at that round of shots in front of the other team as if it was a personal affront.

"Next question," Richard announced. "Blue jeans as we know them today were patented in the 1870s by—"

The green team's horn squeaked, Heather jumping off the sofa. "Levi Strauss! Levi's jeans!"

"That wasn't the question, but correct, blue jeans as we know them were patented by Levi Strauss and Jacob Davis, but why are they called blue jeans? The red team has the question and the opportunity to steal a round of shots." Richard pointed his cards at us.

Before I had the chance to come up with a theory, Esra replied: "*Bleu de Gênes* was the French name for a sturdy blue fabric made in Genoa. The name later developed into the anglicized 'blue jeans'."

"That is . . . correct!" Richard announced in his best show-host voice. He pulled four shots from the green team and set them down with our existing eight. "Red team only needs one more correct answer to win the first round."

"How do you even know that?" I asked. It wouldn't have surprised me if Vivi had gotten that answer right, because she could go on and on about fashion and makeup. She had a personal hand in all the costumes in the park. Esra, however, wore sparkly, borderline-offensive clothing.

"Had a lot of inside time as a kid." She shrugged as if that explained it, when it just left the question why a little girl would spend her time learning about the history of blue jeans instead of playing with dolls or watching TV.

"We're going all the way back in time with this one. The point goes to the first team to correctly quote and name an ancient Greek philosopher."

Esra jumped up and squeaked our horn hard enough for it to make a strangled airy sound.

"I swear by Apollo the physician, and Asclepius the surgeon, likewise Hygeia and Panacea, and call all the gods and goddesses to witness, that I will carry out, according to my ability and judgment, this oath and this indenture.

To hold my teacher in this art equal to my parents; make him my partner in my . . ."

Richard was hanging on to her every word as she clutched the squeaker to her chest. The rest of the room had fallen silent, too, people pausing mid-drink and staring at Esra as she went on.

I turned to Sanny, who was noiselessly giggling, hiding his face behind Zuri's shoulder.

"Hippocratic oath," he whispered when he caught me staring. "She's known the whole thing by heart forever. It was a cute party trick as a little kid. It became less impressive when she got older, so she added the Greek original, and then after my accident, even sign language." He rolled his eyes. "Show-off."

"Hippocrates of Kos." Esra ended her monologue with a deep sigh and collapsed back on to the sofa.

After a moment of stunned silence, people started clapping. Richard blinked from Esra to his cards and back. He'd met his trivia match. "I don't think we'll need to google that to verify." He cleared his throat. "Red team wins the question and the first round of trivia."

More shots appeared in front of us. Richard explained that every player had to drink their rounds of shots. Anyone who tapped out was out of the game. When only three players were left, there would be a lightning round finale.

"All right, I'm out." I pushed the shots back across the table.

"Are you drinking water?" Esra narrowed her eyes at my bottle, having already downed one of her shots and only now registering her surroundings. "If you don't drink, you're out of the game."

"I haven't been *in* the game, princess." I wrenched the claxon from her hand. Her fingernails had left deep dents in the rubber ball at the end of the horn, and it refilled with air with a pathetic hiss.

"Oops." She flexed her hand. "I can let you answer some questions if you want."

"How generous. You'd *let* the rest of your team participate?"

"Don't drag me into this. Esra's brain is paying for my shots." Sinan clanked an empty glass down on the table. "I'm okay being eye candy."

"If you want to answer some questions, answer some questions." Esra threw another shot back, voice growing agitated. "You didn't exactly reach for the squeaker."

"I just don't drink," I said before this thing could spiral into a much bigger argument than it was worth, "so, I'm out of the game."

I climbed across Sanny's legs and took my water bottle back to the kitchen, where I grabbed one of Lucas's bags of chips. Those definitely weren't healthy, and the expiration date didn't help, but I needed a moment of feeling normal. I knew I shouldn't have played. The sour feeling in the pit of my stomach was too familiar. Jealousy. I'd graduated high school by the skin of my teeth. After my mom got sick, I went through a lot, and that included getting wasted and skipping school. I cleaned up my act, but I'd never had much of a chance to make up for those years. I just had to keep moving. I wrote off books and classrooms, just like I wrote off getting drunk and making stupid choices, and I rarely felt like I missed out on anything.

"You good?" Sanny followed me into the kitchen within

a few minutes and grabbed the bag of chips from my hands with a furrowed brow. "Never mind. Clearly, you aren't."

"I hate trivia," I replied.

"You just have to sit back and let Ez answer all the questions for you. She used to spend days in bed reading encyclopedias. I tried to convert her to *Teenage Mutant Ninja Turtles*, all right? But she said comics weren't stimulating enough. What six-year-old uses the word 'stimulating'?"

"What six-year-old spends days reading encyclopedias?"

"Exactly my point," he yelled, some of those shots clearly coming through in his slurred words. "Anyway. Are we still on for painting tomorrow?"

"Sure. If you think you won't be too hungover." I chuckled.

"Okay. Yeah. I think I have to get Zuri home. She's got to be in the office bright and early, and Austin is our designated driver."

"Good call. I'm heading out soon too." I tipped my bottle toward the door, and by extension my perfectly quiet bedroom just across the street.

Sinan's face contorted.

"What's wrong?"

He sighed. "Look, I know that you two hate each other, but . . ."

"Hate?"

"You and Esra."

"Shit, Sanny, she's your family, so I wouldn't call it hate."

He shook his head at me with an amused grin. "What's said on the intercom, never stays on the intercom. There's a pool going on which one of you will snap first."

"Okay, so we're not exactly friendly . . ." And I probably owed Vivi a giant *thank you* for not telling Sinan about me storming into the office the other day, ready to get Esra fired. Seeing the confliction on his face now, I actually felt bad for doing it. I might be an only child, but I still knew what it meant to take responsibility for your family.

"If Zuri and I both go home now, can you just keep an eye on Ez? She's having a good time, and I'm glad she's getting along with everyone, but she's only been here three weeks, she's never lived away from home . . . I know it's only like a two-minute walk. She's probably perfectly fine to get home on her own. I mean, she's an adult, right?"

"I've got it," I said, mostly because I still felt like a dick for trying to get his little sister fired, and partially because the last time Esra and Zuri had a *good time*, she wanted to blow up heads of lettuce with fireworks. Unsupervised, she might end up burning down the whole park.

As if on cue, Esra crowed like a rooster in the next room.

Sinan wrinkled his brow and touched his hearing aid. "Was that . . . ?"

I just nodded, and he sighed before thanking me again and going off to find Zuri.

That ass took my bag of chips.

I snatched up another one and settled in at the kitchen table, keeping an ear on the quiz show in the living room while I scrolled through the social media posts I'd been tagged in. I untagged myself from all the ones that criticized the new Annie Lou.

At some point, Vivi joined me at the table. She'd changed into striped PJs, her blue hair piled into a bun atop her head. Without asking whether or not I wanted to play, she started passing out Uno cards. Two games later, she was barely able to keep her eyes open, and went upstairs to her room.

Judging by the sounds of it, the lightning round was going strong.

I was just going to check on Esra before finding something else to keep me busy for a while, but the display in the living room sent blood roaring through my ears. Not the way Richard stood on an old crate, towering above everyone. Not the way Esra and Lucas stood in the center of the crowd, each of them gripping a bottle in one hand and a horn in the other. But the way Esra had to tilt her head back, because Lucas's white Kit Holliday hat had been crookedly shoved over her wavy hair.

I was across the room in an instant. I wasn't thinking. Some sort of instinct took over as I stopped in front of Esra and grabbed the hat.

"Absolutely the fuck not," I growled.

"What the hell? I'm winning the game." She stuck her full bottom lip out in a pout, and I almost would have fallen for it and backed off if she hadn't pronounced it *win-nin-ing*.

"You're going home," I told her and tossed the hat at Lucas. "Keep your fucking hat to yourself."

"Dude, she took it." He held his hands up in capitulation, but he was grinning widely. I usually didn't mind his antics, but fuck, I wanted to wipe that grin off his face right now. Preferably with my fist. The urge was startling. I didn't lose my temper or get involved in drunken brawls. *I'd promised Sanny to get his little sister home safe.* That was all. And that certainly didn't include Lucas.

"I need a hat 'cause I'm a cowgirl now," Esra giggled, pulling my attention back to her, "yeehaw."

"All right, cowgirl, do you know the hat rule?"

"Yes!" Her whole face lit up and she squeezed her red squeaker, back to trivia mode. "Don't leave a hat on the bed because it's bad luck."

"No." I curled my hand around hers, pressing another squeak from the horn. "You wear the hat, you ride the cowboy."

"Oh." She furrowed her brow as she looked back and forth between me and Lucas, processing that information. Leaning in conspiratorially, she whispered, "I didn't know that."

I shot Lucas a glare, because he sure as hell knew about it—as did everyone in this room—and he'd let her take the hat anyway. "Let's go home before you get yourself into trouble."

"No!" She wrenched her hand and the claxon out of my grip and glared up at me. "I'm winning." *Win-nin-ing.*

This woman was going to be the death of me.

"Are you the only other person still playing?" I turned to Lucas, who nodded in response. "Do you forfeit?"

"Uh . . ." He must have realized how close he was to meeting my knuckles, because he tossed his squeaker to the ground and backed away. "I'm out."

"There. You won," I told Esra and turned to Richard. "What does she win?"

He wordlessly pulled a medal from his pocket. It was a plain purple ribbon with one of the star-shaped *BRAVE* pin badges on it. Esra still squealed and dove for it with grabby hands. She draped it around her neck, smiling from ear to ear.

"Can we go now?" I asked.

"No. If you want me to go home *with you*, you have to pull an Ace Ryder and, like, abduct me because you are boor-ring and I'm having fun and so I'm not leaving with you."

"Have it your way, princess." I didn't give her another chance to blow me off. I ducked, wrapped my hands around her waist like I'd done countless times before, and hoisted her over my shoulder.

Esra squealed and wriggled, her fist drumming into my shoulder twice, before she went slack and started giggling. Behind me, the squeaker and a bottle of beer dropped to the ground. Fully aware that I was causing a scene – and I didn't cause scenes – I maneuvered us out of the room and out of the house without giving anyone another glance.

The second we hit fresh air, Esra started writhing again, but this time she broke into song. She bellowed out 'We Are the Champions', off-key and off-beat, whipping her arms around and shimmying her hips. Her bike shorts were made from a slippery, shiny fabric, so I wrapped my hands tighter around her thighs to keep her balanced.

"Will you hold still, before I drop you?"

"S'this your first kidnapping, cowboy?" she asked and added an extra wriggle to her hips, pushing them against my face.

"I'm not kidnapping you," I grunted as I carried her up the few steps to our house.

She laughed and tugged on the backside of my shirt. "I feel kidnapped. And a li'l dizzy. Ew."

"Don't throw up." I lowered her down until her feet

were firmly planted on even ground and kept my hands on her waist just in case.

Esra blinked, eyes glassy and cheeks pink, clutching the doorframe. "I'm good."

"Sure?"

"Water. I need lots of water. And aspirin. And . . ." She glanced down and wiggled her toes. "Might need help upstairs without tripping."

"Okay. I can do that."

Esra's room was a mess, with only one clear path across the floor from the door to the bed. I had to walk her in front of me, both hands around her middle for support, to get her safely to the mattress. She grabbed the bottle of water from her nightstand and somehow managed to tip it back with enough swing to give herself a shower.

"Damn," she muttered and patted at the spill on her tank top. I left her alone so she could change, while I grabbed a bottle of aspirin from the bathroom for her. When I came back, however, she was sitting in the exact same spot where I'd left her, still prodding her shirt.

"Are you wearing underwear?" I asked.

She pulled at the neck of her shirt and glanced down at herself. "Yep."

I rubbed the bridge of my nose, swallowing the urge to ask what kind of person had to check to see if they were wearing underwear. Instead, I grabbed the large, tangled T-shirt from the corner of her bed and draped it out. "Okay, nothing I haven't seen yet. Arms up."

She followed my command without much protest and allowed me to peel her out of her top. I pointedly kept my eyes on the purple cotton of her nightshirt as I pulled her arms through it, then carefully fit it over her head. Her dark hair bounced out like loose springs. She fished her trivia medal from the collar and smoothed a hand over it against her chest.

"Okay. You have water. You have aspirin. Anything else before you go to bed?"

"Pizza?" She fluttered her lashes at me, those big doe eyes growing to the size of saucers.

"Do you have any pizza?"

"No, but we can order some."

"It's past midnight on a Tuesday, princess, and this isn't New York. Nobody's delivering pizza anymore tonight."

"Oh man," she sighed, deflating, disappointment written all over her face.

"We'll get you pizza tomorrow. Go to bed."

"Ugh, fine." She bent down to take her boots off. Despite the rest of her outfit having changed, she was still in her costume boots. They were comfortable, sure, because Renee knew we wouldn't be able to do the show in ill-fitting shoes, but Esra didn't strike me as a Western boot kind of girl. Then again, she was a cowgirl now. Yeehaw.

"Good night," I said on my way out the door.

Just before it closed, I heard her mumble, "Yeah, whatever, buzzkill sun."

I grabbed myself an apple from the kitchen to get rid of the stale taste of fried potato chips, and then hit the shower, before heading to my room myself. I laid out my painting clothes for tomorrow, texted Sanny that Esra was home safe and sound, and then finally fell into bed.

I'd never been able to fall asleep quickly, often staring at the minute hand creeping forward on my alarm clock, but just when I was about to drift off, heavy knocks pulled me up again. It took a disorienting moment to realize they hadn't come from my door.

In the room next to mine, the door clicked open.

"Hey," Lucas's voice came from the hallway, "so uhm, I wanted to make sure you're okay and everything."

"I'm good. Thank you," Esra replied, words much clearer than they had been an hour ago.

"I brought your bag."

"Oh god, you're so sweet, Lucky. Thank you."

Bag. Of course, she'd had a bag. My goddamn caveman brain had been too preoccupied with getting Esra home to even remember her bag. And now Lucas was the sweet one even though he'd let her wear his hat, knowing full well the implication, and I was, once again, left feeling like a massive dick.

"Any chance I can persuade you to have a nightcap with me?" he asked.

"Only if it comes with food. I'm starving."

"I have microwave pizza," he offered.

"Ohmygod, perfect. I could kiss you right now. Let me put on some pants and I'll meet you at the microwave."

I groaned into my pillow at the realization that this girl just opened her door half-naked again. My mind immediately flashed back to that first run-in when she dropped her towel. *My* towel, to be exact. And then again when she'd opened her door to me in nothing but her underwear. The curve of her hip and the constellations of freckles around her navel were seared into my memory. And now I'd have to hear about them from goddamn Lucas. He wasn't gentleman enough to keep anything private. Not that it mattered.

My insides twisted when Esra's door banged shut, and her footsteps disappeared down the stairs a moment later.

I'd gotten her home safe. I'd done what Sanny had asked me to do.

She sounded sobered-up enough.

Not. My. Problem.

If she wanted to wear Kit Holliday's hat, that was her decision.

I tried to close my eyes, but they flew open again, focused on the light coming through the small crack beneath my door. At some point, Austin came home, easily recognizable because he beatboxed on the way to his room. The light turned off. I kept staring. The light turned back on, and two hushed voices came up the stairs, half-talking, half-giggling. I knew that giggle. Esra's door opened and closed again, but the voices continued, a lot more muffled through wall and wardrobe.

Sourness creeping up the back of my throat, I swung out of bed and shoved my feet into my boots.

It'd be enough to endure Lucas bragging about it. I didn't need to actually hear him having sex with Esra.

Few places were as quiet as Bravetown at night. Once all the guests left, the rides shut down and even the saloon closed, only a few yellow streetlamps still flickered, and the only other people around were the security guards. They knew I checked on the horses after hours, so they never paid me much attention. They mostly made sure none of the hotel guests climbed the fence for late-night park visits.

Someone else had already done night check today, but I still wandered to the stables. Three of the horses in there belonged to me personally, and while they worked in the park, I still made sure to keep an eye on them. Tornado had been with me the longest. We'd been forced to sell all the other horses on our ranch, but I'd never been able to give him up. Renee had allowed me to keep him at Bravetown even before I'd started working here. Last year, Cookie and Crumble, both Tennessee Walkers, had been my first investment back into my family ranch. My goal was to add three more over the next two years.

I slipped into Tornado's stall and he shook his head at me, huffing and puffing. He was annoyed that I was showing up this late, but he hadn't laid down to sleep yet, so I only felt minimally guilty.

"Sorry," I whispered for good measure anyway.

He walked over and sniffed at me, then pushed his nose against the center of my chest.

"No, I'm not upset," I replied.

He knocked me in the sternum again. If I had actually been agitating, he would have pushed his entire face into me. Right now, he was just prodding me to figure out what was wrong. Because he knew that *something* was wrong.

"Just annoyed, okay?" I replied. "It's none of my business what she does, but with how thin those walls are? I don't need to hear her conduct *her* business."

He snorted and lifted his head up, then dropped his chin on my shoulder. It was a particular torture, training your horse to react to different emotional outbursts, and then being on the receiving end when the animal called you out and tried to calm you down.

"I'm not angry either," I lied and grimaced.

Tornado left his head resting in place until some of the tension dissipated from between my shoulder blades.

He prodded my chest again, and I distracted him with an apple before he could take this little therapy session any further.

By the time I'd checked on all three of my horses and got back to the house, it had gone quiet. No beatboxing, no giggling, no other questionable sounds.

At least until the next morning.

I left my room, on my way to meet Sinan, when a loud rumble in Esra's room stopped me in my tracks. Something had fallen. I waited a second for a cry of help or anything; instead the door swung open, and Lucas was shoved out. He stumbled, not even fully balanced before the door banged shut again. I stayed just long enough to register that his clothes were a mess, but they were last night's clothes. He blinked at me in confusion, clearly still half-asleep, and I shouldered past him and down the stairs.

None. Of. My. Business.

The dating pool in Wild Fields was small.

People had limited options.

Sleeping with Lucas was better than hooking up with random park guests. They were both single as far as I knew, so zero drama and zero bad publicity.

I'd gotten her home, just like I'd promised Sinan.

Her early-morning bedside manner could be improved upon, but again, none of my business.

I climbed into my truck and gripped the steering wheel, looking back at the house with narrowed eyes. None of my business, unless I'd fucked up. I'd left. They'd been drinking and I'd left. Lucas wasn't a bad guy, but the Lucas I knew might not be the same Lucas a drunk girl got to see. The way she'd shoved him from her room – had that been regret or resentment? Fuck.

I mentally replayed the moment again and again as I drove through town. I'd been too focused on Lucas to even glance Esra's way. He'd been too baffled, I decided. If something had happened, he wouldn't have been that dumbfounded to be kicked out of her room.

Still, at the first red light, I pulled out my phone and texted Sanny.

Noah: Check on your sister. She seemed upset when I left.
Sinan: Did you steal her chocolate again?

For once I wished this was just about food disappearing from the kitchen.

Chapter Fourteen

KIT HOLLIDAY
SHERIFF OF BRAVETOWN

Kit Holliday is the heroic sheriff of our small town. He keeps the peace and protects the citizens from outlaws. If you keep an eye out for his white hat and shiny gold badge, you might spot him on his daily patrol.

Esra

My head buzzed. Usually it pounded more like a marching band the morning after getting drunk, but today it buzzed like a vibrator on one of those Morse code settings. Ugh. I tried to pull my pillow over my face to muffle the sensation, but it was stuck.

"Shit, sorry, hold on," someone said. "She's right here."

"Hmm? What?" I turned, only to find Lucas lying next to me. His eyes were half-closed but he slapped my phone up against my ear.

"Esra? Who is that man?" Mom shrieked.

Oh. My. God.

"Hold on," I croaked into the phone as pure adrenaline surged through me. I hit the mute button and whirled on Lucas. "Why the fuck are you answering my phone?"

"Sorry. Thought it was mine. Reflex," he mumbled, totally unfazed.

"Get out." I pushed my hands into the mattress and shoved against his stupid long body with both feet. Lucas slid off the mattress, dropping to the floor like a sack of flour. "Get the fuck out. Where do you get off?"

"I didn't? What?"

Who the hell answered someone else's phone? Especially when the caller ID very clearly showed a picture of *my* mother. I barely let him get to his feet before I shoved him forward and out of the room. For good measure, I slammed the door shut.

Idiot.

My right knee buckled as I turned for my bed again. Fuck. I'd been too surprised to pay attention to how I was moving. I had a tendency to over-bend that knee outwards and the misstep from yesterday's show had clearly left its mark. I limped back to bed and collapsed on to the mattress. The marching band behind my temples started its hungover drum roll.

What a shit show of a morning. At least talking to my mother couldn't make it any more painful.

I grabbed the phone, took a deep breath and unmuted myself. "Mom?"

"Esra, why is there a strange man answering your phone in the morning? I thought you were with your brother."

Lucas and I had fallen asleep watching some old Western that I didn't even really remember. Not that my mother would believe me if I told her as much. "Do you really expect me to answer that?"

"Yes, I want answers. This is the first time I get to talk to my only daughter in weeks and then it's a stranger's voice I hear. Where are you? Did you abandon your brother already, just like you abandoned us?"

Wow, we were heavy on the guilt-tripping this morning, and I was too hungover and aching to placate her. "First of all, I didn't abandon you. You cut me off. Second of all, the fact that Sanny and I share the same employer doesn't prohibit me from spending the night with whoever the fuck I want."

"You will not speak to me like that, Esra. Where are your manners?"

"Lost them in Virginia along with the rest of my propriety." There was a joke in there about virgins, but I was too frazzled to come up with it.

"Well, I hope you can go back and find them."

"Huh?" That was a way calmer response than I'd anticipated.

Mom took a deep breath. "Your father has been talking to an old friend of his from college, Rodney Andrews. You might remember him. His family invited us to the Vineyard that one Fourth of July when you were eight. You dislocated your shoulder when you played with Rodney Junior on their boat even though I told you not to get on the pier because it was slippery, but did you listen? Your father spent that night in the ER with you instead of watching the fireworks with his old friend. They invited us again the next year, but I felt so bad for ruining the mood of the entire party and disrupting their plans, we couldn't possibly accept."

"Sure, Mom," I sighed. I vividly remembered Rodney Junior trying to shove me off the boat and feed me to the sharks that he'd sworn were circling in the waters. And I remembered Dad handing me off at the hospital and how I'd watched the fireworks through a window with a nurse, getting two cups of red Jell-O. All of which Mom was perfectly aware of. It wasn't useful to the narrative she was trying to spin right now though, so it'd be a waste of time to remind her.

"Right, so Rodney is vice president of the public health department at Yale, and he thinks you have a perfectly good chance at starting next semester. It's not medicine, but you can transfer your credits toward a grad degree. You're close enough to home if there's an emergency, but far enough away from us for you to have your freedom. There you go."

There you go?

Like she'd done me a goddamn favor by putting me right back where I'd started? More libraries and lectures? And then what? Work as a consultant for big pharma? I hadn't gotten into medicine because I thought the health-care system was so goddamn fascinating, or because I had a massive interest in medical research. I'd worked my ass off for med school because I'd spent the Fourth of July with a nurse; because the doctor at the pediatric ward gave me a big stuffed unicorn for my sixth birthday; because my physical therapist had helped me laugh about silly sex injuries after my first time had gone horribly wrong and I'd felt like I'd never have a single normal experience in my life. They'd wanted me to be happy, not safe.

Medicine had been a personal choice for me.

It had been a safe choice for my parents.

There you go? Go where?

"Mom, I'm too hungover for this. Just send me a link to the program or something."

"Esra Selenay Taner!" Her voice hitched an octave higher, and I could vividly imagine the nervous spasm in her eyebrow. I knew I'd hit a nerve because she continued in Turkish. *You should not be drinking alcohol. What are you thinking?*

"I'm not. That's the whole point," I replied in English.

"Your body—"

"Gotta go. Bye Mom." I hung up before she could ramp up to another lecture.

My notifications showed a missed message from Sinan from just a minute ago. I doubted he'd texted because he'd known Mom was going to call me. She called twice almost every day. I just let it go to voicemail.

Sinan: You good?

Esra: If Mom calls you, don't pick up.

Sinan: That bad? 😩

Esra: She used my middle name.

Sinan: At least you two talked.

I bit my lip, debating what to text back, until I eventually just closed the chat. As much as I loved Sanny, he'd never fully get it. Our parents had always given him more freedom. It wasn't because he was older, since I never aged out of their control. Not even because of my health, since he'd had just as many liberties after the accident that caused his hearing loss, if not more.

The only thing they'd ever expected from him was to look after me. Because I was his *sister*. A *girl*, in need of being kept safe.

I was fully aware that I was only at Bravetown because Sanny was still looking after me, but at least Sanny's version of that was text messages containing five words or less.

He hadn't even tried to stop me from getting drunk last night. Every goddamn celebration at home, every dinner, everyone around me got champagne flutes and wine, and I was handed juice. For what it was worth, Sanny somewhat understood that I was tired of being handled with kid gloves.

I spent the rest of the day feeling like death incarnate.

I took some aspirin but they just reminded me that Noah had thrown me over his shoulder and carried me home last night, and I hadn't made up my mind yet whether that was brutish but thoughtful, or just another instance of him being an asshole control freak. Then thinking about Noah carrying me like I weighed nothing made me think of Ace Ryer and the videos I'd been forcing myself to ignore. And since my mood was already in the dumpster, I started scrolling through socials for the first time in a week.

Every comment made me hike the blanket higher. There were whole video essays dissecting the difference between me and the previous Annie Lou. And they all agreed that I wasn't an improvement.

I only made it out of bed because Adriana lured me to the saloon with promises of free nuggets.

Dino nuggets were good – but nuggets shaped like cowboy boots, hats and sheriff stars were on a whole different level. I was six or seven pieces deep when Lucas climbed on to the barstool next to me. While the saloon was busy, our designated staff area wasn't, so he didn't choose that seat out of necessity.

I sighed and pushed my plate a little toward him, hoping that would be enough of a peace offering.

Lucas was kind of like a puppy. Lively and cute, but also a bit clueless.

"Sorry about this morning," he mumbled, taking one of the star-shaped nuggets and dipping it in ketchup.

"Me too," I said, and offered him a smile.

"This morning?" Adriana asked from the other side of the bar, where she'd been polishing the same three glasses in rotation for the last twenty minutes. She raised her brows and shimmied her shoulders. "All the juicy details, please."

"I accidentally answered her phone when her mom called, so she kicked me out of bed. Literally kicked me. I have bruises." He lifted his shirt, but there was zero bruising. In fact, he lifted it in a way that showed his abs more than the side of his ribcage where I'd shoved my feet.

"We fell asleep watching a movie," I clarified, rolling my eyes at him, "which is all you'll ever do in my bed, so put your clothes back on."

He grinned and ran a hand provocatively down his stomach.

Adriana and I both made gagging sounds at the exact same time, only to then break out in laughter. Lucas grimaced and took another one of my nuggets, poking his tongue out at us.

"You need a real girlfriend," Adriana said and filled one of the glasses with water.

"I'm trying," Lucas whined.

"Sleeping with a girl doesn't make her your girlfriend," she said and put the water down on the short side of the counter, alongside a bottle of beer, without breaking eye contact with Lucas.

It took me a moment to realize Noah had just stepped up to the bar. He took the drinks without a word, then sat down with Sinan in the furthest booth. I'd come to realize that Sanny always preferred that booth because it was the quietest, so the noise from the saloon didn't interfere with his conversations too much. They both had dried flecks of white paint all over their hair and hands. I hadn't been to Sanny's apartment yet, but I knew he'd moved into Zuri's rental, so I doubted they'd been painting anything over there. And paintball seemed way too much frivolous fun for Noah.

I considered going over there for a moment, but my knee was still being a jerk, and I didn't want Sanny seeing me limp around.

"Some Bravetown superfan sliding into your DMs isn't girlfriend material," Adriana replied to whatever Lucas had just said.

"Isn't there anyone in town you actually like? Maybe someone else who works in the park? Vivi? Heather? Morgan?" I asked, jumping back on the conversation.

"Nah." Lucas shook his head. "I've known everyone here my entire life. You just kinda know when there's no one in the mix for you. Maybe I should pull an Adriana. Maybe I'll meet someone on the road."

"Oh yeah? Learned to hold a note yet?" Adriana laughed and popped her hip out.

"No," he huffed.

"Wait. I didn't fall off the horse all week. You owe me answers." I pointed my chicken nugget at Adriana. "What does he mean by *pulling an Adriana*?"

"Phone." She held her hand out.

I pulled it from my pocket and unlocked it for her. Within a few swipes, she had Spotify open.

Adriana winked at me from an album cover that was fifty per cent her wild honey curls and fifty per cent her freckles and big smile.

Adriana Banks – Now/Here.

"I was nineteen when I was 'discovered' by some big-shot producer in Nashville," she said, "so I packed my bags, recorded an album and went on tour to open for Brooks Monroe. I was living the dream for a few years."

"Holy shit." I didn't even listen to country but even I had heard of Brooks Monroe. He was old school. Pretty sure my dad had played his Christmas album on repeat every December for the last ten years, though we hadn't even celebrated Christmas before Sinan had brought Zuri home three years ago.

"Yeah," she sighed, "but then you refuse to take a *private meeting* with some asshole in a suit one too many times, your record label drops you, and you remain a one-hit wonder."

"I'm sorry. That sounds awful." I dragged my eyes from her to Lucas, who was very busy arranging the nuggets on my plate into categories. "But then why are people so shitty around you? They act like you poisoned the well or something."

Adriana bent over the bar and tapped a polished finger-nail against the album cover. "Twelve songs about how I couldn't wait to get out of Wild Fields, about how stifling small-town life is, how the boys have no ambitions beyond drinking beer and driving their daddy's truck – sorry,

Lucas – how I didn't want to be stuck here and pop out two kids, bake pie and go on a family holiday once a year."

"Oh."

"Yup." She shrugged. "Anyway. To get back to the point, Lucas, I didn't find a boyfriend out on the road either. So your options pretty much suck anywhere. Sorry."

"Well, this just got way too depressing. I wanted to have a fun, flirty, fearless summer. So I'm not going to be girlfriend material for you." I pointed at Lucas. "But I will be your fun friend. I will get drunk and watch bad Western movies with you when you need to."

"I'll bring the ice cream if there's room in your bed for a third person." Adriana grinned.

"I'm declaring my bed a *frivolous* fun zone from now on. All *platonic* fun will happen on the sofa."

"Not to burst your bubble, but sofas are much more fun than beds if we're being technical about it," she said. "Like you might want to switch your sex and friend spaces around."

"I'm not having sex on the sofa in a shared living space," I hissed.

"Everyone else is," Lucas threw in, "you just have to time it right."

"What?" I gaped.

Both him and Adriana shrugged as if that wasn't completely insane.

"Ew." I didn't even want to think about who might have done what in the living room, let alone discuss it further, so I just dunked a nugget in ketchup and stuffed the whole thing in my mouth.

Chapter Fifteen

BAKER'S DOZEN

Step inside our bakery and fill your saddlebags with sweet treats fresh from the oven. From cactus cookies to tumbleweed cinnamon rolls and caramel-filled gold nugget pastries, sugary delights await you at Baker's Dozen.

NOAH

"What the hell was that for?" Esra whirled on me the second we made it to Ace Ryder's hideout and the orange light flickered on above the door.

"What?" I barked back even though I knew exactly what she meant.

I'd missed almost all my marks. I'd barely even managed to buckle her in. Every time I got my hands on her, my brain produced images of Lucas's hands roaming over her body instead.

"I almost face-planted out there!"

"Maybe if you were a little more focused on your job—"

"Guys, you're on the intercom," Austin interrupted us, "save it for later."

"I'm not saving anything," Esra huffed and fumbled around her apron for the hidden mic pack. A moment later, she flipped the switch and the little power lamp died. Her head snapped back up, eyes like blazing fires. "What's your problem, asshole?"

"My problem?" Someone spoke my name through the headset. A smarter man would have heeded the warning. Instead, I switched my mic pack off too. "You're my problem. You're treating this place like it's your own personal fucking playground."

"I show up on time. I let myself be hauled through the air. If nobody likes that stunt, that's not on me. I do what I'm told. I do the work. Everything else is none of your business."

"If everything else starts affecting my work, it is my *literal* business."

She was messing with my brain, and it wasn't her fault, not fully. She was insufferable but it was my own damn mind that was hung up on Tuesday night. I couldn't even pinpoint why.

Esra crossed her arms, glaring at me with pure hell in her eyes. "I'm not the one who screwed up out there. I can have my fun, get drunk and wear whatever cowboy's hat I want, and I promise you, I'll still be here and do the work without it affecting you. I know my limits. You're the one who messed up. You're the one who threw me like a freaking hay bale or something."

"Why are you so obsessed with having fun?" I groaned.

"Why are you – incapable – of having – any?" She punctuated her question by poking her finger into my chest repeatedly.

God, I wanted to snatch that finger and— "Why are you so infuriating?"

Her brow was deep and her cheeks tinged bright pink. Her finger stayed burrowed into the center of my chest, leaving a hot, pointed mark. "I could ask you the same damn thing."

For one split second, our surroundings burned themselves into my consciousness. A tiny room the size of a storage shed. Nothing but dust and a table to keep us company. Nobody to hear or see us. And I realized that the blood rushing through my ears would only be quieted by one of two options.

I could kiss her or kill her.

My hand locked hers against my chest and my eyes dropped to her trembling, soft lips.

I had the bandana off my face in one tug. Esra's gaze followed my move. When her hand flattened out against my sternum, I didn't need further invitation, I crushed her mouth under mine. The kiss was neither soft nor sweet. Esra fell back against the door, letting out a startled gasp. That tiny sound echoed through my thoughts, finding a corner to permanently embed in my memory.

I expected a slap across the face.

I didn't expect her tongue to dart out and trace the seam of my lips, asking for entry. I didn't expect her tongue to taste like chocolate and bad ideas against mine.

I kissed her until my burning lungs forced me to pull back. Esra's eyes flew open, anger still flaming in them.

"Is this your idea of fun?" I rasped.

"Hard to say." She pursed her lips. "I think you should try again."

A small voice in the back of my mind reminded me that this was a big mistake, but Esra's slim fingers curled into the front of my shirt and quieted that voice in an instant. I leaned back in and kissed her.

That was no moment of hesitation. Esra hungrily kissed me back, pulling me down against herself until she could wrap her other arm around my shoulder. My hands on her waist, I pushed her back, caging her between my body and the door.

She shifted, her hips grinding over my thigh between hers. Despite the many layers of fabric between us, Esra let out a quiet whimper.

Fuck. That sound destroyed even the last shreds of sanity. The only thing that mattered was her soft body against mine.

"How about now? Having fun yet?" I teased without breaking apart.

"Stop talking, Noah," she mumbled, brushing her lips over mine. "You're so much more fun when your mouth is otherwise occupied."

"You have no idea how much fun my mouth can be, princess."

"Show me." Her eyes flew to the orange light above the door stopping us from exiting too soon. "Seven minutes in heaven?"

I traced my teeth along her jaw to her ear. "Nothing heavenly about what I'm about to do to you."

"Okay," she breathed, "you can use your mouth to say more things like that. I'll allow it."

"Oh, will you now?" I chuckled. She had an entirely wrong idea of who was controlling the situation, but I'd show her.

Whatever was left of our seven minutes would be all

I'd get. I knew that my lapse in judgment had to come to an end as soon as that orange light went out. Until then, I needed to taste as much of her as I could.

I sank to my knees in front of her, trailing her neck and her collar bone with my lips. I kissed my way down the front of her dress and gathered layers of skirts in my fists.

"Noah," Esra sighed as she gazed down at me from heavy lids. She slid her hands from my shoulders to my hair, knocking my hat back.

"This might take a minute, princess." Keeping her skirts bunched around her waist with one gloved hand, I ran the other over the thick straps and buckles that ran above her leggings, around her middle and her thighs. She squirmed as my fingers followed the strap to the insides of her thighs.

"Don't start making excuses now, Young."

"Hadn't crossed my mind." I slid my hand up the curve of her leg and brushed my thumb over the center seam of her leggings. The fabric dipped in, presenting me with a perfect outline of her pussy. I slipped the tip of my finger into the fold.

"Oh god." Esra's fingers tightened in my hair.

"I'll buy you new ones."

"Huh?"

I ripped the center seam of her pants open.

"Hey! What the hell do you think you're do-i-nng?" Her voice spluttered when I gripped the harness around her thigh with one hand and leveraged her leg up, opening her up for me.

"*You* if you'd shut up for a moment," I replied.

"God, you're annoying." Despite her words, her grip on me tightened impatiently.

166

Another quick rip and the scrap of fabric she called panties was gone as well. Her bare skin glistened for me, already wet, little muscle spasms rippling through her. I was desperate to know whether her pussy tasted as sweet as her tongue, but I gave myself a moment to drink in the sight.

I dipped my thumb back into the same spot as before, but now the only layer of clothing between us was the black leather of my gloves. Esra whimpered, the sound rippling through her *entire* body.

I circled my finger over her clit, watching her head fall back and her chest rising and falling fast.

Couldn't blame a man if he became addicted to this sight, these sounds.

"Goddammit," she whimpered, pushing herself against my hand.

I would have loved to draw this out, but we were on a tight schedule. I ran my index finger down the length of her slit to her entrance. And sank it into her. Her tight walls pulsed around me, and she let out a little high-pitched squeal. Shit. Esra brought out a fucking depraved part of me. Because the way her pink pussy gripped the black leather had to be the most intoxicating thing I'd ever seen.

I pulled out slowly, and slid my finger back into her, completely entranced by her sighs and the glistening sheen she was leaving all over my glove.

My own pants strained, my cock hardening just at the sight of her.

"Noah, please," she whimpered.

I didn't need any more than those two little words to spur me on. I curled my finger into her and used it to leverage her against me as I brought my mouth over her clit.

She tasted even better than I'd imagined, bittersweet and intoxicating.

I nibbled and licked, thrusting my finger hard and fast. I wanted her to unravel. I wanted to watch her make a mess of my glove. I needed her to come for me. Just once. Just once and I could move on from the way she haunted my thoughts.

"Noah, wait, oh god," she whimpered. Her fingers flew from my hair to the hand I had around her waist, folding around my wrist for support. She dug her nails into my skin. Her standing leg trembled. I glanced up to find the desire on her face mixed with uncertainty. "I can't."

"Can't?" I asked, stilling.

"My leg's about to give out," she breathed.

A strange relief filled my lungs at the realization that she wasn't asking me to stop.

"I can fix that," I said. Without waiting for her response, I slid my finger out of her. She let out a small moan of protest. It turned into a surprised squeal when I hooked that hand into the other side of the harness and yanked her second leg up. I dove forward again, letting my tongue plunge into her.

I kept most of her weight balanced between my arms and the door, but I let just enough of it come down against my face to feel her every twitching reaction.

"Please, please," she panted.

I groaned, reveling in her desperate need.

"Please, Noah, I need you to . . ." Her breath hitched, and she pulled at my hair just enough to force me to look up, not enough to make me stop. Her dark, glassy eyes found mine. "Please," she whispered.

"Fuck, you're pretty when you beg."

"I'm not begging. I'm polite when I ask for what I want," she protested weakly, trying to tilt her hips in a clear sign that she wanted me to keep touching her.

"Ask me then, princess." I grinned and bit the inside of her thigh, taking way too much pleasure from her responding squeal.

"Would you be so kind as to let me come already?" she huffed, cheeks beautifully reddened from anger or lust – and I didn't care which one. "Please."

"Gladly," I said just before sucking her clit in between my teeth. She writhed in my grip, trying to leverage her weight against me.

Our time had to be up any second now. That orange bulb would switch off, and we'd have to get out of the door within seconds.

I threw one of her legs over my shoulder. Esra instinctively hooked her knee into place and used it to lock me tight against her. My mouth still playing with her clit, I spread her pussy and delved two fingers into her.

"Noah!"

Esra came for me. Her pussy squeezed around my fingers. My name mixed with wordless moans on her lips as I thrust into her and lapped up each drop of her sweet wetness.

When the tremors ebbed, I rose to my feet, careful to lower both her legs to the ground slowly. I kept my hands wrapped around her waist to keep her steady, noting that her nails were still digging into my wrist.

She blinked up at me, breathing hard, face flushed, and lips still swollen from kissing. Climaxing looked damn good on her. I wanted to kiss her again. I wanted to make her taste just how wet she'd gotten for me. But I watched her blink, watched the focus return to her eyes, the haze of the moment giving way to confusion.

At least her lipstick wasn't smudged, or there would have been no mistaking what we'd just done in here.

"I think I just found my new favorite way of having fun," I told her, just as the orange lamp flickered out. I pulled the bandana back over my face, fixed my pants to hide how fucking hard she'd gotten me, and switched my mic pack back on. "Esra's mic is dead. We're coming out now."

"Steer clear of the kitchen," Austin warned from the sofa, not looking up from his phone when I walked in the door that night.

"Why?"

"Because you hate mess."

"Who made a mess in the kitchen?"

On cue, metal clattered to the floor. It sounded like pans and pots crashing together, and Esra let out a loud curse. That answered my question.

Austin looked up then, not toward the kitchen, but at me. Twelve hours ago, that sound would have sent me sprinting to the kitchen. I didn't like mess, and I didn't like it when people *made* messes. It wasn't that hard to keep things tidy. But twelve hours ago, I'd had no clue what Esra tasted like when she fell apart on my tongue – and I wasn't sure how she'd react to seeing me right now, considering we'd gone our separate ways after the show. I was, however, sure that I didn't want Austin to witness that encounter, even remotely.

I flexed my fists and forced my feet to carry me past the door to the kitchen and toward the stairs. "Don't let her burn the house down."

"No promises," Austin replied with a dry chuckle.

Upstairs, I hit the shower and turned up the volume on the old bathroom radio, to muffle the sounds from both outside and inside the bathroom. I finally had a few minutes to myself. An endless loop of Esra's sighs and moans had been echoing through my head all day. While I'd managed to dispel all the intrusive scenarios of anyone else touching her, I was now plagued by the very real memory of her reactions to my own touch. I had to get her out of my system for good.

Fisting my cock, I let my noise be drowned by the shower stream and the music.

"Fuck," I moaned, mentally replaying images of Esra's flushed face and her full lips as she begged for my touch.

I didn't register the lights flicking off at first, but then the radio in the corner died with a whiny squeak, plunging me into silent darkness. Then the yelling started.

"Fuck," I grunted again, for a very different reason, and fumbled in the dark to turn the water off.

The shreds of light coming through the milky window indicated that the other houses still had power. While I wanted to give her the benefit of the doubt, I had an inkling that Esra's kitchen skills were responsible for this blackout.

After finding my phone and turning on the flashlight, I jumped into my jeans commando real quick before I left the bathroom to investigate. I didn't bother with any other room and beelined for the kitchen. Austin had his flashlight pointed right at Esra, who was yelling about *not knowing what was wrong* and *not having done anything*. I slipped right past her. I couldn't look at her. Not when I'd just been jerking off to memories of her.

I turned the oven off and unplugged all kitchen appliances, as well as the phone and tablet she had been charging. I checked the switches on the exhaust and the AC, and turned those off as well. That girl had been sucking enough electricity into this room to power a whole town. Even though the staff buildings weren't too old, they hadn't been built to house a dozen people with multiple supercomputers each.

I wordlessly made my way to the basement. As expected, the breaker for the kitchen had triggered the main one. Both clicked back into place, I waited a moment to see if they'd blow again, but they seemed to hold.

The light flicked on, and I turned to find Esra standing in the door, hand on the switch.

"What on earth were you doing?" I asked.

"Baking."

"Take this as your sign to look for a different hobby."

"Like what?" She propped her hands on her waist, elbows jutted outwards. Maybe that pose was supposed to look intimidating, but it only drew my eyes down to her loose tank top, which was thin enough to expose her lack of a bra. The curves of her breasts were perfectly outlined under the white fabric, and the basement was clearly a few degrees cooler than the kitchen.

"Oh, come on," I huffed and ran a hand down my face,

too aware of the denim grazing over my naked skin as water-drops fell from my hair to my shoulders.

Esra seemed to catch on, her own gaze raking over my bare chest, down my stomach and to the jeans hanging low on my hips. Her throat bobbed. Unlike her, I didn't parade around half-naked, but judging by the way she sucked air through trembling lips, she might have preferred if I did.

"I'm going back to my shower." I stepped around her, careful not to brush even a single hair on her, because if she kept looking at me like that, we wouldn't make it upstairs anytime soon.

Chapter Sixteen

GOODE'S GENERAL STORE

Goode's supplies you with paraphernalia to make your stay at Bravetown the best it can be. Need to replenish your sunscreen stock? Searching for a rain cape to keep you dry? Goode's got you covered.

Esra

I stared at my reflection in the mirror and ran a hand over the buckle around my waist. I wasn't entirely sure how safe it was to wear my leggings over the harness instead of under it, but I was in the *fuck around and find out* phase of my summer. Literally.

Maybe this was the wrong call, but when I hadn't been able to stop thinking about Noah's tongue between my legs, the internet had stupidly suggested baking to clear my mind. My singular attempt at that had only shown that I was not meant to have a clear mind. I was meant to stare at my brother's best friend's glistening wet pecs, completely entranced by the dribble of water from that one white streak above his left brow, and feel the overwhelming urge to lick his stomach.

Screw making sound decisions.

Embrace chaos.

Especially when it felt as good as Noah Young's mouth on my clit.

I just had to adjust my wardrobe. Since I only had two pairs of leggings in tones that worked under the costume, I couldn't let Noah rip up both of them.

I wasn't even sure if he would.

Maybe what had happened in Ace's Hideout had been a blip. I wasn't about to confuse a man pushing his gloved fingers into me with a declaration of love. More like a quick hate-fuck, of sorts, just to get all the frustration out. I still wanted a repeat.

Last night, the moment in the basement had been tense, *sure*, but he'd reverted to treating me like a nuisance.

How on earth did you tell the man you despised that you still wanted his head between your legs?

I know you like me as much as a pebble in your boot, but the way you licked my pebble . . .

We don't have to tickle each other's fancy to tickle each other's privates.

You might think I'm a pain in your ass, but why don't you slap my—

Ugh.

Of course, today's show went perfectly. Noah didn't miss a single cue. Every single move landed exactly as rehearsed. I should have been glad, but by the time we made it to the hideout, I was seething with annoyance. Apparently yesterday hadn't affected him as much as it had me. He'd just casually given me the best head of my life, and then returned to business as usual.

I stomped to the far side of the hideout, putting a few

feet of distance between me and Noah. Maybe this whole thing would be too complicated anyway. Sanny had begged me not to make a mess of things for him here. Asking his best friend to eat me out again was definitely messy.

I turned to look at Noah and clear the air, but startled when I realized he'd followed me. He towered over me, all sharp lines and shadows in his costume.

"Look," I sighed, "about yesterday . . ."

Noah's gloved hand folded over my mouth. I dropped back against the wall, blinking up at cold eyes surrounded by shade. The mask and hat made it impossible to see his expression, and my insides squeezed tight in response. Seeing him like this was the moment before the roller coaster drops you over the edge. The thrill mixed with the biological instinct to take flight. Instead of shaky tracks rattling my nerves, it was his leather glove pressed against my lips, when I knew exactly where that glove had been yesterday. His other hand slid down my stomach, drawing a shaky breath from my lungs. One click, and the headset's quiet buzz in my ear died. A moment later, he shut his own mic pack off.

Right. He needed me to be quiet. Didn't want everyone to hear about our *thing*. It made sense, but I was still a little disappointed.

At least until I realized he wasn't letting go.

His gaze lowered as he watched my chest rise and fall over the sweetheart neckline of my dress. The sharp focus grazed across my skin more intensely than any touch could, raising goosebumps in its wake. With every second my heart beat faster and my breaths came quicker.

When his eyes flicked up again, pale blue through thick

black lashes, they held a question. I'd spent the last weeks pressed against Noah, moving with him and around him, learning to read the shifts in his body language, so I knew exactly what he was asking with his muscles completely still and his eyes locked on mine. I nodded.

Still holding my mouth shut, Noah whirled me around. He locked his other arm around my waist, keeping my back pressed against his chest. My head hit his shoulder. I blinked up at him, the raw cotton of his bandana scraping over my cheek.

"I think I finally understand what bewitching means," he rasped as he walked us forward.

Was he calling me a *witch*? I tried to retort but my voice was muffled by his hand. Any logic and reason evaporated instantly around Noah. That was the only explanation I had for why I clamped my teeth around his thumb. Hard, so he'd feel it through the leather glove.

That asshole chuckled. He didn't even flinch. "Case in point."

The fronts of my thighs hit the table.

"Bend over. Elbows on the table." He loosened his hand from my mouth, and I unclenched my teeth.

"Telling me what to do? How original."

"Do you prefer being handled, princess?"

"Handled?"

Noah left one hand on my waist but slid the other to the back of my neck. With one strong push, he bent me down. I barely managed to slap my hands against the table-top to retain some balance. I swallowed. He'd positioned me flush in front of him. There were too many layers of clothes between us to feel anything more than the heat of his firm body pressed against me, but the mental image was enough to spark the flame in my abdomen. So much better than being given orders.

"Yeah," I breathed, "I prefer that."

"Noted." Noah hiked my dress up. The skirt layers pooled around me, and I braced myself for his touch, but it didn't come. Noah sucked in a sharp breath. "That makes things easier."

"Don't rip these ones too," I huffed. I started pushing myself up, but Noah brought a large hand down on the small of my back, keeping me pinned in place. He curled his fingers into the thick belt of the harness. Something strange and deep unclenched inside me as I realized that I trusted him enough to just . . . let him.

Noah pushed my leggings down my thighs. His gloved hand came back up, smoothing over the curve of my ass and sliding into my panties. He squeezed my flesh, just enough to open me up a little. Maybe I should have felt a little self-conscious about being bent over and exposed like that, but it just sent my pulse racing.

"Fuck," I rasped. One of my arms whipped around. I wanted more of his touch, needed to feel him. My fingertips barely brushed the hem of my panties before he caught my wrist. His grip locked it behind my back, holding my hand alongside the harness.

"Tsk-tsk. Hands off. That's mine," he growled.

"You wish," I huffed.

"Do you let anyone else touch you like this?" His thickly gloved thumb slid to the junction of my thighs. He swirled it around my entrance leisurely. Teasing me.

"None of your business." I pressed my forehead against

the smooth wooden tabletop, desperate for even a little bit of cold. Noah fucking Young set my nervous system ablaze.

His finger brushed over my clit, smooth leather spreading my arousal over my sensitive skin, only for his touch to leave me as he tugged my underwear aside.

"Do you get this wet for anyone else?"

"None of your business," I repeated.

His hand came down against my ass in a fast slap and I squealed as the sharp sting reverberated up my spine. I felt him stiffen behind me – not in the fun way. He was waiting for my reaction, waiting for me to tell him he'd crossed a line. He had no idea that I'd been rehearsing ways to ask him for exactly what he was giving me.

"No one else. And usually not this fast," I answered his question honestly. "I blame the costume. You put on the mask and the feminism leaves my body."

In response, another slap hit my ass and I moaned, the searing pain morphing into an entirely different heat. His hand smoothed over my skin and circled down to my pussy. He brushed over it tenderly, pulling soft gasps from my lips, only to then deliver another slap. He repeated the whole thing, once, twice, three times, keeping me on the edge between gentle and rough. It was too much and it wasn't enough, all at once.

"Noah, please."

A leather glove landed in front of my face just before he thrust two fingers into me. I arched my back, pushing against him.

There'd been something deliciously wrong about his gloved touch, but it didn't compare at all to his bare fingers inside me. His thrusts came hard. The ridges of his knuckles and the precise angle of his fingertips steered me toward my climax faster than should have been possible.

I moaned and gripped the edge of the table for support with my free hand. Noah's hold tightened around my other one, keeping me locked in place when my hips started quaking. The tension in my core clenched tighter and tighter and tighter.

"Please," I whimpered.

"Ask me."

Recalling my words from yesterday, I groaned. Of course they'd come back to bite me in the ass. I hated having to be polite. "Noah, would you please be so nice and— fuck." He shifted his fingers, hitting a deeper angle that had me curling my toes.

"What do you want, princess?"

"Come. I want to come. Please," I gasped, struggling for air.

He shifted behind me. I tried to shake strands of dark hair from my face to see, but the position made it impossible. I didn't even get the chance to ask him what he was doing before his mouth joined his fingers, torturing me. His tongue came down against my clit mercilessly. The taut coil inside me snapped, and I dropped over the edge.

I writhed against him, and I moaned his name, and he didn't stop touching me, licking me, holding me until I stopped trembling, slumped over the table and breathing hard. Bone-deep satisfaction unfurled inside me. I let out a disappointed whine when he loosened his grip on me and pulled my clothes back into place.

"Noah, I . . ." I pushed up, blinking at the hazy room

and the blurred orange glow above the door. My muscles had gone weak, my knees trembling too much to fully keep me upright. But I still wanted more. I wanted him to keep touching me and I wanted to touch him, feel him.

Noah slipped an arm around my middle, steadying me with my back against his chest. I let him take my weight, my head dropping back. I blinked up at him, forgetting what I was going to ask when his blue eyes pierced down at me.

"God, you're fucking gorgeous," he said, his voice breathless and husky.

"Of course," I chuckled, "I am the *Pretty* Annie Lou, aren't I?"

His responding smirk disappeared as he pulled the bandana back over his face. "Don't even bother with panties tomorrow."

Just like that, my dread over having to perform four shows over two days evaporated.

I floated through the rest of the weekend on a cloud of endorphins. The new ankle braces, which perfectly fit into my costume boots, helped with the floating, too. But it was mostly thanks to my new favorite version of seven minutes in heaven.

On Saturday, Noah laid me out on that table and ate me like his last meal. He also discovered that, in that position, he could pull my dress down enough to free my tits. He grumbled something unintelligible when I pushed his mouth away from my chest. His tongue was close to making me lose all coherent thought, but I still wasn't walking out into the park with beard burn all over my cleavage.

On Sunday, I reached for his belt. He grabbed my hands and flattened them against the tabletop instead.

"I want to see how many times I can make you beg," he rasped against my ear in that deep Ace Ryder voice, and I almost fell apart before he'd even touched me.

"I'll beg when hell freezes over," I huffed, fully aware that I was making promises I couldn't keep. Five. Five times over a total of fourteen minutes. There was a line in Ace Ryder's official character description, about how he was known for his silver tongue. And goddamn. They had no idea.

"How are you holding up?" Zuri asked.

We'd settled into Sanny's favorite booth in the saloon. It was fairly quiet in here on Monday nights. Most park guests visited on the weekends, and those who stayed for a couple of days tended to stay in the park until it closed, or they had dinner in their hotel. That, and the ease of access, was probably why Sinan had suggested we should have weekly dinners here. We hadn't spent much time together in recent years. He hadn't been home a lot, and I'd been busy, so we'd just seen less and less of each other. It also hadn't come naturally over the last few weeks unless there was something happening. Putting in the effort felt good.

"I'm fine," I replied, "what about you guys?"

"Do you need me to talk to Renee?" Sanny leaned across the table.

I blinked, only now registering the genuine concern on their faces. There was no reason for it as far as I knew. The combination of ankle braces and boots had been saving me from a lot of pain, so that was fine. And their expressions weren't touched by that hint of awkwardness I'd expect if they wanted to talk to me about my sex life. "Why would you talk to Renee?"

"Because of all those trolls online," Sanny said.

"You look a little tired." Zuri tilted her head, her thick black curls falling sideways. "You're not doom-scrolling the comment sections all night, are you?"

Oh, shit. Right. I'd been getting bad feedback online. Somehow that had completely slipped my mind over the last few days. Just as I considered why that might be, Noah stepped up to our booth and dropped on to the bench next to me with a vague greeting.

"Noah, would you mind giving us a couple of minutes? We're in the middle of discussing something with Esra. It's kind of important," Sinan said, sounding more like a big brother than he had in weeks. Shit. Were the online comments that bad?

"It's fine," I said quickly and motioned for Noah to stay.

I just shot him a quick glance from the corner of my eye. He was the very reason I'd forgotten about the trolls, and why I looked so tired. The show had been exhausting before, but now I was getting an extra workout in every day. Not to mention lying awake, debating whether or not I should just knock on his door to get more than seven minutes. I always ended up slipping my own hand between my legs instead. Keeping this thing perfectly compartmentalized to Ace Ryder's hideout seemed like the best option. I got all the orgasms without any of the emotional or interpersonal mess of hooking up with your brother's best friend.

"It really is fine," I reassured Sanny and Zuri, "I've not

been online much. I don't care. He's the one posting thirst traps for likes." I jerked my thumb at Noah.

"Pointing is impolite," he said and caught my wrist. He pushed my hand under the table and into my lap, where his fingers dropped from my arm to my leg. He squeezed my thigh and his pinky reached high enough to slip up my shorts. It grazed the sensitive skin where his stubble had left its mark. The audacity. Didn't he realize that I was compartmentalizing? Blood rushing in my ears, I glared at him, only for him to pull his hand away and reach for the menu without a single glance in my direction.

"Can we pause whatever feud this is for a few minutes, please?" Sinan waved between me and Noah.

Was *"feud"* the right word to use when you wanted to kill someone by banging their brains out?

Since I could hardly do that here, I held up my hands in mock surrender.

"I'm not doing anything," Noah said and shrugged. I still caught that little twinkle of mischief in the corner of his eye. Yeah, right. *Not doing anything* except feeling me up in front of my brother.

"You're being obnoxious," I hissed.

"I'm reading the menu."

"You've lived in this place for how long?"

"Twenty-nine years in Wild Fields, five years in Bravetown."

"And has the menu changed over the last five years? Or are you going to order a glass of water and a cheeseburger? Maybe a single bottle of beer if you're feeling wild." I wasn't sure why I knew his order, but the fact that I did just annoyed me more.

Both Sanny and Zuri sighed in perfect sync, loud enough to interrupt us, their gazes locking. Some silent understanding passed between them. Putting on a bright smile, Zuri pushed out of the booth and waved for me to come with her. "Let's go get some drinks at the bar."

Ah. They had formulated a Plan B for their "kind of serious" talk.

I debated staying at the table and letting Zuri get the drinks, but I didn't trust myself enough next to Noah. My urge to strangle him had turned into a Pavlovian compulsion to wrap my thighs around his neck instead.

While Adriana was getting our order ready for us, Zuri tried again. "I know you're only here for a few months, but it's still a lot of pressure to play Annie Lou. If you ever want to talk about it, I'm here, you know?"

"Thank you, Zuri. I appreciate it, but I genuinely haven't been online in days. I decided to go the *ignorance is bliss* route."

"Right." She pursed her lips, clearly not fully content with my answer. "If it really bothered you, or you know . . . something else bothered you, there's other people to talk to. Not here, necessarily, but in Nashville. There's a lot of good people in Nashville. You could make a day of it. See the Parthenon. You like attractions, right?"

I blinked, the gist of her ramble computing slowly. "Are you sending me to therapy?"

"You've been through a lot of life changes recently."

"Ohmygod. Please stop talking."

"We just thought it might help you figure things out."

I ran my hand down my face. "Figure what out?"

"What you'll do when summer's over. Do you want

to go back to grad school? Maybe here? Or back home? Change your major?"

"Jesus, did Sanny talk to Mom?"

Zuri's guilty expression was all the answer I needed. Of course. Sinan hadn't actually been interested in spending more time with me. Monday-night dinners were just the Bravetown-friendly version of Mom's Friday-night dinners. She'd probably planted the idea in his head.

Adriana had quietly put the drinks down on the counter in front of us, and I pushed three toward Zuri. "Take these back to the table. Talk to me when your entire life plan has gone up in flames, okay?"

Zuri didn't fight me. She looked genuinely defeated as she carried the drinks back to the booth.

"So," Adriana said, clearing her throat, "as someone whose entire life plan has actually gone up in flames, can I talk to you?"

"Sure," I huffed and climbed on to the barstool across from her.

"Who's the guy?" she asked, grinning widely.

"What?"

"Or girl." She shrugged. "Who are you sleeping with?"

"Guy," I said and shot a quick look over my shoulder to make sure nobody overheard. "How did you know? Is it that obvious?"

"Nah, you just have that exhausted glow of someone who got plowed in the backseat of an old jeep behind a Wendy's. Takes one to know one. Meanwhile, Sinan and Zuri are all rainbows and unicorns. Totally oblivious."

"That was very descriptive, thank you." I laughed, my mood instantly lightening. Adriana was good at that. I figured that it did take one to know one. She knew what it was like when you wanted to leave shit in the past and move on.

"So? Who is it? I'm surprised I haven't heard anything yet. I know for a fact it isn't Lucas." She narrowed her eyes at the room. "The gossip mill is running slow."

"Excuse me?"

"What? Bart's Mart is the only place in town to buy condoms. If someone was suddenly stocking up, the whole town would know."

"That's fucked up. You know that, right?" I groaned and dropped my head on my arms on the counter. "We haven't gotten to that part yet."

"Damn. If your skin glows like that just from . . ." She trailed off, eyes wandering over the people in the staff section. "Who plays guitar? Or maybe piano?" Her fingers strummed through the air to demonstrate why she thought someone with musical skills would also be *otherwise* skilled. Really, she should have looked for muscles. Noah wrangling my body like I was his personal plaything was half the fun.

Instead of replying to her, I pulled my phone out and added a new item to my growing to-do list. I was more than happy to support local businesses, but not if doing so would air my sex life to the entire town.

Summer > Bravetown

To Do

- ✗ Research horse noises
- ☐ Buy Adriana's album

✗ Test new ankle braces for a whole day
☐ Order new leggings
☐ Start budget planner
☐ Buy condoms (out of town!)

Appointments

Notes

- Neigh (also whinny or bray) = normal horse sound, method of communication, mouth open Nicker = lower clucky sound, often used as greeting or in courting
- *Now/Here* by Adriana Banks

Chapter Seventeen

NOAH

I was about to be fired. I should have known that I was too replaceable to get into trouble. Annie Lou's costume was highly specific. It wasn't that easy to switch her out. Ace Ryder just needed to show up dressed in black with a bandana over his face. So when I tailed Esra through the hallways of the office building, summoned by Renee, I knew only one of us was getting fired.

People here hooked up all the time, but not in the park, and definitely not during opening hours.

Had we forgotten to switch off the microphones one day?

The hideout's location wasn't accessible to the public

during shows, but maybe another cast member had heard us from outside. I still would have expected the courtesy of a conversation. Who the hell would run to Renee to tattle right away?

I balled my fists when we walked into Renee's office to see Lucas already sprawled in one of the chairs opposite her desk.

"Oh, hey, Lucky!" Esra's face lit up at the sight of him. She clearly didn't realize what his presence here meant. Or maybe she did, but she was blinded by the fact that she actually liked him, because no matter how many times I made her come, she never smiled at me like that.

"Hey gorgeous." He smiled back.

Sleeping with a girl doesn't make her your girlfriend. I'd heard Adriana tell him as much the day after he'd spent the night in Esra's room. Getting me fired would sure get him a step closer though. Or maybe it wouldn't. Esra was into the costume. Into Ace. Into being handled by the guy in the mask. She liked being the little damsel, had called *herself* Pretty Annie Lou right after I'd made her come the other day. She might just start hooking up with whoever replaced me.

"Sit down everyone," Renee said and closed the door to her office behind us, "we need to talk."

"Do I need a lawyer? Do I get a phone call?" Esra asked with a big grin that didn't quite reach her eyes. She knew as well as I did that we could be in deep shit.

"I know the two of you are active online," Renee said as she sat down, pointing at both Lucas and me. "So you have likely seen some of the posts and comments."

"I turned off the comments on all my videos last week,"

Lucas said and turned to Esra. "I wasn't sure if you watched my videos, but you don't need to see that shit."

"I don't watch your videos, sorry," Esra mumbled, furrowing her brow.

"You called us in here because people have been trolling Esra online?" I asked.

"Unfortunately, yes," Renee said.

Esra and I sighed in relief, garnering confused looks.

Sure, yes, the park's online presence was important, but we'd clearly both been worried about a scandal of a vastly different scale. A few online haters were nothing.

"I've been deleting the comments and untagging myself from any posts like that," I said, unable to keep my smile hidden.

"You've both been getting comments about me?" Esra asked, relief short-lived.

"There are a few very persistent commenters that we can block across all accounts and write off as 'trolls'," Renee said using air quotes, "but the general consensus isn't great either. It's not affecting our numbers. Not yet. But the online chatter has been loud enough for our customer experience team to notice. Once they notice, it usually doesn't take long for word to spread." Renee sighed and trained her eyes on Esra. "I want to make it very clear that nobody thinks you're at fault, okay? You saved us from having to cancel our show altogether after Lindsey left, which would have definitely resulted in booking cancellations. Still, I've decided to put out a casting call to find someone a little more experienced."

"You're firing me?" Esra's voice cracked and, in that moment, I would have burned down the entire internet to keep those assholes hiding behind their usernames far away from her.

"Oh, no, no, honey, no. You'll always have a place here at Bravetown. Just not as Annie Lou. And it will take a few weeks for us to find a replacement and get her ready for the show, which is why I've decided to extend the run until we switch to the Spooktacular Sunset Showdown in late October."

Esra opened and closed her mouth. "Can I keep the boots?"

Seriously?

"She's done nothing wrong," I interjected. Technically not true, but nobody seemed to know what we did when our microphones cut out.

"I know," Renee sighed. "I called all three of you here because I want to try and make the next few weeks a little easier for Esra."

"I've had it easy," Esra said. "I don't really spend much time online, and there's only been a few people who were outright rude to me in the park. Judith shuts them down so quickly. She's great at that. I don't even have to interact with them."

I'd had no idea that she'd been dealing with any vitriol in person. It was one thing for people to say as much to me when I was in costume. They thought they could draw a mean comment from me because I played the antagonist in the town's tale. Making Esra face their opinions was plain cruel. They could consider themselves lucky that they'd only been shut down by Judith.

"I think it would help if you upped your online presence," Renee said. "Nowadays a lot of people come to the park to see the people and characters they found online. Like that *Ren Faire* whip guy who keeps singing pop songs and changes the lyrics to be about whipping, so people come to his shows to suggest really horny songs. He's hot, he's funny, he rakes in the cash."

All three of us stared at Renee. She'd never taken a big interest in our social media profiles. There were a few rules she made us follow to keep the general park image family-friendly, but she'd never spelled out what she wanted to see from us or what she expected for the park. She'd also never questioned whether we made extra cash through our accounts, even though there was probably some legal ground for her to request a cut if we filmed in costume and during work hours.

"I'm not saying you guys should start singing BDSM songs to curb the fallout. Just think of something to make Esra a little more likable. As Annie Lou. You're a likable person, Esra." Renee quickly clarified that last part.

"You just want us to include her on our socials?" Lucas asked and shot Esra a smile. "I can think of a few ways to do that."

"Likable," Renee repeated. "We already have one Heather."

Translation: no half-naked tricks on horseback.

"I might actually have an idea," Esra said, biting her lip, "but I've only taken one year of psychology and wrote only one paper based on the hypothesis that the performative belongingness that comes with being a superfan fulfills the emotional and psychological needs of a person more than the actual subject of their admiration. Plus, that paper focused solely on the fans of three different sports teams, so while I was able to theoretically confirm my hypothesis, I don't know if it can be translated into practice or if it works for fictional cowboys."

I only understood half of what she was saying, but I couldn't look away. It was the Hippocratic oath all over again. The stark reminder that Esra couldn't do her laundry or bake a batch of cookies without putting the whole house at risk but had lived a whole different life before she took this job. Just like many times before, I wondered what the fuck she was doing here. For once, that thought didn't strike because she was somehow unfit for this place, but because I realized Bravetown could never measure up to this girl. She was blindingly bright in ways that couldn't be taught in school. How did someone with a brilliant brain like hers end up running around in a costume in a small local theme park? Why on earth was she letting me touch her every day when she should have been dating Nobel prize winners or something?

"What?" Renee asked after a moment of stunned silence, probably doing both Lucas and me a favor.

"Bravetown is a construct more than a place. It exists online. It exists in that short-lived TV show and in the picture books you sell in the parks. It exists in people's minds," Esra explained, "and to the fans, being part of Bravetown is more important than the individual pieces that created it in the first place."

"Do you think it'll work?" Esra stared up at me wide-eyed and hopeful.

"In some ways, yes." I weighed my answer. "I think it will win over some of the people who are ambivalent about you, and the ones who support you will support you louder than before. It'll help drown out the negativity."

We walked home side by side after spending two hours filming short videos with Lucas. He'd walked off toward the hotel, claiming that was the best Wi-Fi in the park if you wanted to post on social media, but I knew for a fact that the entire park had good signal. I usually filmed my reactions on short breaks at the stables. So my best guess was that some park guest had slid into his DMs with her room number.

"Hmm . . . but the root of the problem remains. Me. I suck as Annie." Esra sighed. "I guess I can say that at least I tried."

We'd just filmed a dozen videos re-enacting snippets from the most popular fanfictions in our category. It had taken Esra only an hour to pull together links, quotes, usernames and screenshots, all neatly organized in a spreadsheet. She'd died twice – once in Lucas's arms and once in mine – and I'd stared deeply into Lucas's eyes for much longer and much more often than I'd ever antici-pated. After the initial awkwardness, theatrically ripping my shirt open, biting down on the stem of a rose and tearing Annie from Kit Holliday's arms had actually made for a fun way to spend the evening. The kitsch of it all reminded me of those pulp Westerns the park was based on.

"Look, from where I stand, only half the comments are valid. The ones saying Annie Lou is regressing instead of progressing," I said, holding open the gate that led us out of the park and directly toward staff housing. It was the only route out we were allowed to take in costume because it was completely shielded from the public.

"And the other half?" she asked and stopped on the threshold.

"Don't think brown eyes are *pretty*."

"Huh." Her lips pursed. "Idiots."

"Exactly."

"Are you saying you think I have pretty eyes, Young?" She grinned and fluttered her lashes at me, still not moving, keeping us locked in the narrow frame of the gate.

"I'm saying we can do something about how pathetic you look on a horse."

"Charming," she groaned and slipped past me.

"Princess, if you want charming, you have to look for a prince."

"No, thank you. I hear *villains* are better at giving head." She cackled and shot a look over her shoulder at me. "So, what? You want to give me riding lessons?"

"Yes, come to the stables tomorrow before the park opens."

"Seriously? Wait. Riding lessons, or *riding lessons*?"

She met my puzzled gaze with a roll of her eyes. Wrapping her fingers around my arm for support, she jumped up to snatch my hat. It dropped loosely over her head, the black brim falling down to her brow.

For just a split second, her intention blazed through me and singed a path down my center, straight to my dick. The heat was quickly doused by the realization that she wasn't wearing *my* hat. She was wearing Ace Ryder's hat. She wanted riding lessons from the *villain*. I supposed she'd already checked the sheriff off her list.

Just like Bravetown wasn't actually good enough for a girl like her, *I* wasn't enough. She was playing make-believe.

It shouldn't have bothered me. I still got her writhing and begging under my touch even if it was fictional for her. And yet . . . that stupid black hat bothered me.

"Give it back," I rasped, holding my hand out.

"What if I want to ride the cowboy this belongs to?" She grinned up at me from below the brim.

"Esra, hand it over."

"Oh, okay. *Serious voice.*" She snorted and flung the hat back at me. "Excuse a girl for trying to be flirty."

"If you want to go around and collect the hats from all the cowboys in Bravetown, go ahead, but there's a name for girls like that."

"What?"

"Buckle Bunnies," I replied.

Her face contorted. Her button nose crinkled up, giving a perfect impression of a bunny as she processed my words. "First of all, fuck you. Second of all, that's sexist on a whole new level. What do you call all the men in Heather's comment section then?"

"Delusional," I muttered, but it didn't stop her tirade.

"And third of all, fuck you. You can't hike up my skirt, slap my ass, fingerbang me into oblivion and then turn around and slut-shame me when I dare suggest we go further than that. Just because you didn't get your dick wet, doesn't mean you were any less of a participant in our bunnying around."

She stormed forward, stomping her feet on the steps up to our house.

"And fourth of all, fuck you!" She slammed the door after her hard enough to rattle it in its frame.

"Did she slap you?" Austin asked from the sofa when I walked in a moment later, his headphones already halfway down his neck. He must have just caught the end of the argument. Esra's boots stomped up the last few stairs and a moment later another door slammed shut.

"No. Why would she?"

"Damn," he grunted, "I have twenty on a good slap."

"You bet on her slapping me?" I asked, strangely grateful for the distraction. If we talked about that, I didn't have to think about the strange fight I'd just had with Esra, when I wasn't sure why I'd reacted that way. I didn't even know when I'd last used the term Buckle Bunny.

"My odds aren't good," Austin said. "Too many people agree with me. If you wanted to throw all of her belongings out the window or mix bleach into her shampoo, I'd make enough money to buy a new car."

"What else did people bet on?"

"Anything from insult to murder, to be honest."

"I just called her a Buckle Bunny, if that helps your financial aspirations."

"Not mine, but I believe Vivi just made twenty bucks." Austin started typing on his phone, presumably to alert whatever group chat had the betting pool going.

"Y'all don't work hard enough if you have time for stupid shit like this."

"Why'd you call her a Buckle Bunny?" he asked, not looking up from his phone. I wasn't sure whether he asked out of genuine interest or if this was part of the bet.

"Her thing with Lucas."

"Lucas? Nope." Austin shook his head and kept typing. "Lucas tried to bet that he could hook up with Esra, and we all told him that was fucked up. He still whined about being friend-zoned, and Adriana ripped him a new one about the concept of the friend zone. Here." He turned his phone around for me to see the chat. I only skimmed Lucas's message on screen, sent the day he stumbled from Esra's room. Well, I'd been wrong about them.

I clicked on the chat menu and brought up the list of contacts. "What the fuck? Even Renee is in this pool."

"She put two hundred on having to reassign Esra to a different house because of you."

"You need a life."

"Oh come on. This is the most entertainment we've had since that year it took Sanny six months to ask Zuri out."

I tossed the phone back into his lap and headed upstairs myself. I probably owed Esra an apology. The fact that she hadn't slept with Lucas didn't even ease the weight off my chest. It didn't matter. She could have fucked the whole damn world for all I cared.

I placed the black Ace Ryder hat on my coat rack, right next to my own brown one. From the corner of my eye, I caught my reflection in the mirror, leather holster around my hips and the black bandana slung around my neck.

I'd lashed out, hurling the first best insult at her, because Esra was only into the fantasy. She wasn't actually attracted to me.

It shouldn't have bothered me.

I was in so much trouble.

Chapter Eighteen

Esra

I hadn't been sure whether he'd show up at the stables. I wasn't even going to come myself. What kind of masochist decided to spend her day off sitting uncomfortably on a wobbly saddle, riding next to the man who had insulted her for wanting to sleep with him? The stubborn kind.

Lucas had sent me an excited late-night message about the thousands of views our first video was racking up. That had made the decision for me. I didn't check the post or the comments to see if people were just hate-watching it. It didn't matter. I just knew that I couldn't let another thing slip away from me. I liked being Annie Lou. I liked doing the shows. I liked meeting the kids and making their good days even better. And even if it was only until October, I wanted to keep doing it. If I had to jump on to a galloping horse to stay Annie Lou, I'd just have to learn how to.

Noah greeted me with a perfectly fine "good morning", but I glared at him hard enough to shut him up. He only spoke to introduce me to Crumble, a caramel-colored horse that was at least a foot shorter than Tornado, and to give me instructions on getting in the saddle. He wordlessly handed me a pale beige cowboy hat made from thick straw, not even looking me in the eye. Since he was already wearing a hat, I doubted this was some sort of commentary on our fight last night. I chose to believe that he was just giving me the hat because the sun was already high in the sky, making the air flicker above the rooftops, and he didn't want me to fall off the horse from sun stroke.

I thought he'd lead the horse around on a leash for a bit to give me a quick *Horseback Riding for Dummies* lesson. Instead, Noah swung himself into Tornado's saddle and Crumble dutifully followed the other horse down a small path and away from the paddock.

I'd sat on Tornado often enough not to panic, but I was acutely aware of the drop to either side of the saddle, and the lack of harness around my waist.

"Where are we going?" I asked, when Noah opened a gate that led out of Bravetown's perfectly enclosed microcosm and on to a signless dirt road. The kind of road an ambulance couldn't get to if you were thrown off a horse.

"It's a beginner's trail," Noah said. "We're basically circling Wild Fields and coming back here."

Okay, circling the town wasn't going to kill me. That was fairly safe. "Shouldn't we do some basics first?"

"No," Noah chuckled. Tornado fell into step beside Crumble, walking slower to make up for his longer legs. "You already know how to move with a horse. You just don't trust yourself to stay in the saddle. So you're going to stay in the saddle for a few hours."

"A few hours?" I echoed, ignoring that he'd seen right through me.

"Don't worry, I brought snacks."

"Oh yeah, because my primary worry about staying on horseback for a few hours is whether or not I will starve to death."

He reached behind himself into the saddle bag and pulled out a beautiful bright-orange bag of mini peanut butter cups. My traitorous stomach rumbled in response as if I hadn't had breakfast. Noah chuckled and opened the bag for me, holding it out. My kryptonite.

I glanced down at where my fists clenched around the reins, and the chasm between our horses that I'd have to reach across to get my hands on the chocolate.

"God, you're annoying," I huffed and straightened out, eyes back on the road.

"They're right here when you're ready," he said and packed them away again. At least he had the decency not to eat any in front of me.

We stayed quiet for a while, and I watched our surroundings change. We left the stockade and Western buildings of Bravetown behind. In their place, lush grassy plains stretched out to my right side, dark emerald hills rolling in the distance, while trees bordered the road on Noah's side. Had he given me the side with the view on purpose?

I was watching a small plane pass overhead when I

realized that this place was quiet. Not artificially so, like the sensory deprivation tank I'd tried once. We were out in the open, but there were neither cars nor people. Only buzzing insects, rustling leaves and two horses trotting along. I wasn't sure I'd ever been anywhere this perfectly, naturally quiet before.

It wasn't until we had to file through another gate and my thighs tensed around the saddle that I noticed I hadn't been squeezing my knees together to stay upright like I usually did on Tornado.

"Something feels strange about riding Crumble. Is it the saddle? Is it because she's smaller? Why does this feel so different?" I asked when Noah led us down a path surrounded by trees. My bare shoulders welcomed the shade. I didn't burn easily, but we'd been out in the sun for an hour or two, and my racerback top didn't cover much skin.

"Crumble's a Tennessee Walker," he explained. "Her breed is known for having a smooth gait. You don't get jostled around as much."

"Oh, yeah, wow. Huh." Crumble's head bobbed up and down but from the shoulders back, she was perfectly balanced out. "Oh my god, this is actually nice."

"You like riding now, princess?"

"I've liked riding for a long time, just not on horseback." The words were out faster than I could recall why we'd been quiet the whole morning in the first place. "Don't reply to that. I don't want to fight."

"Okay."

I watched Noah for any sign of resurgent maliciousness, but he just tilted his head back and narrowed his eyes at the rustling leaves overhead. If I hadn't still been mad at him, I would have stared at the flexing muscles in his neck, the sharp contour of his jaw or the way the warm sunlight brought out a few flecks of green in his pale blue eyes. But I was mad at him, so I bit my tongue and fixed my eyes to my horse's twitching ears.

"Can Crumble do the show?" I asked. "I'd much rather be abducted like this."

"No, she's too small," he replied, "and I'm not starting her in shows."

"What does that mean?"

"Crumble is a great horse for beginners and people who have balance issues. It would be a disservice to make her learn tricks and routines for stunt shows."

"Are you, like, the master of horses at the park or something?"

"No." He laughed, and it was such a chesty and pure sound that I just now realized I'd never heard it before. "Tornado, Cookie and Crumble are my horses. I just get to keep them at the park."

"Really?" I leaned down slightly and carefully slid a hand to Crumble's neck to give her a light pat. "You're so sweet, and you let that grumpy old man sit on you? I hope he's treating you nice. Giving you all the carrots you could dream of."

"The grumpy old man thinks we should take a break over there."

Noah led us toward a small pocket off the side of the track where two benches had been set up. He was off Tornado in an instant and tied him to the back of one of the benches. He looked like he'd done this a hundred times before. Maybe he had. Completely at home on horseback and in the countryside, somewhere between the trees.

Crumble whinnied under me and tapped her hoof against the ground.

"Okay, no need to be impatient," I muttered.

We'd been over this. Swing one leg over the saddle, keep my weight on the leg still in the stirrup, pretend it's a ladder. This was fine. Crumble was smaller than Tornado. Even if I dropped, it wouldn't be far, and the ankle braces inside my boots would absorb the worst of it. I inhaled, closed my eyes for a moment, then swung my weight back.

Somehow, I got both my feet planted securely without getting hurt. I'd done it. A light laugh burst from my chest.

I turned to find Noah just two feet away, hands out-stretched as if he'd been ready to catch me.

"Good job. I think you've earned yourself some chocolate."

Unfortunately, Noah's idea of a snack was all healthy foods, aside from the peanut butter cups. He'd packed fruits and veggies, some crackers, trail mix and two bottles of water. He even had one of those soccer-mom lunch boxes that allowed him to put everything in differ-ent compartments.

I was nibbling on my fifth piece of chocolate and had just slid Crumble one of the carrot sticks when a low rumble overhead made her ears twitch.

"Was that thunder?" I glanced up at the green roof above us.

"Yeah," Noah huffed. He clicked the lid back on to the box. I'd barely unfurled my legs from beneath me by the time he'd packed up. "I thought the birds were acting strange earlier, but the forecast said it wouldn't roll in until tonight."

"Are you trying to tell me that you speak bird language?"

Noah sighed and put Crumble's reins back in my hands. "They get into a feeding frenzy before storms."

"God, you're like a real country boy. Did you get to play outside in the mud as a child?"

"Yeah, of course." He pressed a hand against the small of my back to turn me toward the saddle. "Hop on, so we can get out of here."

Another wave of thunder rolled across the sky, making both horses snort their disapproval. I swallowed. I didn't want to be on a horse during a storm. What if it ran off scared? What if it slipped?

"Sorry, but we have to go," Noah said. His hands slid around my waist, fingers digging in much deeper than usual now that I wore just a thin cotton top. My legs automatically kicked high the second they left the ground, but there was no skirt to maneuver. I still landed in the saddle just as rehearsed.

"Don't make me ride through the storm. Please."

"Trying not to." Noah saddled up and leaned over to take Crumble's reins from me. Great sign if I wasn't even allowed to steer my own horse. Something passed over Noah's features and he turned his head from side to side, regarding the trail. "All right. I know a place. It's closer than the park, but we might still get wet."

"I prefer wet over struck by lightning."

We made it out from the tree cover within minutes. The blue skies and sunlight had been replaced by low-hanging clouds in bruising shades of gray. Noah sped the horses a little, and Crumble wasn't walking quite as smoothly any-more, forcing me to clench my thighs around the saddle and white-knuckle the pommel to stay balanced. By the time the first raindrops fell, we'd reached the corner of a three-rail fence that promised some form of civilization nearby.

Thunder rumbled again and Crumble whinnied, prac-tically shaking her head "no". Noah reached over to pat the side of her neck and cooed soothing words at her. His white T-shirt stretched taut over his arms while he kept my horse calm without taking his eyes off the road ahead. I bet he didn't even have to think about it.

I'd known, logically, that he was a small-town boy who was good with horses, but within Bravetown's perimeter, it hardly mattered. We were all in costume, doing our jobs. At the very most, we were roommates who knew each other's eating habits. We had our little idiosyncrasies, but were all part of the same thing.

Out here, Noah was the amalgamation of years and years of a life completely different to mine.

He grew up outside, with animals and with nature, whereas my mother had taken me to the park every now and again to see a bit of greenery. When it rained out here, it affected his life, it became something he knew how to work around. At home, rain was something I watched through the window and dodged with an umbrella as I sprinted from our front door to a cab.

I'd thought life outside the city would bore me to death, but I could have watched Noah ride ahead of me all day, just to see all the little ways he interacted with the world.

This man had no idea how surreal he was.

The raindrops turned to thin white threads, washing the colors from the world. My hair and my clothes stuck to my skin. I'd just opened my mouth to ask if we'd be there soon when I spotted the pale blue buildings between the trees, at the center of the fence lines. Three buildings. With each step forward, more of the property came into view. A long driveway with paddocks on either side led to a tall, picture-book farmhouse with a wraparound porch and dark blue shutters on the windows. The other two buildings seemed to be a barn and horse stables. More of Tennessee's jade hills rolled out behind the farm. If it hadn't been for the weather, you could have used this as a computer wallpaper.

The entry sign above the driveway read Forever Young Ranch, with a horseshoe replacing the U.

It only clicked when Noah led us down the driveway and my eyes caught his last name on the dented mailbox.

"Is this your parents' place?" I had to shout over the rushing rain.

"It used to be," he replied. "It's mine now. It's a bit run-down, but it's dry."

The implication of his words wasn't lost on me. "Shit, I'm sorry. I didn't know."

"It's fine. It's been years." He looked back over his shoulder and shot me an easy smile to reassure me, only for his gaze to drop along with the corners of his mouth. "Let's get you out of this rain."

"Thank you," Esra sighed as I handed her one of my old shirts. She stood in the small bathroom, wrapped in a large towel, her tan skin glowing from sunlight and cool rain, her hair curling more than usual.

"Do you need anything else?"

"Something to drink that isn't water maybe."

"I can make you some tea. There's peppermint, green tea, or Earl Grey, I think."

She smirked. "Okay, yeah. I've never had a boy offer to make me tea before."

"Right. You meant a drink. Sorry. I might have some lukewarm beer left over, but I don't really . . ."

"No, tea sounds nice."

"Okay."

I knew this wasn't a social visit. We were only here because of the storm brewing outside. But it was still the first time I'd brought anyone home in years without them being here to work. It was the first time I'd brought a girl home. Ever. I wasn't prepared for this.

I kept some bare necessities here in case I worked late and ended up spending the night, but until I got some busted pipes replaced, only one of the bathrooms was remotely operational and the heating wasn't getting fixed until next year. Esra hadn't complained about not getting a hot shower though.

Her wet clothes were draped over the side of the tub. They wouldn't dry properly like that.

I'd changed upstairs and had discarded my own drenched clothes in the sink, but I also didn't need them to make it back to Bravetown once the weather cleared up.

I slipped past her and unfolded the old laundry rack stashed behind the broken washing machine.

"You don't have to do that," she said.

"I do. I'm sorry. This is my fault." I tried not to dwell on the fabrics I was touching as I hung them up to dry. Even if I was hanging her underwear and that meant she was really just wearing a towel right now. "We should have stayed at the park."

"Should have, could have, would have," she mused.

Fabric rustled behind me. She was changing right there. If I turned around right now . . .

"Don't you mind people seeing you naked?"

"Not really. It's just a body. It's not that deep," she said.

"Is that med school talking?"

"Kind of. Actually, no. It's probably part of the whole mindset that made me want to go to med school in the first place." She hummed. "You can turn around now. I'm all covered up."

I did, not prepared for the somersault my pulse did at the sight of her. Esra naked would have been one thing. But Esra standing in my shirt? The plaid fabric hit mid-thigh for her, her smooth legs bare down to the boots. She hadn't buttoned it up all the way, exposing a perfect triangle of skin down to the valley between her breasts, but the rest of the shirt swallowed her. It triggered some sort of caveman instinct in my brain. This woman was wearing my clothes in my house and all I wanted was to get her some tea and some chocolate and shield her from the weather.

"Tea?" She tilted her head, completely oblivious to the ways she fucked with my mind.

Five minutes later, I trailed her through the rooms while she cradled a steaming mug to her chest. I couldn't help but imagine what she must be seeing. Downstairs still needed a lot more work than upstairs. The kitchen was covered in buckets and tools and dust. The doorframes needed to be sanded down and refinished. Some lamps were only light bulbs dangling from the ceiling. It had to look like a complete dump to her.

She leaned through the doorframe into the dining room – or what I hoped would be the dining room someday. Right now, it was just white walls and mismatched old wooden chairs that I picked up whenever I found them cheap or free. They usually just needed some screws tightened and a fresh coat of wax to make them as good as new.

"Is this what you and Sanny were doing when you came into the saloon covered in paint?"

"Yeah, we're fixing the place up again. He didn't tell you about it?"

"No." She turned, but not in time to hide the flicker of hurt. She wandered down the hallway, leaning into each room to get a look. "So you want to be a farmer?"

"No, we're turning it into a therapy ranch."

"You and my brother?"

"Yeah."

Her steps faltered for a moment, but she caught herself on the doorframe to the office – which was just an old desk shoved into the corner, surrounded by boxes. Esra sighed and nodded. "That's why you're training Tornado to be a therapy horse."

"Yes."

The rain drummed against the windows on three sides of the large living-room space, driving home just how still Esra had fallen. She ran a hand over the mantel above the fireplace and circled the old sofa to look out at the back-yard. I wasn't sure I'd ever witnessed her stay completely silent for this long. Even when she'd been quietly riding beside me earlier, she'd constantly let out little sounds of wonder, had greeted a bug that landed on her hand and hummed her approval when the sunlight hit her face. I usually liked silence, but I hated hers.

"If it makes you feel better, Sinan hasn't talked much about you either. Not in detail. I think he's been trying to keep this place separate from his family life."

"Maybe." Esra turned, leaning her back against the window frame. "Will *you* tell me about this place? What's your plan?"

"Sure." I walked over to her, letting my back rest against the other side of the window. "I turned the attic into a master bedroom, so that's where I'll be staying. There's five more bedrooms upstairs. We're planning to put two beds in each. That way they can either be shared or a parent can stay with their kid. There's another bedroom down here that we want to make fully accessible, but the back stair-well is already fitted with a stair lift. A lot of that is where Sanny comes in. He's making sure the house can meet all kinds of support needs."

"That's all renovations. What about the therapy part?"

"I have some plans." I weighed my head from side to side. "Are they secret?"

"No, but . . ." My eyes dropped to Esra's hands, only the tips of her fingers poking out from the sleeves of my shirt as she held an old mug with some car dealership's faded logo on it.

"Oh. You don't want to tell *me*."

"This place, and what it could be, is important to me."

"Right, and I'm just the Buckle Bunny you eat out in the break room."

"Aren't you?" I challenged, not sure how I wanted her to answer. She was infuriating and carefree and irresponsible – and meant for much bigger places than Wild Fields, Tennessee.

Instead of yelling and running like she had last night, Esra held my gaze. She stood, unmoving. Her dark eyes burrowed into me like claws. She stayed.

"I'd never even been eaten out until about five months ago," she said, voice low, still not breaking eye contact. "Which is a very roundabout way of saying that I grew up very sheltered, basically bubble-wrapped, and even throughout college never had even a shrivel of fun. I've been completely focused on school for as long as I can remember. So maybe you think that I'm just easy and in it for a good time, but it's not that easy for me. I'm making conscious decisions every day, allowing myself to indulge in things I've been denied my whole life."

I swallowed and nodded. I had to tell her that the shit I'd said last night wasn't even about her. It was about me and my own stupid hang-ups. But this was the first time Esra mentioned her life before Bravetown in any detail, and I was too curious not to ask for more. "What changed five months ago?"

"Nine months ago, actually, I went to my first anatomy lab class, and I fainted."

"You fainted?"

"It's not uncommon. A lot of med students faint the first time they see a dead body, or the first time they have to cut."

I grimaced.

"Exactly," she laughed but tore her gaze away, back to the dark skies outside the window. The thunder was getting louder, closer. "I grew up on *Grey's Anatomy*. I watched so many surgeries in training videos, so I'd be ready for med school. Confronted with the real thing though? I keeled over. I came back the next week, doubled my OR mask against the smell because I figured it clearly wasn't the visual that bothered me, and still fainted. I thought I'd get used to it eventually. Most people do. I went to the third class, and it was fine at first. I stayed in the back. I was going to ease myself into it. Then when the professor demonstrated . . . well . . . it wasn't . . . That time, when I went down, I fell really badly against some lab equipment and dislocated my elbow. I didn't go back after that. I knew, instinctively, that I wouldn't get used to it. I was done. I'd just spent fifteen years working toward a medical degree, but when I was confronted with a real person, *my own body* was like 'double nope'." Despite her lighthearted phrasing, her voice clogged up. She bit her lip as her next breath stuttered through her chest. "Nobody seems to grasp how much it hurts when you do everything right, everything the way you're supposed to, and your silly body just ruins all your plans. I couldn't *just* switch major. I couldn't *just* go from med school to grad school and pretend it was *just* about finding a different job in the medical field. There was nothing *just* about it. It was unfair."

That same archaic instinct that wanted to shelter her from the storm took over, except this time the storm was inside of her, and I couldn't fix that. I gently freed the mug from her fingers and set it on the windowsill. Esra let herself be pulled into my arms, her face nestled against my collar bone and her fingers splayed across my chest.

"I really wanted it. More than anything," she whispered, brushing her cold nose over my skin, "but losing it has given me the chance to catch up on all the fun I missed out on over the years. I want to feel normal for a bit."

Her words set off a pang in my chest. Normal. I'd never had normal, and I'd envied all the normal people around me for so many years that I wasn't sure I even knew what normal looked like anymore.

"I know that feeling. I didn't exactly have a normal childhood." I brushed a hand through Esra's hair, tracing circles across her back with the other. "My mom was very sick while I was growing up. She had an aggressive form of MS. Horseback riding was good for her though. Even when she couldn't walk anymore and needed help into the saddle, she could still ride on her own. Staying active like that helped with all the other symptoms. It gave me a few more years with her. It was also the only way I could cope. At home, I helped with taking care of her a lot, and in school, I was always the boy with the dying mother. None of that mattered when I was with the horses. That's what I want to offer here. Physical and emotional support that includes care-givers."

Esra slipped her hand around her back to where mine was still tracing invisible patterns over her spine. Her fingers folded around mine and offered a gentle squeeze.

"What about your dad?"

"He wasn't much of a dad, even less so after my mom died. If you want, I'll tell you about him some other time," I said and actually meant it.

The seriousness of the moment was ruptured when her stomach growled loudly enough to compete with the thunder overhead.

"Ohmygod." Esra laughed and shook her head, pushing back just enough to blink up at me. "I can't believe I'm saying this, but I could really use one of your carrot sticks right about now."

"Make yourself at home," I said and nodded toward the sofa. "I'll grab the bags."

When I came back from the kitchen with the saddle bags and a fresh cup of tea, Esra had pulled the throw blanket from the sofa and spread it out on the floor. She arranged the cushions around it to face the fireplace, creating something resembling half a nest.

"We can have a picnic." She beamed. "That feels less depressing than eating veggies on the sofa while waiting for the rain to stop."

"My veggies aren't depressing. They're healthy."

"Those aren't mutually exclusive attributes, Noah." She rolled her eyes at me.

"If you think they're depressing, maybe I should keep them."

"No!" She rose to her knees and stuck her bottom lip out in a cute pout. "I'm hungry. Please."

Heat shot down my center and straight to my dick. Because Esra was kneeling in front of me half-naked, wearing only my shirt, and doing cute shit with her mouth.

"Here." I thrust the lunch box at her and dropped on to the blanket as I pushed away the fucked-up images my brain tried to produce.

She'd opened up to me and she'd let me hug her, and I could be content with that. If that was all she'd ever give me of herself, I'd still have gotten more than I was ever meant to. She could give the rest to Ace Ryder. *I* would have to deal with the way that messed with my head. That wasn't on her. For fuck's sake, she was my best friend's little sister. That was the one detail *I* could easily ignore when we were in Ace Ryder's hideout. A hug was probably the furthest this should ever have gone.

Esra turned the snacks into a spread and squealed in delight when I brought out crackers and a jar of peanut butter. She turned those into a shocking sandwich of cracker, peanut butter, Reese's Minis, more peanut butter, peanuts picked from the trail mix, and another cracker. Her willingness to eat carrot sticks quickly evaporated.

She made me eat one of her chocolates by holding it up against my lips and climbing over my lap when I tried to dodge her. It was supposed to be playful, but the second she straddled my thigh, I remembered that her underwear was drying in the bathroom. So I took the chocolate and shifted her off me.

"Do you think you'd stand a better chance against a bear or a tiger?" Esra asked, lying on her stomach and rocking her feet through the air as she turned the last bit of trail mix into a smiley face in front of her.

"What kind of bear?"

"Uh . . . mountain bear?"

"Then, yeah, bear. The ones that find their way down the

mountains here are mostly black bears. Easy to scare off."

"There's bears here?" Esra stilled, her eyes darting to the window. Water still streamed from the heavens outside, but the thunder and lightning had quieted.

"Not here. They come looking for food. And that won't be enough to lure one out," I said and stole one of her almonds. She crinkled her nose at me. "Would you rather go on *Jeopardy!* or *Who Wants to Be a Millionaire*?"

"Oh, good question," she whispered more to herself as she rearranged the mouth of her smiley face, then said, "*Millionaire*. Less gimmicky. I can just breeze through and walk out with the glory."

"You think you'd breeze through?"

"Unless there's questions about birds predicting the weather, but you can be my phone lifeline now."

"Sure, I'll be waiting for your call."

"Speaking of . . ." Esra scooted up and pointed at the bags. "Do you mind if I check the weather, or do you want to consult with the crows first?"

"Are you making fun of me?" I asked and handed her phone over.

"I'm making fun of the principle. It just sounds so silly. I'm actually genuinely impressed by the skill." Judging by the fact that she was tapping around on her phone, she had no idea what those words meant to me. I wasn't sure I'd ever impressed anyone. "It looks like we might be stuck here for a few more hours."

I angled to check the weather app on her phone. "We'll have to spend the night. We're not riding back after dark, especially not after all this rain. God knows what state the roads are in."

"Tennessee," she shouted out, hand shooting into the air, full trivia mode, "the state the roads are in."

"You're full of jokes today." I chuckled and pushed to my feet. "I'll check on the horses and make sure they're okay for the night. Can you text Renee? Even if we make it back in time for the show tomorrow, Tornado won't be able to pull it off after all this."

"Sure you don't need help with the horses?"

"It'll take me ten minutes." I hesitated for a moment, too aware of how she'd shut down earlier and not wanting to repeat that. "You should also text your brother where you are. I told him that I was taking you on a trail ride. He might start worrying."

Esra

Despite what he'd said, Noah wasn't back within ten minutes. He wasn't even back within fifteen. I'd texted Sinan and Renee to let them know we were stuck at the ranch, and I read three articles about the different kinds of equine-assisted therapy by the time Noah was gone close to twenty minutes, and I decided that he may have been struck by lightning.

I traced my earlier steps back to the kitchen and the side door we'd come in from. I cracked it open, surprised by the crescendo of the rain as it drummed to the ground and into large puddles. Through the curtain of water, I spotted Noah by the stable doors. Not burned to a crisp by lightning but also not really moving.

"Noah?" I called his name, but the rain and the distance drowned out my voice.

The floorboards creaked under my boots as I stepped outside to the very edge of the roofed porch. Some water still managed to splash against my naked legs, but I got a slightly better view. It looked like Noah was pushing his shoulder into the door. He was completely soaked again. So much for not needing help.

My boots were caked in mud by the time I made it close enough for him to spot me.

"Go back inside! You're getting wet all over again," Noah shouted over the rain.

"Too late." I lifted my arms demonstratively. The shirt he'd gotten me was already drenched.

"You'll get sick."

"What's wrong?" I asked.

"Go back."

"Tell me what's wrong."

"The door is stuck," he finally replied.

Inside the stables, Tornado and Crumble neighed. The wind was pushing the rain through the open door and water was pooling down the center aisle of the stables. If it kept raining like this, it wouldn't be long before it reached the horses.

"Stay there. I'll push from inside. On three." I slipped past him and took the opposite door handle. "One, two, three." We both pushed against the sliding doors. They only budged half an inch. I blinked up at the mechanics, water dripping down my nose. "Do you think something's stuck in there?"

"No, it's just rust. I haven't gotten round to fixing anything out here yet."

"I don't suppose you have any vinegar or baking powder here?" Not that it would have even worked in this rain. The acid would have been washed off before it could attack the rust.

"On three," Noah said, and I steeled my grip around the door handle again.

We got another half-inch this time, a full inch by the third time we pushed.

"I need to change position." I flexed my right knee, which had been bearing most of my weight. The hours in the saddle had already taken their toll, but the easily ignored subliminal ache was morphing into sharp pain now.

"Come here. We'll try together." Noah directed me in front of him, my hands right below his on the handle. Despite the rain, the heat of his body still engulfed me as he positioned his feet between mine. "One, two, three."

I threw my weight against the door, expecting another inch at most, but this time, the thing rolled forward. It banged shut and I tried to catch my misplaced momentum. I even managed to land my steps without rolling my ankles. But my feet slipped away in the mud.

I landed with an oomph – not mine.

Noah had gone down with me. His arms wrapped around my waist. He'd absorbed most of the fall while I dropped cushioned to his chest.

"Oh god, are you okay?" I scrambled to my knees. My hands roamed over his shoulders and down his arms, feeling for any bones in places they shouldn't be. "Are you hurt?"

"Just slipped," he chuckled and caught my hands in his. "You good, princess?"

"Are you sure? Did you fall on your wrists? How's your neck?" I asked, still fretting.

Noah pushed himself up on his elbows and regarded me with a furrowed brow. A slow grin spread on his lips. He seemed okay. Of course he was okay. He wasn't me. I took a slow, trembling breath to calm my nerves. Noah was fine, and he had no clue that he'd probably shielded me from a trip to the ER by cushioning my fall.

His hand whipped up faster than I could react. He booped my nose, a wet dollop of dirt hitting me right in the face.

"Never played outside in the mud, Esra?"

"No." I wiped the cold mud off my nose and glared at him. My momentary panic washed away. "Oh, you're so dead." I swung my leg over his hips while grabbing two fistfuls of mud. He laughed, barely even trying to field off my hands as I slapped the mud on to his broad chest and spread it up his neck.

"You're playing dirty," he huffed, mud-coated hands grabbing hold of my legs.

"Who's making jokes now?" I dipped my hands back into the sludge and slid them around the sides of his face. He just let me spread the dirt over his cheeks and stubble. No protest whatsoever. "You know, women in New York would probably pay good money to get an organic Tennessee mud facial."

"I'm *not* joking." His hands roamed up the sides of my legs, leaving a coat of mud in their wake. "This is a very dirty trick to keep me pinned down."

I glanced down, only then realizing what he meant. The rain had soaked me to the point where I couldn't tell where my shirt stopped and my skin started. That strange sensation extended to the fact that I wasn't wearing any clothes other than the shirt. Something Noah was clearly aware of as I straddled his lap.

"Shit. I'm so sorry. My bad." I scrambled backward and pressed my hands into his chest to push away, but Noah's hands tightened around my thighs, keeping me rooted in place.

"Why are you apologizing?"

"I don't want you to think I'm throwing myself at you. You've made it perfectly clear that you don't want me to wear your hat. And now I'm literally sitting on you, like I'm trying to *ride* you."

Noah's eyes narrowed, but they kept me locked in place just like his hands. In one swift move, he flipped us over. My back met the soft ground, but he kept my legs angled around his hips, his weight pressing against my bared lower half. There was no missing the feeling of his rough jeans against my sensitive skin now.

"Do you want this? Do you want *me*?" he asked.

"Noah," I sighed, writhing under him, relishing the feel of his weight and his heat bearing down on me.

His large hand splayed out across my collar bone and slid down my center. The snap buttons of the plaid shirt popped open one after another as he dragged his touch to my navel. If the shirt hadn't been clinging to me, water like glue against my skin, it would have fallen open.

"Ask me for what you want, Esra."

I groaned his name, fully aware that he was getting a kick out of it when I begged for his touch. My skin was prickling, sensitive to every raindrop, every fingertip that pressed into my belly, and it wasn't enough.

"Ask me," he repeated, voice stern enough to send a shiver down my spine.

"Noah," I breathed and couldn't believe the words about to come out of my mouth considering the sheer amount of dirt on both of our faces, but this man was really turning my brain to goo, "could you please kiss me?"

Noah's mouth crashed down over mine, no hesitation, no playfulness. Pure desire. I hadn't understood *desire* up until now. When you hungered for a touch, a kiss, so much, another person became the sole focus of every cell in your body. I wanted him. I *craved* him. He kissed me and with his body covering mine, the storm stopped. I pulled at him, at his shirt, at his hair, pulled him on top of me until I could wrap my legs around his waist again.

He ground down. I gasped when his hips pressed into me, giving me a sense of how much he wanted this, too. The second my mouth dropped open, his moved. He trailed kisses down my jaw to my neck, and let his teeth join his lips. His hand slid in under the shirt, cupping my breast and squeezing.

"More. Please." I reached down to undo his jeans, hesitating after the button only because I was dragging dirt over his clothes. Nothing about this was sanitary. Years of good sense clashed with my need for Noah. I'd never experienced anything like this. This was so much more than some lowered inhibitions. The way I wanted him was raw and primal.

Noah plucked my hands off him, cuffing both wrists in one hand and pinning them above my head.

"Fuck, look at you," he rasped as his gaze traveled down my body and locked on to my spread legs. My chest, my stomach and even my thighs were streaked in mud. There really was only one spot he'd left unscathed. I wanted his touch so bad, even his gaze sent a hot pulse through my insides.

"No more looking. You can admire your finger-painting skills later," I said, trying to pull him back to me with my ankles closed behind his back, and failing. "God, you're like a fucking boulder. Will you get on top of me already?"

His lips pulled into a lopsided grin I hadn't seen before. It put a deep dimple in his cheek. This was worse than the cheeky grin he usually only sported as Ace. This spelled trouble, and I was on the receiving end of it. Goosebumps raced across my entire body in response.

"You want me on top of you?"

"I just said that." I wriggled my wrists in his grasp, just enough to claw my nails into his hand to convey my impatience. He didn't even have the decency to flinch.

"Princess, are you going to let me fill that sweet little pussy with my cock and fuck you out here in the dirt for the whole world to see?"

My mouth ran dry at the images his words painted. Not that there really was a "whole world" besides rain and farmland. But the idea was still there. Anyone coming down that driveway would have been able to see how he had me sprawled out in the mud. It was risky and indecent, and that hadn't even crossed my mind. All I knew was that I needed to feel more of him. And Noah wasn't judging. He was asking permission.

"Yes," I replied, voice hoarse.

"You're going to have to say it." Noah reached for his jeans, pushing them lower without easing up on my wrists.

I used my heels to help him get the denim down alongside his boxers.

I was going to say it. *Noah, pretty please, just fuck me in the mud already.* But his mounting erection sprang free from his pants and wiped my entire vocabulary from my frontal lobe. That thing would *not* fit inside of me. How did he even ride with that? Did he need a permit to carry it around in his pants? Like, that just had to classify as a concealed weapon, right?

Despite all the thoughts racing through my mind, the only word that made it from my brain to my tongue was "Oh."

Noah leaned down, the tip of his nose brushing against mine. So gentle and sweet, the complete opposite to the thick tip of his cock stroking deep through my pussy from entrance to clit and back again. I quivered and moaned into his hovering mouth.

"Say it, Esra," he huffed.

"What if I don't?" I leaned up to catch his bottom lip between my teeth, only to earn myself a harsh thrust over my sensitive flesh. The flames in my core were licking up my spine, making me arch for him. There really was no denying how much I craved him. "Noah, I'm not . . ."

His eyes searched mine for that flicker of hesitation that kept us apart.

"I'm not sure that's going to fit."

He glanced down as if the thought had never occurred to him. "Princess, it'll fit. We didn't get all the way here for you to be anything but perfect for me."

"It's really unfair that you can just say things like that and make my insides melt. God, Noah."

Instead of answering, he kissed me, slow and deliberate, dragging his length over me once more. I shivered at every delicious ridge and vein rippling over my clit.

"God," I gasped and sank my nails into his hand again because I knew I'd need to hold on to something after my next words, "I need to feel you, Noah. Let me have you."

His hand slid under my ass. He gave my cheek a short squeeze before pushing my thigh up. My leg pressed deep into my stomach, turning my breathing shallow, but more importantly, opening my pussy up for him. Noah's own breath labored through his chest as he aligned his tip with my entrance.

That lopsided grin pulled his lips up.

"Beg."

"Stop playing with me, Young."

He slapped my ass hard enough for droplets of water to spray up and hit my face. Unfortunately for my stubbornness, that sharp sting shot straight to my core, eliciting a desperate moan.

"Please," I whimpered, grinding up to get any sort of relief, "please fuck me."

I only got a warning in the split second Noah's grip tightened on my crossed wrists. His hips snapped forward. The impossible fit wasn't entirely impossible. He burrowed himself inside me so fast, my insides didn't get the chance to cramp up. The stretch still seared through me, and my responding cry was more pain than pleasure. By the time my muscles tightened, he'd already sheathed himself several inches deep.

"Look at me, Esra." His fingers pinched my chin and I blinked, unaware I'd even closed my eyes. Rain dribbled from his ink-black hair to my face, cooling the hot blush in my cheeks. He released my wrists and stroked my hair as I adjusted beneath him. With every gentle caress, the tension ebbed from my body. "Can you take more? Just a little."

"Mm-hmm." I nodded, not enough strength to produce words.

He kissed me as he slowly lowered his weight, catching every whimper with his lips. He sank deeper, my inner walls resisting the novel stretch of being so thoroughly filled.

"That's it. Easy, girl. You're doing so good," he rumbled.

His words snapped me back into my mind, pain forgotten. "Fuck you," I hissed, "don't talk to me like I'm one of your damn horses."

"There she is, my feisty little princess." He grinned as he pulled back again, and my thighs automatically jerked against him. "I thought I'd lost you there for a second."

"It'll take a bit more than your—" My voice cut off into a strangled gasp when his hips delved forward, a little further than before. My abdomen felt swollen around him, but the pain wasn't half as bad on the second thrust. By the third one, he was moving just a little easier. My core began to welcome the depth of him.

For a few moments neither of us spoke, lost to the ways our bodies fit against each other. I sank my nails deep into his shoulders, relishing the way even a little scratch could make him change his movements. He retaliated by roaming his hands over my chest, pinching and rolling my nipples until they were so sensitized, every brush against them had me writhing beneath him.

"You're going to be the death of me," he breathed after

my pinky nail left a particularly angry red mark across his neck.

"I'll take that as a compliment."

"Of course, you would."

I huffed and squeezed my muscles around him.

He groaned loud and stilled to stare down at me, surprise mixing with a quiet challenge in his eyes. "That's how you want to play it?"

I painted on an innocent smile. "I don't know what you're talking about."

Faster than I could process, Noah's hands wrapped around my calves, and he hiked my legs up on to his shoulders. He still came down with his face inches from mine, pressing my knees up against my chest. My lips trembled. This tightened his fit again, but I also knew he'd be able to slide even deeper than before at this angle. He rolled his hips back and I braced myself for the inevitable perfect pain, only for both of us to slide across the ground. Without my heels digging in, we'd lost some purchase.

"Oh no, what's wrong?" I asked in mock-surprise and squeezed him inside me again. I'd won that round.

"Fuck. Goddamn rain." He slapped his hand against the stable door. The wood creaked but stabilized his position enough for the next thrust to push to an exquisite deep spot that knocked the air from my lungs. He bottomed out inside me with a groan.

I couldn't breathe through the fullness. He was everywhere. In the heat coursing through my blood. In the cold water dripping from his round shoulders. In the hot air that traveled from his mouth to mine with every gasp.

"Noah." My voice came strangled.

"I know, baby." He delivered blow after blow, hitting that same perfect spot that stole my breath.

My mouth dropped open, desperate for air. My spine arched high, and my feet scrambled for some sort of hold, but I couldn't breathe. I couldn't. I cou— I fell over the edge with a primal scream, my lungs filling and emptying through the same sound. I was drowning. Wave after wave of pleasure crashed over me, keeping me under the surface, cut off from oxygen, only for me to come up again with loud cries.

Noah's pace increased. I was sure he was calling my name, but the waves drowned him out. I held him through the perfect storm. "Esra, I'm about to . . ." he rasped against my lips. His hand brushed over my cheek, pulling me from my blissful daze just enough to meet his hesitant gaze.

"Yes." I knew what he was asking, but I couldn't form more eloquent words to reassure him with. Those three simple letters occupied my every thought. "Yes," I repeated and closed my mouth over his. "Yes." I kissed him longer, kissed him again and again as I echoed how much I wanted him, all of him. "Yes. Yes. Yes." I grasped at his neck and wrapped my legs tighter around his shoulders as he spilled himself inside me, riding out his own waves.

When we stilled, it felt like my body was floating, tingling and limp and warm.

"Fuck, that was . . ." Noah pressed his forehead against mine, breathing hard.

"Wholeheartedly agree." My voice came out scratchy. "Wanna go for round two?"

"Woman, I haven't even pulled out yet." He chuckled and stole a quick kiss from my lips and leaned back. One hand lazily roamed down my sternum to my navel while he carefully untangled my legs before shifting out of me. I whimpered at the sudden cold emptiness.

"We may have a problem," he mumbled, kneeling between my legs.

"It's okay, I'm on the pill," I said because I felt the hot trickle of his release that he probably had a prime view of.

"Good to know, but no." Noah's fingers trailed over my stomach, tracing patterns to expose my skin under the layer of mud. It took me a moment to recognize the pattern. He was connecting the distance between my freckles, brushing the dirt from them as if he knew exactly where to find each one. "There's no hot water, remember?"

Cleaning up without running hot water sounded like *torture*. Noah didn't take me to the bathroom though. He sat me on the kitchen counter and brought the tea kettle to boil, then mixed the hot water into a sink full of cold water. Using a dishtowel with little horses printed all over it, he gently brushed the mud off my skin. He started with my face, only to ruin his progress when he leaned in to kiss me, so he let me clean his face, too. His lids fluttered shut under my fingers and I spent more time cleaning him than I actually needed, just to keep touching him.

Bit by bit, he made his way down my body. He peeled me out of the plaid shirt and caressed every inch he cleaned with soft kisses. When the sink looked worse than the skin on my belly, he put the kettle on again and kissed me until he could continue dabbing me down with hot water. The real torture was the fact that he wouldn't let me touch him back because he was still covered in dirt.

When he got to the space between my thighs, he took out a fresh dishtowel and carefully washed that part of my body, too. He paid every cleaned inch extra attention with his kisses, until I was clutching the edge of the counter for support and moaning his name again.

The comforting haze he wrapped me in drowned out everything else until his touch made it down my calf and he unzipped my boot.

"Wait," I gasped and pulled my leg away from him.

His brows jumped up, but he didn't move to grab my boot again.

I could run to the bathroom and take the boots and braces off and stash them somehow. Or I could just say that I had weak ankles. Sounded a bit Victorian but it might work. At least until tomorrow morning, when I'd need painkillers to get out of bed after everything I'd put my body through today.

"I have a thing," I sighed and watched Noah closely.

"For boots?"

"No," I laughed, grateful for one last joke before his perception of me changed. "Less kinky, more medical."

Noah reached for my foot again, and I placed it in his palms. He pulled the boot off and brushed his fingertips over the thick black brace that had been perfectly hidden by the snug leather. "Did you sprain your ankle?"

"No, uhm . . ." I pulled the socked foot from his grasp and replaced it with the other one. Noah took that boot off, too, and tilted his head when he found another brace underneath. "Remember how I said that I had a lot of inside time as a kid and that I grew up bubble-wrapped? That was slightly more literal than metaphorical. I constantly

232

got badly hurt as a kid and even had some surgeries you usually don't need until you're middle-aged, and they couldn't figure out what was wrong with me for a while, but uhm . . . I basically have weak tissues. Like, the protective lining that's keeping my body held together isn't great at doing its job. For me, it's mostly my joints, so I kinda *bubble-wrap* them when I need to. Hypermobility means I'm super bendy though. So prepare for some mind-blowing sex." I grimaced after adding that last part. I'd never done this, and I was making it so awkward.

Noah stayed quiet for a moment, processing, thumb still circling over my ankle. "Can I take these off? Your socks are soaked."

"Yeah." I nodded and waited for his reaction.

Noah carefully undid the Velcro to unwrap my ankles. I couldn't stop the deep sigh that escaped me. Those things were kind of like bras. Supportive, preventing unwanted jiggles, but, god, it felt good when they came off at the end of the day.

He placed my socks and braces on the counter and ran his hands back up my legs until he stood between my knees, his expression still neutral.

"Tell me what you're thinking."

"Is that why you wanted to become a doctor?"

That wasn't one of the questions I'd expected him to ask.

"Yes."

He seemed to consider my answer while his fingers feathered over my right knee, finding the faint surgery scars from years ago. "Are you in pain right now?"

"Just the normal amount."

"The normal amount should be zero."

I shrugged. I didn't want to turn this into an even bigger pity party by pointing out the chronic part of chronic illness.

He weighed his head from side to side. "Would you rather have bendy mind-blowing sex on the sofa or in bed?"

I grinned. Even though the sofa might have been more conducive to what he had in mind, I wasn't going to turn down soft sheets and a blanket right now. "Bed."

Noah stripped out of his own dirty clothes, granting me a look at all the sloped and hardened muscles I'd only ever felt through fabric. His was the kind of body earned through physical labor, not sharply defined, but sculpted to a width and strength you couldn't get at the gym. God, I wanted to run my hands over every inch of him.

Instead, I watched him clean off quickly. He wasn't as meticulous as he'd been with me, toweling off the mud with rough strokes, but that didn't stop the water from pearling down his sun-kissed skin. And it certainly didn't stop the burning heat from pooling at the base of my spine again. If anything, I wanted those rough hands on me.

Noah knew what he was doing to me. He pinned me in place with a cocky grin, not breaking eye contact once until he tossed the dishtowel in the sink. My toes were curled tight in anticipation when he finally whisked me off the counter and carried me to the large bedroom under the roof. The sloped ceilings and beams across the gable were made from a warm wood that gave the entire space a cozy feeling even if there wasn't much more to it than a bed with white sheets and blankets. It was placed right under a large skylight almost the same size as the mattress itself,

234

letting in plenty of light and offering a breathtaking view of the storm clouds still hanging low in the sky.

He set me down in front of him slowly, chest pressed against my back, his forearm still braced around my waist from behind.

"It's not much," he started to say.

"It's perfect," I cut him off and tilted my head back to get a look at him. He furrowed his brow as if he was trying to puzzle out whether I was teasing him, but for once, I wasn't. "It's perfect."

Leaning down, Noah grazed his lips over mine. "I know this isn't what you're used to."

Huh. Considering Noah's closeness to my brother, it hadn't crossed my mind that he'd feel awkward about our different backgrounds. *I* didn't. "In case you haven't noticed, I ran away from everything I'm used to. I'm choosing what I like for myself. And I like this. I like your home. I like the way you make me feel, Noah, the way you touch me."

Maybe I even liked *him.*

I wanted to strangle him half the time for being rude and domineering and stiff, but he was also determined and selfless and always there to catch me. He was physically strong, and that was great, sure, but after everything he'd told me today, seeing this place, I also understood how much quiet strength he carried. He was resilient. And, god, he was beautiful.

I ran my hand into his hair, twirling his white streak around my finger, and pulled him to me. My lips bridged the last gap between us as I *chose* to kiss him.

Tension ebbing, Noah sighed against my mouth and

the sound weakened my knees. If his arm hadn't still been wrapped around my waist, I would have melted to the floor.

His tongue nudged mine, finding all the ways he could kiss me and tease needy sounds from me. The kiss was passionate, but it was also patient. He wasn't just consuming me; he was exploring me. I'd never been kissed like this. I wanted to savor it. The longer he kissed me, the harder I clenched my thighs, fighting the heat simmering in my core, just to prolong the moment.

He was holding himself back, too, if the growing erection pressing against my backside was any indication.

"Oh god," I whimpered as his teeth cut a sharp crescent across my bottom lip.

"You're intoxicating, Esra," he rasped, a large hand brushing over my flushed cheek and tugging stray curls behind my ear. "I don't think I'll ever get enough of the way you taste."

"Then don't stop." I pulled him back to me, but instead of kissing me, Noah lowered his mouth to my neck. Goosebumps raised in the wake of every kiss.

His hand brushed down to my chest. Fingertips feathered across my skin, tracing slow circles around and around my nipple until it peaked into the air without him even touching it. He kissed a searing path across my shoulder and repeated his slow play around the other nipple. I squirmed against him, needing more than what he was giving me.

I was suddenly way too aware of being completely naked, in the middle of an almost empty room. All I felt were cold floorboards against my soles, warm air tickling my skin, and Noah's hands and lips, his body pressing into me, his heat mingling with mine. I couldn't even push him against a wall or pull him into bed with me. Everything was so far away.

"Noah, please," I breathed.

"I get more than seven minutes today. I'm taking my time." His voice dropped to a low rumble. This wasn't up for discussion, apparently, and that firmness just made my inner walls pulse with need for him.

I tried to turn, to at least align us face-to-face, but his arms kept me locked in place.

"No-ah," I whined, reduced to pure petulant need as his finger circled my nipple, closer and closer, but never touching, never giving me that rush of heat I craved.

"Not yet," he chuckled.

Pushing one foot in between mine, he nudged my legs apart. Just enough for me to feel the soft air against the wetness at the crest of my thighs and between my legs. God, I was covered in it, Noah's cum mixed with my own resurgent arousal.

Torturing me, his fingers kept mapping my breasts, as I stood, exposed and open and desperate for more.

Apparently, I had to do it myself if I didn't want to die from sexual frustration. I dropped a hand, but before I could touch myself, Noah snatched my wrist. He tugged my arm behind my back and locked my hand at waist level. Not only was he denying me my own pleasure, but his grip just made me want him more, made me want that muscle strength on top of me again. I let out a frustrated groan. He responded with another chuckle.

Fine. I could be mean, too.

I rose to my tiptoes and writhed my hips against him,

shimmying until I felt his cock align perfectly between my cheeks. Noah moaned and bit my shoulder.

That seemed to have done the trick. He eased me forward, walking us toward the bed without releasing me from his embrace.

"Anything else I should know about before I screw you six ways to Sunday, princess?"

I knew he was really asking whether he needed to change the way he touched me. Whether he needed to be more careful. I loved that he didn't ask like that though. He made it clear that he still had every intention of thoroughly fucking me. "Don't go gentle on me now, Young. I'm perfectly capable of letting you know if I'm uncomfortable with anything. Don't hold back."

"All right. Get in bed, down on your hands and knees."

I narrowed my eyes at him as his grip loosened around my wrist. "Stop telling me what to do," I hissed.

He heaved a sigh that was so perfectly raspy and grumpy that I couldn't help but grin. "You'll tell me if I hurt you?"

"Yes." I rolled my eyes at him just to drive home the point that he was hovering. "And if my mouth is somehow otherwise occupied, I'll flip you the middle finger, okay?"

He nodded and dipped his face to me. His lips skimmed over mine and my mouth readily fell open, but before I could close the kiss, he grabbed my waist and picked me off the floor. Noah tossed me up like he'd done many times before. This time, however, he let go. I was suspended in the air just long enough for panic to surge through my chest, only to land in the softest cloud of a duvet. My heart still racing, I tried to rise on to all fours, but Noah's weight came over on the back of my thighs, and his large hand pushed against the small of my back, holding me down.

"You look so fucking perfect in my bed," he groaned, pushing the thick head of his cock into the narrow gap between my thighs, barely deep enough to find my entrance. "I think the only way you'd look better is covered in my cum."

I moaned and buried my face in his sheets. I grasped the fabric with both hands. No part of me had ever expected to be turned on by a man wanting to come all over me. It seemed so lewd, almost degrading, but Noah was coaxing new cravings from me. Whether he yanked my skirts up during our breaks in Ace Ryder's hideout, fucked me in the mud, or tossed me into his bed, I *liked* being at the receiving end of this sexual desire.

It was freeing to let myself want his filthy words and all the indecent things he could do to me . . .

There was *some* of the aforementioned mind-blowing sex, but we spent more of the night talking than anything else. Noah told me about working summers in the park when he was younger, and Renee offering him Ace Ryder after his dad passed and he couldn't keep the ranch running. I told him about my parents wanting me to go to Yale and how I couldn't fathom spending any more time in lecture halls if it wasn't medicine. We kissed and touched and dozed and talked more, about Wild Fields, about Manhattan, about the logistics of running a therapy ranch, the strangest park guests we'd encountered and stars we could spot through the window once the clouds cleared up.

Chapter Nineteen

ARMADILLO ICE CREAM PARLOR

When you need to cool off from the heat of adventure, treat yourself to a delicious scoop of our traditional ice cream, served in a freshly baked waffle, cup or cone, or find refreshment with one of our creamy milkshakes or floats.

NOAH

Esra was going to occupy my mind no matter what. I could try fighting it, try and be nothing but her live-in co-worker, get annoyed at her laundry forever being left in the washer – but why bother when the alternative meant getting to drag my tongue all over her body while she lay in my bed solving crosswords in old newspapers? I accepted my fate. I was done. She was sinking her claws into me, figuratively and literally, and I was going to say thank you and ask for seconds.

After that night at the ranch, Esra spent more time at the stables. Not only did Crumble walk a lot smoother than Tornado, but she was also smaller in every way, which meant Esra was physically more comfortable, and by extension less nervous.

Even with her newfound interest in learning how to ride, part of me had expected her to show up every other day, get on the horse for thirty minutes, and then run off to go about her life. Instead, she stuck around the stables. She asked me about feeding schedules and brushing manes, and I overheard her asking the other people working with the horses about saddle types and horseshoes and the difference between ponies and horses. She didn't shy away from physically helping out either, though after she twisted her wrist when trying to lift the wheelbarrow, I assigned her to grooming and cleaning tack – both of which she accepted without protest.

I managed to pull her aside for quick kisses, but the stables were generally too busy and too open for more than that. We still had our "seven minutes in heaven" – as she called them – every day, but they got more frantic as we tried to make the most of the limited time we had to ourselves. There always seemed to be way too many people around.

". . . so it's cool that you're technically a mutant, but it's really nothing you should be worried about," she told Cookie while brushing his mane. I leaned against the stall door and watched her. I'd cleaned Crumble's hooves in the next stall over and had listened to Esra educate the horse on *heterochromia*, the condition that meant he had one blue and one brown eye. Her interactions with the animals were so goddamn pure. She'd gone from recoiling and calling Tornado a cow to treating my horses like her best friends. I could have watched her braid manes and ramble about everything and nothing all day, and I'd end up with facial cramps from smiling. Her lightheartedness was becoming intoxicating like that.

"Night, guys! Turn off the lights when you leave, okay?" Hector called from the front of the stables.

"We got it." I waved and nodded at him. Once he was gone, I turned back to Esra, who had stilled with the brush mid-air, eyes on me.

"Were you watching me?" she asked.

"Yes."

"I'm not sure if that's sweet or creepy."

"Based on what I was thinking while watching you, very sweet actually."

"Oh?" She wiggled her brows. "Are you *sweet on me*, Noah Young?"

Her question shattered my smile even if she was only teasing. I wasn't sure what I was when it came to her these days. I knew what I shouldn't be. Because of her brother. Because she'd be leaving soon. Because I had nothing to offer to a girl like her.

"Would you prefer me watching you while thinking about how I want to tie you up and edge you until you can't even remember your own name?" I deflected.

Esra grinned and popped her hip, all sass. "Tie me up? Are you going to rope me in with a lasso?"

"Maybe." I opened the stall door and nodded for her to come out.

Esra grabbed the grooming basket and slipped past me. She raised her brows. "I think I just found my hard limit, and it's getting naked in the stables."

"Mud is fine, but stables are the limit?" I asked and latched the door to Cookie's stall.

"It's the smell."

"Noted."

"That said . . ." She dropped the basket and brushed her hands off on her shirt. It read "I was put on this earth to be hot and smart" in bright pink letters, and I couldn't disagree with it. Esra fluttered her dark lashes at me and wrapped both arms around my neck. The text on her shirt disappeared as she pressed her perfect soft body into me. ". . . I wouldn't mind being tied up. I think."

My responding groan rumbled deep. As if her big doe eyes blinking up at me, and her tits against my chest, weren't enough to set me on edge. "We'll have to take a raincheck on that until the next time I can take you to the ranch. I have a feeling someone would notice if we didn't come home tonight."

She scrunched her nose up. "Fine, then just take me home."

We'd been walking from the park to staff housing together a lot the last few days, but we always split apart as soon as others were around. As far as most people knew, Esra and I had struck up a truce at best. We may have spent some time together out here, but most of the stable staffers were older or lived on the ranches surrounding Wild Fields, so they had very little to do with our roommates — or Esra's brother.

"I'm not taking you to my room," I said and wrapped my arms around her waist.

"Why not?" She stuck her bottom lip out in that silly pout of hers. I caught it between my teeth this time. Esra let out a whimper that almost made me forget my self-restraint. The sound embedded itself in my mind, to be replayed again and again whenever I'd get myself off. I was close to throwing her over my shoulder and carrying her to the tack room, just to spread her legs and see how many more desperate little noises I could draw from her.

"If I got you in my room alone, and you let me tie you up, I'd fuck you so thoroughly, my sheets would smell like you for days. I love the way you scream for me, princess, but those walls are thin. And that's the worst possible way for Sanny to find out that I'm knuckles-deep inside his little sister every single fucking day."

She swallowed, eyes dropping to my lips. "Not on Wednesdays."

"Yet."

Last Wednesday, Sinan had joined me at the ranch again to continue painting, nixing any notion I had of getting Esra back to my large bed in my very private bedroom. I had plans for us though. On our next day off, I'd make her come in each room of that house, until every miserable memory was replaced by visions of her body sprawled out under mine.

Her eyes narrowed, a wicked little smile kicking up her lips. "How do *you* feel about getting naked in the stables?"

"Why? Are you reconsidering letting me tie you up and fuck you senseless?"

"No." Esra licked her lips and glanced left and right to make sure we were all alone. Instead of answering, she loosened her arms from my shoulders and sank to her knees in front of me. "But there are other ways you can be inside of me."

I opened my mouth to respond, but my tongue ran dry when she pulled a hair tie from her pocket and quickly twisted her brown waves into a stubby ponytail without breaking eye contact. She was prepared for this to get messy. Images of painting that pretty face of hers in cum immediately flooded my thoughts. That probably wasn't what she had in mind. I couldn't help it. This woman was activating every primal instinct in me, making me want to mark her in every way possible.

Esra's hands roamed over my jeans, up my thighs. She popped the button open, but didn't touch the zipper. Instead, she leaned in and slotted her teeth around the tiny piece of metal. Eyes on me, she lowered the zipper inch by inch, her hot breath sinking through the fabrics. This was the sight I'd come back to. It didn't matter that my dick wasn't in her mouth yet. Was this what it was like to be seduced? This wasn't about Ace Ryder or even her own pleasure. She was doing this for me, and it sent my pulse into overdrive.

"Fuck," I grunted when she tugged my jeans down, only to bite down on the elastic of my boxer briefs. Her teeth grazed over my skin, then she pulled her head back and let the fabric snap against my skin. I hissed at the momentary sting. It sent a hot rush straight down to my cock.

"Kiss to make it better?" She fluttered her lashes with faux innocence and licked the spot right above the waistband.

I needed something to hold on to and only found the back of her head. Esra actually smiled as I gripped her hair in both fists. She skimmed her teeth along the top of my briefs and continued her little trick on her way across the width of my hips. Bite, pull, let it snap, lick. Repeat.

By the time she'd made it from one hip bone to the other, I was rock hard and straining against my underwear.

"What are you doing, princess?"

"Just enjoying myself. I like your little moans."

I involuntarily let out another one because she *liked* it.

"Open that pretty little mouth for me," I huffed and pushed down the last fabric barrier between me and her tongue. Drops of pre-cum already clung to my tip.

"Stop telling me what to do," she sing-sang with a big smile and rolled her eyes at me. Little brat. Fuck, I loved how much fun she was having even when I got rough with her, both with my words and my actions.

"Fine. I'll fuck that grin off you." I pinched her chin and guided her face right in front of me. When she still kept her perfect pouty lips sealed, all cheeky and proud of herself, I pushed my thumb in between them. She lapped at me without further prompting, so fucking eager.

I pushed her tongue down, wrenching her mouth open just enough to guide the head of my cock to her parted lips. They were so soft and rosy and pretty. I couldn't wait to ruin them.

"Same as last time," I breathed hard as I pulled my hand out and slid it back into her hair, "you flip me off if it's too much."

Esra gave me a small nod and one of those bunny-nose-scrunches.

And I buried myself inside the heat of her mouth.

She gasped and clawed at my thighs for a hold. Stroking her hair and her jaw, I gave both of us a moment. For her to adjust. For me to control the tension down my center that urged me to sink myself deep down her throat.

The second her tongue flicked against the underside of my cock, that control slipped. I thrust into her. Esra's breath stuttered. I knew my size could be uncomfortable, and I pulled back instantly, but she only gave me two inches before delving forward again herself.

A muscle I hadn't even known existed unclenched deep in my chest.

She wanted this, wanted me, didn't give my insecurities the chance to sneak in.

Her lips tightened around me as she sucked me deeper. My cock was wrapped up in her hot mouth, and her tongue lapped at me, spurring me on. My thrusts sped up, and Esra met my movements with little huffs.

And then she cupped her fingers around my balls and sent a red-hot shiver down my spine.

"Esra," I groaned.

She giggled – actually giggled – and let my cock spring from her lips with a *plop* like a goddamn lollipop. She'd soaked it, and the fresh air teased my exposed skin. Between the chill and her warm fingertips working my balls, a short white ribbon shot from my tip. I moaned and gripped her hair tighter.

Fuck.

A girl who deserved all my patience, and I was close to busting within minutes. My abs had tightened, my core tense, every muscle desperate for release.

The first rivulet of cum had hit the corner of her mouth, and her tongue darted out to lick it off. Esra hummed in delight, smiling up at me. "Thanks," she chirped.

"How are you real?"

In lieu of replying, she ducked her head and licked the underside of my cock from root to tip.

I groaned, my hips buckled, and another streak of cum shot across her cheek. Esra was still smiling up at me, biting her lower lip.

"God, I really love the way you moan," she said.

"Princess, I'm about to——"

Esra wrapped her free hand around the tip of my cock and cut off my words. She pumped down my length and rubbed her thumb deep into my sack. I moaned, completely at her mercy. A third white splatter hit her face, and she didn't even flinch.

"That looks so fucking good on you."

"Yeah? If we were alone at your ranch, I'd let you come all over me."

"Shit. Get back here before I lose it," I groaned and directed her head back into position. This time her mouth parted readily. I sank my hands knuckle-deep into her hair, messing up the perfect ponytail, and pulled her against me at the same time as my hips snapped forward.

Esra squeezed my balls in the exact moment I hit the back of her throat.

Heat rushed over me.

My muscles spasmed.

I fired my release down her throat in hot pulses. She kept kneading my balls, working shot after shot of cum from me as the orgasm rocked through my body. I grabbed at her, leaned into her, reveled in her warmth. My vision was swimming, my senses shutting down, until I could only feel her. She was everywhere. In my veins. In my lungs. Behind closed lids.

I was still trembling and gasping for air when she leaned back.

The ruined mess of her ponytail, the smudged mascara around her eyes and the pink swelling of her lips were blatant signs of what we'd just done, but it was the specks of my release that still clung to her skin that elicited another groan from my chest. All mine.

"Are you okay?" she asked. She wiped her fingers over the wetness on her face and brought them to her lips to suck it off.

I laughed, because she was still being unreal. She'd just swallowed what felt like the biggest cum shot of my life, was licking the rest of it off her face, and she was asking *me* if I was okay.

"I've just been to heaven and back. I'm more than okay."

"Good." She beamed and wiggled her shoulders in a happy little dance. I had no idea how she switched from being the hottest combination of all my fantasies to being the cutest little thing in a matter of seconds. But it shot a bolt of lightning right through my chest.

"Come here," I huffed and helped her back to her feet. One hand wrapped around the back of her neck, I used the other to slide the cherry red scrunchy from her hair. I pulled it over my wrist instead.

Esra smiled up at me, watching intently while I fixed her hair. Couldn't let her walk out of here looking all roughed up. Her flushed cheeks and swollen lips I couldn't do anything about, but I also swiped my thumbs along the underside of her eyes, catching some of her mascara.

She just kept those warm brown eyes on me, all big and shiny.

"Stop looking at me like that," I muttered as I tucked the last pieces of hair into place behind her ears.

"Like what?"

"Like I hung the moon or something when I just fucked your face."

Esra giggled. "You're doing my hair."

"Yeah. I'm the one who messed it up. It's my job to fix it."

She shook her head at me and wrapped her arms around my shoulders again, curving her body into mine. "You're so earnest. When it doesn't drive me up the wall, it's actually incredibly sweet."

"Who's sweet on who now?" The words were out before I could stop them but, unlike me, Esra didn't seem to panic.

She stole a quick kiss from my lips and grinned. "Selective hearing much? I also said you're driving me up the wall. But fixing my hair is very sweet."

"I chose to focus on the positives."

"Ooh, a gentleman *and* an optimist. I like that." She brushed her nose against mine before she stepped back and took my hand. "Come on. I need food and a cold shower."

If she kept telling me how much she liked all those things about me, liked my home, liked the way I touched her, liked the sounds I made . . . I'd have to start believing her.

Neither of us brought up what this was or how we might feel again on the way home. It wasn't like we were going on dates or holding hands in public. *We* only existed in the moments we were alone.

Vivi may have accused me of becoming a hermit before, but I'd never wanted to be more reclusive than now, just to get more alone time with Esra.

Chapter Twenty

ESRA

"This place is beautiful," I said when I'd finished wandering around Adriana's house and come back to the kitchen. She didn't want to play tour guide, but she'd allowed me to explore the bungalow by myself. There wasn't a single white wall in her home. It was drenched in sunset colors, mossy greens and warm browns. The furniture was all mismatched and covered in throws and fabrics. Instead of bright overhead LEDs, it was lit up by cozy fairy lights and vintage table lamps with colorful glass shades. Suncatchers dangled in every window, reflecting rainbow prisms everywhere, and outside, lush flowerbeds bloomed around the entire house.

"Thanks," Adriana said. "My mom's the one with the green thumb."

"Does she live here, too?" I asked and glanced around for any sign of a parent living here. Not that I knew what to look for. The main trace my parents left behind was spotless minimalism.

"No, over there." She pointed her spatula at the window, toward a twin bungalow, separated from this one by hedges and trees. It couldn't be more than a three-minute walk from door to door, but it felt like just enough distance for some privacy. "My record deal wasn't massive, but it paid for these places, so that's pretty cool."

She shrugged as if that wasn't a big deal, so I wrapped my arm around her shoulder and squeezed.

"Yeah, that *is* pretty cool, Adriana."

"Thanks." She grimaced and rolled her shoulders out of my embrace. "I'm trying to cook here."

"Do you have a problem with affection?"

"No," she scoffed, very focused on poking at the risotto in the pan, "I'm hella affectionate."

"Uh-huh." I grinned and grabbed one of the wine glasses she'd set out.

Getting to know Adriana was like getting to know Shrek. Or peeling an onion. Layers. Lots of layers. I wasn't sure if she'd always been this opposed to letting people get close to her or if that was a side-effect of being the town's black sheep, but she was worth being patient with. She'd been nothing but kind and supportive since the day I got here. Case in point: inviting me to dinner because I was either eating at the saloon or surviving on pasta and cereal.

"And while we're on the topic, who are you getting all affectionate with, huh?"

"I wouldn't exactly call it affectionate."

"Down and dirty?" she asked.

"More like it." I weighed my head from side to side. Being with Noah wasn't unaffectionate either. Earlier today we had spent our entire seven minutes making out like teenagers. No orgasms at all. Just giggles and kisses. And in the little privacy we managed to carve out, a minute in the kitchen, or a moment when I got out of the bathroom and he got in, we brushed hands, and he told me I was beautiful, and I asked him about his day – and genuinely cared about his answer, too.

In some ways, I was grateful that those affections were short-lived. I wasn't sure if I could compartmentalize our thing as easily otherwise. We were just hooking up. Colleagues with benefits. The way my stomach fluttered when he looked at me from across the room was just physical attraction. He was hot, and he was good in bed, and he was likable enough. That was all.

It had to be all.

If it wasn't, then I'd have to start considering Sinan's plea not to mess up his life here. Or the fact that summer was already in full swing and I'd be leaving soon. Or that I had no idea what I'd be leaving for, or where I'd go.

So . . . nope.

Compartmentalizing.

Noah and I were just having sexual, sneaky, totally meaningless fun.

"Hello-ho?" Adriana snapped her fingers in front of my face, rings and bracelets jingling. "Earth to Esra."

"Sorry." I shook my head to clear it. "What?"

"God, I miss having the kind of sex that scrambles your brain like that."

"I'm sure Lucas would volunteer if you mentioned it in front of him," I said as I accepted the plate that she must have been holding out in front of me for a while.

"I've known Lucas since he wet his pants in kindergarten. He was the one who pointed out that I had a massive stain on my jeans when I first got my period on a class trip. There is no universe in which I could forget those things long enough to let him in my pants." Adriana faked a shudder and sat down at the small dining table with four mismatched chairs around it. "Besides, brain-scrambling sex requires more than just sex."

"Please enlighten me," I laughed.

"You need someone you trust enough to take you right to the edge of your comfort zone. That's where your brains get scrambled." She narrowed her eyes at me and I could practically hear the cogs turning inside her mind. "It's not Daddy Mayor, is it? You know Richard's married, right?"

"Ew, Adriana," I moaned around a forkful of delicious risotto.

"What? He's hot, you work with him every day and you both have a hard-on for trivia. It was a valid assumption."

"He's like twice our age."

"Yeah, but he parties like he's in his twenties. And he's hot. Don't pretend he isn't."

"Ew," I repeated and scrunched my nose up at her. "At least now we know the real reason you won't ever hook up with Lucas. You have daddy issues."

"Can't have daddy issues if you don't have a dad." She rolled her eyes at me as if I was ridiculous – and clearly to cover up the little layer she'd just peeled back for me. "Fine. I'll stop guessing. As long as you promise me he isn't married."

"He isn't married."

"Hmm." She chewed and tipped her head from side to side. "Big dick?"

"Yes," I laughed.

"Good for you."

"We should sign you up for a dating app." I reached across the table to grab her phone, but she snatched it away.

"Hell, no. I don't need all the tourists passing through the saloon to see my bikini thirst traps when they open Tinder. I'll just live vicariously through you until some hot older man from out of town comes around and whisks me off my feet."

After dinner, we spread out on the thick carpets on her living room floor. Adriana had one of those record players that looked like a little suitcase, and she played me her favorite country albums, musing about lyrics and chords and musical influences. I followed some of her explanations, but I mostly let my mind wander while my eyes roamed the pictures on the wall, of her on various stages and with various musicians. She was so young in some of those pictures, cheeks still round and her curly mane much shorter.

"Do you have a plan?" I asked, interrupting her monologue about Dolly Parton.

"What do you mean?"

"Did you give up on music? On all this?" I gestured at the wall of pictures. "Or are you just taking a break?"

Adriana's shoulders tightened and her lips flattened into a thin line. I thought she wouldn't answer, keeping all those layers wrapped tightly around herself, but she heaved a deep sigh instead. "Making music always felt right. It made me feel safe. And then it didn't anymore." She vaguely nodded toward the guitar stashed in the corner of the room, wedged between the sofa and the wall. "I can't touch it."

"Do you want to?"

"Not right now." She smoothed her hand over the vinyl sleeve in her lap. "But I know that I don't want to be a small-town music teacher who plays the open mic night circuit. Maybe it's juvenile not to settle, but I loved touring and playing for big crowds and working with insanely talented people."

"No, I get that." I nodded. "I don't want to work for big pharma just to sort of be in the medical field."

"If I never touch my own guitar again, I might become a sound tech. Or a producer. Or something else that tickles the same spot for me. I just don't want my hometown to still hate me when I do."

"I think people are warming up to you."

"One drink at a time," she agreed and tipped her glass at me. She took a long sip before she launched back into her declaration of love for Dolly Parton. Apparently, this was all the heartfelt conversation I'd get out of her tonight.

After another glass of wine and a deep dive into musicians who started out by playing in honky-tonks, Adriana produced a variety of long fruits and vegetables from the kitchen, trying to get me to find the closest size-match to Noah. I ate the banana and questioned how on earth a butternut squash was supposed to fit. She just laughed and ended up carrying the squash around for the rest of the night. She didn't get an actual answer from me though.

The rest of the night passed in a happy blur, but my thoughts kept circling back to her words. She could see herself doing something that *tickled the same spot* as making music.

Playing Annie Lou was fun. It even came with its own sense of fulfillment, but it didn't give me the same purpose that medicine had. There were some parallels when I boiled it down to making a person feel better, whether that was a patient or a park visitor, but I wanted more than that. I wanted to make a real difference in people's lives.

Adriana shrieked and my gaze snapped to the squash that had exploded at her feet. "Not my Grammy."

"Grammy? I thought it represented a massive dick."

"No, I decided it was a Grammy ten minutes ago," she giggled. "Keep up."

"Guess you do have to go back to making music, so you can win another one."

"Meh." She shrugged. "I can just buy another one in the veggie aisle. Ooh, we should go to the store. We can find you a vegetable, too. It can be an Oscar. Or a Tony. Or a Nobel— why are all the awards named after men? That's so sexist."

"I'm good," I laughed. "And there's the Emmy."

"Okay. Yes." She clapped her hands together, then turned and grabbed the cucumber off the counter. "The winner of the primetime Western Country Theme Park category is Esra Taner, for her breathtaking performance as Annie Lou."

My balance wavered a little as I got up and accepted the cucumber with a gracious smile and a small nod. "Thank you. Thank you. I have to thank the Academy, and also my best friend Adriana. Adriana, if you're watching this at home, it's time for bed."

"Watching this at home?" she scoffed. "I'm your plus one."

"No, you're not. If I'm going to the Emmys, I'm taking No— Nobody; I mean, *someone* to have crazy ballgown bathroom sex with during the commercial break." I was *not* going to worry about how Noah's name had almost slipped from my tongue. I had definitely *not* automatically imagined him in a hot three-piece suit, walking the red carpet with me. Nope.

"Ugh. Fine. Commence your speech." Adriana rolled her eyes at me but couldn't keep down a big smile. "You were just about to tell the world what an awesome friend I am."

I'd think about making a difference later.

Having fun was good enough for now.

Chapter Twenty-One

THE HAUNTED MINES

The gold mines around Bravetown have made many people their fortunes, but legend has it the mines demand payment in return. Every once in a while, miners disappear and only their screams remain within the deep tunnels. Are you brave enough to seek the treasure and the truth within the caves?

NOAH

With each passing day, it became harder to stay away from Esra, even if we might get spotted. I found myself wishing for more shows, just to have more of those heavenly seven minutes with her when we were out of everyone's sight. I went to game night and dinner with the rest of the cast, things I usually sat out in favor of working on the ranch or with the horses, just to spend a bit more time with her under the safe cover of a group outing.

I even proposed that we film more videos with Lucas. Maybe I could sneak in a fanfiction in which Ace and Annie kissed. Just for the cameras, of course.

"Come with me." I grabbed Esra's wrist when she walked out of the saloon on Monday night. Sanny had specifically asked me to stay away from tonight's dinner, give him and Esra some time to talk. He thought my presence would only provoke another fight.

I'd waited outside the saloon in the shadows like a goddamn stalker, watched Sanny leave fifteen minutes ago and stuck around for his little sister.

"What are you doing here?" Esra's head whipped around but the only other person outside the saloon was an older guy smoking and scrolling his phone.

"I want to show you something. Come on." I laced my fingers through hers and tugged her toward the park gates.

"I'm not hooking up with you in the park at night. I don't need one of the security guards catching us. I've met them. I know them. Deacon's wife makes sure to keep some Reese's Minis back for me if they're low on stock at Bart's Mart. I could never go back if he caught me giving you head behind the popcorn cart."

"God, you're cute." I shot a quick look around to make sure it was safe before I leaned down and pressed a quick kiss to her lips. "Everyone knows everyone here. There's very few secrets in this town, and people still show their faces in public."

"I'm serious," she huffed but let herself be pulled through the gates. They clicked open without issue, thanks to our badges.

"I won't ask you to give me head behind the popcorn cart," I promised.

"Noah . . ." She squeezed my hand and blinked up at me, shadows circling beneath her eyes. "Sinan caught wind that Renee wants to replace me, and he's not a fan of the videos and me putting my face out there like that. I've just sat through a very exhausting dinner. Can this wait until tomorrow?"

"I'm sorry." I didn't say more because we never talked about her brother, but I cupped her face in my hands and turned us, so anyone outside the gates would only see the silhouette of my shoulders from afar. Her lids fluttered shut and she leaned into my touch. I knew that if I could only kiss her, touch her, I could make her feel better in seconds, but we were still out in the open. "The thing I want to show you only happens once a year, but it might cheer you up."

"Oh?" Her interest was piqued enough for her to look up again.

"Come on."

We only walked a bit further into the park when the noise started giving it away. Esra's face snapped up. Her eyes narrowed on the dark roller coaster. The tracks were barely illuminated by a few security lights, but the train still rattled as it plunged downwards. She spotted the children's carousel next, twirling round and round, the horses moving up and down, but no doodling music and no lights giving it its usual charm.

"It's an insurance thing. Once a year, all rides are run for twenty-four hours straight to keep track of any technical issues that might not pop up otherwise," I explained. "When I was a kid, someone told me that we had to open the park for ghosts one night of the year to prevent it getting haunted the other 364 days."

"That's cute," Esra laughed.

"It scared the crap out of me. I circled that day on my calendar and stayed far, far away from the park."

"Why? Look at them." She pointed at the roller coaster. "All the little ghosts are having the best time ever."

"Little ghosts? Maybe they're big and murderous."

"No." She shook her head decisively and turned me by the arm toward the carousel. "I think that's a sweet thought. I had a friend at the hospital when I was little. Juliet. She died of some genetic thing. I didn't really get it back then. She was always there when I was, so I always had someone to play with. And then she was just gone, but people checked in and out of the hospital all the time, so it didn't really register with me. That said, if people stick around as ghosts, I think it would be nice for the little ones to get free rein here for a night."

She smiled and the sincerity in her eyes needled its way right to my heart.

"Well, now I feel bad. I was going to say we can ride any attraction you want tonight, but I don't want to take a seat away from a ghost child."

Esra seemed to genuinely ponder for a moment. That either made her the most unhinged or the most considerate person I'd ever met. Jury was still out. Both seemed to work for me though.

"Haunted Mines," she said, "because if I was a ghost on my day off, I wouldn't want to deal with any inaccurate depictions of ghost hauntings."

"Of course. That's the only logical solution."

She slapped the back of her hand against my chest. "Don't make fun of me and my ghost children. I just want them to be happy."

"I want your ghost children to be happy, too," I said and caught her wrist to kiss her knuckles. I kept her hand against my chest as we made our way over to the Haunted Mines, reveling in the bit of casual physical contact. One of the security guards walked past us, and I just greeted him and told him we'd have to check on the horses. He didn't seem to care that the stables were at the opposite end of the park.

The entrance to the Haunted Mines was shaped like a skull carved from stone, and we had to walk through the gaping mouth to get to the carriages. Unlike the roller coaster's train, this ride had individual carts, each shaped like an egg. The bottom part looked like a hollow boulder with a bench inside, while the top half was made from metal grating. The cage kept guests from reaching out to touch stuff, but it also allowed staff members to jump out of the shadows and rattle the cart a little. That was the most thrill you got on this ride. There were no drops or loopings. The carts only went in one direction and swiveled left and right.

Without anyone attending the controls, we had to sprint for a cart, get in and latch the door within seconds. We made it by the skin of our teeth. My heart pulsed in the back of my throat. Raw nerves told me that we'd been too close to jamming the ride. Meanwhile, Esra collapsed on top of me on the bench, half-sprawled out, laughing.

"We did it. That was so close," she wheezed, brushing a tear from the corner of her eye. Her laughter reverberated through my chest, easing some of the tension there.

"Yeah," I breathed, "so close."

"You okay?" She pushed herself up but not off me. She slid deeper into my lap, back resting against my chest, and kissed the side of my face.

"I just realized how irresponsible this is." We could fuck up the whole insurance thing. I was pretty sure it wasn't cheap to run the whole park at night without the ticket sales to offset the running cost. If we fucked that up somehow, it would definitely be grounds for firing.

I usually wasn't this reckless, but I'd wanted to spend the evening with her. Alone. Having fun. Somehow, the possible consequences hadn't even crossed my mind.

"Too late to back out now," Esra whispered as the cart rounded the first corner and we were greeted by a sinister voice relaying the history of the mines. She settled in and pulled my arms around her waist in lieu of a belt. Getting to hold her like that immediately eradicated all worries about the potential fallout of this date.

The Haunted Mines were a very child-friendly attraction, but Esra's stomach still trembled under my hands as her eyes drank in the story. I watched her face light up in shades of red and purple through the ride, mouth slightly ajar. I tightened my hold on her when she jumped at the mechatronic spider monster that shot out from one of the caves.

"Was this your first time?" I asked as we rattled toward the exit.

"Nope. I think I've been two or three times. I love it. I keep finding new little details that I missed before."

"You still jumped at the spider."

"Because spiders are scary, even when you know they're there. Duh."

Her weight lifted off me. Rather than dashing for the exit, however, Esra slid back into my lap, facing me this time. Her knees hugged my thighs on either side and her fingers grazed into the back of my shirt.

"Hi." She leaned her forehead against mine. "I missed you."

"I missed you, too, princess."

It was a ridiculous thing to say. I saw her every day for hours on end. But I missed holding her and touching her the way I had at the ranch. I'd gotten a taste of more when she'd fallen apart for me in the rain. How was I supposed to come back from that?

Our cart rolled past the exit and back into the dark tunnel, granting me at least a few more minutes alone with her.

"Would you rather kiss a ghost while a girl watches, or kiss a girl while a ghost watches?"

"Since we've already established the ghosts aren't murderous, I'll kiss the girl. Let the ghosts watch for all I care."

"You'd kiss a murderous ghost?" She laughed and her sweet breath tickled my lips.

"Survival instinct. I figure it wouldn't kiss and kill me."

"Of course. Only logical."

Nails biting into the skin of my neck, Esra pulled me to her for a kiss. It was gentle at first. Lips and noses brushed soft and slow. I let my hands roam down her sides and into the hem of her top. The second my fingertips connected with her skin, a switch flipped. All sweetness dissipated from her mouth. We'd both been starving for each other and the kiss turned from hungry to ravenous in seconds.

When she leaned back to catch a breath, her lips were red and swollen. God, the things I wanted to do to those lips. I'd have to get another night with her, just so I could kiss and bite and fuck those lips.

My jeans strained against the pressure building in my groin. I knew Esra felt it too, because her eyes dropped, and she shifted her weight slightly. She ground herself against me, the friction of fabrics almost painful on my hardening dick.

"Fuck," I hissed.

"Remember how you said we could go on any attraction?"

"Yeah," I replied warily. The exit was only a corner away, but I didn't want to leave yet.

"Your thighs are the real main attraction, you know?"

"My thighs?" I asked, running my hands up hers, which seemed far more interesting than mine as I pushed her little skater skirt up to her hips. She wore a pair of thin lacy panties underneath that just begged to be ripped off.

"Yeah, I get the whole riding-the-cowboy thing now." She shrugged, not taking her eyes off me as we entered and passed the exit hall. "It's those juicy thighs you get from sitting in the saddle. Your lap was made for me to sit on."

"I don't object to the sitting, but there has to be a better word than juicy."

"No, they're juicy." She wiggled her brows and leaned in to kiss me. Her tongue flicked against my lips just before pulling back again with a sassy grin. "Thick and juicy."

"I'm going to shut you up now, silly woman." I took her by the back of the neck and pulled her to me for a kiss that left no room for sass. She squealed and braced her hands against my shoulders. She pushed back just enough to whisper *"juicy"* one last time before her mouth was back on mine and her body shuddered against me.

The Haunted Mines officially became my new favorite ride when I tied Esra's wrists to the cage's roof with my belt and denied her release until she was flushed and breathless and unable to get the word *juicy* past her lips.

Chapter Twenty-Two

THE MOONLIGHT CASINO

Place your bets and try your luck in the Arcade at the Moonlight Casino. Purchase your gold tokens at the booth and then step right up! Make the daily high-score board, compete against friends, and take home adorable prizes.

Games are evaluated for content using American Amusement Machine Association (AAMA) standards.

NOAH

The next time the Stallions put on their cowboy burlesque show at the saloon, all the girls were there again, including Zuri. Things had been a little tense between Esra and her brother. I hadn't asked for more details, but seeing her and Zuri become more talkative and smiley over cocktails was good. If things turned sour between them, I wasn't sure where I'd stand anymore. A few weeks ago, I would have automatically sided with Sinan on everything. Now . . .

I hung back by the bar just so I could walk Esra home after the show. The stage lights swiveled through the room too brightly for my taste, the music was too loud, and I definitely wasn't interested in the shirt-ripping on stage. At some point one of the ladies from accounting came up to me and offered to set me up with her nephew – because why else would I be at a male burlesque show – but I barely even looked at her, too focused on Esra leaning over the balcony to point at something, drink sloshing in her glass. If Adriana noticed me staring while she refilled my water, she didn't say anything. She and Esra had gotten close, so for all I knew, she was already aware of what was going on and had been sworn to secrecy.

Two of the dancers spotted Vivi wearing a crown and sash for her birthday and made their way to the staff balcony. Somehow their cowboy hats, oiled chests and body rolls had all the girls whooping and hollering. The pink and blue cocktails may have been at fault for that too. Watching from afar, sober and straight, the whole thing just gave me second-hand embarrassment. Right up until one of the dancers swung a leg over Esra's chair to give her a lap dance. His denim Speedos were keeping things contained by a thread. I clenched my fists, ready to rip this man off my girl.

I could. For all anyone knew, I was just making sure Sanny's little sister wasn't getting whipped in the face by a stranger's dick.

"Down, boy." Adriana slammed a bowl of nuts on the counter in front of me.

"Excuse me?"

"It's supposed to be funny and embarrassing." Adriana clasped my underarm on the bar, keeping me rooted in place even as Esra clearly shook her head and waved the dancer's unwanted attention off. "They actually have a very strict contract about not getting frisky with any of the saloon guests."

"How do you know that?"

"Because that guy grinding up on Esra is called Sam. He has a pierced dick. And I'm not technically a guest at the saloon." She whipped her hair over one shoulder and shrugged.

"I get why you and Esra get along so well." I shot another look at Sam, but lucky for him, he shimmied his way over to the next lap. Esra had a hand clasped over her face, laughing. "She told you?"

"Nope. Well, only that she's getting it good, but thanks for confirming."

"Fuck. You're not part of the betting pool, are you?"

"Technically, yes, but I put my money on her punching you in the nuts. We'll just have to wait and see on that one."

"Great, thanks."

"Hey, if you keep up the jealous watchdog act, I might get my payout sooner rather than later."

Instead of rising to the bait, I turned around and put my attention back where it belonged. Every now and again, Esra looked over her shoulder and scrunched up her nose or gave me a smile, just to acknowledge my presence.

Every single look squeezed the air from my chest. Maybe I was jealous after all.

The second we were home and in our hallway, and I was sure no one would see, I pulled her into my bedroom. I just needed her to myself, just for a few minutes.

"Ooh, scandalous! Are you going to rip my clothes off, Young?" She twirled in the center of my room, swaying lightly.

"You're gonna have to be quiet, princess," I whispered and furled my arms around her, shushing her with the kind of kiss I'd wanted to break out in the saloon, in front of everyone, just to mark my goddamn territory. She tasted like sugar and champagne.

"Then you have to keep my mouth busy." She grabbed her shirt and started pulling it up, but I pushed her hands back down.

Esra let out a little whimper and stuck her bottom lip out. She was learning far too quickly what that pout did to me, my dick stirring just at the sight. I still kept my hands on hers, leading her to my bed fully dressed. She let me guide her to sit on my mattress and her hands were immediately on my belt.

Again, I pushed her eager fingers away.

I deserved a gold medal for self-restraint.

"I'll keep your mouth busy in a bit," I promised and sank down in front of her. "Give me five minutes."

"I'm not going to be quiet if you eat me out," she replied at full volume. "Impossible, sorry."

"Will you please be quiet for just a second?"

She let out an annoyed groan but let me pull the baggy jeans off her hips and the boots off her feet. Her perfectly curved, smooth legs tried to wrap around my shoulders, and I pushed them down with a chuckle. I loved how much she unabashedly wanted me, but she was too tipsy for me to act on it. Instead, I methodically unlatched the Velcro on her knee brace, wiggling it to the right first, so I could take it off without the scratchy bits irritating the scars.

"Oh, that's nice," she sighed and dropped back on the bed.

"Just you wait until I get to the ankles."

"That's some next-level dirty talk, mister."

I'd helped her with the braces a couple of times. She wore the ankle braces for every show, but the knee brace only came out when she was dealing with some pain and needed the extra stability. Mondays seemed to be bad, after the double shows on weekends, but the other day it had been enough for her to try and turn in the middle of walking up the stairs, twisting her knee in the process.

"How's that?" I asked after freeing her ankles too. I crawled on to the mattress next to her, brushing my hand through her hair. Her eyes had already fallen shut but she smiled and leaned into my touch.

"You make me feel good," she mumbled.

"Good." I kept stroking her hair, listening to her little comfortable hums. "You make me feel . . . confused."

She didn't reply again, now peacefully asleep in my bed.

Probably for the better. I wasn't sure I even wanted to know how she'd respond once I admitted that I was getting jealous of other men, that I was looking forward to every minute with her, that I felt protective of her in a way I had no right to be.

I contemplated taking a shower, or at least brushing my teeth, but I didn't want Esra to wake up alone and half-naked in a bed she didn't recognize. So I just shucked off my jeans and boots, pulled her up on the mattress and tucked her against me.

The next night, my door creaked open just after midnight and Esra tiptoed to my bed. She peppered little kisses along the underside of my jaw and slipped her cold feet between my legs.

At least I wasn't the only one who couldn't keep my distance.

I stayed in her room one night, but that dissolved quickly the next morning when I started picking up the most basic laundry around her room. I earned myself a pair of socks against the head before she kicked me out the door for playing housekeeper.

Austin had walked past me standing in the hallway with my arms full of women's socks, had merely shaken his head and started typing on his phone. If someone in his group chat had bet on me developing a foot fetish, they'd owe me a goddamn drink.

After that, Esra slipped into my room exclusively at night. I was too aware of the betting pool though. If people were already watching us, I didn't need them listening to us, too. As fucking hot as it was, Esra wasn't quiet when she climaxed, and I didn't need Sanny to hear about us sleeping together because Austin had fifty bucks riding on it or something.

So I let her hands slip under my shirt and I wrapped mine around her back and I made her tell me about her daily meet and greets. It was supposed to be a distraction. But it turned out that, now that we were posting more videos with Lucas, some park guests had started asking her uncomfortable questions and filming her reactions. They usually revolved around the Kit/Annie/Ace triangle. Talking it out seemed to help her unwind.

"I promise it will die down if you don't acknowledge it," I whispered against the top of her head after she detailed a group of teens that her meet and greet assistants had struggled to keep under control. They were eventually kicked out of the park for some of the lewd gestures they made.

"Yeah, easy for you to say. You just get women swooning over you." Her hands balled into fists over my stomach.

"People get bored, trust me. When I first started posting online, I had people come to the meet and greet just to tell me their detailed fantasies about being kidnapped and tied up by Ace Ryder."

In retrospect, maybe that had fucked me in the head, considering how much easier it had been for me to believe Esra wanted the fantasy, not the reality. I didn't want this to leave a similar mark on her.

She tilted her head back, her nose sporting a dangerous rosy sheen. Fuck. Was she about to cry? What did I do? What did you do with a crying girl? Chocolate? There was an emergency stash of peanut butter cups in my nightstand as of three days ago, when I'd learned the definition of hangry.

"Don't cry," I pleaded and smoothed some hair back from her forehead.

"I'm not," she rasped, voice dangerously clogged. "It was just worse because it was teenagers. Teens are scary, man. I didn't even get them when I *was* a teenager."

"As someone who did a lot of fucked-up shit as a teenager, I can promise you that none of that was about you today."

"You? Fucked up? Like, you ate your dessert before the main course?" She snickered.

"Hmm . . ." I brushed my lips over hers. "I stole a cow once."

"A cow? Like, from a farm?"

"No, that's what made it so funny. Mr. Wilkens had her

in his backyard. She was some pageant cow. Had won prizes for the shiniest coat or something. But she was stuck all alone in his tiny backyard, so I got her out of there and set her free to roam in the high school's football field. She frolicked around the whole weekend before anyone noticed."

"Are you making this up to make me feel better?"

"They couldn't calm her down enough to herd her out of there. By the time they got someone down from the cattle ranch, she'd completely ruined the grass. I cost the school a whole season of football games."

"How did you get her in the stadium in the first place?"

"Put a rope around her neck one night and walked by her side from Mr. Wilkens' to the school. No problem. She clearly knew that I was leading her to greener grass."

Esra let out a quiet little giggle, more breath than sound against my collar bone. "If that wasn't about the cow or Mr. Wilkens, why did you do it?"

"Because I could. My mother was dying and my father was on a bender, and everyone knew. They let me get away with anything. I just wanted someone to give a shit."

"I'm sorry."

"Don't be. I'm just telling you because teenagers aren't scary. They do dumb things to deal with their own issues."

"I give a shit," she whispered and nestled against my chest, quiet for a few moments while drawing slow patterns across my stomach. "Can't believe I'm sleeping with a real-life cowboy."

Saving horses. There was a joke about how she was saving horses in there. My mind stumbled over itself as it tried to come up with the wording, still blanking by the time her breathing evened out and her hands stilled. Maybe

I was wound too tight. After years of holding it together, I wasn't sure if I was even able to unwind. Maybe the part of me that was supposed to be fun and carefree had rusted into a rigid, unmovable thing.

I lay awake for a while and stared at the ceiling because somehow Esra had turned me into a man agitating over coming up with "save a horse, ride a cowboy" jokes just to hear her tired little giggle again.

It was irrational. I was fully aware of that. If I hadn't been, the two dozen people trailing me across the park would have been a dead giveaway. Anna and CJ had shot me panicked looks. They had protocols on how they should handle guests going rogue – not cast members. There were very specific schedules and routes mapped out for the character meet and greets, but my rationale was gone after last night. I was back to the caveman instincts that told me to protect Esra from the storm. The storm just took the form of shitposting teenagers now.

"Excuse me, miss?" I drawled in Ace Ryder's voice as I walked up behind Esra just as she finished taking pictures with a little girl in a matching Annie Lou costume.

Esra turned, eyes wide. Her gaze raked over me, those full lips falling open. I had the bandana around my neck, but I was in the full-length duster that I only threw on for photographs, that she usually didn't get to see. So, yeah, okay, the costume still did it for her. We'd have to do something with that at some point.

"Me?" she asked, blinking rapidly as she caught herself.

I saw the phones going up and noted the people behind me falling quiet, but I kept my sole focus on Esra as I slightly tipped my hat. "Yes, miss, please excuse me for being so forward, but you look like your daddy's got money."

Esra's cheek twitched but she kept her expression schooled in the perfectly polite Annie Lou smile.

"Don't tell him!" A little girl in pink sparkly cowgirl boots raced around me and waved her hands in front of Esra. "He's the bad guy!"

"A bad guy?" Esra feigned surprise. "I don't know about that. He said, 'please excuse me'. Those are some very good manners. Sir, would you please tell this young lady that you have no bad intentions."

"I suppose that depends on your definition of *bad*, miss. I do enjoy being a little bad every now and then, just like everyone else."

"Annie, that's Ace Ryder!" The girl tugged on Esra's sleeve, only for her father to scoop her up and whisper something in her ear as he pulled her back to the sideline of the little circle that had formed around us.

"Ace Ryder? Where have I heard that name before?"

"Does it matter? Surely you don't rely on other people's opinions," I said, walking around her back, letting one gloved finger trail along her shoulders, "when you can form your own impression?"

All those fanfiction videos we'd been doing must have gone to my head. I was shamelessly flirting here. Esra's eyes fluttered, and she swallowed visibly as her gaze followed my finger lift from her shoulder and touch my lips.

"I don't mean to be rude, but I have guests waiting. They are visiting Bravetown and, as the mayor's daughter, I really should greet them." She vaguely gestured to the crowd, who let out some cheers at being acknowledged.

"The mayor's daughter, you say?" I tilted my chin up and ran my hand along the bandana just to remind everyone where this whole thing was going to lead. "I would love to hear more about your father's beautiful town. Maybe I can stay and help you greet the visitors, and you can tell me more."

Somewhere the little girl from before shouted a heartfelt "No!"

"I'm not sure. Let me ask them." Esra turned to the crowd with a big smile. "Would you mind if my new friend, Mr. Ryder, and I welcomed you in town together?"

Of course they cheered. They were getting a two-for-one photo opportunity. But Esra still seemed a little relieved at the positive reaction when she turned back to me and gave me a small nod.

"All right then, Mr. Ryder. You may greet them with me."

"Please," I said, taking her hand and bowing low to kiss her knuckles, "call me Ace."

Chapter Twenty-Three

Esra

"Eat something." Noah set a lunch box down next to my
thighs alongside a glass of iced tea. I was prepared to give
him shit for his sliced vegetables again, but the little compartments in the lunch box actually held a whole variety of
snacks today. Sure, carrots and cucumber and red radish,
but there were also cheese cubes, dino nuggets and a few
pieces of my favorite chocolates.

If I hadn't been already becoming obsessed with this
man, the dino nuggets would have tipped the scales.

"Two secs," I said as I set the PDF to print double-sided.
I sat on the floor of his so-called office at the ranch,

surrounded by a new printer, some of the articles I'd printed on equine-assisted therapy, and three actionable lists of next steps divided by renovations, therapy and admin.

On our last few days off, Sinan had come here with Noah to paint, or fix lights and fences, which had totally robbed us of the chance to spend time alone. *Quality* time alone. Noah had his own place, far away from the rest of our roommates, and I was still going purple with sexual frustration. Maybe not sexual frustration. We still got plenty of orgasms in. Intimacy frustration? I wanted to climb into Noah's lap and rest my forehead on his shoulder and feel his chest against mine without time limits or worrying who might see us.

Zuri had taken Sanny to Nashville today to get some stuff for his birthday party, so we were completely free. We'd come here first thing in the morning, before anyone else was awake and would see us leave together, both of us practically vibrating with pent-up energy on the drive over.

He didn't even let me get out of the car myself. I'd just opened the passenger door, and he was there and lifted me up without so much as a strained breath. He carried me up to his attic bedroom and didn't let me come up for air for what felt like hours. Knowing how fast he could get me off if he wanted to, made it so much more excruciatingly delicious when he kept me on edge until I was red-faced and sweaty. He still cradled me afterward like I was the most beautiful thing he'd ever seen, and he hadn't just fucked me like he hated me. I drew swirls in the smattering of hair on his chest while he whispered kisses and plans for the ranch against the crown of my head.

Noah wanted to enroll in a therapeutic riding instructor course for proper accreditation, but he'd never taken a course of any kind, so he'd asked me to take a look at the brochure in his office. He had no idea of the monster he'd unleashed on his paperwork. If there was one thing I was good at, it was studying. Dissecting texts, streamlining information, creating study guides for maximum efficiency? That was my jam.

Now I sat half-naked, wearing only his T-shirt, in his office, grateful for the cool floorboards against the hot, sore skin of my backside.

He had some entirely wrong forms in his files, which frustrated me at first because it seemed like a stupid oversight, but I quickly understood once I saw the useless mobile versions of the government websites he'd downloaded them from. And Noah didn't have a computer. I used a good chunk of my last paycheck to order him a refurbished one, which should make all of this easier. He could even use it for his course. If I'd known ahead of time, I would have brought mine from home. I'd barely touched it since clicking ctrl+a+delete on last semester's study notes.

"Where did you learn all this?" he asked when I pushed the printer away and reached for a cheese cube.

"I can tell you, but you might see me differently afterward."

"I see you differently every day I learn more about you. So far, it's working in your favor." He settled down next to me, his large hand wrapping around my thigh.

"Gee, thanks."

"I mean, I haven't learned anything about you that could make me like you any less."

"You *like* me, cowboy?" I teased.

"You're deflecting."

"You're so observant." I playfully rolled my eyes at him and looked over my neatly sorted piles. "I figured out early on, thanks to many clueless doctors, that having the right knowledge at the right time can be vital. I realized that the best way to learn as much as I could was by learning *how* to learn first. The other kids around me were starting to get into simple division, and I was reading textbooks on metacognition, analyzing my own way of absorbing information, and then reading up on different learning styles that I could apply to my specific way of thinking. I figured out that I don't necessarily need a live teacher, or auditory input, but visualization in text or examples helps." I held up the printed-out articles.

"Esra, you're a massive nerd," Noah chuckled.

I opened my mouth to reply but he stifled my words with a kiss. He pinched my chin to tilt it just right for access, his tongue teasing mine.

I broke out of the kiss. "I'm reformed though. You can't think of me as nerdy anymore."

"I've known you were secretly nerdy since that drunk trivia game. Still had to whisk you out of there the second I saw someone else's hat on you. You're *my* secret nerd, princess."

My stomach fluttered at the thought of being *his* anything, but I wasn't sure if that was nerves or butterflies. I cleared my throat. "Okay, well, it's going to stay a secret. I've started a new chapter in my life."

"I'm great at keeping secrets these days, don't worry."

Our eyes locked. There it was. We were a secret. This

was the first time either of us had properly addressed the issue other than that time he told me the walls of the staff housing complex were too thin for us to hook up in the comfort of our bedrooms. There had been a silent understanding that *we* were not a public thing.

Sinan had clearly been on both of our minds. I didn't see that conversation pan out well.

And beyond that . . . we weren't exactly throwing roses at each other's feet and talking baby names.

What if he wanted that though? Did I?

I shook my head and cleared my throat before my mind could run away on that train of thought.

"Anyway. Thank you," he said, and gestured at the stacks.

"You're very welcome." I smiled, grateful to get back to safe topics. A little bit of organization was nothing, and if it made his life easier, I might as well crank out those skills.

He kissed the tip of my nose. "I don't know what I'd do without you."

That was not a safe choice of words. Not when he'd put the other thought in my mind. I wasn't sure where we stood, and I sure as hell wasn't sure what my life was going to look like two months from now. Maybe he'd have to make do without me. My attention dropped back to the stacks of paper and suddenly it didn't feel like *nothing*, it didn't feel like *skills*. It felt like routine.

"I can show you the app I use to stay on top of things," I said, needing to offload all this work. "It's customizable, so you can make folders and lists the way they work for your brain."

"Metacognition," he echoed.

"Yup, exactly." My voice came out clipped. I brought up the app on my phone and handed it over.

Summer > Bravetown

To Do
- [x] Research horse noises
- [x] Buy Adriana's album
- [x] Test new ankle braces for a whole day
- [x] Order new leggings
- [ ] Start budget planner
- [ ] ~~Buy condoms (out of town!)~~
- [ ] Set up social media account for Annie?
- [ ] Buy birthday present for Sanny

Projects
- FanficQuotes.zip
- EATherapy books.pdf

Notes
- Neigh (also whinny or bray) = normal horse sound, method of communication, mouth open Nicker = lower clucky sound, often used as greeting or in courting
- *Now/Here* by Adriana Banks
- Birthday present ideas: wallet, Pass the Pigs, wedding bow tie

He leaned his chin on my shoulder as he read. "Your summer to-do list included buying condoms?"

"That was before we'd slept together. They were meant

for you though." We'd at least both discussed our STD-free bills of health since, so that item had dropped off the list altogether. I hadn't missed the fact he caught the folder's title though. He'd called it my *summer* to-do list.

Shit, shit, *shit.*

Did he want to ask about that? Was he going to ask me to stay longer than the summer?

I wasn't sure what I'd say if he did.

I hadn't found anything yet that filled me with the same sense of purpose as medicine, so I didn't really have a reason to leave. But I didn't want my summer of fun to end with me settling into a lifestyle that I hadn't actually chosen for myself – not at Yale, and not here. Even if staying meant that I got more of Noah. I'd get more of the little smiles that he reserved for when he thought no one else was looking. I'd get more soft pats high on my thigh when I sat on the horse and he told me I was doing a good job staying in the saddle. Heck, I even wanted more of his grumpy eye-rolls.

Or maybe he'd meant the opposite.

Maybe he meant to imply that he was just seeing this as a summer fling.

We had to rewind. Those last five minutes were too close to bursting our perfectly compartmentalized boxes. If I had to throw myself on top of those boxes like they were grenades, I would. Get back to being obsessed with his tongue between my legs, and his moans and the way he could cuff both my wrists in one of his hands – without any of the mental gymnastics of what it might mean.

I had no forewarning as Noah pulled me into his lap and spread my legs to either side of him. I yelped as he slipped a finger into me, still sensitive and hot.

"I'm glad you didn't get to buy any. I much prefer you bare like this anyway."

"Good," I gasped, only referring to the fact that he had clearly panicked just as much as me, and sex seemed like a safe change of topic right now.

He slowly moved back and forth, teasing my muscles until they relaxed enough for him to add a second finger. I shuddered under the perfect strain, letting the feel of him engulf my every thought.

"You should know that I have a to-do list, too, princess."

"Oh yeah, cowboy?"

I leveraged myself against his shoulders, so I could tip my hips against his hand. Each move stirred the crushing current of my orgasms back up after it had quieted only an hour or two ago. This felt good. Sex was easy.

"I'm going to make you come in every room of this house."

I gasped a laugh because that to-do list was ridiculous – and it sounded perfect. My laugh turned into a moan when he pushed down to his knuckles and curled his fingers. He hit that sweet spot. My pussy clenched around him, and I dropped my forehead against his.

"Okay," I whimpered and closed my eyes, trying to piece together words through the blood rushing in my ears, "that could take a while. Do you have a specific plan?"

"No," his breath mixed with mine, our lips skimming but not closing to a kiss, "I just want to replace every awful memory of this place with good ones. I want to walk into every room and be reminded of how prettily you fall apart for me."

He wanted to make memories with me? In his family

home? That was not the kind of plan you made with a summer fling.

He caught me off-guard. My eyes flew open and my grasp on him slipped. Still mid-thrust, the momentum shot my right arm forward over the top of his shoulder. Before I could react, my hand collided with the edge of the windowsill. The wood bit into my palm. I should have been able to use that to my advantage, grab the windowsill and catch myself – but my wrists weren't made for that kind of support. Instead, my upper palm caught but the heel of my hand still jutted forward and bent my wrist at an unnatural angle. The back of my hand slanted toward my arm. Pain shot through my wrist. And then the heel of my hand finally collided with the wall under the windowsill, breaking my momentum.

"Ah, fuck!" I yanked my arm back, cradling it to my chest.

"Shit. Are you okay?" Noah's hands wrapped around my middle, just a moment too late to steady me.

"Yeah, I'm fine," I grumbled as the immediate strain ebbed into a thickly pulsing pain. This had to be the stupidest way anyone had ever sprained their wrist. Barreled into a sex injury by fear of commitment.

"Let me see," he said and tried to reach for my arm.

"Noah," I shrieked and leaned back, "your fingers are covered in . . . well . . . us."

He hesitated, hand still mid-air. His index and middle finger glistened with the remnants of my arousal and his previous orgasm.

"Fair enough." He awkwardly reached across with his other hand, and I just groaned and turned away from it.

I didn't need to be babied. If he didn't know about my stupid issues with my tissues, we'd be laughing right now, and having silly sex. "Esra, at least let me see if you need an ice pack."

"I'm fine," I sighed and lifted the sprained wrist up to his eye level. It was *maybe* swelling up, minimally, but if I had to make an educated guess, the pain would mostly be gone within three days. Sooner if I wrapped it up nice and tight.

Noah leaned forward and brushed his lips over the inside of the wrist. "Kiss to make it better," he said with a small smile.

A cynical part of me wanted to roll my eyes and tell him to move on, but there was something so genuine and soft about the moment that my heart beat loud enough to drown out everything else. He was comforting me in the simplest way.

"Again," I whispered.

Noah complied. He carefully closed his lips over my pulse point.

My chest seized as it tried to contain the wild beating in my ribcage.

"Again."

Noah smiled and kissed the inside of my palm, and every bit of pain dissipated from my body. All I felt was my heart fluttering like a hummingbird.

Oh.

Oh no.

That wasn't supposed to happen.

When Renee cited me in for a talk, I'd expected her to introduce me to my replacement, but nobody but her waited in her office for me. I wasn't entirely sure how all the online things were going. Lucas was very good at only keeping me in the loop on the positive feedback we got. That included people now actually submitting their fanfic snippets and even writing little scenes for us to act out. It was fun to engage with people like that. We were all playing make-believe in the same little universe. But there might be just as many negative comments, and I'd have no idea.

"I want to talk to you about two things today," Renee said, gesturing for me to sit, "but I know it's scary when the boss calls you in, so let me reassure you that your job is safe."

"Okay . . ." I drew the word out. That wasn't reassuring at all. That meant there were two issues other than finding a new Annie Lou.

I glanced down at my bare wrist. I'd only worn my brace around the house the last two days, and the sprain hadn't impacted the shows, so I doubted this was one of her reasons.

"Let's start with the harder one." She cleared her throat and tilted her head, watching me intently. "I thought it might be easier to talk to me than to a stranger in HR, but I've never had to deal with something like this, so please excuse my directness. Are you being pressured into a relationship that you may not feel comfortable with?"

"What?" My mouth fell open. Surely, she couldn't mean . . .

"There are security cameras in all our rides. Most people don't realize that they run even when the park is technically closed. I did my monthly spot-check, and, well . . ."

Oh shit. I felt the color drain from my face. All the blood rushed to my heart, making it beat a thousand miles a minute.

"I am so sorry, Renee. I . . . I have . . ."

She held up a hand to silence me. "If this is a consensual relationship, we can discuss next steps. There's no problem with employees dating, but we'd have to figure out some consequences for the . . . indiscretion. I mean, beyond your responsibility to represent Bravetown as a family-friendly environment at all times when you're in the park, there's also the very improper use of park machinery that I didn't think we'd ever actually have to include in the employee guidebook. Even if so, my money would have been on the spouting fountain, I mean . . ." She cut herself off and took a deep breath. "Look, I am aware that there are some difficulties between you and Noah. He's older and he's more experienced at the park. I'd be a fool to disregard a certain power imbalance there. I haven't reviewed the full footage, of course, but what I saw did make me want to talk to you."

"Right," I breathed. The footage where he practically tackled me into a cage, tied me to it with his belt and made me come until I couldn't get out a single word. That footage. The very same night he told me he wanted all my ghost children to be happy and I could practically feel my ovaries fist-fighting my birth control. "Could you delete that video?"

"Are you sure? If you want, I can delete it from our servers but give you a copy if you change your mind."

"Yes, I'm sure." I nodded. "Noah and I . . . we haven't told anyone, but we have been seeing each other."

It was the first time I'd admitted anything like this out

loud. And while it was the most non-committal phrasing I could come up with, my silly heart still bounced around in my chest.

"All right then." Renee nodded, a smile playing across her lips and relief sagging through her shoulders. She liked Noah, I realized, and she had still given me a chance to speak up. "I'll schedule a meeting for next week, with Noah and HR this time, so we can figure out how to handle this."

"Could you hold off for a day? I want to talk to Noah in person first. We were obviously sneaking around because we aren't ready for people to know about us. I'm seeing him tonight at Sinan's birthday party, so I'll talk to him then."

"Of course."

"Thank you."

"The other thing . . ."

The other thing boiled down to our online videos doing well. Not just ours, but the ones guests had captured over the last week, when Noah kept crashing my meet and greets. I knew he did it because I'd been facing some rude visitors. It worked. Once he was beside me, people weren't so bold as to ask insulting questions. And Ace Ryder was such a shameless flirt, people were eating it up.

Somehow the small fact that Ace was now flirting with Annie before the show had drowned out many hate comments. It wasn't about my stunt skills anymore or whether or not Annie was an archaic damsel in distress. It was about his hands around my waist and the way his face was right next to mine when he growled threats at me.

Renee wanted to know if I was comfortable expanding on that and making it a permanent staple in the park.

Thanks to the aforementioned *indiscretion*, she hadn't wanted to suggest anything before she was sure that Noah and I were on good terms.

I told her I needed to think about it.

Noah and I *were* on good terms. At least I thought so. But I wasn't sure I was comfortable with anything permanent right now . . . though I was even less sure if I could stomach leaving Bravetown at the end of summer season only to see Ace flirt with another Annie via a shaky phone video.

Only my brother would think that turning twenty-nine in the height of summer combined with a guest list consisting mostly of people who wore costumes every single day at work meant that his birthday party should be a costume party. I scratched my head on the way up to his and Zuri's apartment. Hairspray and a dozen bobby pins kept the tight bun in place.

I'd gotten a sparkly white prom dress at Goodwill. Two thin straps held it on my shoulders while the skirt fluffed out around my thighs in an explosion of tulle. With the updo and the plastic crown on my head, I looked like a cartoon ballerina.

"What are you?" I asked when Sanny opened the door in a beige tank top and green cargo pants. His hair was parted down the middle and big round glasses balanced on his nose. "Nerd soldier?"

He heaved a deep sigh. "It's Milo. I knew it only worked as long as I'm glued to Zuri's side."

As if on command, Zuri materialized next to him in a shimmering silver wig and a tiny blue two-piece co-ord. They wore matching glowing pendants around their necks, and that finally made it click.

They were dressed like the couple in *Atlantis*, Sanny's favorite film growing up.

"If this is the twenty-first-century version of the Princess Leia bikini, if he's making you wear this against your will, blink twice," I told Zuri.

She laughed and drew me into one of her hugs, perfect and soft and only slightly awkward considering she was wearing a tiny tube skirt and tinier tube top.

"Don't be silly. It's his birthday present." She fluttered her lashes at my brother and that told me everything I needed to know.

"Please spare me the details," I laughed and shoved the little gift bag at Sinan. "Happy birthday!"

"You didn't have to get me anything."

"Don't get too excited. I literally got this in one of the park gift shops." I'd noticed his wallet falling apart and Bravetown had some leather ones that seemed durable enough. Plus, staff discount.

"Ah, you're joining an age-old tradition." He looped his arm around my neck. His breath already smelled like whiskey and the party had only started twenty minutes ago. He pulled me down the hallway to the large living room with windows overlooking the town square. Back home, this room alone would be rented as a loft shared between four people. I'd know. I'd checked rent prices before agreeing to move here for the summer. "You work here long enough, you'll find yourself drinking from Bravetown mugs, wearing Bravetown socks and somehow never running out of Bravetown gift-shop cookies. Case in point."

He lifted a plate of pink-frosted cowboy-hat cookies from the side table of gifts, where I noticed at least two more boxes of cookies with bows on them.

I grabbed one and let him lead me over to some of our friends on the sofa. Adriana, dressed as some superhero in a red leotard and pink tights, narrowed her eyes at me when I refused a drink and bit into my sugar cookie instead.

"I'm not pregnant," I groaned.

"Ugh." She grimaced. "He's rubbing off on you."

I stilled, but it didn't look like anyone else had tracked her words. The others were chatting and laughing and doing shots over some dice game. It wasn't hard to guess who she was talking about. Not a lot of other cast or staff members refused a drink. After the bits and bobs Noah had dropped about his absentee father, it wasn't hard to guess why he generally preferred staying sober and only indulged in a beer here or there.

"Relax. My lips are sealed. You could have told me though." She patted my thigh. "Just don't become too boring, okay? These country boys will wife you up and put a bun in your oven like that." She snapped her fingers in the air.

"Thanks for the advice," I mumbled and stuffed my face with another bite of sugar cookie. So not what I needed to hear right now.

I was definitely going to get drunk later. I needed to let loose. Have fun. Dance on the table or something. I just had to get the whole sex-tape conversation over first.

My eyes kept darting to the door whenever the bell rang,

but Noah was noticeably absent from the party. By my third or fourth sugar cookie, the music got so loud that it completely drowned out any other sound, and I had to remind myself to periodically check the room. He might not come over to me on his own if he was trying to keep up the pretense.

Staying sober made the party a lot less enjoyable. Especially when a mermaid and a gorilla started grinding against each other in the middle of the living room and everyone went wild for it.

"Oh, come on dude, that doesn't count as a costume!" Sinan shouted from the far end of the sofa.

I followed my brother's attention to the large silhouette darkening the living room doorway. My insides shot heat down to my abdomen faster than my brain could process Ace Ryder striding into the room. And it was Ace Ryder. Dark hat, black bandana mask, long leather coat, and the shift in his hips and tilt to his chin that was *nothing* like Noah.

"Better than yours," he retorted in that dark, gravelly voice.

Oh. Fuck. There went my ovaries.

His gaze locked on to mine. I couldn't see behind his mask, but judging by that little crease under his eyes, he was grinning.

That bastard knew exactly what he was doing to me.

"And what are you?" he asked.

"Three guesses." I tapped my pink plastic scepter against my pink plastic crown.

"Princess."

Of course he knew. I'd told everyone who asked that I was a ballerina, but Noah knew better. "Bingo."

He pulled his hat off and bowed his head slightly. "Your highness."

That . . . yeah, that worked on me. Damn. I shot up from the sofa before anyone caught a whiff of the waves of pheromones my body had to be shooting through the air. Adriana laughed and choked on her drink, but I didn't turn around.

"No, Esra, stay. He wasn't making fun of your costume. Noah, tell her," Zuri pleaded, "play nice."

"I know exactly what he's doing," I said, unable to look at Noah-as-Ace. "I'll be right back."

I booked it to the kitchen to get myself some ice water to cool down, but I could still see him through the archway. What a sight he was. The broad shoulders in that leather coat, the veins in his neck when he turned his head – nope, no. I had to stop. This was exactly what had gotten us into this mess. I had to resist his stupidity-inducing hotness.

I just had to get away from him and splash myself with some cold water.

I tried the guest bathroom in the hallway, but the door was locked, and someone yelled profanities at me from inside. Okay, then. The door to the bedroom was closed, but it was unlocked, so I quickly slipped through that, grateful that no drunken party guests had discovered this dark and quiet corner yet. All right. Master bathroom, cold water, and then a calm and collected conversation about the fact that we'd been filmed having sex and Renee knew about us and all the compartmentalizing in the world couldn't get us out of this. No biggie.

I flicked the lights on in the bathroom, my eyes needing

a moment to adjust to the brightness. It was a really nice bathroom. Large rain shower on one side and a double sink with a huge mirror above it on the other. Maybe I'd have to come here to take long, hot, muscle-soothing showers in the future.

I turned to close the door, only for it to bang against something hard. My eyes dropped. A boot?

Before I made sense of it, a gloved hand wrapped around the door, forcing it back open, pushing me backward. Noah stepped through, startlingly tall and dark in the bright bathroom, and shoved the door shut behind him. He twisted the lock.

"You can't run from me, princess," he said in his stupid sexy-villain voice.

Fuck.

I swallowed.

Some primal part of my brain told me to run. That this was a tall, heavy man behind a mask, who oozed viciousness. And another — very different — primal part responded by sending a hot shiver down to the base of my spine, way too excited by the fact he'd locked us in.

"Look, Noah—"

A gloved hand over my mouth cut me off. Noah shook his head slightly, icy blue eyes never leaving mine. I got the meaning. Not Noah.

Strange relief fluttered through me. If he wasn't Noah right now, I had a little bit more time before I had to blow up our neat boxes, putting an end to whatever comfortable limbo this was. It was a slightly unhinged concept, but it was an easy out.

I twisted my chin out from under his hold. "Okay, two

things. First, I just need you to tell me whether you're having some sort of mental-breakdown identity crisis." If that was the case, I should probably run.

He shook his head again and his hand slid down my jaw and around my neck. His fingers barely rested against my skin, but the position alone was enough to make me squirm.

"All right. Second. I don't need you to do this. You know that, right? I'm not going to deny that this whole Ace Ryder package works for me, but it's only because, *god*, the Noah Young package works for me. I got naked for Noah way before I even knew about Ace."

"Are you done talking now, your highness?"

I nodded.

"Good." He squeezed his fingers together slightly, just to affect but not restrict my airflow. Enough to send a spike of adrenaline through my system, making my nerves come alive.

"You're going to be very quiet now." He used his hold on my neck and a hand flat against my stomach to walk me backward until my ass hit the bathroom counter. "You're going to watch me fuck you in that tiny dress until your pussy is bright red and stretched wide for me." He jerked me around to face the mirror. I jumped. Seeing Ace Ryder in front of you was one thing. Seeing yourself in a fluffy dress, blushing, with his chest pressed against your back and his hand wrapped around your neck, was surreal on another level. He chuckled at my reaction, pressed his nose against the side of my head and inhaled deeply. Noah had breathed in my scent plenty of times. This was different. Ace Ryder smelled fear. And I shivered against him.

"After you've come on my cock, princess, you're going to get on all fours, open those plump lips for me and swallow every last drop I give you." His hand slid up my neck until he could push his thumb in between my lips. I may have had goosebumps rising, from my ears to my ankles, but I was no pushover. I opened my mouth, lapped at his thumb once, then bit down.

The asshole laughed in my ear. His other, non-bitten hand slid up my stomach and down the front of my dress. One of the straps snapped as the neckline was shoved down. He roughly palmed one of my breasts before pinching down hard on the nipple. My sensitive nerve endings shot white-hot flames through me. I spluttered around his thumb, my knees going weak for a moment. He held me caged between his body and his hands though, keeping me upright.

"Get feisty with me. I dare you. It'll be so much more fun."

Oh god, I felt the heat blooming between my legs, and he'd barely even touched me yet. This mind game was really going to be my undoing.

But I was all for having fun. So I bit down again.

His hand moved to the other side of my chest, knocking the second strap off my shoulder in the process. The top of my dress fell down to my waist. In the mirror, I could see his glove stretch taut as he grabbed my other tit roughly and twisted the peak of it between his fingers.

"Fuck," I gasped, releasing his thumb, my entire body jerking again.

"Didn't I tell you to be quiet?"

"I'm not great at following orders."

His head tilted down, and the brim of his hat hid even his eyes from view. Our reflection showed nothing but a faceless man, clad in black, gripping my exposed flesh, and it sent another hot shiver through me. He traced one languid finger down my spine, only to come back up and wrap the hand around the back of my neck. He pushed down, my hips jutting backward automatically as I bent.

"Take your panties off," he ordered.

"Do it your fucking self," I countered and earned myself another rough push downwards until my cheek brushed the cool granite countertop. Oh, he was good. An inch further and I would have walked out of here with an angry bump on my temple. Apparently spatial awareness was now one of my turn-ons. This man was ruining me.

"Take them off, princess."

I reached down, too impatient to keep protesting. I wanted this. Wanted him. Both versions of him. The rough one he'd never show the rest of the world and the perfectly controlled one that knew every limit. With his hand on my neck still keeping me bent down, I only managed to wriggle my underwear a few inches down my ass. The second I struggled to push further, he grabbed hold of my panties and ripped them off.

"Those were new," I whined.

"Don't worry, I'll treasure them even if they're broken." He pulled my hips back. My tits slid across the countertop, the cold stone sharp against my oversensitized nipples. I gasped and tried to get my hands under me, but he pressed me down again, not a pocket of air between my chest and the counter.

He shifted behind me. I blinked up through some fallen

strands of hair, trying to catch a glimpse of his reflection, but the mirror hung a few inches too high for me to see from this angle. Hadn't he promised me that I got to watch him fuck me? And now he had me bent down with his hips pressing into my ass? That was not what I'd signed up for.

I blew out an angry breath. "Is that your gun or are you excited to see me?"

"If you can't tell the difference, we have an issue." He turned me around and hoisted me on to the center of the counter in one smooth move. Instead of seating me on the edge though, where I could easily spread my legs around his hips, he pushed me to the very back until my shoulders aligned with the mirror. He grabbed both my ankles and hooked my feet into the twin sinks, spreading me wide.

Dress bunched around my middle, I was completely exposed in front of him.

And the way his eyes raked over my center just added to the wetness already pooling for him.

"Hand," he demanded, a split second before grabbing my left wrist, the uninjured one, and pulling my fingers to his groin. At least he was as turned on as I was. He didn't just do this to fulfill some sort of fantasy for me. He pushed himself into my palm and let out a low growl. "That's what excitement feels like."

He jerked my palm up to the smooth handle on his holster. With his hand over mine, he wrapped my fingers around the revolver and made me pull it out.

"This is what a gun feels like," he growled as he pushed our entwined hands, and the pistol by extension, toward my pussy.

It was pointed right at me.

"Please," I hissed, not sure what I was pleading for.

I knew it was a prop. I knew it only had a little compartment in the back that, if loaded, produced nothing but a pop and a bit of smoke right by the trigger. A pretty toy. That knowledge didn't stop the surge of panic as the cold metal kissed the hot skin of my inner thigh.

Every instinct told me that guns were dangerous. And yet, I didn't try to pull my hand away or use my leverage on the grip to fight him. I knew he'd stop if I did. He wouldn't push me further than I was willing.

I let his hand steer the barrel. The metal scraped a winding path up my leg. Inch by inch my heart beat faster. It was so close. My breath stopped when the tip of it bit into the soft flesh of my outer lips, nudging them apart. He had to have a prime view of the pulsing heat between my legs, half instinctive fear, half arousal.

The barrel kissed my clit. The hole at its tip slotted right over my swollen bundle of nerves, and I couldn't keep down my whimper.

"Look at how fucking wet you are for my gun." He lowered the cool metal to my entrance, sending another pulse through my inner walls. "I'm starting to think you're just a princess on the outside."

"I . . . hmm . . ." Words were impossible with the gun swirling slow circles around and around my sensitive opening.

"I think you're an outlaw on the inside." He held my gaze, and pushed the barrel in. It wasn't thick, but it was cold and ridged and *entirely wrong*.

"Oh fuck." My head dropped back against the mirror. My core squeezed tight around the metal shaft. *So right.*

"Your majesty, you're making a mess." He brought his other hand against me to catch my dripping arousal with his thumb and circled it over my pulsing clit.

"Please."

"Please what?"

"I don't know."

He chuckled and slowly moved the revolver back and forth. That thing was definitely not meant for thrusting, but that tiny bit of movement was already enough to remind me of its hard shape inside me.

"Oh god," I moaned. My free hand clutched for a hold on his collar. My hips rocked on their own accord, meeting each of his movements.

"Come for me," he growled, playing my sensitive flesh like an instrument he'd mastered for years.

"I can't. It's a fucking gun."

"Yes, you can. I know you're already there. Just let go." There was a hint of Noah in his voice, and I locked my eyes with his, finding the familiar trust and affection there.

My body shuddered as the first wave of the orgasm crashed over me. My moans were muffled by warm fabric. By a mouth. He was kissing me with his mask on. And fuck if it didn't make the next wave more intense as I fell apart for him. My muscles spasmed, my mind blanked and I drowned and drowned in the pure bliss of him.

"That was the most beautiful thing I've ever seen, Esra," Noah rasped against my lips when I came up for air, dazed and heady.

The gun clattered into the sink next to me.

"My turn now," he said, voice dropped low again. His arms came around me and he hoisted me around like I was nothing but his plaything – and I was too warm and fuzzy to care. He positioned me in front of him, facing the mirror, knees spread apart on the counter. My reflection was a disheveled mess of the princess I'd been earlier. My crown hung crooked in my messy updo. My dress was torn. Mascara smudges ringed my eyes. And I thought I never looked better when his gloved hand wrapped over my mouth again. I was going to bite him just for the audacity, but then I felt him align the tip of his cock between my legs. Another full body shudder rippled through me, the afterquakes of my orgasm not quite over yet.

"Ssh," he hushed by my ear. "It'll just hurt for a second."

I knew he was right. That first thrust always stung. No matter how much he warmed me up.

He'd promised me that I was allowed to watch though, and right now, all I could see was tulle.

I reached down to gather my skirt up, giving myself a prime view of how his thick head parted my folds. He was so pretty. Maybe that was an odd thought when it came to a penis, but he really was just so perfectly pink with ribbed veins running down his length and a little droplet of pre-cum glistening at his tip. Skirt gathered in one hand, I reached the other down, desperate to touch him and show him just how nice a cock I thought he had.

My fingertips barely brushed his tip when my arm was wrenched back. I whimpered at the short sting in my shoulder, but once again, he knew exactly just how far he could push my body. He brought my hand behind my back and fixed it in place. Goddammit. Now I really wanted to bite him. Or scratch him. But I couldn't even wriggle the hand behind my back and if I let go of my dress, I'd miss the whole show. Besides, I wasn't sure he'd still let me watch if I scratched him.

"Move your hand and I'll stop, got it?" He placed my hand on his belt buckle.

I nodded and gave the hand over my mouth just a tiny nibble. Just enough to let him know I was still enjoying myself here.

He reached down in front of us, and I watched, fascinated, as his fingers worked me open. My arousal already swirled together with his pre-cum, wetness glistened all over my skin.

"Keep breathing," he warned right as he rocked into me.

I squealed into his hand and squeezed my eyes shut, my insides resisting that first deep stretch.

"Ssh, look at you, princess. Look at how perfect you are for me." His fingers wrapped around the hand on my back again, pinning it in place as he slowly dragged in and out of me. "Open your eyes for me."

I blinked away the tears cresting on my lashes and let my gaze drop to the junction of my thighs. My skin was stretched taut around him, but he was right about how perfect it looked. He pushed in slowly, showing me exactly just how deep he could bury himself inside me before he hit that perfect spot that wrangled a moan from my throat.

The sound was muffled by his glove. As was every subsequent one as he picked up his pace and my thoughts started swimming away, sensation overtaking my body. I couldn't look away from our reflection. Each thrust rocked my entire body. My tits were reddened, nipples peaking into the air, bouncing as he slammed home.

A knock on the door froze us in place.

"Esra?" Zuri's voice came muffled through the door. "Are you in there? Is everything okay?"

Fuck. I knew the door was locked, but in that moment, I still saw this whole scene through her eyes. I was restrained and muzzled, exposed and spread wide in front of the mirror with Ace Ryder's cock several inches inside me. The prop gun in the sink was still shiny, covered in my wetness.

How had Adriana put it? Zuri and Sinan were unicorns and rainbows?

This was about as far as you could get from it.

"Esra?" Zuri asked again, the doorknob jiggling.

"Answer," he growled low by my ear as he loosened his hand from my mouth.

"I'm okay," I called back, only to gasp when Noah thrust up hard. Asshole. "Give me like ten—" Thrust. "Minutes, okay?" Thrust. "Just dealing—" Thrust. "With a-h situation." Thrust.

Noah's hand wrapped over my mouth again and I crumpled into him with a whimper.

"Okay, uhm, there's hygiene stuff in the drawer under the sink," Zuri replied. "Let me know if you need anything."

Noah kept rolling his hips into me, stoking the tense heat building at my core, but he didn't speak again until we heard the bedroom door fall shut.

"You really think you're going to last ten more minutes?"

He didn't give me enough space around his glove to reply verbally, so I dropped my skirt and grasped at his arm with my free hand until I found the sliver of skin between his glove and his jacket, and I sank my nails in.

"Oh, you're going to regret that," he drawled in the

deepest Ace Ryder voice. My pussy clenched up around him all on its own. "Pull your dress up again."

I did but definitely because I wanted to watch and not because he'd told me to. Not that it mattered.

He loosened his grip on the hand behind my back. On the next thrust, his fingers whipped against my exposed clit. Stars exploded across my vision as I bucked into him. If he hadn't held my mouth firmly shut, my scream would have echoed off the bathroom tiles.

He repeated the move, sending another shockwave through me, and another. My vision blurred as the sharp jolts turned to shivers.

"Noah," I pleaded his name, but my voice strained against his hand. It didn't deter me. All that pressure had to go somewhere and begging for release seemed like the only option. "Noah, please."

"Do you want to come for me?"

I nodded frantically under his grip.

"It hasn't been ten minutes yet," he taunted and delivered another blinding slap to my raw nerve endings.

I shook my head. I didn't care that it hadn't been ten minutes. If he even took one minute longer, I'd pass out from the overstimulation.

"Look at me."

I craned my neck, leaning on to his shoulder to meet his gaze. The second our eyes locked, he sheathed himself in me with enough force for my body to jolt forward, only to buck right into his waiting hand, so he could pinch my clit. I cried into his hand as the rush of pain and pleasure took over. When my eyes threatened to fall shut against the overwhelm of sensations, Noah jerked my chin up. He forced me to keep my eyes on him as he fucked me through an orgasm that crushed my bones and turned me into a trembling mess. If he hadn't been holding me, I would have shattered across the floor in a thousand shards.

When the only sounds coming from my throat were nothing but soft gasps, he gently lifted his hand off my mouth, tugged the bandana down and kissed me. His lips soothed mine, soft and slow, even as his thrusts into me came faster. I felt the way he hardened and jerked deep, right before he moaned my name against my lips and released himself inside me.

"Liar," I huffed.

"Hmm?" Noah's forehead dropped against mine while he caught his breath.

"You promised me a blow job."

"Changed my mind when I realized how fucking tiny this dress is." He nipped at my ear, then at the skin right beneath it, as he pulled back just enough to slide out of me. "And you'll walk out of here with my cum dripping down your thighs."

"You're kinda deranged," I mumbled and pressed a kiss to his cheek.

Noah grinned as he grabbed his prop gun from the sink. He brought it up to his lips and ran his tongue down the entire length of it before he holstered it. "You're kinda delicious."

Yeah, I got the point, we both were a little messed up.

Noah helped me fix the bobby pins in the back of the updo with careful fingertips and took it upon himself to make sure my crown was straightened. I found a safety pin in one of the bathroom drawers to keep my dress in place.

He didn't give me back my panties though. And he made me walk out first, just so he could be sure I wouldn't stay behind and clean myself up.

As soon as I was out in the hallway, I busied myself by rearranging the cookie plate. I didn't want to go back to the sofa without underwear, and I was also sort of waiting for Noah. I couldn't help myself. Maybe we were both a little messed up, but at least we were a matching pair.

And after this, the sex-tape conversation didn't feel as threatening anymore.

The bedroom door had just swung open when another arm wrapped around my shoulders.

"Hey, can I talk to you for a second?" Sanny boxed me into the kitchen, but it wasn't lost on me that Noah stopped in his tracks and leaned against the wall right outside, even if his back was turned to us.

"What's up?" I asked and pushed myself against the counter in a way that hopefully hid the way I squeezed my thighs together for dear life.

"I know that, uh, you and Noah got caught at his family's place during the storm, right?" His words were slightly slurred, but his eyes were locked on me with complete focus.

"Yeah, we did," I answered, not willing to give up more information than need be.

"I don't know if he told you, but uhm, I'm working with him on it. We're turning it into a therapy ranch."

Oh, thank god, at least I didn't have to face *that* conversation just yet.

"Yeah, he's told me something like that," I said, trying to sound nonchalant.

"I hope you're not mad at me."

"Why would I be mad?"

"Because I'll be leaving Bravetown, and I just got you this job here. So, like, I don't want you to think I'm abandoning you or anything."

"I thought the therapy ranch wouldn't open for another two years?" My eyes skipped from Sanny to Noah. If I'd gotten that detail wrong, I'd have to go over the deadlines on the to do lists I'd created again.

"Yeah, yeah, yeah, give or take." Sanny nodded vigorously. "And so, I was thinking, maybe you'd want to come work with us. We can all switch over from Bravetown. But you have experience with chronic pain and injuries and such. Like, personal experience. And we don't."

"Why don't we talk about this tomorrow when you've sobered up a little?" I tried to sound calm and collected, but that same panic that had been creeping in for two days was thrumming loud in my ears.

"You don't have to worry about Noah. I already asked him. He's cool with it."

"You asked him?"

My eyes snapped back to the archway, where Noah had taken the Ace Ryder hat off and was now watching me, not even trying to hide his eavesdropping. He'd talked about me to Sinan, about my future. He'd talked to my brother before talking to me.

"Yeah, and there's all kinds of jobs you can do if you don't want to work with the horses. I think we have a list of jobs. I think Noah has a list. He has lists. You'd like them."

"Uh-huh." He sure had a list of jobs. The one I'd put together so he could start looking into the hiring and training processes for various positions he'd need to fill. Had he looked at that and considered which role to assign me, so he could keep me around?

"Yeah, and then you'll be taken care of no matter what, you know? You'll always have a job. And he said he'd be nicer to you. And you don't have to go back to school like Mom wants you to."

I'd be taken care of. The words cracked through my chest, leaving a deep chasm behind.

It was never going to be about what I wanted.

I'd never get to just *live* without someone hovering over me.

For years, I'd accepted my parents' specific brand of overprotectiveness because I'd been comfortable. I'd been on a clear path toward a future I wanted, which happened to fit their vision of a perfect little daughter. Hell, Mom had mentioned, more than once, that by going to med school, I'd probably meet a nice surgeon to marry one day, and we could be a doctor power couple or something. I'd ignored those comments for years. I'd ignored that they didn't let me go to birthday parties. I'd ignored that they didn't let me drink alcohol. I'd ignored every single tie they'd slung around me, not realizing how hard it had become to breathe.

And I'd fallen into the same trap again.

Taking a job at Bravetown had been a comfortable option. I'd wanted a fun summer, so I ignored that Sinan and Zuri had been needling me about my plans for the future. That he voiced his disapproval of the choices I made, to play Annie Lou or to film videos with Lucas and Noah. I'd even accepted that he didn't want me to make a mess of *his* life, so I'd put *my* life second, sneaking around with Noah for weeks when I'd wanted to spend every second of every day with him because he was making me feel things I'd never experienced.

Only for Noah to do the same thing as the rest of them.

I'd be comfortable staying and taking a job at his ranch. I'd just have to ignore that he and my brother would be planning my life behind my back because they viewed me as someone who had to be taken care of.

The betrayal hit me in the stomach like a fist. Bile burned the back of my throat. I blinked through the sudden tears blurring my vision and pushed away from the counter, leaving Sanny in the kitchen without another word. I stormed past Noah, peripherally aware of how he said my name and touched my elbow. There was no way I could talk to him. No way I could even meet his eyes right now. My heart was too weak; I'd accept the offer to stay and work at the ranch, and I'd let him take care of me, just to be with him. So I kept my eyes straight ahead. I was done compromising on my independence.

I beelined for Adriana, who was dancing with a plush anaconda draped around her neck. "I need to get out of here."

To her credit, Adriana took one look over my shoulder, presumably at my brother or his best friend or both of them, and dropped the anaconda to the floor. "Where we going?"

"Somewhere fun."

Chapter Twenty-Four

THE SUNSET SHOWDOWN

Immerse yourself in the story of Bravetown and experience the dangers and thrills of the Old West in this spectacular show. When Ace Ryder and his bandits cause mayhem in town, it's upon Sheriff Kit Holliday to save the day. From horseback stunts to pyrotechnics, the showdown will leave you breathless.

For access to the dedicated space for disabled park guests and to find out more about our accessibility program click here.

NOAH

I had barely slept in three nights.

Esra had left the party with Adriana on Friday and not come home.

After weeks of stealing every moment we could, she hadn't spared me a second to say goodbye, to explain, to let me in. She shut me out and I didn't know why. Maybe I had read too much into it, but the way she'd let me touch her in the bathroom had felt like it meant something. She'd trusted me through the costume, to my core, knowing I wouldn't hurt her, wouldn't let anything happen to her.

But when something *had* happened, I wasn't the person she'd turned to.

I'd waited in the living room that first night and fallen asleep on the sofa, not caring who might see and draw their conclusions. I couldn't care less about some betting pool when Esra was god-knows-where, emotionally riled up, wearing a tiny dress held together by a safety pin. Maybe I wasn't who she turned to for comfort, but I'd be ready to give it nonetheless.

Her brother had said something to upset her at his party. I'd only caught snippets of their conversation, but he'd told her about his plans to work on the ranch with me. I'd already told her as much, so that could hardly be why she bolted. Sanny had downed a few too many shots to piece the conversation back together himself.

No matter how often I called, Esra wasn't picking up her phone. Adriana had texted Sinan both Saturday and Sunday to let him know they were fine, just so he wouldn't call the cops.

If she'd told him where they were, I would have driven out there myself.

Esra was hurt or angry or sad, and I didn't know why, and I couldn't fix it.

My own incompetence stifled every other thought that weekend. All I could focus on was that she was gone, and I couldn't bring her back or make her feel better from afar. She hadn't just run away from her brother, or from the park; she'd run away from me, and if I hadn't been worried sleepless, I would have been hurt.

Monday morning, I dragged myself into the kitchen, muscles aching from tossing and turning the third night in a row. I swiped my finger across my phone screen to refresh my messages – as if that would magically produce a new one. My gaze snapped up at the sound of cutlery. Not Austin. Not Lucas. Not any of the other people I'd lived with for years. A small, hooded creature crouched at the table, and even though I'd known her less than three months, I distinctively knew the ebony shade of the hair cascading from under the hood, and the soft lips closing around a spoonful of cereal. Esra just sat at the kitchen table with a bowl of sugary, crunchy breakfast as if I hadn't been calling her non-stop. She didn't even look up. Just kept shoveling spoon after spoon of chocolate crap into her mouth and staring into space.

She had a hoodie jacket around her shoulders, but she was still in the same sparkly white dress she'd worn Friday night. Shit. That had to be a bad sign, right?

Adriana's texts may have said she was fine, but she didn't look fine. She looked like death with pale cheeks and dark circles under her eyes.

"Esra?" She didn't respond, so I stepped closer. "Where have you been?"

"None of your business," she mumbled, still staring ahead and seeing nothing at all.

I'd seen that look before. Many times. In my father's eyes when he'd remember our address long enough to come home and change. She wasn't my dad. She was the girl who put researching horse noises on her to-do list and actually checked it off. She'd gone through something. Must have. And if she told me what was wrong, I'd figure out how to fix it.

"Are you okay? Are you hurt?" I asked.

"I'm not hurt." She grimaced as if I'd just poured salt over her cereal. "Why the fuck is that the first conclusion you jump to?"

"Shit, Esra, I don't know." A bitter laugh hiccupped up my throat. "You were gone all weekend. You missed four shows. I had to cover for you with Renee."

"I didn't ask you to do that," she responded without a hint of emotion.

"I did that because I didn't want you to get into trouble."

"That sounds like a you-problem, Young."

"A me-problem? Are you listening to yourself right now?" I wasn't sure what was happening with her, but I knew that I'd done *this* before. The moment you realized that you were about to be left behind. It had happened once with my mother, and dozens of times with my father. I'd known it was coming with Esra, too. I'd just thought we'd get the rest of summer and then she'd breeze off and leave me with enough memories to make the end sting less. Only a tiny voice in the back of my mind had allowed itself to hope that maybe, just maybe, I'd get a bit more time than that. "What the hell is wrong with you?" The words came out more vicious than I'd intended, but she was leaving, and I was not okay.

"Right now? I'm incredibly hungover. This guy I have no memory of meeting or giving my phone number to keeps blowing up my phone. And you're yelling at me."

So her phone definitely hadn't been dead the last two days. She'd just ignored me. She had looked at her phone long enough to see some other guy's messages though. I tried to swallow the bitter taste that left in my mouth but couldn't hold the bite from my words. "Great, partying and getting blackout drunk around random men, then coming back here hungover when we have to be at work in three hours? That sounds like you made all the right choices this weekend."

She wasn't Dad. *She wasn't Dad.* She was just a normal twenty-three-year-old who partied with her friends. I'd seen her hang out with the others and stop after one or two drinks. She'd made some bad choices this weekend. Normal people got drunk and made bad choices every now and again. Maybe she could come back from it. Come back to me. Give me the rest of summer.

"Yeah. I had a great weekend, actually," she quipped and pulled a feathered pen from her jacket pocket. "I got this from Adriana's Stallion. They put them down the crotch of their Speedos. I had to pull it out with my teeth."

My gut twisted with jealousy at the image of Esra's teeth anywhere near another man's crotch. We hadn't talked about being exclusive, but the last few weeks hadn't felt casual. *We* hadn't felt like there was enough empty space between us for another person to slip in. Not some stranger she gave her number to, and definitely no fucking Stallion.

I blinked at the pen, then at her tired smirk. She really was ending it. She had to know that I'd been developing real feelings for her, so she was putting me back in my place. "Do you even realize how many people worried about you this weekend? Missed you? God, you're selfish."

"Yes. So what if I am? It's my life, isn't it?" She tossed the stupid feathery pen across the table, brows drawn deep. "I should be allowed to live my life however I please. I can go wherever I want and do whatever I want."

"And apparently do *who*ever you want. Is that what

317

you want me to say? Do you want me to ask whether you fucked some Stallion covered in body glitter and feathers this weekend?"

"Isn't that what Buckle Bunnies do?" She pursed her lips.

"I'm not rehashing that with you just because you want a fight. I shouldn't have called you that. I know you better now. We moved on." I pinched the bridge of my nose. "Will you just tell me what the hell is actually going on?"

"Yeah, you know me better," she bit the words out, teeth showing. "Is it because you actually bothered to get to know me? Or because you talked to Sinan about me behind my back?"

"What?" I'd barely mentioned Esra to her brother. At first, because I'd been too worried about keeping our hookups secret – then, because I was sure I wouldn't have been able to mention her name without smiling like an idiot.

"I know that my parents can't handle me. I know that I'm too much for Sanny. But you knew what you were getting into. You can't fuck Esra and expect to wake up next to perfect little Annie Lou. And Sinan can't help you turn me into her either."

It took me a second to follow her train of thought. Annie Lou was Little Miss Perfect, and she hadn't been interesting until Esra had breathed new life into her. This wasn't really about her role in the park though. This was about the fact that I should have known all along that she wasn't here for anything serious. I'd fucked her and now I got jealous if she went out and had fun all weekend. I'd fucked her and I wanted commitment. I'd fucked her and

I'd talked to her brother about her staying in town. "Is this because Sinan asked me to give you a job at the ranch?"

Her face dropped into an expression that was too neutral. She was clearly trying not to let it show that I'd hit the spot.

"You don't want to stay here? You want to run off and fuck around? Fine. Leave. I don't want to work with whatever the fuck you've got going on right now anyway. Not in the park and not at the ranch." I grabbed a trash bag and tore open the cabinet we kept our food in. I dumped the contents of her shelf in the bag one after another. No point delaying the inevitable if she didn't want to be here. "You need to get your shit together."

"I had my shit together for twenty-two years! Shit fell apart. My life is an explosion of shit. Shit is dripping from the ceiling. I don't want to keep it together anymore."

"You have a job here. You have friends. You have family. You have me." With each phrase I counted off, another item landed in the trash bag. "Other people would consider themselves lucky to have all that."

"Yeah, well, good for other people," she scoffed and pushed herself off the table. "I don't want it. Not like this."

I dumped the bag of groceries and followed her when she marched upstairs. "Like what?"

"Like I'm just exchanging my overbearing parents for an overbearing brother and an overbearing boyfriend. Why does everyone always think they need to handle my life for me?"

She'd just called me her boyfriend. Kind of didn't matter when she was about to leave, but it still pulled a string inside my chest that had been coiled tight for weeks.

"When did I try to handle your life for you?" I asked.

She whirled around in the doorway to her room. Now it was her turn to count items off. "When you did my laundry. When you tried to stop me from drinking at the saloon *and* then stalked me home afterward. When you literally threw me over your shoulder to carry me home after the cast party. I mean, I could go on about the ones I know about. But then there's the ones that happen behind my back. When you told Sanny to send me back home after my first week here. When you ran to Renee's office to get me fired – yeah, Vivi told me about that. And when you started planning a whole future for me with Sanny without consulting me. Anything else that I should know about?"

"Have you ever paused to consider that I do those things for you and for Sanny? That I care?"

"If you care about someone, you let them make their own decisions."

"If you care about someone, you consider how your actions affect them instead of acting like an entitled brat!"

She threw the door shut in my face.

I deserved that for calling her a brat. Fuck. If I'd had any hopes of her staying before, they'd been completely eradicated now.

Rubbing my chest, where that taut string still trembled after she'd called me her boyfriend, I automatically turned and left the house. There was only one place that had always been safe when the world around me went to shit, when my mother got sicker and needed more care, when my father pawned our car to afford another bottle of Jack. There was one place quiet enough for me to sort through my thoughts, where I could allow myself to feel hopeless and angry for a few minutes before I had to make plans to fix things.

I made my way through the staff walkways and to the stables in a daze. It was still hours before the show – and I wasn't sure if we'd do the watered-down version without Annie Lou again – but I knew that spending that time with Tornado would soothe my nerves. It always had, even before I'd officially started his therapy-horse training.

I barely made it into his box before he pushed his face into my chest. My arms closed around him instantly. I let his slow breathing and heartbeat radiate through me, quieting my own pulse. Just when I thought I was getting a handle on myself, I stroked through his mane and knocked my knuckles into the string of faded beads there.

"Well, shit," I breathed.

I'd let Esra braid them into his mane this year, but the beads were older than Tornado himself. They were one of the last things my mother gave me. Her physical therapist had her threading these big colorful wooden beads to help her fine motor skills as long as possible. She'd lost the ability to move her own wheelchair shortly after making her last beaded lucky charm.

The beads were mocking me now.

A glaring reminder that caring for someone didn't mean taking care *of* them and handling their every issue yourself. Caring for someone meant providing them with tools. It meant helping them live independently as much as possible.

I could practically hear Mom's disappointed sigh from beyond the grave.

Esra may have pushed my buttons to bait me into a fight, but she hadn't been wrong. She'd trusted me. She'd told me how much it hurt that her family expected her to move on from her dream and settle into another profession they approved of, when all she wanted was some time to find herself without that dream. Only for me to turn around and help Sanny do that exact same thing. Because if she had settled for a job at the ranch, she would have settled for me.

"I fucked up," I muttered against Tornado's forehead.

He huffed in agreement.

I went back to the house, half-expecting Esra's room to be completely cleared out. Her door stood ajar, but the inside still looked like her suitcases had exploded. That was a good sign, at least.

She wasn't in any of the shared rooms. I even checked with Lucas to see if she was in his room, but she must have taken off shortly after me. I checked the saloon and the dressing rooms but couldn't find her. I eventually had to go change into my costume, and just hoped that she'd be in the park as Annie Lou.

This morning had been a shit show. We were good at butting heads because we knew how to get under each other's skin. In the best and worst ways, apparently.

She didn't show up for her meet and greet. My jaw locked up at the thought that she might be using the time slot to pack her things and disappear while most of us were working. After everything we'd said, I wouldn't be able to handle an Irish goodbye.

I needed to talk to her.

I went through the motions of my own meet and greet. I knew how much these characters meant to all the guests – and how important they were for the park – but for once,

I couldn't care less. Inwardly, I was already preparing to come clean to Sinan about the last few weeks. If she was gone from Wild Fields by the time the show was over, he'd know where she'd gone, and I didn't want to come across like an ax murderer when I pried that information from him.

Tornado felt my nerves when I saddled up for the show. His ears twitched and he danced on the spot for a few moments before letting me get on. Not ideal, but I was working with him to stay calm no matter who sat in the saddle, and he had the routine of the show down. My mood shouldn't be impacting him too much.

He calmed down beneath me the second I saw her. Ace Ryder and the bandits rode into the town square, and I forgot to draw my gun, because there was that tell-tale blue dress disappearing into the bank. She was here. I couldn't take my eyes off the bank building and missed so many of my marks that Renee hissed in my ear on the intercom.

When it was finally time to storm the bank, I was first through the doors. I beelined straight to her and yanked the damn bandana off my face.

"I need to talk to you about this morning," I said, knowing that every single person on the intercom could hear me.

"I have nothing left to say to you, Noah," Esra whispered, avoiding my gaze.

"You can listen. I have some things I want to say."

Before Esra could respond, Richard started pushing us toward the exit by the shoulders.

I'd never hated the show before that moment, but god, I just needed a few minutes alone with her. Esra went rigid when I touched her to take her hostage.

"Mask," she hissed.

I was really out of it. Fuck. I pulled the bandana back over my nose. Okay, I just had to get her to the hideout. I had to keep my shit together until then, and then I'd have seven minutes to tell her that we could work this out. I'd let her make all her own decisions. I'd let her do her own laundry.

We managed the first bit of our act, only for Tornado to side-step when we got close enough for me to lift Esra on to the saddle. "Easy." I patted his side. Two agitated riders would be rough, but it was just for a few minutes. Tornado seemed to still a little, and I hoisted Esra into the saddle. I followed behind her and signaled for him to start walking. Only to realize my mistake when Esra scrambled for the hidden straps on the saddle. Shit. I grabbed them from her hands and buckled her in just moments before Tornado broke into his canter.

"Sorry," I whispered.

I had to get my head in the game. She could have gotten hurt. What the hell was wrong with me?

We made it to the hideout, and I slid out of the saddle first. When I reached for Esra, she swiped my hands away. "Touch me again and I will kill you," she hissed, unbuckling herself.

"Fair," I muttered, considering I had just almost gotten her thrown off the horse. So instead, I braced my hands in the air, ready to help her out of the saddle if need be. She'd been mounting and dismounting Crumble without a hitch, though, and her movements were just as smooth as she swung herself out of Tornado's saddle.

I saw it in the split second before it happened. In the

way Tornado's shoulders tensed. I lunged forward, ready to catch her, but my horse danced three wobbly steps to the side in the exact moment Esra still had one foot in the stirrup. My fingertips brushed her elbow, just before she went down.

With one leg still up, she crashed sideways into the ground.

Esra screamed.

I sprang into action, grabbed her foot and pulled it from the stirrup before the horse could drag her off.

Esra was wheezing. On the ground. She was on the ground, and she was clutching her shoulder and my horse had just thrown her and . . . dread squeezed my lungs as I dropped to my knees.

"Don't move," I said and cradled her face. Head and neck injuries were the most dangerous when falling like that, followed by spinal injuries. Even worse for someone like her. She could be seriously hurt.

Guilt joined the panic in my chest. I hadn't controlled my feelings or the horse I'd been riding for years. I hadn't lifted her off the saddle like I was supposed to, like I'd done countless times before.

"Noah." Esra grimaced and squeezed her eyes shut as silent tears started running down her cheeks. "Help me up. Now."

"I don't think that's a good idea."

"Get me inside. I'm not a goddamn spectacle."

I felt around the sides and back of her head, but there was no blood. And judging by the way she was jerking her chin at me, her neck was likely fine too. She had her left arm slung around the right one though.

"Okay," I breathed and pushed my arms in under her. She buried her face against my chest as I carried her, and I tried hard not to interpret anything from that. Inside, I sat her down on the table with her back propped up against the wall.

"Shit. Austin?" I fumbled for my microphone.

"I saw. Is she okay?"

"We're gonna need an ambulance," I said.

"I can finish the show. Give me ten minutes," Esra sniffed.

"You fell off the horse. You're not going anywhere but the hospital."

"I fell from like halfway down the horse." She shot me a withering glare.

"What on earth is going on?" Renee's voice came online. "Esra, are you all right?"

"Yeah," she breathed through a straining chest.

"No, she's not. She's crying. She's white as a ghost. And ..." Something was wrong with her arm, and if I'd understood her correctly about her chronic illness, her joints were fragile as fuck.

"Don't," Esra warned.

We locked eyes.

Her diagnosis wasn't mine to share, but I wasn't going to sit idly by while she pretended it didn't exist, just so she could feel more normal. Not when she was clutching her arm like it might fall off. "She needs a doctor. I think her shoulder's dislocated. Get us an ambulance."

I knew she'd hold this against me later as another instance of me trying to manage her life. If she couldn't see that her own stubbornness was working against her, maybe some doctor would agree with me that her injury required immediate medical attention.

Esra tore her gaze away, another wave of tears spilling down her face, and something told me those had nothing to do with her arm.

ESRA

Noah tried to climb into the back of the ambulance with me, but I had the EMT kick him out. Even if I ignored the fight and everything that had come before I fell off the damn horse, I'd seen the shift in his eyes when he picked me up.

It was the moment I'd expected the day he'd removed my shoes in his kitchen.

He thought I was fragile now.

I knew my shoulder was dislocated, even without an X-ray. It had happened before, and it would happen again. Not that anyone believed me, because god forbid a young woman with a medical file thicker than most med-school textbooks actually knew what was wrong with her own body.

Waiting for the X-ray to confirm what I already knew – nothing broken – took longer than the rest of the treatment at the hospital. A nice doctor jabbed me with an anesthetic, popped the shoulder back where it belonged and outfitted me with a sling for my arm. They also tried to prescribe me pain meds, but I told them that over-the-counter would work just fine for me.

"There's a young gentleman waiting outside for you," the middle-aged nurse said as she helped me back into my dress.

"Is he wearing a costume, too?" I asked.

"He is."

"Tall, dark, broody, kinda looks like he could rob a bank?"

"Honey, we might live a few towns over, but we all know Bravetown like the back of our hand. That's the young man who plays Ace Ryder."

"I don't want to see him," I said way too quickly.

"He's been here for hours, waiting for you."

And under different circumstances, he probably would have gotten to me if I'd just been in the ER. But despite canceling my credit cards and practically kicking me out of the house, my parents didn't have the heart to boot me off their insurance. Their very expensive insurance that paid for all the little extras, like private rooms.

"Could you give me a minute to myself?" I asked the nurse and offered her a polite smile.

"Of course, honey."

As soon as she was out of the room, I released a long, stuttering breath.

God, I hated hospitals.

I stared at the door, picturing Noah's long limbs folded into one of those tiny hallway benches while he waited for me. Because he couldn't help himself. He'd feel responsible for the fall, and he'd feel responsible for me.

I closed my eyes, steeling myself for the conversation I was about to have, then pulled out my phone. She picked up on the second ring.

"Mom, I'm hurt."

"Canım benim," she sighed, "which hospital are you in? Do you need surgery? I'm getting Dr. Garibaldi on the phone."

"Mom, please." I pressed my lips together for a second, registering all the questions she didn't ask. *Hurt, how? What happened? How do you feel?* A week ago, I would have clashed with her over it, but I was tired. I was just so tired of constantly having to fight for air. At least I had two decades' worth of experience in handling her specific brand of stifling.

I took one last deep breath of freedom.

"Can I come back home?"

Chapter Twenty-Five

PARK HOURS: SUMMER SEASON

June 1 – September 30

9 a.m. – 9 p.m.

Last entry: 8 p.m.

Select the date of your visit in the calendar below to see a list of available activities, attractions and shows on that day.

Our helpful staff members will let you know when it's time to end your adventure in Bravetown and ride off into the sunset.

Please note: Due to safety concerns, visitors discovered in the park after gates have closed will not be allowed to return to the premises.

ESRA

"Your brother wants to talk to you." Dad thrust his phone at me, and I accepted it before I had the chance to process his words.

Sinan's face lit up the screen.

"Huh? No, Dad. Dad!" I turned in my chair and tried to hand the phone back, but Dad was already walking out the door, waving a hand over his shoulder at me.

I sighed and closed my eyes for a moment, phone still angled away from me.

I didn't even get a say in which phone calls I accepted.

Apparently, declining every single one of Sanny's FaceTimes over the last couple of days hadn't made it clear that I had nothing to say to him. So now he had to go through our parents. Cheap trick. I turned back to the dining table, where I'd set out my reading materials and balanced the phone against my half-empty glass of water.

"Hey Ez," he said, trying to paint his voice with faux friendliness.

"Hey," I replied because the door to the living room stood ajar, and I was sure Mom would lecture me if I didn't have at least half a conversation with my brother. Never mind that we could have a whole conversation in sign language. I'd have to actually *talk* to Sanny to appease our nosy parents.

"So . . . what's up?" Sanny ran a hand through his already messy hair.

"Why did you want to talk to me?" I asked, fighting the urge to cross my arms. The right one was still in a sturdy sling.

"Just checking in, you know?"

I rolled my eyes at him. This couldn't be more awkward. He had never checked in like this before. I wasn't sure if the in-person overprotectiveness hadn't worn off yet, or if this would end up being a thinly veiled attempt from our parents to get some answers from me.

I hadn't exactly been talkative the last few days . . . To get them off my back, I blamed my mood on the pain I was in. In reality, their every comment grated down my spine. Mom didn't even have to mention Yale or my future or *that place*, as she referred to Bravetown, for my jaw to clench up. Yesterday, she'd been going on and on about the dresses she'd found for me at a small boutique by an up-and-coming designer that none of her friends had discovered yet, and how I'd be ahead of every trend. I'd stormed to my room and put on a T-shirt that said "great tits" across the chest with an image of two great tits, the birds, underneath. It had been one of the first items of clothing I'd bought myself. Now I felt ridiculous for letting my mother clothe me for over twenty years.

"Ask her," Zuri hissed from off-screen.

Great. Because we needed even more witnesses to this train wreck of a phone call.

Sinan huffed and squared his shoulders. "Are you coming back?"

"Why do you want to know?"

"Because I feel like it's kinda my fault that you left."

I bit my lip and glanced over at the living-room door. Was it just me or had the TV been louder a few moments ago? Not that it mattered. Sanny was part of the reason I'd left, but he wasn't the whole reason. "I was always going to leave."

"Yeah, no . . ." He fell quiet and switched to signing. "I don't think that's true. I think you liked it here."

"Do you think you know my life better than I do?" I signed back.

"No, that's not what I meant," he signed and groaned.

"I just thought you liked this place and everyone here. I thought you'd want to stick around. That's all."

I narrowed my eyes at him.

"I'm looking through the Yale grad school course catalog, so you can answer your own question." This time, I replied out loud, because I wanted Mom to hear, and I demonstratively held up the brochure I'd been reading.

"Shit, okay." He sighed and glanced up to something – or someone – on the other side of the phone. Was that Zuri? Or was Noah there, too?

Before I could give in to my stupid heart, which still fluttered at the thought of him, and ask about Noah, I bit my tongue hard enough for it to sting.

"What's on your list?" Sinan asked after an awkward moment of silence.

"What list?"

"You know, the list to go with the catalog. The courses. I don't know. I'm just . . . I don't want to go back to only speaking to you every other month. Just keep me in the loop. I can tell you about everything that's been going on here if you want me to. People are worried about you."

"I don't want you to," I muttered and slid the course catalog aside. I had stacked it on top of a brand-new pink legal pad to carry it to the dining table, but I hadn't even written down a heading for the list I should have been making. My gaze circled the table. I hadn't even brought a pen with me.

"And the shoulder? Are you back in PT? I know you've dislocated it before, but—"

"Sanny," I cut him off, "I'm actually okay not talking to you for two months at a time until you figure out that I don't need you to take care of me." I ended the call and let the phone clatter to the table face down. I didn't even want to know if he called back.

I drummed my fingers against the empty notepad and glanced at the open catalog next to it. I wouldn't even know what to put on the list. I'd somehow made it halfway through and didn't remember a single course description. Well . . .

I tore the first page off the legal pad, making sure to leave a messy edge behind.

If my parents asked, that page contained the list of courses I was genuinely interested in – and it wouldn't even be a lie. They just wouldn't expect that list to equal zero. I folded the piece of paper into a small square and pocketed it before I wandered back to my room. I slipped off the arm sling I'd been wearing for the last five days and flung it in the box with all my braces and bandages, just to crawl into bed and indulge in my new favorite kind of masochism:

I opened Noah's social media profile.

Seeing his face was enough to reopen the stitches of my barely healing heartbreak. I was giving myself emotional open-heart-surgery – but I hadn't actually gone to med school, hadn't studied under a world-class cardiothoracic surgeon, so I was just poking and prodding my poor heart, hoping it would stop beating faster at the sight of him. Because how could both be true? How could he be the reason for the pressure on my chest that stole the air from my lungs, and yet I still loved him?

The only relief I got was that he hadn't posted in over a week. Since before Sinan's birthday party when everything had gone to shit. I'd checked Lucas's and Heather's profiles, and they'd both been uploading videos, so it wasn't like Renee had put a halt to it after my accident. Noah was the only one who had gone silent online.

I wouldn't be able to stomach the day I'd open his profile and spot a new video thumbnail.

I wasn't ready for him to move on.

Chapter Twenty-Six

404

Oops! Page not found!

The site you were looking for has been removed.

NOAH

I set the last of my boxes down by the door and dropped on to the splintering porch steps. I'd have to fix these at some point. Right now, I needed a minute to breathe. Not physically. I'd managed to get all my things from the staff housing complex to the ranch in two drives. But I wasn't coping well with the change. I was returning two years sooner than I'd anticipated. The house was supposed to be completely overhauled by the time I was going to live in it again. It was supposed to be new and wholly mine.

Now, it was neither.

The front door was still notched where my father had thrown an empty liquor bottle against it. Half the kitchen was still covered in construction materials. My bedsheets still smelled like a girl I'd only dream of from now on.

It wasn't the place I'd wanted it to be when I moved back in.

I glanced down at the ailing wood beneath my boots,

held down by shiny new nails for now. Maybe clean breaks and fresh starts were all lies. There'd always be jagged edges that you just had to build your life around.

If that was the case, this wasn't the worst place to build a life. The sun was just beginning to set, lowering toward the tree line that separated this place from the rest of Wild Fields, and it bathed the entire estate in golden light. Sprawling grass as far as the eye could see, birds swooping through the air, and the kind of quiet you couldn't get anywhere else.

I wanted a future here, but my throat constricted every time I remembered that she wouldn't be in it.

My attention snapped to the driveway when the crunching of tires on gravel disrupted the silence. Sanny's car rolled to a stop next to mine. He'd offered to carry boxes with me today, but I had to do it for myself. I'd made the decision to move here, and each box had helped turn it from a far-off concept into my new life.

When he'd insisted on helping anyway, I'd sent him to the hardware store.

"You look tired," he said by way of greeting as he jumped out of the car.

"Thanks, always good to hear," I called back.

Sinan just grinned and shrugged before he grabbed a paper bag from the passenger seat. He set it down on top of the box I hadn't bothered carrying inside yet.

"Have you talked to Esra since she left?" he asked and sat down next to me.

My throat momentarily tightened at the mention of her name.

"No." I'd wanted to. I'd opened her contact details

multiple times a day, only to lock my screen and shove the phone back in my pocket. I wanted to hear her voice and her laugh as she told me about her days, and for her to call me *cowboy*. I also owed her an apology, but even if she agreed to talk to me, it wouldn't change the outcome. She'd always meant to leave after the summer. I had to live with the jagged edge that remained. So I swallowed everything I wanted to say to Esra and every detail I wanted to pry from Sanny, and asked, "Why?"

"I tried today, but she hung up on me." He sighed and scratched the back of his neck. We hadn't talked about his sister since the day I landed her in the hospital, after he'd informed me that his parents had booked her on a red-eye back to New York. "I think I messed up."

"Yeah . . . I think we both did."

"What did you do?" He sounded genuinely puzzled.

I raised my brows at him. He may not have known that we'd been together, but he had seen how I'd let her fall off the horse just like everyone else in the park that day.

"Because of the accident? Man, that wasn't your fault."

"We fought over her disappearing and partying all weekend, and the tension between us affected Tornado. I shouldn't have let her sit on an agitated horse, Sanny. I should have helped her out of the saddle." My throat tightened again and turned my voice hoarse. "I really fucked up. I'm so sorry."

"Noah, with all due respect . . ." He whipped his flat hand over the back of my head. It was barely hard enough to cause me to nod.

"What was that for?" I groaned.

"Just trying to smack your brain back into place." He

laughed and shook his head. Clearly this hadn't been torturing him like it had me. "Accidents happen. It sucks that the outcome tends to be worse for her, but that doesn't change the fact that it was just an accident. She could have just as easily slipped in the mud and still dislocated her shoulder."

My gaze snapped past him to the stables, where we had lost our footing and dropped into the mud. She had panicked and prodded at me until I reassured her that I was fine. It just clicked now. Esra lived with the constant awareness that one bad fall could seriously injure her.

"Tell her that I'm sorry anyway, okay?" Even if he didn't blame me for the accident, I'd still caused her serious pain. "I'm sorry she got hurt."

"She doesn't want to talk to me. I think I get it though." He grimaced and rubbed a hand over his knuckles. "I called my dad yesterday. *I* called *him*. My parents, who have called every single day all summer, haven't actually reached out since Esra went back home."

"I'm sorry."

"I'm not. Made me realize that I let them treat me like an extension of the tight leash they keep on her."

"They bubble-wrap her," I echoed the words Esra had used to describe her upbringing.

"Yeah, kind of." He slapped his hands against his knees. "Anyway, I have the rest of the shower curtain stuff in the car. They didn't have oil-rubbed bronze, only Venetian bronze, but they look the same to me. The Home Depot guy said the color variation . . ."

His words faded into the background as we walked around his car and I grabbed the curved curtain-rod pieces from his trunk. They would come together in an oval to hang above the tub in the master bathroom. It was a cheaper option than getting a glass wall fitted under the slanted roof, and Esra had called it *farmhouse chic*. In another life, I didn't care that they were the wrong shade of dark brown. In this one, however, this wasn't the color Esra had picked and put on the list of renovations, and it felt wrong.

Sanny would probably smack me over the head again if I asked him to return this. I didn't even have an image of the right color in mind.

All I knew was that these were the incorrect bronze, and Esra was gone, and I didn't have so much as a picture of us, and I couldn't tell my best friend that my chest felt hollow without her here. And it was like we never even existed.

I glanced at the stables again, wishing I could walk over and let Tornado steady me. But the stalls were far from ready, so my horses were still in Bravetown's care for now. Even the one comfort I'd always relied on was gone, and I only had myself to blame. Because I couldn't stomach staying in Staff House B and waiting for someone else to move into Esra's room, fill *her* cupboard with healthy foods, hang a towel on *her* hook in the bathroom. They couldn't just replace her.

She hadn't just left her job at Bravetown. She had left me.

And I wasn't ready for my world to move on without her.

Chapter Twenty-Seven

Esra

There was a perfectly good chance that Rodney Junior had grown up into a normal adult without murderous tendencies, but I could hardly listen to a word he said as he led me and my parents around campus. He hadn't even acknowledged the sling around my arm. Considering he was the boy who'd caused my very first dislocated shoulder, I would have liked at least one little joke in a futile attempt to leave the past behind us. *Silly kids*, and all that.

Nothing.

The fact that he seemed so normal with his polo shirt and brown loafers just made it harder to believe that he actually was. He could be Yale's own Patrick Bateman.

"What do you think, Esra?" Dad asked, smiling at something Rodney Junior had said.

"I'm not sure yet," I said. I had no clue what they were talking about, but sounding critical always seemed to work on the academics.

Rodney beamed, his teeth bleached to the point of glowing blue. "You're absolutely right to be skeptical. Never trust someone else's word when you can make up your own mind, right?"

Bingo.

I almost laughed at how easy it was to feign interest as we wandered down the hallways of the School of Public Health. Apparently, Rodney Junior was trying hard to follow in the footsteps of daddy dearest, so he was doing his old man a favor by playing tour guide for us all day.

Yay me.

I was just here because after two weeks of carrying the course catalog around like an alibi when I was really just wallowing, my mother had decided it was now time for me to *start working on my future.* I still had zero interest in going back to school. But I figured if I went on one campus tour, I could get my parents to back off with a little *hmm, I'm not sure yet* for another month or so.

The only thing that really stood out to me about Yale was the lack of air conditioning. Sweat slowly trickled down my back and I fanned myself with my brochure as we walked down one long hallway with doors and into another long hallway with doors. Everything about it felt narrow. It was irrational. All four of us could comfortably walk side by side, but I wanted to clench my shoulders to squeeze through these halls, scared of getting stuck.

"Didn't you say this was a particularly green campus?" I wasn't sure if he'd said that, but I doubted he'd admit it if this place was a concrete wasteland.

"I was just getting to that," Rodney chuckled and winked.

"Yeah, can we get to that now?" The air was disgustingly thick in here.

"Esra!" Mom scolded me under her breath. Easy for her to do. She didn't look like she was about to melt into a puddle. Maybe Tennessee's superior air conditioning had absolutely spoiled me.

"Of course," Rodney replied, completely ignoring my mother, "there's a beautiful green space right behind the building. The students love sitting outside for lunch or to study in the warmer months."

"Stop waving that thing around like a madwoman," Dad hissed at me after Rodney Junior had already set off toward the elevator.

"Aren't you hot?" I asked, brows raised at the thick suit he was wearing. He'd dressed up more than me. I'd already compromised on a plain white T-shirt after Mom had refused to let me leave the house in the one that said "medical professional" on the front and "ask me about my mouth-to-mouth skills" on the back.

"You'll cool down outside," Dad said with the kind of authority that didn't leave room for protest. Okay then. I'd cool down outside.

Except the green space I had been promised was a glorified strip of grass between a bunch of concrete blocks and a busy street. Cars were honking, somewhere music was playing from a window, and the little bit of lawn there was, was covered by people. They sat a foot or two away from each other at most.

This was not the kind of place you went to get fresh air.

This was the kind of place that you searched for Waldo.

"I think that's a very nice offer, thank you, RJ," Mom said and patted Rodney Junior on the arm.

"Hmm?" I raised my brows because three pairs of eyes were trained on me.

"Then it's a date. Maureen is said to be the next Meryl Streep," Junior said, still smiling at me.

"Isn't Meryl Streep still the current Meryl Streep?" I asked, confused.

"Maureen is on the Yale theater program. In the play RJ just invited you to," Dad pressed the explanation through gritted teeth.

"A play? What about?" I gasped. Why was the air conditioning not working? My lungs felt like they were being wired shut from heat. *Oh, right.* We were outside.

"It's a deep look into the human psyche as told through the points of view of consumerist goods."

"Huh." I nodded, fanning myself faster. "Any kidnappings? Bank robberies? Something fun?"

Rodney Junior laughed as if I'd just made the best joke he'd ever heard. I hadn't been joking. Why would I watch a play that wasn't at least a little bit exciting? I just wanted a good villain in it.

Something was wrong.

Not only with Rodney Junior, on a very deep psychological level, but with me.

No matter how much I fanned, I couldn't cool down. I felt the wind against my clammy skin, too, and saw the rustling leaves on the strategically placed five trees. There *was* air. It just didn't get to me.

Was this a panic attack?

I needed to get out of here. This was wrong. Everything about this place was wrong. This wasn't a green space. I'd seen green spaces. First of all, they required space, not a patch of grass between buildings. Fields of nature and birds and insects. You were supposed to be able to ride through them on the back of a golden horse named Crumble.

And I missed the sky. Ever since coming back to the city, I just wanted to get a car and drive out of the concrete jungle, find somewhere where the sky took up most of my field of vision. I missed the blues of the day and the burning reds and oranges of the sunset.

I tilted my head back to check the sky above New Haven, only to be greeted with a murky soup of low-hanging gray. Of course.

I missed looking at the sky from Noah's bed. I missed Noah's bed. I missed—

My chest constricted.

"This is wrong," I croaked, pressing my palm against my flushed face.

"I'm sorry, what is?" Junior asked.

"This. This place. This school. That play. This T-shirt. You. You're so wrong for me."

"Excuse me?" For the first time all day, Junior's mask slipped. His perfect polish vanished and gave way to a shocked, gaping carp's mouth.

"I'm sorry, RJ," Dad cleared his throat and forced a

painful-looking smile. "Esra is clearly a little overwhelmed by all this today."

"Esra, honey, do you want to sit down for a moment? Let's have a little chat." Mom stepped toward me, and I stepped back.

"I don't want to have a chat."

"Esra," Dad warned.

"I need to go. I can't do this. I'm not meant to be here." I backed away from all three of them. Thank god there was a busy street right next to this oh-so-green campus. I had hailed a taxi before my dad had finished yelling at me to "come back here".

"Where to, miss?" the cabbie asked.

I glanced out the window to where my mother was throwing up her hands and shaking her head, while Dad talked at Rodney Junior, inches from his face. Neither of them was even trying to come after me. "Nearest airport to get a flight to Nashville."

"That would be Hartford."

"Hartford it is. And could you crank up the AC? I feel like I'm about to go up in flames. Thank you so much."

It was about an hour to the airport, plus check-in and security times, which meant the only flight to Nashville I'd catch was the last one of the day. Damn. There were a few shuttle buses that ran from Nashville to Wild Fields, Bravetown in particular, but none that late. And with the stupid sling, I couldn't rent a car.

I had a few hours to come up with a way to apologize to Noah. But in the meantime, I'd have to start somewhere.

I called Adriana and got sent to voicemail within two rings.

346

I called her again and got the voicemail on the first ring.

For someone who had made many enemies by ditching town, she was good at holding a grudge over me for the same thing.

So I sent her a text instead.

Esra: Think I might be pregnant.

My phone immediately started ringing. *Gotcha.* I picked up with an innocent "Hello?"

"Tell me you're lying right now. I told you not to get knocked up by a country boy," Adriana shrieked into the phone.

"Yeah, I was lying. I just needed you to pick up the phone."

"Lies aren't a great start if you're calling to make amends," she said.

"What if I win your love back with a drink tonight? You'll just have to drive my car to Nashville," I offered, mirroring the same tactic she'd used all summer to weasel her way into everyone's heart.

"I'm listening."

Chapter Twenty-Eight

THE HUDSON FAMILY HOME

Step back in time as you walk through this historically accurate replica of a family home in the Old West. You won't find electricity or running water here, but that doesn't mean it was a wholly uncomfortable place to be. The house's inhabitants will be more than happy to answer your questions on how they live and spend their days here.

Noah

"Oh, come *on*," Sanny groaned and let his screwdriver clatter to the floor to pick up his phone instead. He swiped over the screen, shaking his head at whatever message had just come in.

I'd stopped asking. They were never from Esra.

I didn't have to ask though. He turned his phone around and showed me a picture of Esra walking next to some polo-shirt-wearing guy with way too much gel in his hair. It was taken from behind their backs, so I assumed at least one of his parents was there too. That couldn't be some super-romantic date. Or maybe it was. I'd never really asked Esra how her parents felt about her dating life. I knew they had been vehemently against Sinan living with a woman unless he'd put an engagement ring on her finger.

"Who's that?" I asked, trying to sound nonchalant.

"They're making her tour Yale."

I wanted to yell at him that that didn't answer my question. I wanted to know who the fuck the smarmy guy was and why the hell he was standing so close to Esra. Instead, I just said, "Huh."

"I hate this guy."

"Oh?" *Smooth.*

"I mean, I don't know him now. But he was a walking shit stain when we were kids. Whacked me in the face with a tennis racket once and pretended it was an accident. I had two black eyes for weeks. One summer, he put Esra in the hospital when he shoved her off his family's boat."

"Then why the fuck's she talking to him now?"

"I think he goes to the school she's touring or something. I don't know."

"She shouldn't be around this guy," I said.

"Which is why my first reaction was *'oh, come on'.*"

That was not an appropriate reaction if you asked me, but I was also losing all common sense when it came to Esra. She was probably perfectly safe. Little kids with violent tendencies didn't always grow up to be violent adults.

I still wanted to rip that phone from Sanny's hands, call his parents and tell them to get her the fuck away from that man.

Sinan sighed and picked the screwdriver back up, then went back to putting my new drawers together with me. Well, *for* me, because I wasn't doing much other than staring at his phone right now. If I could have, I would have asked for hourly updates, just to make sure that guy wasn't trying anything.

Unfortunately, I'd already asked Sinan to build this wardrobe with me due to my unrelenting obsession with his little sister, so I was all out of sister-related favors. I hadn't spelled it out like that. But after Esra left the staff housing complex, I didn't want to stay either, so I had to make the ranch livable.

I'd lived in the Bravetown staff house for five years, but after a few weeks with Esra, I could see her standing in every corner, walking through every door, sitting on every surface and dangling her feet.

I'd been close to asking for his parents' address once or twice now, but every single time, her pained scream echoed through my mind. Sanny may not have blamed me, but I should have held Tornado still that day. It was horsemanship 101, but I'd been so in my head about losing another person I cared about, I'd fucked up. Maybe Esra didn't need someone who took care of her, but at the very least, she deserved someone who wouldn't endanger her. She deserved better than me.

Sanny took off in the late afternoon to pick Zuri up from work, leaving me alone at the ranch. There was always something to work on, so I wandered past the to do lists taped up in the hallway and picked an item. The gate of one of the stalls in the stable had come off its hinges. That seemed easy enough and matched the unhinged thoughts I'd been harboring since seeing that photo on Sinan's phone.

One day, I'd install completely new horse stalls out here. I wanted to get the kind of doors that allowed you to open the upper half, so the horses could stick their heads out. They were going to be great for first-time riders to meet the animals. For now, I focused on getting the place fixed and polished.

I was packing up the tools after the light of day had faded from the stables when the sound of tires down the driveway gave me pause. Sanny and I were the only two people who ever came here. As far as I knew. I grabbed the hammer from my toolbox and inched toward the stable doors.

A small car stopped right by the front steps of the main house. It looked familiar from the Bravetown parking lot, but I couldn't place it yet. It was almost dark out, and the porch light didn't shine bright enough to illuminate the license plate either. So I waited. Nobody emerged from the driver's side.

It wasn't until I stepped outside and could see a head of dark hair through the windows, the car lit up from inside, that I remembered who it belonged to.

My throat closed up.

The hammer dropped from my hand and landed in the dirt.

The woman inside the car turned, finally ready to open the door, and her big brown doe eyes met mine through the window and across the distance.

We stayed locked like that for a moment, neither of us moving.

She was here.

How was she here?

It didn't make sense.

But she was here, and her shoulders rose and fell in a

deep sigh, and she was here, and she tilted her head and shrugged, and she was here, and the car door clicked open.

At the sound, my muscles sprang into action instinctively. I jogged down the small slope toward her.

"Esra?"

"Hi." She climbed out of the car but leaned against it heavily, her head flopping to one side. As I got closer, I could make out the dark crescents under her eyes and the shadows hollowing her cheeks. She looked exhausted to the point of collapse. "I prepared something that I want to say. I just don't remember it right now."

"What are you doing here?" I asked, stepping closer with outstretched hands because I didn't need her falling down again. She probably shouldn't even have been driving with her shoulder still in a sling.

"I need to apolo—" Her good intentions were cut off as she swayed dangerously and closed her eyes. Her left arm waved through the air, grasping at the car for support.

I jumped forward. My hands closed around her middle, steadying her frame before she could topple over.

"Oh no," she gasped.

"Let's get you inside." I wasn't sure what was going on. She'd just been touring Yale with that walking hair gel tube and now she was close to fainting in my driveway – but she needed to lie down.

"No, no, no, I need to get this out, please."

"Do you need to throw up?"

"Not like that." She straightened back up and took a wavering step backward.

My fingertips brushed across her stomach as I untangled myself from her unusually bland T-shirt, only for me to hesitate and bring the back of my hand up to her forehead. "Jesus, Esra, you're burning up."

"Yeah." She hiccupped a laugh. "I thought I was having a panic attack. But I think I'm getting sick."

"I think you already are sick. Let's get you to bed, come on."

"One second, please." She held up a single digit, then grabbed my forearm for support. Her nails dug into my skin as another dizzy spell had her leaning on me.

"Well, at least the manners are impeccable, princess."

She giggled, then moaned and clutched her hand to her chest. "Ouch. No laughing."

I maneuvered Esra on to the sofa and got her a bucket just in case she threw up, but that was as far as she let me take care of her. I tried offering a cold compress and she swatted me away.

"I need to apologize," she huffed. Her face was flushed bright pink, tiny beads of sweat cresting above her brows.

"We can talk later, Esra. You should really be lying down." I knelt in front of her and tried to take her shoes, but she kicked my hands off.

"No, look, I had a whole apology mapped out. It's on my phone." She patted her pockets, only to realize there was no phone. Her glassy eyes moved to the front door.

"I'll get it," I said.

"Stop. Will you just stop? I'll do it myself later. Just sit down and let me tell you that I've fallen stupidly in love with you."

I froze. "What did you just say?"

"Oh, you heard me, Young," she snapped and squeezed her eyes shut, bending forward. She gripped the edge of the sofa cushions until her knuckles turned white. "Now can I please apologize for leaving the way I did?" She yelled those words into the space between her knees as she tried to keep her body from swaying. A little dizzy spell was one thing, but she couldn't even sit upright.

"Listen to me, you stubborn woman," I sighed and sank down in front of her again. This time, I held her feet firmly enough so she couldn't shake me off. I pulled her tennis shoes off first, then the ankle braces. "You're sick. You're actually acutely sick. So I'm going to take care of you, and you're going to let me. Because, right now, you need someone to look after you and make sure you get better. That has nothing to do with me being overbearing. I'm used to being the one who takes responsibility, so sometimes you might have to roll your pretty eyes at me and tell me to relax. But you'll have to accept that sometimes you just need help. And I'm going to be here to help you because I love you too, so you're stuck with me."

"Fine," she mumbled and slowly blinked through tired lids, "but you might have to repeat all of that tomorrow."

"I'll repeat it every day if you need me to."

"God, I hope this doesn't last that long."

"I'll be right back, okay? I'm going to get you something to drink."

By the time I came back with a cup of water, Esra lay sprawled out on the sofa. She flipped the hem of her shirt up and down to cool off, but soaked strands of hair stuck to her face and the flush had spread from her cheeks down her neck. When I brought the cold compress to her forehead now, she didn't try to fight me off.

"I thought you were at Yale today with some wannabe boat murderer."

Her eyes cleared for just a flash. "Have you been keeping tabs on me?"

"Yes." No point in lying.

"I don't know if that's creepy or sweet," she muttered. "I was touring the campus, but I just couldn't see a future in that kind of place anymore. I guess I never did. It had always been about the end goal, but grad school was never going to make me happy. It was so stifling." She gulped down some water, then lay back with her eyes closed. "I got the first flight I could to Nashville and Adriana picked me up from the airport. I went home, but you weren't there."

Home. She thought of Bravetown as home.

Whatever kind of apology she had drafted on her phone, this was already more than I'd ever expected of her.

"I moved in here a couple days ago," I explained.

"You don't even have a hot shower." Her face contorted and I smoothed the tension back out with my fingertips.

"I didn't want to live next to anyone that wasn't you, princess." I climbed on to the sofa and draped her legs over my lap. "Besides, I bought a makeshift electric shower. It'll do for now."

"Huh. That wasn't on the to-do list."

"I added it and then I crossed it off."

"Good."

Esra slipped into a quick sleep. For a short while, I just watched her. I was worried she'd wake up and spit the water back up when she really needed those fluids. I also considered that I was merely hallucinating her and if I looked away, she'd be gone again. Only when I was somewhat certain that neither was the case did I leave her to go have a conversation that was long overdue.

Sanny picked up on the first ring. "She's with you?"

Jumping right into the deep end. Not sure how he'd come to that conclusion, but it saved me the preamble. "Yeah."

"Good." He let out a long breath. "She's not picking up her phone and Dad's going berserk."

"She left her phone in the car."

"How is she?"

"Sick. I think she has a virus or the flu or something." I glanced down the hallway toward the living room, but nothing stirred at the other end of the house. "She's asleep now."

"Okay. I'll stop by first thing tomorrow."

"You don't want to know why she came to the ranch?"

"Aw man, give me some credit. I have more than two brain cells. I know she didn't ditch our parents and come back here for the horses." Sanny laughed, apparently completely unbothered by the revelation. "I'll see you tomorrow."

That went better than expected. There was a possibility that he'd just been relieved Esra hadn't gone missing, and I'd still get sucker-punched tomorrow, but I'd deal with that when the time came. For now, I just wanted to get Esra through the night.

I got her phone from the car and left it in the kitchen to charge before returning to the sofa. I rearranged the cushions on the far end, so I could settle in somewhat comfortably without costing her any space to stretch in all directions. Someone else's body heat was probably the last thing she needed right now, but I wasn't leaving her side. She woke up four or five times that night, sweating through her shirt and downing water. I kept refilling her cup, refreshing her cold compress and smoothing the sweaty strands away from her face.

"Noah?" she whispered around 4 a.m., stretching until her toes reached my thigh. I cupped her ankle. Even her usually freezing feet were unnaturally warm.

"I'm here." I'd left the light in the hallway on, so she could have easily spotted me, had she opened her eyes.

"How's Tornado? He was so nervous that day."

"He's all right. He picked up on our mood, that's all. I should have held him still while you were dismounting. I'm so sorry."

"It's not your fault. I was just so worried he was getting sick." She heaved a deep sigh, turned her head and went back to sleep.

How was a sane man not supposed to fall for her when she did things like that? She was on the brink of delirium, but what was important to her was my horse's wellbeing. The horse she'd fallen off after he sidestepped her, no less. Something she didn't blame me for, either. The guilt that had been wrecking me unhooked one of its sharp claws from my chest. I still felt responsible, but at least Esra wasn't holding the accident against me.

She had just fallen back asleep when Sanny showed up the next morning. Instead of using his key, however, he knocked on the door. He never knocked on the door.

I opened it for him, brows raised in a silent question.

He sported a wide, shit-eating grin. "I didn't want to interrupt anything."

The implication was obvious, but I only shook my head. "She really is sick. Her fever seems to have gone down a bit, but she's passed out on the sofa."

Sinan walked in and paused in front of the to do lists taped to the wall. He'd praised those lists not too long ago and had tackled a few tasks with me. Today, he narrowed his eyes at them, wandering along the wall toward the living room to inspect them. His gaze swiveled to me, then in the direction of the living room. It finally clicked. I hadn't just magically become a list person.

"You're not going to rip my head off, are you?" I asked, only half-kidding. Knowing that his little sister and I had become an item was one thing, but he had to realize how long it had been going on. That we'd been lying to him for months.

I watched him, my shoulders tense as I waited for his reaction.

Sanny rolled his eyes at me in a move that reminded me a lot of Esra. Funny. A few months ago, she had reminded me of her brother. But now all her little movements were the benchmark and Sanny could only try to live up to them.

"Why would I rip your head off? Noah, you and I, we're planning a whole future here together." He circled his hand through the air to indicate the ranch. "I know who you are behind that resting-bitch-face. So, in my opinion, out of all the men my sister could date, you're the best-case scenario. You're practically already my work husband. Might as well make you my real-life brother-in-law."

He was jumping many steps ahead. So was I, but in a different direction: "What if something happens between her and me, or between you and me, and you end up having to choose sides?"

"Jeez, we have to work on your optimism, cowboy," Esra croaked from the living room.

I slipped past Sanny without another word. Esra had a magnetic pull on me. "Good morning," I said, even though she'd technically been awake twice before today. Her eyes had cleared up a little. That was a good sign.

"Hey, remember how I told you not to be messy?" Sanny leaned over the back of the sofa, grinning down at his sister. "You owe me a drink. The new Annie Lou is a Mess. Capital M. She can do the horse tricks but can't stay in character for shit."

"I didn't know there was a new Annie Lou already." Esra's voice quivered, and she pushed herself up on the sofa. Even that bit of movement must have been too much, because the little color in her cheeks turned pale and she squeezed her eyes shut again. "That was quick."

"Let's get you better before you think about getting back on the horse," I said. "For what it's worth, you're a much better Annie."

"Thank you," she whispered.

I arranged the cushions around her until they held her upright.

"Look, Ez, I talked to Mom this morning." Esra groaned but Sinan carried on undeterred. "I think I got her off your back for a while. It's not an ideal solution, but it'll buy you some time until you're ready to deal with her yourself."

"What did you tell her?"

"Zuri and I set a date. So Mom will be in wedding mode for a while."

"What? When? I thought you wanted to wait a bit longer."

Sanny reached over to pat Esra's head, then wiped his hand off on the sofa cushions when he realized that her hair was drenched in sweat from last night. "Consider it our apology to you for meddling."

"Thank you. Genuinely." She sighed and offered him a small smile. "Can you please send my wedding invitation here?"

I'd held myself back from the conversation, but my spine straightened at those words. Esra fixed her gaze on me. "If that's okay with you."

Those renovation to do lists in the hallway were about to grow tenfold. I didn't care so much about running hot water or window condensation for myself, but if Esra was moving in, I'd turn this house into a palace for her. "That's very okay with me, princess."

Chapter Twenty-Nine

BROOKS MONROE: ONE NIGHT ONLY

Brooks Monroe (41) returns to the stage for the first time in three years after his unexpected retirement from touring. The former Sexiest Man Alive, three-time Grammy and nine-time Country Music Award winner officially announced the "One Night Only" show on his social media profiles, but if you were hoping to snag tickets and see the country legend in concert, you may be out of luck.

Many fans expressed their disappointment in the choice of venue and the limited ticket availability . . .

Esra

I spent four days drifting in and out of sleep. The third day was the worst, when the fever spiked again and even the joints in my fingers burned to the point where I couldn't hold my phone anymore. Noah barely left my side throughout the whole thing. He couldn't take the entire time off, but he had someone else handle his work with the park's horses and check on Tornado, Cookie and Crumble, so he was really just gone for the few hours he had to play Ace.

Once I was well enough to get out of bed, he helped me

into the tub in the master bathroom and showed off his electric hot-shower contraption. It was made for camping grounds, but it worked well enough for him to wash days of sweat and grime off my skin and out of my hair. His fingers carefully combed along my scalp and through the knotted ends. I let my head fall back, every molecule in my body humming with comfort.

"The dark bronze looks great," I mumbled as I blinked up at the shower rod he'd installed.

"Yeah? You like it?" he chuckled.

"Mm-hmm, yeah." I let my eyes fall shut, soaking in every soothing touch. I didn't care that much about the shower curtain fixture, but we'd chosen it lying naked in his bed while he'd tried to distract me with his tongue. In the end, I'd just picked one, so he'd finally sink his head between my legs. Lucky enough, the dark brown *did* look great in the bright rooftop space.

He rinsed my hair and rubbed a towel through it before helping me up and out of the tub. I smelled like him now. I was going to use his shampoo for the rest of my life if it meant getting to smell him whenever I whipped my head around.

It took another week for my body to fully recover, but despite the bland diet and early bedtimes, that week was one of the best of my life. I wore Noah's shirts around the house and wandered barefoot through the backyard. Noah made me tea and cradled me in his lap while I sipped it, and we watched teen horseback-riding dramas on Netflix. And we lay under that beautiful skylight, tangled in the blankets, sharing secrets and stories from our lives while we tried not to get distracted by all the kissing we could do for hours on end without interruption.

By Tuesday, I felt well enough to leave the house with Noah as he went to work. He said he'd smuggle me through the staff entrance, but I waved him off and headed to the ticket office instead. Even Stephanie at the counter tried to tell me that I could just go through, but I insisted on getting a ticket. I'd left. I was just like any other guest. Almost. I felt a bit like Clark Kent. I'd put my hair up in a high ponytail and had borrowed Noah's big aviators just to be safe. I didn't want to shatter some little kid's illusion on the off-chance they knew my face.

The crowd in the park seemed denser than usual. Maybe it was just the height of summer season. Part of me couldn't help but think it was because people preferred the new Annie Lou. I took a bite of my horseshoe pretzel to swallow the bitterness down as I stood in line for the meet and greet. His smile didn't falter until I got to the front of the line and flipped my sunglasses up.

"Hey Lucky."

Lucas shook his head, the smile returning slowly. "Hello gorgeous."

I handed my phone to Clarence, who was assisting with Lucas's crowd, and went up to get my picture taken with Kit Holliday.

"Are you coming back?" he asked when I was close enough for only me to hear him.

"If you'll have me," I said and meant it. I was going to talk to Renee later, but Lucas had spent so many hours on those videos with me, trying to help me find my footing here, that I wouldn't blame him if he never wanted to see me again after the way I took off.

"Yes, please," he said and put an arm around my shoulder

for the picture, leaning in to whisper, "you can be my wing-woman, so I can finally pull myself an Annie Lou. The new one's kinda hot. I have dibs."

"You're incorrigible," I laughed.

Clarence handed back my phone and Lucas sent me off with a big smile and an "I'll see you later."

I considered staying for the show afterward, but my throat closed up at the thought of seeing someone else in my costume. Playing Annie Lou wasn't what I'd envisioned for myself, but it was so much fun. Between the excited kids and the show itself, I also got to spend all my time with the people I cared about in a place designed to make everyone's days brighter. Maybe it wasn't what I was going to spend the rest of my life doing, but I wasn't ready to give it up yet.

That's what I had to talk to Renee about.

"I want to come back," I said in the firmest voice I could manage. I sat in Renee's office, shoulders squared and hands clutched together to stop them from trembling. I hadn't even been this nervous for my med school interviews. Those had been based on my merit and my grades, which had been impeccable. My Bravetown record wasn't as impeccable though. "I know that leaving without a heads-up after the accident was a horrible thing to do, but in my defense, I wouldn't be able to do the show right now anyway, or even help in the stables or anything. With the shoulder, I mean. So I would have been useless either way. But when I'm better, Noah and I will do the Ace and Annie thing permanently if you still want us to."

It was the one thing I knew I could bring to the table.

Over the last few days, Noah had given me a bit more insight into his profiles. He'd been putting in very little effort since day one. All he had to do was raise his brows, smirk, flex his gloved hands and his biceps, and the views tumbled in. It was an easy side hustle for him. Or had been. After Lucas's footage of the three of us had run out, people kept asking for more. Both their comment sections were full of it. A lot of them were particularly asking for a part two of a video that had gone a little viral. That dynamic was the one thing I brought to the table. Especially since Noah said there was no one else he'd ever indulge like this. I was the only one who got more Ace Ryder if I asked him for it.

Renee tapped her pen against the open file on her desk, with my almost empty CV at the very top of it. "Well, I think we need to clear something up first. It says medical leave of absence in your employee file."

"I'm sorry?"

"Judging by the way you just tried to talk me into giving you a job, it sounds like you resigned. But I never received a resignation from you."

"But I left. I didn't even tell anyone. I just . . . I left."

Renee crossed her arms in front of her chest and regarded me with raised brows. "Well, I have no written resignation, and as far as I know, you're recovering from an occupational injury. Where and how you do that is legally none of my business. I do have some insurance forms for you to fill out, though, and a meeting with HR you'll have to attend. Once you feel well enough."

"Oh. Wait. So I'm not fired? I'm still Annie Lou?" That didn't seem right. Sure, I'd had an accident, but besides being inconsiderate, I must have broken a bunch of clauses in my work contract by running off without notice. At the very least, they would have needed a doctor's note to confirm my medical leave.

"Yes, Esra," Renee sighed, and her face softened into a smile, "you're still the Pretty Annie Lou."

"And that other girl . . ."

"I've decided to start casting understudies for our lead roles. I hear they're becoming quite popular."

"Oh." *Oh.* I still had my job. I got to come back. The bridges I thought I'd burned seemed just a little charred. Tears started pricking in my eyes. Everyone had just welcomed me back. Unconditionally. "I guess I should tell you that I won't need my room anymore. You can reassign it."

"All right. You'll need to get your stuff out. I believe your parents tried to send someone to pick up your things, but I hadn't heard from you and I couldn't find your signature on any of the paperwork. And then the movers had the audacity to throw a tantrum." She smirked and twirled her finger by her temple. "As if I was going to let a bunch of strange men on to Bravetown property to rummage through my employee's belongings."

"It's all still there?" Dad had only said he'd hired movers and that they were delayed. He'd taken on the task and had never even mentioned that my signature might be needed.

"Just as you left it." Renee held out a box of tissues. I hadn't noticed the tears spilling down my cheeks. "Before you leave, we should discuss the consequences for your . . . mishap in the Haunted Mines."

Shit. I'd forgotten about that. It felt like forever ago. "Of course. Again, I'm so sorry," I croaked as I wiped my face clean.

"I think a paid suspension will do. Six weeks, starting three weeks ago. You can come and go as you please, but you're not allowed to work."

"So I come back to work in three weeks? When my shoulder is better?"

"If a dislocated shoulder that didn't require surgery takes six weeks to heal before you're allowed physical activity, and that recovery time just so happens to line up with the suspension, then yes." She tried to put on a nonchalant face as she waved her hand through the air. As if I hadn't noticed her explicitly mentioning it was a *paid* suspension as well.

"Thank you, Renee." I wasn't sure what I'd done to deserve this place or these people. "What about Noah?"

"I don't have an understudy for him yet. I might suspend him over Christmas. We'll see." She sighed. "I'll have a firm talk with him as well and then we'll have to get the two of you booked in for *that* HR meeting. You're really making sure Liz works for her money this year, huh?"

"You haven't talked to him yet?" I'd asked her to give me the chance to discuss the situation privately first, but I would have expected her to disregard that after I left.

"No, not yet. I figured it could wait until you felt better." She snapped the file on her desk shut, signaling that she was pretty much done talking to me. "And Esra?"

"Yes?" I braced myself for one last jab about how I'd disappointed her or how she'd expected more from me.

"Welcome home."

"Thank you." Another tear spilled over my lashes, and I quickly wiped it away with the tissue.

When I walked out of Renee's office, Vivi was about to leave her desk as well, but she took one look at me and sat me down in her chair.

"You look like you just got fired and I know you didn't," she said and opened one of her desk drawers. It was filled to the brim with makeup. She had me fixed up and looking better than before in less than ten minutes.

"Please teach me your ways," I said as I inspected the perfectly sharp winged eyeliner in a tiny compact mirror.

"If you stick around, I will," she said with a certain note of challenge. She wasn't the most talkative person, but she also left little room for nonsense.

"I'm planning on it," I said.

"Good. Then let's go. I don't want to be late."

"Late for what?"

"Saloon night." She snatched her bag and nodded for me to follow.

That didn't make sense. Every night could be saloon night if you wanted it to be. It wasn't a Wednesday either, so it couldn't be time for another burlesque show from the Stallions unless they'd changed the schedule when I was gone.

We walked out to the parking lot, and I forgot all about the saloon. Noah waited for me, perfectly drenched in the bright colors of the sunset, looking like a picture-book cowboy in his hat and a plaid shirt he'd rolled up to the elbows. Those tanned forearms with the veins running down to his knuckles belonged in a museum. Noah could make me stop dead in my tracks any day, but this casual

368

version of him was quickly becoming my favorite. Vivi kept walking and said she'd save us a seat, but I couldn't even glance her way to thank her.

"Hi cowboy," I said, unable to resist the smile Noah put on my lips.

"Hi princess." He lifted his arm for me and let me nestle against his side. "How did it go?"

"Turns out, I forgot to quit when I left." I filled him in on all the details on our way over to the saloon. I'd just finished explaining about the accidental sex tape and how he might get suspended over Christmas for it, and how Renee made it sound like she'd always expected me to come back, when we reached the park's main entrance.

I stopped short at the crowd that had gathered in the square outside the Rattlesnake. The saloon was crowded, too. Guests spilled out the door, packed into a tight formation of heads and shoulders. And out here, people were putting down picnic blankets and fold-out chairs. That couldn't all be for the Stallions. Especially not considering the number of middle-aged men who, demographically, usually steered clear of the saloon during their shows.

Noah had to wave his cast-member badge at a lot of disgruntled people who were trying to squeeze closer to the Rattlesnake's doors. Noah kept one arm braced around my shoulders as we shuffled through and up the stairs to a staff section that was almost as packed as the public section.

"What's going on?" I asked when we made it to the table by the balcony where many familiar faces were already waiting. Including Zuri and Sinan, who usually preferred the table in the back.

"Adriana got us Brooks Monroe for one night only at

the Rattlesnake Saloon," Zuri explained after drawing me into a long, perfect, warm Zuri Hug.

"Seriously?" I turned toward Adriana. For once, she wasn't standing behind the bar. She leaned against the railing in a floaty dress, her curls falling free, her arms and neck decked out in enough gold jewelry to turn her into a disco ball whenever one of the stage lights swung her way.

"It was getting really expensive, buying everyone drinks to make them like me. I figured this would do. Brooksy still owed me a favor."

Brooksy.

I knew she'd been the opening act on his last tour, but from the way she talked, I'd assumed she'd completely left that part of her life behind. Apparently, she hadn't left country legend Brooks Monroe behind though.

What kind of favor did you have to call in to get a superstar like him to give a concert in your hometown?

I narrowed my eyes at Adriana. "Is that favor why you're so dressed up?"

She flipped me off and turned away, but I still caught a glimpse of the grin tugging at her lips.

Vivi had kept her word and saved us a seat. One. Singular. Noah didn't go off to look for another chair or make a show of offering it to me like a proper gentleman. He just wrapped an arm around my middle and pulled me into his lap. We hadn't actually talked about how we wanted to handle us being together in public, but after everything, even one minute of pretending that we weren't seemed like too long. I wanted as much of him as I could get. So I settled against him and folded my fingers over his hand resting on my thigh.

"All right, pay up, suckers." Sinan stretched his hands across the table, palms up. One after another the people around us were taking out their wallets or fishing money from the back of their phone cases.

"No, you didn't," Noah grumbled behind me, his fingers tightening around my thigh.

"What's happening?" I asked louder and signed the question, certain that Sanny hadn't heard Noah. Stacks of cash were building in Sanny's hands.

"He made a bet about us. They all did," Noah explained, then asked louder. "What did you put your money on?"

"Austin, will you do us the honor?" Sanny grinned as he smoothed the bills out.

"The winning bet was – drumroll please . . ." Austin pulled out his phone and waited until someone finally drummed their fingers against the table before he read the aforementioned bet out loud: "*Noah and my sister will be together by the end of summer season, like together-together, so that trumps Vivi's hookup. Betting $50.* And you just saw who took the bet. There was an emoji system for different tiers. I'm not getting into that."

Austin shrugged as if gambling via emojis on someone's love life wasn't even a little crazy.

My eyes narrowed on Sinan, who was grinning at his winnings like a mouse with a fat chunk of cheese.

"I don't know if Sanny won that bet," I mused and playfully tapped my finger against my chin.

"Hey!" Sinan's fists clenched around the money. "This is for Zuri's wedding dress."

"Yeah, but are we *together-together*?" I blinked innocently at Noah over my shoulder. "I thought I was more like your live-in casual non-exclusive sexytime hookup."

"I don't wanna think about what that means," Sanny groaned.

Noah's grip on my thigh tightened, hard enough to make me squirm and remind me of all the other perfect moments when he grabbed my legs like that. His dark brows drew deep over his eyes. "Don't even joke about that, princess. We're exclusive and anything but casual." His voice was a low rumble that sent goosebumps rippling down my arms.

There really was nothing casual about the pull Noah had on me. I tilted my head back to meet him for a kiss. Noah needed no further invitation. His hand slid into my hair, cupping the side of my face, and he pulled me to him for a breathless kiss. He was staking his claim. He was showing everyone that we were *together-together*. Even after his lips had left mine, and it felt like my mouth was bruising, he kept his eyes on me. "Clear?"

"Crystal," I answered, heart still racing, and grinned a stupid, giddy grin.

"Ugh. Gross. Are you going to be one of those disgusting PDA couples?" Adriana asked, pulling me out of the moment and back to earth.

"Yes," Noah replied without missing a beat.

I cleared my throat and turned to Sanny. "I can't believe you bet on us."

"I knew this was going to happen the very first time Noah complained about you." He leaned over, speaking louder as the volume around us rose. "You remember what you said to me?"

"I'm not sure. That you should send her home to your parents?" Noah replied, just as loud. As if he wasn't perfect enough already, he tried to sign his reply. You couldn't always verbatim translate to sign language, but he'd clearly picked up a few words.

"I remember." I sat up straighter, so I could properly look at both Noah and my brother. "You said 'She's careless and irresponsible. Don't let her blow through your life like a tornado.'"

"I'm sorry, princess," Noah whispered and pressed a kiss to my shoulder.

"No, but exactly." Sanny grinned. "Noah has, like, a sixth sense for weather. Loves a storm. And rides a *Tornado* every day."

I groaned at the implication and shot Noah a withering glare. "Please don't tell me that you like me because I remind you of your horse."

"You're more stubborn than any horse I've ever met." Noah's chest shook with laughter.

I made a show of getting up, but Noah pulled me back into his lap and tightened an arm around my hips, locking me in. He tilted my chin up only to smile at me with so much warmth in his eyes, the air spluttered from my lungs.

"I like a good storm," he said.

"Perfect," I corrected him. "Unusual chains of events and rare conditions all coming together with perfect timing, resulting in an exceptionally strong storm."

Something must have happened on-stage because the people around us were jumping up in their seats and cheering, but Noah stayed perfectly still under me, holding my gaze. The tips of our noses brushed together before he closed his lips over mine. It was a quick kiss, in the middle of a bar, with people jumping around us, and it should have felt casual. In his arms, it was the most intentional I'd ever been kissed.

"Perfect storm," he whispered against my lips.

I nodded and despite the rising noise and excitement around us, I chose to stay seated, chose to kiss my cowboy again, chose Noah.

Epilogue

NOAH

One Year Later

"Okay, I've narrowed it down. Primary Motor Cortex, which would be movement-related, Cortex for short. Or Broca's Area, which is all about expression through speech, Broca for short."

"You're not naming your horse after brain parts," I replied and tried to shoot her a warning look from the corner of my eye.

Esra sat cross-legged in the passenger seat and tapped her pen against her notepad, where she'd doodled more swirls than listed actual name options. I only knew that those "names" were terms for brain sections because she'd hosted trivia night a few weeks ago and turned out to be better as a participant. All her questions had been incredibly niche.

"Why not? All this information in *my* brain has to go somewhere, and both would be therapy puns. Physical therapy or psychotherapy. Get it? The horse helps you move and express your feelings."

"Part of therapy is bonding with the horse. I'm not asking someone to bond with *Primary Motor Cortex*."

"Killjoy," she huffed.

"Better name than Cortex, but not exactly trust-inspiring."

I turned the car on to the road where we were picking the horse up, checking back over my shoulder to make sure the trailer made it around the corner without issues.

"What if we let him choose?" Esra suggested. "I'll call out a bunch of names and we'll see which one he responds to."

"Just because you pitch your voice higher on 'Cortex' and he whinnies in response, doesn't mean he actually likes the name."

"Can you be certain? Have you ever asked your horses if they like their names?"

I parked the car near the paddock's gate, and only then turned to Esra and tried to give her my most exasperated look, but the way she was grinning quickly stole the air from my lungs.

"Come here, woman." I leaned over the center console and pulled her to me by the collar of her shirt. *My* shirt. She was always wearing my shirts. I was constantly doing laundry, but it was so worth it for the caveman part of my brain getting tickled by the sight of it. I kissed her, fist still wrapped up in the fabric, and her mouth readily fell open.

She was breathing hard by the time she pulled back. "Slipping me the tongue won't win you the argument. Nice try, cowboy."

"I have my ways of persuasion." Hands around her waist, exactly where they belonged, I lifted her out of her seat and on to my lap. She squealed but easily slotted over me, my hips between her knees.

"Oh, do you?" she challenged and popped open the

top button of her shirt. "What if I keep moaning Primary Motor Cortex in your ear until you love the sound of it?"

"I'm willing to let you try."

She crushed over me in another deep kiss. Her hair fell around our faces and her hips ground down on mine until I was willing to let her name even our future children after body parts.

A sharp knock on the car window interrupted our anatomy lesson.

"Sorry. That was . . . sorry," Esra laughed when she popped the door open and climbed out of my lap.

"Yeah, yeah, I've seen men buy their girlfriends horses before." The middle-aged woman who was selling the horse rolled her eyes at us. "You can continue thanking him later."

Esra grinned at me over her shoulder and reached her hand out to tug me along toward the paddock. Neither of us mentioned that, technically, her parents were buying her the horse.

I'd first met them when we visited them for their New Year's celebrations. While I was fairly certain that Esra's father hated me before I'd even opened my mouth, solely because she lived with me and didn't have a ring on her finger, her mother seemed to be more accepting after interrogating me. I wasn't divorced, nor did I have any illegitimate children. I owned land. I had savings. And thanks to many late nights around the kitchen table with Esra, Zuri and Sinan, we had a structured business model for the ranch.

They'd also flown in for Sinan and Zuri's wedding in the spring, which we'd held at the ranch. Esra had introduced her parents to everyone, and both of them seemed genuinely surprised by the laughs and the hugs and the bubbling excitement she garnered – which seemed ridiculous, because Esra was easy to like. I'd just taken longer than everyone else to realize that, but I made up for it now by loving her more than anyone else could.

She also gave them the grand tour before the reception. We'd renovated most of the house by then and even had some of Zuri's family staying in the guest bedrooms. Seeing everything in person seemed to change something for her parents. Especially when Esra sat her dad down to show him her two binders full of research into equine therapy.

One binder was about managing the symptoms of hypermobile EDS through physical therapy, and how horseback-riding actually covered most of those needs.

The other binder was full of market research on how most therapy ranches weren't even equipped to provide for people like her, because every single one of her joints had different support requirements and even the shape of the stirrup could determine whether or not she'd walk pain-free the next day.

She flat-out told her father that she needed a specific kind of horse, narrow with a long gait, and specific gear, so she could become the *leading expert* on the topic. Her words. She said, if he was going to pay for her degree, he might as well pay for a horse, because she wasn't going back to school but she was going to publish her research one day, and it was going to change the life of every little girl with hEDS who never got the chance to become a "horse girl" because she was too afraid to fall, when she just needed the right tools and skills to stay in the saddle.

I'd leaned back against the fridge with a big smile on my lips and watched her plead her case, so fucking proud of her. Even if her father was going to say no, she'd found something she was passionate about and she wasn't too stubborn to ask for the support she needed to go after it.

Three months later, we found her this chestnut-colored Missouri Fox Trotter on a ranch just a few hours north of Wild Fields. We'd visited last week to make sure he was as calm and easygoing as the ad had promised. I didn't exactly know how, but Esra and that horse had fallen in love at first sight.

Today, he rushed over the second she climbed up on the gate and clicked her tongue at him.

"Hi Peanut," she cooed at him, both hands immediately on his face while she peppered kisses on his forehead.

"Peanut?" I asked.

"Peanut Butter, technically. Peanut for short," Esra explained with a big smile.

"You had that name picked out all along, didn't you?"

She giggled and scrunched her bunny nose up at me. "You just make it so easy."

"All right then," the previous owner sighed and scribbled the new name on to the stack of papers in her hands, "Peanut Butter is all yours. Do y'all need help loading him up into the trailer?"

"That would be great," I said.

"Do we have to already? Can I get five more minutes with him out here?" Esra called over her shoulder without looking away from her horse, completely besotted with him.

"Oh jeez . . ." The woman smacked the stack of papers

at my chest. "I'll be in my truck. Five minutes, then I'm leaving."

I rolled the papers up and stuck them in my back pocket, so I could wrap my arms around Esra from behind. She stood on one of the gate's rails, meaning I didn't have to bend down to her for once. Peanut only acknowledged me with a huff, too focused on getting ear scritches from Esra.

"You'll have plenty of time with him, princess. He's all yours now," I said and kissed the back of her head.

"I know," she sighed, "I just wanted him to have a good memory of meeting me before he gets taken away from his home."

"He'll have a new home and you'll make a lot of good memories together there," I whispered in her ear.

"Speaking from experience?" she asked and leaned her head back to brush her lips against mine.

"Mm-hmm, yeah," I replied, trying to catch her mouth under mine, but she tilted her face, and I kissed her cheek instead.

"Noah?"

"Hmm?"

"He's mine. Don't even think about stealing my Peanut Butter, got it?"

Acknowledgments

This is my third time writing acknowledgments and I still don't know if there's a right way to do it.

So many people are instrumental in turning a story idea into an actual book, and while my name is on the cover, I've had so much invisible help: hands-on support at home, friends taking care of my mental and emotional stability, and the brilliant professionals in the publishing industry.

First and always: PB. My person. Thank you for bringing me snacks and cleaning the kitchen and looking after the dogs when I'm off riding Phantom Manor in the name of research. Your kindness and generosity and spirit are forever inspiring me. It's been like twenty-three years and I can't believe you aren't tired of me yet.

This book wouldn't exist without Bethany. We actually managed to reduce our 2 a.m. phone calls. Look at us making healthy choices. Thank you for letting me unabashedly be myself, from the bitchiest version to the corniest, and riding with every version. And a big Bravetown-specific *thank you* for answering my theme-park employee questions!

I also have to thank my mother, not only for taking me to Wild West cities and big theme parks when I was a little kid and sparking an obsession, but specifically for the last year. My health hasn't been this bad since I was a little kid, but unlike Esra's parents, you have supported me through it unconditionally and have let me make choices you might not agree with. That's a pretty big deal. I hope you know that.

My unending gratitude to Soraya and Imi. You have read and loved this book before anyone else, have offered rational advice when I was an emotional mess, and have kept me going when I wanted to yeet the book (and myself) out the window. I don't want to know what the inside of my brain would look like without you two.

Thank you to my agent Hayley for believing in my work and in me. My brain's always whirring at a thousand miles per hour and I'm so lucky to have met you, someone who doesn't only keep up with it but who sees it for the asset it can be.

This book wouldn't be more than a Word doc without the entire team at Penguin Michael Joseph who have worked tirelessly on this release. It's my first traditionally published novel, in big part due to my editor, Phillipa Walker. Thank you for stumbling across a single-sentence summary of this book and seeing what it could be. Your trust in my ideas has blown me away from the start, and your vision made Bravetown, Esra and Noah so much stronger. Thank you to Alicia Clancy, who was meant to find this book, and the amazing team at Dell Romance for bringing Bravetown to life across the pond!

There are so many more people who have had a hand in making this book what it is today, whether that's through offering advice, providing feedback on a few chapters, body-doubling or just being on the receiving end of my rambles, so thank you: Aiysha, Amelie, Annabel, Autumn, Ava, Bailey, Bec, Caden, Cee, Courtney, Elliot, Emma,

Georgia, Grace, Ki, L., Maren, Meg, Romie, Ruby, Zarin. I'm sure I forgot someone – I'll buy you a coffee to make up for it!

An extra shoutout to the Disney Imagineers, who share so much of their expertise and passion in the Theme Park Design and Imagineering courses. I've never had this much fun with worldbuilding!

And a thank-you to Channing Tatum (again) and to the Ranch Hands – for inspiring the Stallions.

Last – but most importantly – I have to thank *you*. Whether this is the first book of mine you've picked up or just the latest, you're the reason I get to do what I love every day. And I hope that if you take anything away from this book, it's this: It's completely fine if you have to make some detours to find the thing, the place and the people you love – enjoy the roadside attractions on the way.

Dic(k)tionary

The following chapters include sexually explicit content:
Chapter Fifteen
Chapter Sixteen
Chapter Eighteen
Chapter Nineteen
Chapter Twenty-Three

Sexual themes and kinks explored in this book include:
Light bondage; harnesses; mask kink; mud play; role play;
improper use of a prop gun.